Lord Ash

Books by Sally MacKenzie

THE NAKED DUKE

THE NAKED MARQUIS

THE NAKED EARL

THE NAKED GENTLEMAN

"The Naked Laird"

THE NAKED BARON

THE NAKED VISCOUNT

"The Naked Prince"

THE NAKED KING

"The Duchess of Love"

BEDDING LORD NED

SURPRISING LORD JACK

LOVING LORD ASH

Published by Zebra Books

Loving Lord Ash

SALLY MACKENZIE

ZEBRA BOOKS
KENSINGTON PUBLISHING CORP.
http://www.kensingtonbooks.com

ZEBRA BOOKS are published by

Kensington Publishing Corp.
119 West 40th Street
New York, NY 10018

Copyright © 2014 by Sally MacKenzie

All rights reserved. No part of this book may be reproduced in any form or by any means without the prior written consent of the Publisher, excepting brief quotes used in reviews.

If you purchased this book without a cover you should be aware that this book is stolen property. It was reported as "unsold and destroyed" to the Publisher and neither the Author nor the Publisher has received any payment for this "stripped book."

All Kensington titles, imprints, and distributed lines are available at special quantity discounts for bulk purchases for sales promotion, premiums, fund-raising, educational, or institutional use.

Special book excerpts or customized printings can also be created to fit specific needs. For details, write or phone the office of the Kensington Special Sales Manager: Attn. Special Sales Department. Kensington Publishing Corp., 119 West 40th Street, New York, NY 10018. Phone: 1-800-221-2647.

Zebra and the Z logo Reg. U.S. Pat. & TM Off.

First Printing: March 2014
ISBN-13: 978-1-4201-2323-4
ISBN-10: 1-4201-2323-8

First Electronic Edition: March 2014
eISBN-13: 978-1-4201-3414-8
eISBN-10: 1-4201-3414-0

10 9 8 7 6 5 4 3 2 1

Printed in the United States of America

For my boys and my daughters-in-law,

For grandparents everywhere,

and

For Kevin, as always.

Chapter One

Never jump to conclusions.

—Venus's Love Notes

The March wind stung his face, but the Marquis of Ashton, heir to the Duke of Greycliffe, still paused when he rounded the curve in the drive that led to Blackweith Manor.

Zeus, he loved this house, especially with the late afternoon sun limning its classical facade. It was so orderly and controlled. No one could look at it and not feel calm—

Oh, God.

The image of Jess's milky white thighs—and Percy's naked arse between them—shoved to the front of his thoughts. Again. He'd been battling the memory every minute of every hour on this blasted journey.

He shifted on his horse, making the animal toss its head. The jangling of its bridle sounded unnaturally loud in the quiet.

There was nothing calm or controlled about the place. It was a wasp's nest—smooth and beautiful on the outside, but a mass of stinging, painful chaos on the inside. He should go back to Greycliffe Castle. A wise man didn't poke a wasp's nest. He'd left this problem alone for eight years; why couldn't he leave it for another eight?

His fingers tightened on the reins. Because he needed

an heir, of course. He'd just turned thirty; Jess was twenty-eight. It was past time to set up his nursery. Running back to the castle would not give him a son to carry on the title.

He nudged his horse forward. Hell, he couldn't run back even if he wanted to. He'd never had such a cursed journey. What with the snow and the mud and the washed-out bridges—not to mention his horse coming up lame, forcing him to hire this slug he was currently riding—a trip that should have taken two days had stretched to over a month. Even the few interesting buildings he'd seen along the way hadn't made up for the slow pace and maddening detours.

Well, he was here now. Surely he and Jess could come to some agreement. He was only asking for a couple years of her life. Once she gave him his heir and his spare, she could go back to doing as she pleased. It was a very common arrangement among the ton.

A cloud drifted in front of the sun, bringing a chill to the air, turning the manor's warm stone dark and forbidding. His stomach tightened with each step the bloody horse took up the drive.

His brother Jack had said the London idiots were taking bets on what he would do about his union with Jess. It was a particularly delightful situation for the gossips because Mama was the Duchess of Love, the ton's premier matchmaker and the author of *Venus's Love Notes,* mortifying leaflets of marital advice. How ironic that her oldest son had made such a damnable muddle of his marriage.

Yet everyone but his mother knew love didn't last. . . .

Love. He scowled at his horse's ears. If he didn't feel this wretched, stupid love for Jess, everything would be much simpler. He wouldn't have married her in the first place, or he would have had a calm discussion with her about her duty as soon as they'd left the church. But he *did* love her. He loved her—and he hated her, too.

He was such a bloody fool. He had no one to blame for this mess but himself.

He stopped at the front of the manor and waited. When no one came to take his horse, he dismounted.

The horse stomped its front hoof and gave him a nasty look.

"Don't complain. I'll grant you this is irregular, but I'm sure someone will come out and take you to the stables shortly. It's not as if you exerted yourself. A slower hack would be hard to find in all of England."

The animal snorted and tossed its head, but it couldn't dispute the truth of the matter.

Ash shifted his shoulders, trying to ease the kinks out of his back. God, every one of his muscles ached. If only Inigo hadn't pulled up lame—

No, it was just as well. If he was going to bring Jess back to the castle, he'd have to take a carriage, and this way he wouldn't be tempted to ride instead of sitting inside with her. He didn't want to spend one more moment astride this bag of bones.

The horse found a few blades of grass to nibble, so Ash was confident the animal would stay put for the time being. He climbed the stairs to bang on the front door.

Nothing happened.

He scowled. The servants either did not expect visitors or the butler was deaf. Well, he would have a word with Walker, the estate manager, after he spoke to Jess. If he remembered correctly, he was paying for a full staff. He expected anyone working for him to be competent.

He tried the latch; the door opened easily. Good God! This was the country, but even so, leaving the door unlocked and unattended was not wise. Perhaps he'd have to make a list of things to discuss with Walker.

Sadly, this was what happened when one didn't visit one's estate regularly. He stepped over the threshold.

"Hallo! Is anyone here?"

He heard an odd sort of yelp and some scuffling, and then a large man hurried out from the back of the house, tucking in his shirttail and fastening his fall as he came.

He stopped when he saw Ash, his hands still on his buttons. A slow grin spread across his face. "We-ell, who do we have here?" His eyes swept Ash from his boots to his head and back.

Was the fellow drunk? "Ashton. I've come to see my wife."

"W-what?" The man's jaw dropped.

He must be a half-wit. It would be just like Jess to insist Walker take on a man who wasn't employable elsewhere. She might lift her skirt for anything in breeches, but she did sincerely care about the less fortunate. Perhaps it was the artist in her; she saw people who were invisible to most everyone else. But she also gave little thought to her own safety. She'd very likely never considered how she'd be at this fellow's mercy if he became violent.

Once they came to an agreement about their marriage, he would have to discuss that with her. Perhaps the man could be moved to the fields. At least then he wouldn't have the run of the house.

"I'm Lord Ashton." Ash spoke slowly and distinctly so the fellow could comprehend. "I'm here to see Lady Ashton. Your mistress."

The man's brows snapped down, and he snorted. "And I'm Prinny himself. You'll have to try harder than that to fool me, my fine fellow. Anyone will tell you Lord Ashton never comes to Blackweith Manor." The butler, or whatever he was, stepped forward to grab the door. "Now turn yourself around and be off, or I'll help you on your way with my boot."

"I am not going anywhere." Ash stood his ground and

glared. Good God. He'd never expected to have to prove his identity.

"Who is it, Charlie?" Another man, also fiddling with his fall, came up behind the first.

Charlie sniffed. "Some scoundrel who says he's Lord Ashton, Ralph." He glanced out the door at the broken-down nag and curled his lip. "I don't know what your game is, sirrah, but you won't cozen Charlie Lundquist."

Ash clenched his fists, struggling to keep a hold on his temper. This was ridiculous. "I don't *say* I'm Lord Ashton, I *am* the marquis, and if you don't move aside at once, Charlie Lundquist, you will find yourself on your arse next to that poor hack."

Charlie was not easily cowed. "Brave words. Now let's see you try—"

"Charlie." Ralph had been studying Ash. Now his eyes widened, and he grabbed Charlie's arm.

"Let go." Charlie tried to shake him off, but Ralph hung on.

"Charlie," he hissed, "he does look bloody like the painting in the library."

Charlie paused and examined Ash more closely. "I . . ."

"And look at his clothes. They're muddy, but they're quality."

Charlie's eyes narrowed. "But the marquis never visits."

"He has now," Ash said. "And I will tell you that you and Mr. Walker will be looking for new positions if this is how matters are handled at Blackweith Manor." He took a savage sort of satisfaction when Lundquist paled at his use of the estate manager's name. "Now take me to my wife."

"Ahh." Charlie looked at Ralph, and then they both looked up the stairs. They turned back with identical expressions of horror.

"Please forgive me, milord," Charlie said, pulling a

handkerchief out of his pocket and mopping his brow. "If you will just come along to the parlor, you can be comfortable while Ralph tells Lady Ashton you're here."

Any fool could see they were trying to hide something from him. "I do not wish to go to the parlor; I wish to see my wife."

"Yes, of course, milord. It's just that Lady Ashton is a little busy at the moment." Charlie nudged Ralph toward the staircase. "I'm sure—"

Bloody hell! He could guess what Jess was busy with. He lunged forward and grabbed Ralph's arm before the man could escape. "On second thought, I shall announce myself. You may attend to my horse."

Ralph stared at Ash's hand as if it belonged to Death.

"But, milord," Charlie sputtered, "please. You will truly be much more comfortable in the parlor while Ralph fetches Lady Ashton." He smiled nervously. "I'll bring you a nice bottle of brandy."

"No." Ash knew what he would see upstairs, but he needed to see it. He needed to feel the pain to remember why he could not let Jess stay in his heart. "Where is she?"

Charlie and Ralph looked at each other again, their shoulders slumping as they realized the futility of resisting him.

"The studio, milord," Charlie said.

There hadn't been a studio when he'd lived here. "Where?"

"Top floor," Ralph said. "First door on the left."

Where the nursery had been. Damn.

He dropped his hold on Ralph and started up the stairs.

Jessica, Marchioness of Ashton, mixed brown into the white paint on her palette. She could not get Roger's skin color right today. She swiped her brush with the new tint over his stomach.

No, that was wrong, too.

"You really should talk about it, you know."

Jess glanced up from her easel to glare at Roger, reclining naked on a red chaise longue. "Talk about what?"

Roger just lifted an eyebrow.

He knew, of course. She'd been in a foul mood since before Valentine's Day. It was a bad time every year, but this year had been by far the worst. Her fit of the dismals had lasted over a month.

She dropped her eyes back to her canvas. "There's nothing to say."

She did not care what Kit did. If he wanted to fornicate with Ellie—

Dear God! She squeezed her eyes shut at the thought's all too familiar pain. How could Ellie climb into Kit's bed? Kit was the heir to a duchy; everyone knew the aristocracy lived by different rules. But Ellie was a vicar's daughter, and she'd been Jess's childhood friend.

Jess plopped more brown paint onto her palette.

But people changed, didn't they? She'd never have guessed Kit would turn into such a rake; he'd been brilliant, but rather awkward and shy when they were growing up. Now, though, the Marquis of Ashton visited too many ladies' beds to count. The London papers had been full of his exploits—so full she'd stopped reading them.

If he had a proper wife, perhaps he'd stay in his own bed.

She mixed the paint with short, sharp strokes. Yes, perhaps he would.

She was not one to make excuses for herself. After that dreadful scene with Percy, it was perfectly obvious why Kit wouldn't wish to have anything to do with her.

But then why had he offered for her?

She shook her head. No matter what his reasons, she should not have accepted him.

This year Kit had turned thirty. Time was passing. He would want to start his nursery.

He would have to divorce her.

Finally, her marriage would be over—and *that* was what was causing her stupid heart to feel as if it were made of lead.

She frowned at her palette. Painting and drawing had always been her escape. She just needed to focus. She'd feel better eventually. Not happy—she couldn't remember the last time she'd felt really happy—but at least not so morose.

Hmm. Roger's skin was closer to olive. Maybe she should try a touch of yellow? She mixed in just a little. . . .

Oh, blast. Now the color looked like what her dog hacked up after eating grass.

Roger snorted, shifting position slightly. "There's plenty to say, as well you know."

"Don't be an ass. And keep still. I'm never going to get this painting right if you fidget." She started over, mixing brown paint into white again.

Most people would say she'd landed on her feet. She'd had a roof—a very comfortable roof—over her head and food on the table for eight years, as well as plenty of paint and canvas and brushes. For someone who was the daughter of an Irish groom and a seamstress, it should have been a dream come true.

But she had dreamt of more. She had fallen in love with Kit, with the future Duke of Greycliffe, and had imagined her life by his side, not as a duchess but as a wife.

Stupid! She should have weeded her ridiculous love out of her breast the moment she'd first felt it. By the time she'd tried to do so, it had been too late. It had grown like thistle; its roots deep, spreading into every corner of her life.

"If you want me to be still," Roger said, "you'd best put

more coals on the brazier. I don't know why you insist on painting me without a stitch of clothing when the snow has barely melted from the fields." Roger leered at her. "Just can't resist my manly physique, can you?"

She slammed down her brush, causing a bit of brown paint to spatter over her palette. "Don't flatter yourself. A still life of a dead bird would be far more tempting—and easier to paint. Damn it, why can't you be as pale as a proper Englishman?"

"Blame my Italian mother."

"Your poor mother." She started for the coal bin. "She—*ack!*" Oh, hell, she'd forgotten Kit, her enormous black dog, was stretched out at her feet. She tripped on him, pitched forward, and went crashing to the floor.

Kit's deep, loud bark almost drowned out Roger's cursing. They'd both leapt up and were now staring at her.

"Are you all right?"

"Yes, of course. I'm fine." Her lace cap had been knocked askew, and a large quantity of her straight, thick hair had escaped its pins—it was hard enough to keep under control in the best of circumstances.

She sat up and ripped off the cap, letting her hair tumble down her back. She clearly wasn't going to get any good painting done today. She might as well give up. Maybe if she went for a long walk, the cold air would shock some sense into her.

Kit licked her cheek, and she wrapped her arms around him, burying her face in his long, black coat. He'd been her loyal companion since she'd got him as a puppy, a few years after she'd come to the manor. "Oh, you big Fluff. I'm sorry I tripped on you. Are you all right?"

He barked again.

"Not in my ear, you silly dog! You'll deafen me."

"Here, let me help you up." Roger extended his hand.

His male bit dangled right at her eye level.

She admired all aspects of the human body, but this poor part was ungainly and, well, ugly. It really was best hidden by a fig leaf or a pair of well-fitted pantaloons. And it wasn't only Roger's that was unattractive; she'd painted enough of the male servants to know the organ's homeliness was universal.

Percy's certainly had been—

No. She would not think about that disgusting blackguard.

She forced herself to smile up at Roger, which had the added advantage of taking her eyes off his least attractive feature. The rest of him was lovely. He had long limbs, broad shoulders, and well-defined muscles. He was by far her favorite model.

She let him haul her to her feet.

"You're certain you're all right?" he asked.

"Yes, of course." She tugged on her hand, but he didn't relinquish it.

"I was afraid you'd hurt yourself."

She made a face at him. "The only thing hurt is my pride." She tugged again.

"Well, that's good." He finally let her go, but only so he could grab her shoulders. He shook her a little. "Jess, you know you can't keep living this way."

"Living what way?" She dropped her eyes to his collarbone. She'd definitely mixed too much brown into the white paint. If she—

"You know. Married, but not married."

Her eyes snapped back up to scowl at him. Blast it, she knew everyone in the house worried about her, but until now everyone had been kind enough to hold his tongue. Why was Roger bringing the subject up when he knew she was so terribly out of sorts?

"I don't want to talk about it." She put her hands on his chest and pushed, but his grip on her shoulders only tightened.

"In the four years I've been here, I've never seen you really happy, Jess. Dennis and I were just discussing it last night."

Dennis Walker, her—no, *Kit's* estate manager—and Roger's lover.

"I *am* happy. Why wouldn't I be? I have a houseful of servants to do my bidding." She looked him in the eye. "And I bid you drop this topic."

His mouth was set in an unpleasantly mulish line. "But you don't have a husband."

"I *do* have a husband." That was the whole problem.

"But not in your bed."

A hot, odd yearning exploded in her stomach. "Damn it, Roger. Didn't you hear me? I do not wish to talk about my marriage."

Roger ignored her. "Every year, when the marquis's birthday approaches, you get quieter and quieter. This year has been the worst. Valentine's Day is more than a month gone, and you're still dragging around as if it were yesterday."

"You are mistaken."

Roger lifted his damn eyebrow again.

"And even if you're not, it will pass."

He tucked a strand of her hair behind her ear. "Until it comes again next year and the year after and the year after that. Your life is drifting away, Jess. Is that really what you want?"

"No, of course not." Damnation, her voice broke. She bit the inside of her cheek and willed herself not to cry. She was tired, that was all. She hadn't been sleeping well lately.

"Dennis and I think it's time you faced your husband."

Dennis and he had been far too busy about her business. "No."

"I don't know what he did—"

"He didn't do anything." Her predicament was her own fault. She should never have let things with Percy go so far. She just hadn't been thinking clearly. And then Kit had come in at precisely the wrong moment.

Why *had* he offered for her?

She'd wondered that for eight years. All she could surmise was the proposal had been a momentary lapse in judgment, Kit's generous heart speaking before his considerable intellect could silence it. And once the words were said, he couldn't unsay them and maintain his honor. She'd realized that even then.

And selfishly, she'd leapt to accept. She definitely should not have, but she'd been young and stupid and in love. She'd known she had some beauty; she'd seen how the other men looked at her. She'd even stolen a few kisses. She'd thought she'd have no trouble getting Kit to fall in love with her.

Youthful hubris.

"—but he should settle things now. And if he won't come to the manor, you need to go to him."

She stared at Roger. Go to Kit? Go to Greycliffe Castle and see the duke and the duchess and Ellie and Kit's brothers and perhaps Percy?

She was going to throw up.

"You can do it, Jess. You have to."

"No, I . . ."

But things couldn't get any worse than they were, could they? It was just a matter of time. Kit was going to divorce her anyway. Why wait?

She took a deep breath and nodded. "All right."

Roger grinned. "That's the spirit." He threw his arms

around her, apparently forgetting he was naked, and hugged her.

She hugged him back, since leaving her hands on his chest was uncomfortable and letting them dangle risked encountering portions of his anatomy she'd rather avoid. And she did love him. He was the brother she'd never had. He was funny and kind and maddening and sometimes overbearing.

And he had terrible timing.

The door flew open right at that moment, and she jerked her head around to see who'd come all the way up to the studio.

Oh, bloody, bloody hell.

She stared directly into her husband's furious eyes.

Chapter Two

The angrier the man, the more desperate his love.

—Venus's Love Notes

Shock, longing, horror, mortification. The emotions flashed through Jess, keeping her frozen where she stood—with her arms around a naked man.

Oh, damn. This was almost as bad as the scene with Percy. Why did she have such horrendous luck?

She shoved Roger away as if he'd caught fire. "Ash, what are you doing here?"

How easily she fell into using Kit's title. She'd been the only one who'd ever called him by his Christian name, but that was only when they were alone, back when they'd been friends.

They were not friends now. His face was like granite, his eyes hard gray chips. He looked even harsher than he had that terrible time with Percy.

Or maybe he looked harsher because he was older. His blond hair had darkened, his face was leaner, and there were lines around his eyes and mouth—likely caused by her and their doomed marriage.

But she also saw a glimmer of the Kit she'd loved—the shy, intense, brilliant boy with the heart-stopping smile who had befriended her even though she was only the groom's daughter and had taught her to draw. She saw that boy's face in her dreams at night and had ached to see him again in person.

And now she had, in such damning circumstances.

His lip curled. He probably saw her face in his dreams, too—or rather, his nightmares.

Roger stepped naked between them. "The door was closed, sir. A gentleman would knock and beg admittance."

Kit's eyes narrowed, his anger so intense Jess would swear he vibrated with it. "A *gentleman* would not fuck another man's wife."

Jess gasped. She'd never heard Kit utter such an ugly word.

"Wife?" Roger said. He turned to look at her. "Wife?"

"Yes, wife." Kit stepped forward threateningly. "Or didn't you ask if she was married before you—"

"That's enough!" None of this was Roger's fault. Jess pushed him aside and faced Kit squarely. "Lord Ashton, I'll thank you to—"

Her sharp voice alerted her dog that some threat had entered his territory. He started barking, great deep woofs that echoed off the studio's wooden floor and bare walls, and came over to vanquish the interloper.

"It's all right, Kit." Jess glared at her husband. "Lord Ashton is harmless."

"Er, Jess," Roger said. He'd had the good sense to grab the blanket off the chaise longue and wrap it around his waist. "I wouldn't say he's harmless precisely."

Kit ignored Roger. His eyes had widened, and he stared at Jess's pet, which was leaning protectively against her side now, and then up at Jess. "You named your *dog* after me?"

"She does like the dog," Roger said helpfully. "It's rather a compliment."

The look Kit gave Roger could have frozen fire. "You bloody—"

"My lord, Charlie said you'd arrived." Dennis Walker appeared in the corridor behind Kit. The poor man's face was flushed, and he was panting as if he'd run up the stairs. He wrung his hands—and carefully avoided looking at Roger. "What a surprise." He smiled weakly and cleared his throat. "A *wonderful* surprise, of course. But you must be hungry and thirsty. Why don't you retire to the study, and I'll have some refreshments sent to you?"

Kit turned his glare from Roger to Dennis. "Refreshments will not be necessary; I am leaving."

"But, my lord—"

"However,"—Kit cut Dennis off, and suddenly Jess could see the duke in him, though His Grace had never been this cold—"I shall require a moment of your time before I depart, Mr. Walker. If you would be so kind as to await me in the study? I shall not be long here."

Dennis opened his mouth to argue, but must have realized he'd be wasting his breath. Kit had made up his mind.

He pressed his lips together, gave Jess a worried look, and then bowed and departed.

Jess listened to Dennis's heels echo down the corridor as she looked at Kit's stony countenance. So this was it. It was finally coming. Her heart stilled. It felt like a fragile glass ornament that would shatter in a moment with the words she knew were coming.

She sniffed and swallowed sudden tears. Stupid. She should have given up her foolish hope of a miraculous happily-ever-after a long time ago.

"Madam," Kit said.

Damn it, he sounded as if he were addressing a servant—no, not even a servant. A poor, dirty cur.

Her heart lurched back into motion, anger beginning to smolder in its center. Good. Anger was better than tears.

"Madam," he said again, "I came to tell you that I am initiating divorce proceedings. I apologize for taking so long to do so." His nostrils flared, and he looked at Roger—poor Roger standing barefoot in the cold studio with a red flowered blanket wrapped around him.

Kit looked back at her. "I must also inform you that if you become *enceinte,* I shall deny the child is mine. I have plenty of witnesses who will swear we never shared a bed."

Her temper flared. How dare he talk to her—to any woman—this way. "Oh, do you need a bed to accomplish the deed?"

For a moment, she actually thought Kit would hit her.

"Jess, I'm not sure that's what you wanted to say," Roger muttered.

Well, she'd wanted to say it when the words had left her lips, but now she wished she'd kept her tongue between her teeth.

Kit finally managed to loosen his jaw enough to spit out a few words. "Good day, madam. I don't believe we need ever meet again, a fact for which I'm certain we are both profoundly grateful."

Then he turned and walked out of her life.

Ash had to make a detour on his way to the study. He ran down the back stairs—fortunately he didn't encounter anyone, but then most of the servants were probably gathered in the kitchen, gossiping about how their cuckolded lord had finally appeared after so many years—and out the back door. He took a few quick steps and then bent over a nondescript bush and emptied the meager contents of his stomach.

He couldn't as easily disgorge the memory of Jess's

arms around that naked lecher. Or her long hair, black as night, sweeping down to skim her derriere. Or her violet eyes so full of anger and passion.

Bloody hell. He rubbed his hands over his face. Now he had something besides Percy's arse to haunt him.

Dissipation should show in a person's appearance, but Jess was as beautiful as ever, perhaps even more beautiful. Her face had matured. It had character—

Evil character.

And the worst of it was he *still* wanted her so badly his damn ballocks burned. Desire pounded in his chest as hard as anger.

He heaved again, but there was nothing left to come up.

He should take her to bed and cure himself of her once and for all. It was his right. He was her husband—

No. He was the worst sort of fool, but he wasn't *that* stupid. His cock did not—had never—ruled his will. If he bedded Jess now and she bore a child in nine months, he'd never know if the babe was his or that blackguard's upstairs.

Being a cuckold was bad enough, but passing the duchy on to some filthy rake's get—no. He could not do that.

But Jess might be barren. It seemed likely, given how many men she'd reputedly entertained over the years. Or perhaps she merely knew the light-skirts' tricks for avoiding conception. He could scratch his itch—

His stomach twisted again. She might be no better than a whore, but he couldn't use her as one. He had loved her once and, to be honest, he was afraid that if he went to her bed, he'd discover that he loved her still.

He straightened, pulled out his handkerchief, and wiped his mouth. He was making too much of this. His problem was solved simply enough—at least the problem of his aching cock. All he needed was an accommodating bit o' muslin, a girl who didn't pretend to be anything other than what she was.

He'd kept his marriage vows all these years, but now he considered himself well and truly free of them. He'd have a word with Walker, and then, when he got to the inn, he'd see if any of the serving girls were interested in a little bed play. It was long past time he lost his virginity.

He stood in the chill March air a few more minutes, waiting for his head to clear and his passions to subside—and his nether regions to return to their proper proportions.

When he met with Walker a few minutes later, he was in strict control of himself. He sat down at the desk, pushing a stack of papers aside . . . papers that carried his wife's handwriting.

What were they? Notes to her many lovers?

He picked one up to read.

Walker cleared his throat. "My lord, that is Lady Ashton's correspondence."

"I see that." And Walker was correct. He should not be reading Jess's letters. It was beneath him.

This was merely a note to a shopkeeper in London, ordering more painting supplies. Perhaps she kept her personal correspondence—her *love* letters—in a desk in her room.

He turned his attention to Walker. "Who the hell is that bounder upstairs?"

Well, perhaps he wasn't in *strict* control of himself.

Walker turned a bit green about the gills, but at least he didn't pretend to misunderstand. "Roger Bagley, my lord."

"Bagley." That surname sounded vaguely familiar. . . .

He thought for a moment, his finger tapping the desktop. No, he couldn't recall where he'd heard it before. Well, if the reprobate had any connection to the nobility, it was probably as a very small twig on a very distant branch of some very minor family. "What is his position here—besides his position in my wife's bed?"

Walker went white and braced himself on a chair. "Rog—" He cleared his throat. "That is, Bagley is a footman, my lord." He swallowed. "And I assure you he has never been in Lady Ashton's bed."

"Do you need a bed to accomplish the deed?"

Damnation! Would he ever be able to get those words out of his head? Clearly his clever wife could "accomplish the deed" in many inventive ways.

His blasted nether regions suddenly turned as hard as stone. Thank God he was sitting down.

"Walker, I may be slow, but I am not an imbecile. A woman doesn't embrace a naked man simply because the poor fellow has taken a chill." He grabbed an oddly shaped paperweight off the desk.

Walker stepped behind the chair he'd been gripping.

Did the man really think he'd throw the object at him? Ash glanced down to see what kind of weapon he had.

Zeus! It was the smooth piece of sandstone he'd given Jess when they were children. He remembered the day; they'd been drawing by the lake when he'd found it—

And that had been many years ago. He dropped the stone. The girl Jess had been—or at least the girl he'd thought she'd been—was long gone. Why in God's name did she still have the worthless thing? It was only a piece of rock and rather ugly at that.

"Rog—I mean, Bagley—"

He looked up at Walker. The man was clutching the back of the chair with both hands now.

"Bagley was merely posing for Lady Ashton, my lord. She is a painter, you see. She likes to paint Bagley."

"I'll bet she does."

Walker shook his head a bit desperately. "She paints all the men, my lord." He paused, quite likely hearing his words and realizing how they sounded. "That is, there is nothing special about Bagley, my lord."

"So you admit my wife has been sharing her favors with the entire staff?"

Walker looked as if he might cry. "My lord, no! None of the staff would ever do, ah, what you are suggesting even if Lady Ashton asked them to—which she would not because she is completely faithful to you." He took a deep breath and visibly steeled himself. "She loves you, my lord."

That was too damn much! Ash surged to his feet and planted his hands on the desk, sending Jess's papers flying every which way. "Mr. Walker, you forget yourself."

Walker staggered as if his legs had given out. "My lord."

"I want Bagley gone."

"But, my lord—"

"Tonight." He could not dismiss everyone, much as he might wish to. And he certainly couldn't dismiss Walker out of hand. He relied on him to run the manor, though it clearly was time to find his replacement.

"But, my lord." Walker's Adam's apple bobbed a few times. "Tonight?"

He must remember it was not just Bagley's fault. Jess was a Siren. A succubus. Look at how much he still wanted her, even with clear evidence of her perfidy. "Very well, he may stay the night. But I want him out of Blackweith Manor by noon tomorrow. Do I make myself clear?"

"Yes, my lord."

"Good. Now have my horse brought round."

"But, my lord, wouldn't you be more comfortable here? I can have the master's rooms made up for you in a trice."

The master's rooms with their connecting door to Jess's chambers. "No, thank you."

He had to get to the White Stag and see about losing his virginity. He was not so base as to do so with one of the maids in this house.

He frowned. He hadn't seen any female servants, had he?

Well, he hadn't seen any servants at all besides Bagley, Walker, and the two men that had greeted him—

Ah, yes. Those two.

"Walker, I expect a footman on duty at the main door at all times, especially if it is unlocked. There was no one there when I arrived."

"Yes, my lord. I shall discuss the matter with Charlie."

It was odd that Walker referred to the fellow by his first name, but he was beginning to think there was a great deal that was odd about the management of Blackweith Manor. Well, he couldn't worry about that now. He'd put this house in order once he'd dealt with the disorder of his marriage.

"And be sure he and the other man—Ralph, I believe it was—understand the importance of looking presentable. I don't know what they were doing, but they were both adjusting their livery when they finally appeared in the entryway."

Did Walker blush?

"Yes, my lord. Indeed. I will be certain to speak to them."

The White Stag was like any other inn. It was dark and smelled of cooking, stale ale, and smoke.

Winthrop, the innkeeper, looked up as Ash entered. His eyes widened. "Milord, we haven't seen ye in many a year."

In eight years, to be precise. He'd deposited Jess at

Blackweith Manor and then spent the night here, alone, before returning to Greycliffe Castle.

He didn't want to think about that night. He'd been furious with Jess and with himself. Desire had cramped his loins; desolation had echoed in his soul.

He'd felt much as he did now.

"I need a room for the night."

"Not staying at the manor, then, milord?"

He just looked at Winthrop. He bloody wouldn't be standing here if he were staying at the manor.

Winthrop comprehended. The man's face paled slightly. "Right, then. Would ye be wishing to go up straightaway, milord?"

Yes.

No. He was going to find an accommodating serving girl, wasn't he? He was going to lose his damn virginity.

"I'll take a glass of ale and something to eat in the common room."

Winthrop nodded. "Very good, milord. I'll just have your bag taken up, shall I?"

"Thank you."

The common room was crowded, but there was one empty table in the far corner by the window. Ash made his way to it, ignoring all the stares and whispers. Damnation. He'd hoped no one would recognize him, but of course everyone did. He might not have been here for eight years, but Jess's scandalous goings on had kept him present in people's minds.

He gestured for the barmaid's attention, not that he needed to do so. She was staring at him like everyone else.

He watched her approach. She had blond hair and large breasts and a saucy swing to her generous hips. She was nothing like Jess.

Thank God.

"What can I get ye, milord?" She leaned forward so he

could admire her breasts more thoroughly and gave him a suggestive smile.

Good. This would be easier than he'd thought. She was clearly expecting to be invited into his bed. He wouldn't have to spell it out.

If only she didn't smell quite so much of onions and garlic.

"I'll have a glass of ale and some roast beef."

"And would ye like some of Cook's trifle, too?" Her pink tongue peeked out to slowly wet her lips. "Or would ye rather have something else for dessert?"

This was quite bold.

But boldness was a good thing. He forced himself to smile. He should say yes. He cleared his throat. "I'll, er, think about it."

Her brows rose in surprise.

"To see if I'm still hungry." Oh, God, he hadn't said that, had he?

She stared at him a moment longer, clearly puzzled, and then shrugged. "I'll just be getting yer food then."

He watched her swing her hips back to the kitchen. All the other men watched, too, and then turned to look at him before resuming their conversations.

He looked out the window. It was too dark now to see anything but his own reflection.

If he took this woman up to his room, everyone would know it. He would shame Jess—

He clenched his fists. Hell, she'd shamed him. He'd only be giving her exactly what she deserved.

The thought did not make him happy.

He looked down at the scarred table. The lump in his stomach was just nerves. He was the only thirty-year-old male virgin in England, if not the world. Once he got this girl into bed, nature would take its course. He would enjoy the experience, just like all men did. He certainly had dreamt of it often enough.

And always with Jess.

Blast it, he was not going to be having sexual congress with Jess ever, and he did not wish to go to his grave a virgin. He couldn't. It was his duty to get an heir.

At least it looked as if his brother Ned would marry Ellie, so the burden wasn't entirely on him any longer.

The barmaid was back. He'd swear she'd tugged her bodice lower; he could almost see her nipples. Her breasts were huge white globes, like engorged cow udders.

True, he'd never particularly admired large-breasted women, but that was not the point here. The point was to rid himself of his lamentable virginity.

She leaned over to deposit his plate and mug. Now her breasts reminded him of someone's buttocks.

That was not what he was supposed to be thinking.

He took a large swallow of ale. Courage. Determination. "What is your name?"

"Nan, milord." She batted her eyelashes. "I've a few minutes. Would ye like me to sit with ye while ye eat?"

His stomach twisted. "I don't want to keep you from your work."

Idiot! He was supposed to say yes. Yes, please.

She shrugged and her breasts threatened to hit him in the nose. "Fanny will wait on the other lads for a while."

He looked over toward the kitchen. An older woman was watching them. She smiled and waggled her brows. Oh, damn. Clearly there was no such thing as privacy at the White Stag. He might as well jump onto the table and announce his plans.

Well, there was nothing for it. "Very well. I could stand to have—"

She plopped down on the bench next to him.

"—some company."

She pressed up against his side. The smell of onions and garlic—and, sadly, body odor—was overwhelming.

He stuck his fork in his beef. He should eat. He hadn't had any food since he'd broken his fast this morning.

The meat was tough and stringy. The inn hadn't been known for its cuisine eight years ago, and it appeared the cooking had not improved.

"Have ye come to fetch Lady Ashton, then, milord?"

He put his fork down. He had no appetite at all. "No."

He did not wish to discuss Jess.

The girl nodded. "That's what we figured." She looked at him from under her lashes. "Ye know we're jealous of yer lady, milord. She has all those handsome men around her at the manor. She must be sorely tempted." She batted her lashes. "Not that ye aren't as handsome as any of them, o' course, but ye've been away." She looked down and put her hand on his thigh, quite close to his cock—his sadly flaccid cock, completely unmoved by her nearness. "Ye must know people say she's had no trouble keeping warm at night."

The image of that bloody footman, Bagley, slammed into his mind, quickly followed by the vision of Jess with her hair hanging down her back . . .

That image caused his cock to stir.

He shifted so Nan's hand slipped off his leg. "I do not discuss my wife."

The girl's lower lip jutted out. "I only wanted to offer ye some comfort, milord. Ye must be lonely."

He was lonely. Terribly lonely.

He looked over the room. The men, who'd all been watching as avidly as any London gossip, returned their attention to their meals.

He *should* take Nan up to his room. Jess deserved it.

But Nan didn't deserve to be used in such a fashion.

She should be taken in love or at least in lust, not in anger. Not because he wished to hurt his wife.

And in any event, the question was academic. It would not just be Jess who would be mortified if he brought this girl to his bed. His cock was clearly unwilling to rise to the occasion unless Jess was involved. It now lay between his thighs as if dead.

He felt dead. All he wanted to do was take a bottle of brandy upstairs and get blindingly, numbingly drunk.

"Thank you, Nan, but I find I am not feeling quite the thing. I believe I'll retire for the night."

She smiled hopefully.

"Alone."

Chapter Three

Fear is rarely a good companion.

—Venus's Love Notes

"It's over, blast it. It's finally over. I'm bloody *happy* it's over." Jess threw her private sketchbook, the one she used for the drawings only she would see, at the fire, but the pages caught the air, and the book fluttered to the floor, inches short of her target.

Roger, leaning against the mantel, bent over and picked it up.

"Give me that." She almost stepped on Kit's tail in her hurry to grab the book, but Roger held it over his head.

"No. You've been drawing in this for as long as I've known you, Jess. It must be important, since you never show it to anyone. I will not let you consign it to the flames."

The book was full of pictures of Kit. She stretched to grab it from him. "Don't you dare look inside."

"Of course I won't." Roger's expression was a mixture of disgust and pity. "You know me better than that."

She did know him better. What was the matter with her? She pushed her hair off her face. "I'm sorry."

"You're merely feeling a trifle overset," Dennis said, pausing in his pacing by the door.

They were in her bedroom, which looked like a whirlwind

had hit it. Her valise was open on her bed, and everything she owned was strewn about. She had pulled things out of drawers, then put them back, then pulled them out again, all while arguing with—and sometimes shouting at—Roger and Dennis.

Her maid, Dennis's older sister Helena, had fled an hour ago, unable to stand the battle raging around her. Kit was hiding under the bed—all of him but his tail.

"A trifle overset?" Roger snorted. "She's dicked in the nob." He glared at her. "Get back to packing, Jess. You need to go after your husband tonight if you want to have any hope of saving your marriage."

Roger was the bedlamite here. "Didn't you hear Lord Ashton? It's already too late. He wants nothing more to do with me."

Kit was going to divorce her. She was going to lose him forever. Oh, God. Pain lanced through her, so intense she could barely breathe.

"Of course I heard him," Roger said. "Surely you weren't surprised? Zeus, Jess, I was stark naked, and you had your arms around me. Of course he said he's washed his hands of you."

"But it meant nothing." She dragged her hair out of her face again and tried to breathe. "It was completely innocent."

Why the *hell* had Kit arrived at that precise moment? Damnation, she really did have the world's worst luck. The time with Percy, that, she'd admit, hadn't been innocent. Stupid, desperate, but not innocent. But this time—

Oh, what did it matter? Kit would never believe her. He would divorce her, and Roger . . .

"You should not lose your position over it, Roger. You were only trying to help, and now Lord Ashton is throwing you out of the house."

"But not until tomorrow," Dennis said.

"And Roger should be *happy* for that?"

"Jess," Roger said, "I *am* happy. I'm damned relieved. For a moment there, I was certain your husband was going to tear my head—and other precious parts—from my body."

"Yes." Dennis gripped the doorjamb. "I was terrified Lord Ashton would do Roger an injury."

Of course Dennis would worry about Roger. They were like an old married couple.

"Oh, you needn't have been concerned. Lord Ashton doesn't fight." She'd flown to Kit's defense on more than one occasion when they were children and Percy had been teasing Kit, not that he'd ever thanked her for her efforts. And the time she'd seen Percy and Kit actually come to blows, Percy had bloodied Kit's nose.

If she were being truthful, she'd admit she'd always admired how calm, rational, and controlled Kit was, but his lack of reaction was also infuriating. If he'd railed at her when he'd found her with Percy, she would have yelled back, and perhaps they would have settled what was between them.

Who the hell was she trying to fool? There was nothing between them—the feelings were all on her side. A marquis couldn't love a groom's daughter.

But they had been friends once.

"I'm sure with enough provocation Lord Ashton would fight—and he was extremely provoked today." Roger grinned. "I'd wager my next quarter's wages—if I were going to get any wages next quarter—that he'd strip to advantage."

"Oh, yes." Dennis sounded far too enthusiastic. "He's one of those tall, wiry men who are often surprisingly strong. And well muscled."

"Mmm." Roger nodded. "Lean and long. And controlled—

don't forget how angry he was. I wouldn't mind watching him go a few rounds."

Were these two lusting after her husband? "Well, you're both wrong. I told you the marquis doesn't fight. I doubt he knows how to."

Roger raised a brow. "When have you seen Lord Ashton fight?"

"A few years ago." Why were they looking at her that way? "When we were children."

Roger snorted. "Children? Come, Jess. Your husband is not a child any longer." He grinned lasciviously. "I suspect you'd find him most, ah, inspiring if you were to paint him without his shirt and pantaloons."

An odd, embarrassing heat bloomed in her gut. Her skin—her breasts—suddenly felt overly sensitive.

And then a thin finger of panic curled around her heart. She could not let herself think of Kit that way. If she did, the emptiness in her life would swallow her.

"He was only angry because he thought you'd cuckolded him, Roger. You hurt his pride. Hopefully he'll reconsider by tomorrow and let you stay on."

Roger gave her a long look. "You don't believe that, do you?"

"What do you mean? Of course I believe it. It's the truth."

"No, it's not. I wouldn't have thought it, since he's stayed away so long, but your husband loves you, Jess."

Hope fluttered momentarily in her breast.

She squashed it. Roger couldn't know. She'd never told him about Percy. She'd never discussed the details with Dennis, either. "No, he doesn't. Trust me, our marriage was a mistake Lord Ashton regretted the moment the offer left his lips." She pushed her hair out of her eyes again. Where was the blasted cord she used to tie it back? Her pins had fallen all over the floor.

Ah, there it was. She stepped over Kit's tail and snatched it off her pillow.

"I think Roger's right," Dennis said. He almost always thought Roger was right. "The marquis has very strong feelings for you, Jess."

"Yes. Hatred and disgust."

"No," Roger said. "Love and passion."

What was the matter with the man? He wasn't usually as thick as a post. "Damnation, Roger. You can't know what Lord Ashton is feeling. You aren't . . . that is, you don't . . ."

She jerked her hair back and tied it with the cord. Roger wasn't the least bit interested in women. When she was painting him, his male bit was floppy and small. But let Dennis walk into the room, and it sprang up, growing to twice its size. It was very annoying if that happened to be the part of him she was painting at the time.

And it wasn't just Roger and Dennis; all the men at the manor were that way. Dennis had explained things in a rather roundabout fashion when she'd arrived.

At first she was shocked, but she soon realized the situation was very much to her advantage. The men were polite, neat, and orderly, and she never had to repulse an improper advance. She felt safe. Yes, the neighbors talked, but they'd talk even if she had only female servants. There was no avoiding the fact that she was the Marquis of Ashton's discarded bride.

Well, all right, the neighbors wouldn't say quite the same things if her servants were all female. Everyone thought she had a male harem at the manor. It was annoying, but there was nothing to be done about it. She certainly wasn't going to tell anyone what was really going on. Men of Dennis's and Roger's ilk weren't safe in society if their true interests were known.

"I may not be attracted to women," Roger was saying,

"but I still understand love and passion." His gaze rested on Dennis.

She wished Kit would look at her that way.

And then he looked back at her. "Trust me, Jess. Lord Ashton loves you rather desperately."

"No, he doesn't." Roger was at heart a starry-eyed romantic who, like the ancient Roman poet Virgil, thought love conquered all. Ha! If she went to Kit now and threw herself at his feet, he'd just kick her in the teeth.

It was over. Hell, it had never begun. She needed to move on, to make plans. First she'd need a place to live, but where could she go?

She studied Roger. He had his hands on his hips and a look of extreme exasperation on his face.

Hmm. Kit was tossing him out, too. It was unlikely he'd find a situation like the one at Blackweith, but if he went back to London, his mother would be after him to take a wife. He was actually a baron, and his mother understandably thought he should be busy getting an heir, even though he had a perfectly pleasant younger brother to inherit and ensure that the title continued. It was one of the reasons he'd left Town—that, and the fear that his, er, special interests would be discovered.

A sham marriage might be the perfect solution to both their problems.

"Roger, will you marry me?"

Roger's eyebrows shot up. "*What?* Are you daft?"

"No. Think about it." It was a good idea. Not a great one, but at least it would keep her from sleeping in the hedgerows. And she did like Roger. "Once Ash divorces me, I'll be more of an outcast than I am already. I won't even have a roof over my head."

"Lord Ashton would never turn you out." Dennis sounded shocked. "I'm sure he'll find some place for you to stay." He frowned and looked at Roger. "Though not at the manor. I suppose there will be some changes here."

"Exactly," she said. "Things won't be as comfortable for anyone at Blackweith if the marquis starts taking an active interest in it."

Dennis rubbed the space between his eyebrows, a sure sign he was upset. "It's true the marquis was quite displeased with me."

"He shouldn't hold you accountable for what he perceives to be my sins," Roger said, his voice now rough with anger.

Dennis shook his head. "I'm the estate manager. I'm sure he thinks I shouldn't let such things go on. Well, I know he feels that way. He told me years ago to keep an eye on Jess and tell him if she was engaging in assignations."

"See?" Roger said, looking at Jess. "The marquis is jealous."

She couldn't let herself believe that. "He's just interested in protecting the succession."

Dennis pinched the bridge of his nose. "And he was most displeased that no one was at the door when he arrived." He looked miserable. "It did make the manor appear poorly managed."

"Damnation." Roger sighed. "I suppose Charlie was on duty."

Dennis nodded. "But he was off with Ralph."

"You know those two have no sense and less control."

"Yes, but they're young. I was hoping . . ." Dennis let out a long breath. "But now everything will come tumbling down. If the marquis finds out exactly what's been going on here, we may all be let go . . . or worse."

Even Roger was looking glum now.

"But if you marry me, Roger, you can hide in plain sight. You can return to London and your place in society.

Then you can take on Dennis as your secretary or valet or something. You could even hire the rest of the men. No one need know how things really are."

"I would not risk having Charlie or Ralph in London," Roger said.

"But you could employ Archie and Barnabas and Walter and Philip and any number of the others."

Roger looked at Dennis.

"It might not be a bad idea," Dennis said, somewhat hopefully.

"And what would everyone say when there were no children, Jess?" Roger raised his brows. "Or were you hoping I'd manage to give you a child or two?"

"No, of course not." She hadn't thought of children.

No, she *had* thought of children—Kit's children. Warmth curled around her heart. . . .

Zeus! Kit was going to divorce her. There would be no children, ever. "I have my painting to keep me busy. Children would be a distraction."

"But won't people wonder?" Dennis asked. "Roger will be expected to get an heir."

"You've heard the rumors. Everyone assumes I'm barren, since I've supposedly had relations with hundreds of men and never conceived."

"Bloody gossip." Roger didn't bother to protest that no one believed it, because they all knew everyone did.

Her dog, perhaps hearing the distress in her voice, crawled out from under the bed. He leaned against her, and she laid a hand on his head, taking comfort from his solid, furry presence. At least she had one friend who would stand by her. "So, Roger, will you marry me?"

He looked at her for a long moment and then nodded. "Assuming your husband doesn't throw up any legal barriers to our nuptials, yes, I'll consider it—on one condition."

Her heart plummeted. Blast it, she should be happy.

This was the solution to her problem. She forced her lips into a smile. "Why would Lord Ashton object?"

"Because, as I said, he loves you."

"He does not."

If only Roger were right . . .

But he wasn't. If Kit had ever felt anything remotely like love for her, she'd killed it when she'd made her ill-considered decision to encourage Percy.

"And you love him."

"No, I—"

He pointed at her sketchbook. "If I did look inside this, I think I'd find the truth of it."

She bit her lip. She could lie, but her pencil could not. "So what's your condition?"

"That you spend six months in his company."

"What?" Kit wouldn't spend six minutes—six seconds—with her. "Are you mad?"

Kit—her dog, Kit—whined and looked up at her. She stroked his ears and took a deep breath, swallowing panic.

Roger caught her gaze with his. "Jess, you've loved this man your whole life. You can't give him up without at least trying to mend matters."

She shook her head. "It's too late." Perhaps if Kit hadn't walked into the studio when he had—but there was no changing that.

"It's *not* too late." Roger crossed his arms and leaned back against the mantel. "Why do you think he's here?"

"You heard him. To tell me he's going to begin divorce proceedings."

"He could have done that via the post—isn't that right, Dennis?"

Dennis nodded. "Yes. Now that you mention it, that's what I would have expected."

"Exactly." Roger lifted one blasted eyebrow. "Do you want to know why I think he's here?"

Oh, splendid. Now Roger wished to play guessing games. "If I say no, you'll tell me anyway."

He grinned. "I think he wants an heir."

Her dog whined again as she stiffened. An heir. Oh, God. A baby. Kit's. Warmth spread round her heart again—and round a point rather lower in her body.

Fool! She was letting her dreams lead her to false hope. "Don't be ridiculous."

"He needs an heir and a spare, doesn't he? And you are his wife."

"His discarded, detested wife."

Roger actually rolled his eyes. "Not detested."

"He hates me." She saw Kit's beautiful gray eyes again, hard with disgust, as he looked on her in Roger's arms.

"Sometimes what looks like hate is just frustrated desire."

"And sometimes what looks like hate is just gut-twisting loathing."

"But it's passion. Don't you see? If your husband didn't care for you, he wouldn't be so angry."

Roger was purposely being obtuse. "He'll be angry enough to slam the door in my face if I follow him to the White Stag. He certainly won't want to . . . that is, there is no way he'd want to . . ." She swallowed. Damnation, the warmth had moved to her cheeks now.

"Not right away, of course. You heard him—he thinks there's a chance you might be increasing. He'll want to wait until he can be certain any child you carry is his. But that is to your advantage. It gives you time to get to know him again and to be certain how you feel." Roger shrugged. "A man can change a lot in eight years. You've likely changed, too."

"Yes." That was her way out. "He's changed. I've changed. As I said, it's too late."

Roger came over to grip her shoulders. "That's fear talking."

She opened her mouth to protest, but . . . Roger was right. She *was* afraid.

"Don't let fear determine your life, Jess. Go talk to your husband."

"He won't want to see me."

"Make him see you. Make him hear you. Bargain with him. I think he'll listen to you. A divorce is long and expensive and very, very messy. You'll be a social outcast—"

"I already am that."

"—but so will he, if to a lesser extent. It's in his best interest to make a marriage with you work." His grip tightened. "What do you have to lose?"

What *did* she have to lose? She'd already lost everything.

"And if you find he doesn't love you—or if you discover you don't love him any longer—then we can discuss a sham marriage."

"All right." She'd never let fear rule her before, had she? Well, perhaps she had in these last years, but she didn't like that thought. Not at all. "I'll go."

When Roger pulled the horse to a stop outside the White Stag half an hour later, Jess clutched the side of the wagon. She looked at the light spilling out of the inn's windows.

Kit was inside.

Her stomach churned with a mixture of excitement and dread.

Dread won. "This is a bad idea."

"No, it's not." Roger climbed down and came around to

her side. "Pluck up your courage, Jess." He grinned as he offered her his hand. "The marquis doesn't stand a chance. I know all too well how stubborn you can be when you decide on something."

But this was Kit. No one had ever mattered as much to her, and failure had never been so frightening. "But what if he refuses to see me?"

"He won't, but if he does, you must dig in your heels and refuse to be refused. Camp outside his door. Follow him when he leaves. Demand his attention."

She let Roger help her down, and her dog leapt down to stand beside her; she put her hand on his big furry head to steady herself. Roger was correct. She did have a backbone—she just needed to find it.

He took her valise out of the back of the wagon. She had only one small bag. Most of her things were old and paint spattered, so she'd left them behind.

"Stop worrying. Believe in yourself, for God's sake. You always have before." Roger clasped her arm briefly. "Remember, you hold the winning card in this game. The marquis wants an heir, and you are his most expedient path to that goal."

"I don't know. . . ." Panic clawed at her throat again.

"It's only to give you time, Jess. To give you both time to get to know each other again. You are doing Lord Ashton a favor, too."

She swallowed, forcing the panic down, and nodded. Yes, it was time to settle this, if only so she could finally move on with her life.

She might have been in love with a phantasm all these years.

And she hadn't been the only one at fault. Kit had chosen to marry her. He'd offered, even if it had been only a charitable impulse. Not all marriages were built on love.

They could have worked out an arrangement if he had been willing to try.

He should not have abandoned her. He bore some responsibility for their current situation. "You're right."

Roger grinned. "Of course I'm right. Now here is your bag. I'd walk you to the door, but I don't believe my presence will help your case."

She took her valise and frowned. "Have you decided what you are going to do?"

"Yes. I'm going back to London. That way if you do wish to discuss a liaison later, I'll have resumed my place as Baron Trendal."

She smiled, glad to feel happy about some decision, even though it wasn't her own. "Your mother and brother will be delighted to see you."

"Yes, I think they will be. And, Jess," he said as she turned to go into the White Stag.

"What?"

"I put something in your bag."

Damnation, Roger had a very amused expression. Surely he wasn't pulling some prank? He did have an odd sense of humor, but this was not the time for foolishness. "What is it?"

"I thought you might need some help with Lord Ashton, so I'm loaning you my favorite advice sheets. Please take good care of them—I want them back."

"Yes, of course." Advice sheets? How ridiculous. She would put them away in a safe place and try to be convincingly appreciative when she returned them.

"Oh, and I wouldn't let Lord Ashton see any of them if I were you."

"Very well." There was little chance of that, especially as she had no intention of consulting them.

He grinned as if he knew exactly what she was thinking. "And remember when you deal with old Winthrop, or anyone else who may try to keep you from your husband, you are the Marchioness of Ashton, a very important, very exalted personage."

The *discarded* Marchioness of Ashton. "And I have a very large dog."

He nodded, and his grin widened. "But when you are with Lord Ashton, you are just his wife." He leaned toward her, all humor dropping from his voice. "Jess, you've been in limbo for eight years. This is your chance to settle things. Don't let anything or anyone stop you."

She *had* been like a leaf spinning in an eddy, caught by her connection to Kit from moving downstream. Even her art had suffered. Her pictures felt flat—pretty enough, but lacking much emotion. "Yes. I shall try."

Roger gave her a quick hug, and then climbed back into the wagon. "Good luck."

She waved as he drove away, and then she looked down at her dog. There was no turning back now.

"Come, Kit. It's time to see if your namesake will listen to me."

When she opened the inn door, Mr. Winthrop did not look happy to see her. "Lady Ashton!" He frowned at her dog and then at her valise. "Where is your maid?"

She was not going to get into a discussion of the proprieties. "Where is my husband?"

The innkeeper sniffed as if he smelled something unpleasant. He'd never liked her—well, none of the local people had. "I'm not certain that is any of your concern, madam."

Her temper came to her rescue. She leaned forward as menacingly as she could—and it helped that Kit growled low in his throat and bared his teeth slightly. He was the best of animals, quite gentle unless he sensed that she was threatened.

"I am still *Lady* Ashton, sirrah, so I believe the location of Lord Ashton is very much my concern."

"Ah." Winthrop stepped back. "Er." He looked at her

dog and paled. "Very well. If you must know, he's upstairs in number ten." And then he managed to leer at her. "Though I'm not certain he's alone."

Oh, God. She did not want to walk in on Kit in bed with a whore. That would surely kill her.

But she had no choice in the matter. Roger had left. She was stuck here. "Thank you. I shall go up directly."

"Perhaps it would be better if I go up first and tell His Lordship ye're here."

Perhaps it *would* be better, but she'd promised Roger she would not let anyone stop her, and Mr. Winthrop looked like he would do exactly that. "That won't be necessary."

She started up the stairs before she could lose her nerve.

The last time she'd been in an inn with Kit was on their wedding night. He'd been taking her to the manor. She'd ridden alone in the carriage all day, but she'd kept her spirits up thinking she could make things right with him once they stopped for the night. She'd got ready for bed, leaving off her nightgown, and waited for him to come to her. When he hadn't, she'd gone to him—and found his door locked.

She'd been young. She'd allowed her anger to carry her down the stairs in the morning and back out to the carriage. When Kit had deposited her at the manor that afternoon, she'd not said a word.

Nor had he.

She'd thought he'd come back the next day.

The next week.

The next month.

He hadn't.

Well, this time things would be different. They had to be. This was her last chance. If Kit didn't listen to her now, he never would.

Her feet felt like lead, but she kept her chin up. She

couldn't retreat even if she wanted to; she would not give Winthrop that satisfaction.

And, in any event, her dog was behind her, blocking her escape.

She reached the landing and turned right. Number ten was at the end of the longest corridor she'd ever encountered, but she forced herself to keep walking.

What if Kit was with a whore?

Perhaps that would be a good thing. It should cure her of this infatuation with Kit, and she would be able to tell Roger tomorrow that she knew beyond a shadow of a doubt that she was ready—anxious!—to be done with the marquis. They could begin to make plans. It would be a while before she was free to actually marry, of course, but it would be best for Dennis and the other men to know that they would eventually have a place to live.

She stopped in front of number ten. "This is it, Kit." She was talking to her dog—and perhaps her husband. She raised her hand to knock.

Chapter Four

*Sometimes opportunity's knock
sounds most unpleasant.*

—Venus's Love Notes

Ash was halfway through the brandy bottle when some idiot knocked on his door.

Maybe if he ignored the nodcock, he'd go away. Or *she'd* go away. Surely that barmaid hadn't been so bold as to come to his room? He took another swallow of brandy.

The cabbage-head knocked again.

Damnation, was the fellow—or female—going to keep at it all night? Clearly there was only one way to deal with the fool. He lurched to his feet—and steadied himself on his chair as the room spun round.

Perhaps he should have eaten something after all.

Too late for that now. He lurched over to the door and flung it open.

Good God!

He felt his jaw drop, but he was powerless to stop it. His eyes were likely starting from their sockets as well.

Jess stood in the corridor with her valise and her bear-like dog.

"Good evening, Lord Ashton. May I come in?"

Jess wanted to come into his bedchamber? His cock leapt with joy.

He should *never* have drunk so much brandy. "No."

She looked momentarily nonplussed, but then her expression hardened as it had so many times when they were children and Percy or Jack had told her she couldn't do something.

"Nonsense. We have things to discuss." She brushed past him.

He should have blocked her way, but surprise delayed him and then her dog stepped on his foot.

Pain paralyzed him. Black specks danced before his eyes; he couldn't even find the breath to curse.

"I suggest you close the door, my lord, unless you wish to treat the entire inn to our discussion."

Yes. Close the door. He pushed it shut and leaned his forehead against it, striving for control. He'd never done a woman injury, but Jess's pert tone made him want to wrap his hands around her throat and squeeze. As soon as he got over the pain of having his foot mashed, that is. Her dog must weigh over ten stone.

He heard the soft rustle of cloth behind him as Jess removed her coat and bonnet, and his cock throbbed.

No, he didn't want to throttle her. He wanted to strip her out of her dress and stays and shift, lay her on that bed that was just a few steps away, and bury himself deep inside her.

If only he'd opened the door eight years ago when they'd stopped at the inn on the way to the manor. He'd heard the latch rattle. It had taken all his control—well, and the bottle of brandy he'd consumed—to keep him sprawled in his chair. If he'd let her in, hauled her into his bed . . .

No. She'd been with Percy. She might have had Percy's get growing in her womb.

She was his wife. He had the right to her body. She'd

come here and bade him close the door so they could be alone. She was asking him to take her.

He pressed his forehead harder against the door. No, she wasn't. He didn't know why she was here, but it wasn't for that. And even if it *were* for that, he couldn't give in to his urges. Just like the last time they were in an inn together, she might be carrying another man's child.

"Are you ever going to come away from the door?"

Control. He needed control. He took a deep breath and let it out slowly.

"I do not see the need for discussion, madam." He turned to face her. Zeus, why the hell did she have to be so beautiful? "There is nothing to say."

He'd always loved how her dark hair contrasted with her pale skin and how her eyebrows tilted up at the ends. And she had such lovely cheekbones and a straight nose that was perhaps too strong for beauty but which fit her face perfectly....

Blast it, she *was* a Siren. He'd caught her twice in the arms of a naked man, and yet he still wanted her.

Her jaw flexed. "There is much to say." She glanced down to pat her dog and then met his eyes again. "You arrived at a very awkward moment."

God give him strength. "At least this time your legs weren't spread for the fellow. I count myself fortunate to have missed that sight."

He thought she flushed, though it was hard to know for certain in the flickering candlelight.

"Roger is a friend. He poses for me when I wish to paint the male form."

Ah, yes. Painting the male form, just as she'd been supposedly painting Percy. "He's your friend, is he? Your *very special* friend, no doubt."

Her dog did not care for his tone. The animal growled.

"Hush, Kit. Lord Ashton is just barking; he won't bite. Go lie down by the fire."

He half wished she was wrong about that, but she wasn't. Even her extreme provocation could not move him to violence. If only the damn footman were here. He'd very much enjoy beating *him* to a pulp.

He watched the dog amble over to stretch out on the hearth. "Why the hell did you name him after me?" And to use his Christian name . . . Jess had been the only one ever to call him Kit. Even his parents used his title. Hearing her say it now, and to an animal—

He'd thought she couldn't hurt him any more, but she kept finding new ways to turn the knife in his gut.

She ignored his question. "Yes, Roger is a very special friend, Lord Ashton. I love him . . . as a *brother*."

Zeus! "It is a very good thing you have no brothers then, madam. He was *naked,* for God's sake."

"Of course he was naked. I was painting him."

"You were embracing him." Did she think him a complete dolt? Perhaps she did. He'd married her after he'd caught her with her skirts around her ears and Percy between her thighs. She likely thought he would forgive her any sin. Well, she was very much mistaken.

"No. *He* was embracing *me*."

"Oh, really? It looked to me as if you were an enthusiastic participant. Your arms were around the man."

"Yes, but that was only so I wouldn't—" She bit her lip, grasped her hands in front of her, and actually glared at him. "Roger was only hugging me because I'd agreed to finally seek you out to discuss the state of our marriage. There was nothing at all salacious about it."

Their marriage. Yes. Their nonexistent marriage that he was going to put an end to. She was trying to distract him, pretending she'd been thinking of seeing him. Hell, her constant lies were as bad as her whoring.

He forced down his rage. He would *not* lose control. He would treat her to an icy silence.

His mouth had other ideas. "Just as there was nothing salacious about your encounter with Percy?"

He most definitely should not have drunk so much brandy on an empty stomach.

"Yes. No." At least she had the grace to look guilty. "Nothing actually happened with Percy."

A red haze bloomed in front of his eyes. He clenched his fists, digging his fingernails into his flesh. "Forgive me for doubting you on that, madam. I was there, if you will remember. I *saw* him swiving you."

His stomach twisted, threatening to rid itself of the brandy he'd drunk. He swallowed determinedly. He would not so embarrass himself before this jade.

The jade had the gall to scowl at him. "No, you didn't. I stopped him before it came to that."

"He said he'd had you." Percy had got up and offered them—him and Morton, one of Mama's guests, and Alfred, a footman—their turn with her since he was done.

Oh, God. His stomach rebelled again. That had been the worst few minutes of his life. He'd wanted to think it was rape, but Jess had not been struggling, and when he'd accused Percy of violence, she hadn't disputed the man's assertion that she'd been a willing participant.

He shoved the memory away.

"He was lying. I . . . he . . ." Jess was definitely flushing now, as well she might. "I stopped him."

How stupid did she think he was? He might be a virgin, completely inexperienced with women, but he knew copulation when he saw it. He'd grown up in the country. He'd observed enough animals busy about the business.

"Percy was naked and between your thighs. I think we both know how the thing is done."

"But it *wasn't* done. I said I stopped him before he"—she looked away—"before it came to that."

She'd said that at the time. He hadn't believed her then, and he didn't believe her now. There was no way in hell a man in Percy's position would stop. And that wasn't all.

"Jesus, Jess. Your poor father wasn't even cold in his grave." O'Brien, her father and their head groom, the best horseman in the county, had broken his neck going over a jump just days before.

She narrowed her eyes. "I know that. Why do you think I—" She pressed her lips tightly together.

Zeus, had she been holding on to her virginity so as not to embarrass her father? He'd heard she was a bit of a flirt and that some of the footmen and male guests had stolen kisses, but he'd never completely believed the whisperings—she'd certainly never flirted with him—and even so, he'd never thought she'd go beyond kisses.

He was a naive idiot.

"I'm surprised you knew about my father," she said now.

Did she sound hurt? "Of course I knew. My father told me as soon as I got home."

"Oh? I thought—" She bit her lip again. "Never mind."

"You thought what?"

"That you would have come to see me." Her voice was a bit shrill; her dog lifted his head at the sound and gave a muted woof. "Though of course you were much too busy, and I was only a groom's daughter."

He felt a twinge of guilt. He'd wanted to seek her out. He'd been shocked by her father's death, and he knew—or he'd thought—she'd be distraught. Her mother had died when she was very young, before she'd come to the castle, and she'd always been very close to her father.

But Mama had been having one of her matchmaking house parties, and Lady Charlotte, the daughter of the Duke of Delton, had stuck to him like a burr. It hadn't been until the next afternoon that he'd been able to free himself of her dogged pursuit and slip off to the cottage he and Jess used as a studio, and then Morton, who fancied himself an artist, had invited himself along. To make matters even worse, Alfred happened upon them just as Ash was opening the cottage door. Jess and Percy had had quite the audience.

Oh, *God*. Every time he remembered that scene, his stomach twisted.

There'd been no hope of hushing up the scandal. Morton might not have mentioned it—Jess *was* only a groom's daughter—but Alfred would have spread the tale far and wide. The footman was as bad as the worst London gossip. Ash had made it clear he was not to breathe a word of what he'd seen, but he wasn't certain the man could hold his tongue for long.

Not that he should have cared. Jess deserved everything she got. But . . .

If word had got round, she would not have been able to find a husband or get a position, even if Mama would give her a reference, which he hadn't been entirely sure she would. Jess would have been alone and unprotected.

Which had been no reason for him to sacrifice himself to save her, damn it.

"I did come see you—and look what I saw you doing."

She flinched as if he'd hit her—and then her jaw hardened.

"It was more than a day after you arrived home." She looked over at her dog again. "Not that it mattered."

"I had responsibilities." He didn't need to explain himself to her.

"Yes. Of course. Your mother's guests."

Good God, was she trying to make him think that her spreading her legs for Percy was somehow his fault?

He should have washed his hands of her, but she was his

friend and, yes, he'd loved her. She'd looked defiant and angry that day, but also lost, standing there with her hair falling out of its pins and her clothes awry. And he'd seen something he'd never seen before in her eyes—fear and despair. He'd offered for her without thinking.

And see where it had got him? Married to a woman who was no better than a whore. Was there a man within a ten-mile radius of the manor that she hadn't graced with her favors?

"Why did you do it, Jess? Why did you let Percy touch you?"

She flushed. "I thought Percy loved me."

"Percy?" He laughed. "Come, madam, you must know Percy loves no one but himself."

She did know it.

No, that wasn't true. She'd thought Percy cared for her. It might not have been love, but she would have sworn it was more than lust, though he did lust after her as well. He'd been pursuing her since she'd turned fifteen and grown breasts.

She looked at the tall, angry man still standing by the door. It had never mattered if Percy had loved her or not. She had always loved Kit. She'd thought—or perhaps she'd only hoped—that he'd felt something for her, too, something maybe not quite love but more than friendship.

But she'd never had the courage to find out. She hadn't wanted to risk losing his friendship. If she'd flirted with Kit and he'd repulsed her, she'd be left with nothing.

Apparently she'd always been afraid to risk too much with him.

And then her father had died, and she'd panicked. Could Kit understand that?

No. Her husband was the Marquis of Ashton and would

someday be the Duke of Greycliffe. He had wealth and property and prestige and a family who loved him. His position in the world was assured. He likely had never had to worry about anything.

She was the only spot of tarnish on his silver spoon.

But he had married her. She might have made a mistake with Percy—she *had* made a mistake—but Kit had not been compelled to offer himself as a sacrifice. It was his fault they were wed.

Well, and hers, too. She should have told him no. But she'd been desperate, with her father dead and no family to turn to, no way to earn her living. And she'd wanted Kit. She'd thought their friendship and her love could trump her lack of social standing.

She'd thought she could persuade him to love her.

Roger had said he already did, but Roger was mistaken. Lord Ashton did not look at all amorous at the moment. He looked disdainful and angry.

Well, she was stuck here, and she'd promised Roger—and herself—that she would try to reach a bargain with the marquis. She clasped her hands together—she *would* keep a tight rein on her temper and her unruly tongue—and took a deep breath. Best to start with an apology. "Lord Ashton, I deeply regret the scene with Percy you saw so many years ago."

He snorted. "And do you also regret what happened with your footman just a few hours ago?"

Could the bloody man be more supercilious? He looked like he had a poker up his arse.

"Damnation, Kit. How many times do I have to say it? *Nothing happened with Roger!*"

All right, perhaps she wasn't going to be able to control her temper. Unlike Kit. His expression hadn't changed. The blasted man never lost control—

Except when he'd seen her with Percy, and again today with Roger. Then there'd been a crack in his almighty restraint. Maybe he *did* feel something for her besides his current disgust.

And maybe fairies painted the grass with frost in the nighttime.

"You can say it as many times as you wish, madam. Repetition will not make it true."

If he called her madam once more, she would kick him in the shins.

"Why the hell did you marry me, Kit, if you find me so revolting? You weren't the one who compromised me—not that a servant can really be compromised. And I certainly didn't expect you to offer for me."

Blast, she hadn't meant to say that, either.

Kit's brows shot up and then slammed down again. He looked away. "I don't think you're revolting." His voice was strained. He shrugged. "But I'll admit offering for you was a mistake."

Pain lanced through her. So he agreed . . .

And he was looking down his aristocratic nose at her again, blast it all. She was tired of it.

"It's not as if you've been a saint either, you know. I've read the newspapers and heard all the rumors."

He looked surprised. "And what do they say?"

He must know very well what they said. "They go on and on about your countless amatory exploits, of course." Some had even suggested Kit loved men as well as women, but she'd discounted those stories. Roger or Dennis would have told her if that were the case. "And they claim you've had a long-standing liaison with Ellie."

She was very happy she'd been able to say Ellie's name without her voice breaking.

Kit snorted. "That's ridiculous. There is nothing between Ellie and me."

Oh! He was either an excellent actor or what he said was true—at least now, because she believed him. She started to smile—

Wait. Ellie wasn't the only woman who he'd been linked to. He'd consorted with many ladies, some as highborn as he . . .

"Between you and someone else then? Is that why you want to end our marriage now—because you're in love?" Oh, God, yet another thing she hadn't meant to say, but the notion had just popped into her head. It made perfect sense. It hadn't been his birthday, but his heart that had sent him riding to the manor.

She'd thought her own heart couldn't get any heavier, but she'd been mistaken.

His face twisted with distaste. "I do not believe in love."

It would be sadly ironic if the Duchess of Love's oldest son truly did not believe in love, but Jess was happy to hear it hadn't been that emotion that had sent him journeying to the manor.

Perhaps there was still hope for her marriage.

"Jess," he said, finally coming away from the door, "let's not argue. You don't have to worry. I'm not going to throw you out on the street. I'll make arrangements—settle some money on you. You won't go hungry or homeless."

He would, too. He'd find her a nice little cottage and likely keep her in paint and brushes as well. It was what she wanted, wasn't it? To be left alone to paint.

No. She'd tried over the years to convince herself that was indeed all she wanted, but now, having seen Kit again . . . Roger was right—she needed to decide if she still loved her husband, and if he could be persuaded to love her.

She took a deep breath and grasped her courage with both hands. "I have a proposal for you."

His eyebrows rose. "A proposal? What—"

Someone knocked on the door. Kit looked at her. "Is that whoever brought you to the inn checking to see if I've murdered you?"

She'd wondered when Kit would realize he was stuck with her, at least for the night. "Oh, no. Roger left after he dropped me off. I don't know who that could be."

Good God. He stared at Jess. She was here until the morning. Here in his room. In his *bed*room.

Surely the inn had another chamber available.

The idiot in the corridor knocked again, blast it. Ash turned, grabbed the handle, and flung the door open.

Winthrop stood there, his hand raised to knock once more.

Good. He could ask the fellow about procuring a room for Jess.

The innkeeper was looking her up and down as if she were a clod of horse dung someone had tracked into his inn. "Milord, would ye like me to have this woman removed?"

Jess made a small, pained sound. Anger surged through Ash.

"'This woman,' Winthrop, is my wife, the Marchioness of Ashton, as well you know. You will show her the proper respect."

Winthrop's eyes widened and he ducked his head, bowing in a disgustingly fawning manner. "My apologies, milord. I thought—"

"Don't." Ash looked over at Jess. "Have you had your supper yet, madam?"

Jess smiled at him—the bright smile she used to give him when she was a girl—and shook her head. "No, my lord."

He hadn't managed to choke down a single bite in the common room, but now he found he was famished—but not for Winthrop's stringy beef. Perhaps the kitchen could do better with something else. "Send up some roast duck, bread, and vegetables, Winthrop, and a bottle of Madeira."

"Very good, milord." Winthrop bowed and departed.

Jess was still smiling at him. "Thank you for not letting Winthrop throw me out."

Her smile was doing very odd things to his heart. "I would never let you be treated in such a fashion. I don't know what got into the man."

Jess shrugged. "I'm afraid the local people don't approve of me."

Of course they didn't approve of her, but he didn't wish to start that argument again. It would be far too exhausting to squabble about it anymore, especially if she were really going to stay until morning. . . .

How *would* they get through the hours until daylight?

One obvious activity presented itself—

He would not think about that now, or about the bed that took up a good portion of the room. The White Stag did not cater to the aristocracy. His bedchamber was simply that—a room with a bed. There was no separate sitting room.

"How are things at the castle?" she asked, looking at the brandy bottle.

Was she nervous? She'd never been at all reticent around him when they were children. It was one of the things that had first drawn him to her. Not that the other children deferred to him, precisely, but there had always been a distance, even with his brothers, that had never been there with Jess. With them, he was Ash, one day to be Greycliffe. With Jess, he was Kit.

Or perhaps he'd just been fooling himself.

"Well, I think. I left after Mama's Valentine party."

Jess's eyes widened. "That was over a month ago."

"Yes." It was his turn to study the brandy. "I've been traveling."

"In all the snow? You must have left right after the blizzard."

He shrugged. "It did make things more difficult. That's why it took me so long to arrive at the manor. Well, and I stopped along the way for a few days."

"Find some interesting architecture?" She smiled.

He grinned. She did know him. "Yes."

The servant arrived then with their food, breaking their brief rapport.

"Thank you," Ash said. "That will be all. We shall serve ourselves." They certainly didn't need one of Winthrop's people eavesdropping on their conversation and spreading the details throughout the countryside.

"Yes, milord."

Once the fellow left, Ash held Jess's chair while she took her seat. Mmm. He smelled lavender, the same scent she'd worn as a girl—he smiled—when the scent wasn't overpowered by the smell of oil and turpentine and paint.

He sat and carved her a slice of duck. "I don't suppose you know if Winthrop's kitchen does better with this than with beef? I tried some of that downstairs earlier. It was inedible."

"No." She took a spoonful of peas. "I don't leave the manor except for Sunday services."

"You don't have any female friends in the area?" That seemed too bad, though now that he considered it, Jess had been somewhat solitary even as a girl.

She met his gaze directly. "I don't have *any* friends, male or female, outside the manor staff."

"Ah." The rumors said otherwise, but perhaps her early

success with the area's male population had faltered. Hell, she didn't need any "friends" besides that damn footman and the rest of the male servants.

"Might I have some of the Madeira?"

"Yes, of course." He poured her a glass and then reached for the brandy.

Jess concentrated on cutting her duck, not that it required much concentration. At least the inn's cook had had better success with this dish. It was almost palatable.

For a while, the silence was broken only by the scrape of their utensils. It wasn't a companionable silence, but he couldn't think of something to say that wouldn't just pitch them back into an argument. He could ask her about her proposal, but he wasn't certain he wished to hear what she might say.

"So was your mother's party successful?" Jess finally asked.

At last, a happy topic. "Yes, indeed. After years of trying, Mama managed to bring Ned and Ellie together. We celebrated their betrothal at the closing ball."

Her eyes darted up to his and then back down to her plate. "Is that why you broke things off with Ellie?"

"What?" Oh, that's right. She'd mentioned that ridiculous rumor about his relationship with Ellie Bowman. "Jess, Ellie is my friend. That is all she has ever been to me—except now she will be my sister-in-law as well. Didn't you know she's been in love with Ned since we were children?"

Jess frowned. "But Ned married Cicely."

"That didn't change Ellie's feelings." But then Jess hadn't been at the castle to see that. She hadn't been invited to Ned's first wedding, and she hadn't been there when Cicely and the baby had died.

Perhaps that had been badly done of him, but he'd felt

the only way he could manage the pain was to cut her out of his life entirely.

And now here he was, sitting across a table from her, getting ready to make their separation permanent.

He should do so without a qualm. How many more naked men did he need to find her with to understand divorce was his only option?

And yet . . .

She was so beautiful and so familiar. His idiotic heart still wished to find a path to happiness with her, to children and years of marital love.

Stupid, stupid heart.

He took a swallow of brandy. "You said you had a proposal."

Chapter Five

*Once you see the glimmer of an opening,
shove your foot into the crack.*

—Venus's Love Notes

"Yes." Jess leaned forward, her expression suddenly hardening into what looked to be determination while the candlelight made her skin glow.

God, she took his breath away.

"You need an heir."

He inclined his head. "Obviously."

"And procuring a divorce is an expensive, messy, lengthy business."

His heart—or, more likely, another organ—urged him to reach across the table and run his thumb over her lips. Instead he clasped his brandy glass more tightly. "Which is why it is time I got started with it."

Jess's lovely brows snapped down.

Zeus! When she was a girl, she used to frown like that at anyone who didn't fall in with her plans immediately.

Her fingers tapped the table. They were long and slender, and for once she'd managed to get all the paint off them.

She'd always been so happy with a brush in her hand. Her paintings, like her, had been full of life and color. That passion had been one of the things that had attracted him to her. His life had seemed dull in comparison, drawn in measured lines, painted in pale watercolor.

Perhaps he shouldn't be surprised she'd taken to depicting naked men.

"It will be painful and embarrassing for you and your family, Kit, especially your mother. She's the Duchess of Love, after all. Think of all the fun the wags will have with that."

"Yes." He had thought of it and had hoped to avoid it. It was one reason he'd made the trip to the manor to see if he and Jess might come to an agreement.

But what he'd seen was Jess with that naked footman.

He took a swallow of brandy.

"The talk will affect you, too," she said.

He shrugged. "Yes, but I'll wager the ton will forgive a future duke."

Her frown twisted into an expression he'd not seen on her face before—self-mockery. "I'm sure you are correct. They will likely forgive you even more quickly since your first wife was a servant."

She'd mentioned that earlier. "You weren't a servant, Jess. I never thought of you that way." She had always been Jess, his friend.

His love.

"Of course I was. My father was the head groom." She looked down at her plate and pushed a few lonely peas around. "Though I grant you I couldn't have found a position anywhere, unless someone wanted a painter who wasn't very good at making people look better than they are."

He had to smile at that. Cicely had been extremely put out—and Ned upset on her behalf—at the painting Jess had done of her when Cicely was fifteen. Jess had always thought the girl rather insipid, and it showed in her portrait.

But that was then, before Percy and the naked footman.

"What is your point, Jess? As you say, I need an heir." He took another sip of brandy. "Are you offering to give me one?"

"Yes."

The brandy went down the wrong way. Jess started to get up to thump him on the back, but he held up his hand to stop her.

She frowned. "Are you all right?"

He nodded. He was still coughing.

"I didn't mean right away about the heir, of course. We should take some time to get reacquainted." She leaned toward him. "If you're not in love with someone else—if you don't believe in love at all—then why not see if we can salvage this marriage? If we try and find that we can't, then you can proceed with the divorce."

This had been his initial plan, but he wasn't certain it was a good one. "Why do you want to try?" In another woman, he'd suspect a desire to maintain her status as marchioness and duchess-in-waiting, but he could not believe Jess cared for that.

She looked away and shrugged. "We were friends once—or at least I thought we were."

"We *were* friends." She'd been his best friend, the only friend who seemed to see him—Kit, not the Marquis of Ashton. "But we were children then."

Her eyes were dark in the candlelight. "I'd like to see if we could be friends again. We haven't seen each other for eight years; perhaps if we spend a few months together, we'll find we can at least tolerate each other."

He would like that, too, but was friendship her true reason for proposing this plan? It seemed unlikely, especially when he could think of another more pressing one.

He took another sip of brandy. "Are you increasing?"

"No!" She looked as if she was going to throw her glass at him. "I am not."

This was obviously not the best way to begin a reconciliation, but he must be very clear. "I cannot allow another man's child to become the Duke of Greycliffe."

"How many times do I have to say it? I am not in the family way."

He'd swear Jess's teeth were clenched. Her hands definitely were. He would prefer not to push the point, but while in the past he could argue he'd never been physically close enough to get her with child, now it looked as if they would have to share this room—this bed.

"Then you'll not object to signing a paper stating that any child you may bear within the next nine months isn't mine."

Her mouth flattened into a hard, thin line; she was going to refuse.

Disappointment knotted his gut.

Hell, he was a pitiful arse, wasn't he, to want her back so badly? He should—

"Very well, I will sign your blasted paper." She spat the last word as if it were a curse. "Have you a sheet and quill handy? I have a few clauses I wish to include myself."

He should be angry at her tone, but he was mostly relieved. He stood. "I didn't bring any writing materials, but I shall ask Winthrop—"

"Don't bother," Jess said, getting up also. "I packed my stationery set."

This was a stupid idea. She should go back to the manor, though Kit would probably still insist she sign something since they'd been alone together—in a bedroom, no less. Surely she could persuade Roger to forget about waiting six months once she told him what a blockhead Kit was.

But Kit *had* walked in on her in two very damning situations. She must remember he had some grounds for his asinine behavior.

She threw open her valise. Damn it, her stationery must be at the bottom. She dug for it, jerking out her sketchbook—

A packet of papers tumbled out. What was this? She bent to pick it up.

"May I see what you've been drawing?"

Kit had followed her. When she looked up, he had her sketchbook in his hands and was opening it—

"No!" She lunged, grabbing the book and shoving it and the papers back into her bag. If Kit saw her drawings, he'd know how stupidly in love with him she was—or, had been. She wasn't feeling much love at the moment.

"I beg your pardon." Kit sounded like he had a poker up his arse again. "I did not mean to pry."

She didn't trust herself to answer. Instead, she closed her valise and carried her stationery case over to the table. Fortunately, Kit followed her.

She pushed aside her plate, pulled a sheet of paper and a pencil out of the case, and, as Kit looked over her shoulder, wrote: *Jessica, Lady Ashton, swears that she is not with child, but if she were, that child is not her husband's.*

"Will that do?"

"And add that you swear not to engage in sexual congress with any other man during the months we are together."

She glared at him.

Kit had the grace to blush. "If we should come to an agreement, I will still need to be certain our first two sons carry my blood. After that you may do as you please." He cleared his throat. "You don't have any reason to, er, think that you can't have children, do you?"

Idiot. "No. Do you have any reason to think you can't?"

His brows snapped down. "No."

"Fine. Here you go, then." *She further swears she will not allow any man into her bed—*

"You said you didn't need a bed to cuckold me."

Oh, dear Lord, she had. Her lamentable temper.

"So I must ask you to refrain from allowing any man but me access to your person."

Access to her person? She glanced up at Kit; he looked stiff and uncomfortable. She'd never fit into his orderly life, had she? He preferred things to be all straight lines and right angles where she was swirls and shades of colors. But she'd loved him anyway . . . or perhaps she loved him because he was so different from her. She'd always found him steadying. When she got caught up in her emotions, his was the calm voice of reason.

Which had been why she'd so wanted to see him after Papa had died.

"All right." She changed it to *any other man access to her person*. "Does that suit?"

"Yes, that will do. Now if you will just sign it, we can—"

"Oh, no, I'm not finished yet." This would never work if she were the only one making promises. She started writing again: *I, Christopher, Marquis of Ashton, in consideration of my wife forsaking all others, swear that I will not*—hmm, how to put it? Perhaps best to be as blunt as he had been—*that I will not engage in sexual congress with any other woman.*

Kit made an odd, strangled sound.

She put down her pencil. "It is only fair."

"The situations are not the same."

Of course they weren't. She understood why he needed to know any child she might bear was his. If it were a boy, the baby would inherit the vast Greycliffe holdings someday. The poor mite. The nasty ton would likely look down their damn aristocratic noses at him for being the grandson of an Irish groom.

Well, they would have her to contend with if they tried to do so . . . unless Kit exiled her to the manor again once she'd done her duty.

Ha! If he tried to do that, he'd have quite a battle on his hands. She wasn't going to desert her children.

If she ever had any.

"That is true, but I find I don't care to be just another woman you spill your ducal seed into."

Which she wouldn't be if she kept saying things like that. She *must* learn to control her tongue.

Kit's head jerked back. His mouth twisted in disgust, but his eyes had an odd, intent, almost hot gleam. "Ah, but my seed is only ducal when it's spilled into you, isn't it?" He looked away. "Or into my wife, whoever she should be."

She barely heard his qualification; she was too busy trying not to drown in the heat that suddenly flooded her. Oh, dear God. Her breasts felt swollen and sensitive, but worst, the place between her legs ached, throbbed—

She was losing her mind.

She hadn't felt like this when she'd had her horrible encounter with Percy. Then she'd felt nothing but desperation, her heart numb from her father's death and Kit's absence. She'd been willing to do anything to guarantee she'd have a place to live and food to eat.

And then she'd discovered Percy had never been offering marriage at all.

"Very well," Kit said. "I am willing to control my carnal urges if you are."

Carnal urges? She'd like to show him some carnal urges. Very, very much—

No! No, she would *not,* or certainly not now, before they had settled anything. And he would just reject her if she were to be so bold; he thought her base enough to break her wedding vows with Roger and countless other men.

And she thought the same of him . . .

But that was different. Men—especially the male members of the ton—weren't expected to keep their wedding vows. Even back when she was a girl at the castle, she'd heard the servants talk about how the guests behaved—or, rather, misbehaved—and how unusual it was that the Duke of Greycliffe was faithful to his duchess. He was the only peer in England who never strayed, they said.

Hell, she knew firsthand of the ton's profligate ways. If she wanted to be the loose woman everyone thought her, she'd have no shortage of married nobles eager to oblige her. She'd had to turn far too many offers of that nature down, sometimes with the aid of an elbow or other sharp object.

"Of course." She signed the paper and handed Kit the pencil. "Will we be returning to the manor in the morning?"

Kit shook his head as he signed, too. "I don't wish to share a house with your beautiful footman."

"Why?" Kit was far more handsome than Roger. "And I thought you'd let Roger go."

"I'll admit I was too precipitous in that." He stared at her, his eyes the color of slate, as he folded the paper and put it in his pocket. "If I punish him for falling prey to your wiles, I likely would have to replace the entire household."

"Blast it, Kit. If you are going to continue to insult me, our deal is off."

He looked at her, his face expressionless, and then nodded. "I apologize. You are quite right. Since we have agreed to try this, we should give our plan the best chance of success, which is why I do not wish to return to the manor. Forgive me, but I prefer not to test your willpower so quickly." He reached for the brandy bottle.

If only Kit knew he was more likely to be the target of

the staff's amorous attentions than she was. "May I have a glass as well?"

His brows went up. "Do you drink brandy?"

"Occasionally." She and Roger and Dennis sometimes shared a bottle in the evenings.

He poured her a glass. She took it and looked around. The room had hardly enough space for the table and the bed. . . .

Oh, damn. Where were they going to sleep?

She wouldn't think about that now.

"Then if we're not returning to the manor, where do you propose we do go? To Greycliffe Castle to live with your mother and father?"

Kit scowled as he sipped his brandy and leaned back against the bedpost, focusing her attention on the bed again.

The bed that suddenly looked very small.

Something hot and needy shivered low in her stomach.

"Yes, that's what I had thought," Kit said, "but now that you put it that way, I can see it is perhaps not the best idea."

She nodded. "And Percy's estate is nearby." The thought of Percy cooled any misplaced ardor she might be feeling. She did not wish to see Percy ever again.

Kit's thunderous expression indicated he agreed with her. "True. And Percy has been short of funds recently, so he might be rusticating." He shook his head. "I think our only choice is to go up to the London house."

"London?" Good God. She'd never been to Town—and she never wanted to go. "Are you mad? What about the ton? What about all those dreadful gossips?" Perhaps it *would* be better to go to the castle. It was a big place with extensive grounds. Maybe they could avoid the duke and duchess most of the time.

But could she avoid Percy? Given the opportunity, he was sure to make a nuisance of himself.

"I grant you it is not ideal, but we won't be going to any society events. If we're careful, we should be able to elude the gabble-grinders." He smiled. "And I confess I wouldn't mind seeing some of the sights, especially the new building that's been going on."

Kit had always loved architecture; he'd even named his horse after the famous British architect Inigo Jones. "Have you designed anything recently?"

He shrugged. "Nothing of import. It is only a hobby after all."

"But you used to enjoy it so much." She'd marveled at how he could create such detailed structures using only his imagination; she needed to look at a model when she painted. "Remember when you built that snow castle Ellie and Cicely and I played in until Percy decided to attack it?"

Kit had actually lost his temper that time. He'd pushed Percy, and the two of them had fallen to the ground, rolling around and swinging at each other and knocking down the castle walls. Cicely had cried, of course; she was always crying. Ellie had been sad, too, but Jess had laughed. She'd grown bored playing pampered princesses and had been on the verge of dropping snow down Cicely's back, so the fight was a welcome diversion.

"Yes, I remember. I built a fort at this year's Valentine's Day party, too; it's so seldom we get snow that packs down well."

Ah, yes. The Valentine's Day party to which she was never invited. Not that she wanted to be, of course. Percy would be there—he was Ned's brother-in-law—and she didn't wish to spend even a moment struggling to be polite to him.

She took another swallow of brandy, but its warmth didn't quite melt the cold knot in her stomach.

"Does the manor have a serviceable traveling coach?" Kit asked.

"No."

He frowned. "How do you travel?"

"I don't." Did he think she went tooling around the countryside? "I've had no reason to undertake a long journey."

She might be happy enough to miss the duchess's house parties, but she hadn't been invited to Ned's and Cicely's wedding either. She'd admit to having shed a few tears over that. Not that she'd truly cared to see them marry. Cicely had been an annoying milksop and Percy's sister as well, but being excluded from such an important event underlined the fact that she was not and never would be part of Kit's family.

"The wagon was good enough for getting to Sunday services."

"But for getting to London . . ." Kit shook his head.

"What? You don't think it will suit your consequence for the Marquis of Ashton to arrive in Town in such a plebeian conveyance?"

He looked at her sourly. "I don't think it will suit my comfort. London is several days' travel, as well you know, and while the roads must be better than when I came here, they will still be rutted and likely muddy. Does the wagon have any springs whatsoever?"

"N-no."

"Then you have to admit every inch of our persons would ache if we were to attempt the journey in it."

There was no point in arguing the obvious, so she merely nodded.

"I will arrange for a suitable coach when we get to the next inn. The White Stag clearly doesn't have any for hire." He looked over at her small valise. "Is this all you brought?"

"It was all I could carry." Especially as she was half expecting him to toss her out on her arse. "But I don't have anything suitable for London anyway."

Did Kit look a little guilty? He shouldn't. What use would she have had for fancy dresses at the manor?

"Well, since we'll be avoiding the social whirl," he said, "it shouldn't matter too much, but I'll have Jack point us to a good mantua maker once we get to London."

So it was decided. He was going to take Jess to London. They were going to see if they could salvage their marriage. If they could be friends and then lovers.

It was a good thing the room was shadowy, because that thought was having the predictable effect on his anatomy.

"I assume your maid will come as well?"

Jess shook her head. The candlelight gleamed on her hair. He'd like to see it down again, and run his hands through it. . . .

"Oh, no. She won't leave her roses."

"Roses? We've just had a blizzard, and the manor doesn't have a hothouse. There can't be any roses."

Jess laughed. God, how he'd missed that sound.

"True, there aren't any flowers yet, but the plants must be watched and tended and coddled so they will produce the very best blooms when the time comes."

She had a dimple in her right cheek that peeked out when she found something ridiculous.

"I begin to think the manor is a very odd household."

Damnation. He hadn't meant to make her flush and look away.

He hadn't wanted to make her sign the blasted paper that was in his pocket, either. He wanted to believe her when she said she wasn't increasing, though if she'd been busy with the naked footman just today, she couldn't yet know if she was or not. He had to protect the succession.

"N-no. The house runs quite well. Mr. Walker does an excellent job of overseeing things."

He took leave to doubt that, given the very peculiar behavior of the butler or whoever that was who was supposed to be answering the door. Not to mention Roger, the notorious footman.

No, he would not think about that rogue. Jess was correct. They would not make any progress if he kept holding her past over her head, and he definitely wanted to make progress. Once he was certain she wasn't carrying another man's child, he'd like to make very certain she was carrying his.

Bloody hell. If he kept thinking like that, he'd never be able to get an heir. His cock and ballocks would have exploded long before he had the opportunity to give it a go, poor virgin that he was. It was rather amusing that she thought *he* had a past.

He saw that she'd finished her brandy, so he swallowed the last of his. "I suppose we'd best get ready to retire. I don't believe either of us wishes to stay at this miserable inn any longer than necessary."

"Yes." Jess stood up and looked at her valise.

"I shall go into the corridor to give you some privacy, shall I?" Of course the room was too small to offer a dressing room or even a screen.

"Thank you."

He stepped into the hallway and pulled the door closed behind him. Blast, this was a bad idea. Nan, the barmaid, was coming toward him, arms wrapped around a thick-set fellow he recognized from the common room.

"Did yer lady toss ye out then, milord?" She grinned at

him. "I'm sure Alf here won't mind sharing if ye want to come with us."

Alf looked distinctly alarmed at that thought.

"No, thank you. I was just going to"—what would be a good excuse?—"I'm just going to stretch my legs before retiring."

Nan looked skeptical. "Ye'll need yer overcoat, milord, and yer hat. It's cold outside."

Very true, but it was too late for that.

"Ah, but I enjoy a good brisk walk." And he set off briskly down the corridor.

Winthrop looked up as he came down the stairs, but had the good sense not to say a word. Ash stepped out into the night.

Nan was right—it *was* bloody cold.

He managed one quick trip around the inn yard and a visit to the stable to check on his horse, contentedly eating his head off, before heading back inside. Surely he'd given Jess adequate time to change.

She was still fully dressed when he reentered their room, though her dress was oddly twisted and she looked furious.

"What the hell have you been doing?" He blew on his hands. Here he'd been a gentleman and frozen his arse off, and she'd been twiddling her thumbs.

"What does it look like I've been doing? I can't get the blasted dress off."

"What do you mean?"

"I forgot it buttons up the back. You'll have to help me."

"Ah." Undress Jess? It was a wonder his blasted cock didn't poke a hole through his pantaloons. He took a breath, swallowed, and tried not to sound like a lust-crazed madman. "Of course."

"Thank you." She blushed and turned away from him.

He stared at the long row of cloth-covered buttons. Good God, there must be a hundred of the tiny things. His fingers suddenly felt as big as his cock and just as stiff. He swallowed again and stepped closer.

Jess bent her head forward so he could reach the top button.

Her neck was so slender and elegant. A few stray strands of hair had tumbled free of her coiffure to brush over her nape. They tickled his fingers as he reached for the buttons, sending lightning flashing through him to lodge in the obvious—far, *far* too obvious—place. He breathed in the scent of lavender and, yes, a hint of oil and turpentine and paint.

Pure lust pulsed in his brain. He wanted to turn this into a seduction. The bed was just steps away. Jess was his wife.

And she might also be carrying that footman's child. There could be no thought of seduction until he knew she wasn't *enceinte*.

His cock had never ruled him before. He would not let it rule him now.

His fat fingers fumbled with the first button. He tried to touch only fabric, but he could not avoid brushing against Jess's soft, silky skin. He heard a sharp intake of breath. Had it been his or hers?

He wanted to brush his lips where his fingers had been, to move them over the fine, downy hair of her neck past her delicate earlobe along the smooth line of her jaw. . . .

"A-are you always this slow?" Jess sounded rather breathless.

"Slow?" He beat back the fog of desire in an attempt to understand her words. "What do you mean?"

"You haven't managed to get the first button open. At this rate I'll still be standing here come morning."

"The blasted things are too small. It's not as if I make a habit of unbuttoning ladies' gowns."

Jess looked over her shoulder at him. "Oh, no? Everyone says you do."

He was not about to tell her he was a virgin. Zeus, how embarrassing that would be! But he couldn't let this story stand, either. With her own vast experience, she'd discover it was a lie in short order. "I don't know who 'everyone' is, but they very much mistake the matter. Now stop squirming."

"I am not squirming," she said, but she turned to look forward again.

It took what seemed like an hour, but was probably only several minutes, to get the bloody buttons undone. One, unfortunately, did not survive the ordeal. It went flying off into the shadows.

"I hope you didn't need that."

Jess sighed as she held her dress to keep it from sliding to the ground. "They aren't there for decoration, you know. I have another dress in my valise that I can wear tomorrow. I'll sew the button back on when we get to London. Did you see where it went?"

"I think it ended up under the table. I'll look."

It took a little searching—the button was very small and the light was dim—but he finally found it. "Here it is. I'll—" He turned and forgot what he was going to say.

He just about forgot his name.

Jess was standing in front of the fire by her snoring dog, spreading her dress over a chair. Her shift was either of very fine lawn or somewhat threadbare, because the firelight shone through, outlining her long legs and the curve of her hips very, very clearly. He even thought he caught a glimpse of a dark patch where her legs met. . . .

His nether organs were definitely going to explode.

"If you'll just loosen the ties on my stays," she said,

apparently oblivious to the view she was affording him, "I can take them off as well." She smiled at him as she approached. "I've decided to sleep in my shift tonight; it will make getting dressed in the morning that much easier, and you won't have to leave the room again while I get on my nightgown."

"Ah." He nodded. At least now he couldn't see her legs, though unfortunately their outline seemed to be burned into his memory.

She presented him with her back again. Thank God the laces weren't tangled or exceedingly tight, so he was able to make short work of them.

And then she went back to the chair by the fire to lay her stays on top of her dress.

He shouldn't look. He *knew* he shouldn't look, but he was only a poor, lustful man. His eyes followed her as iron shavings follow a magnet.

She raised her arms to pluck out her hairpins, and he saw the outline of her small, soft breasts.

"Which side of the bed do you want?"

Oh, God. Her hair cascaded in silky strands down over her shoulders to her waist. He wanted to bury his face in it—

"Kit!"

"What?" He snapped his eyes back to her face; she was glaring at him.

"What are you woolgathering about?"

Fortunately it was a rhetorical question.

"I said, which side of the bed do you want?"

"Oh." Bed. Jess. Together. "It makes no difference to me. You choose."

"Very well."

She gathered her hair up, thrusting her breasts against her shift. Ahh. Did she know what she was doing to him?

Likely she did. She was a temptress, after all. She'd been to bed with many, many men.

Somehow that thought wasn't having its desired effect on his cock. Instead of shrinking in disgust, it was swelling with enthusiasm. Apparently, it would like to be one of the multitudes. If he gave it its head, it would drag him over to cup her lovely breasts, press her body against his, run his fingers through her long hair, and—

"What are you waiting for?" she asked.

"W-what?" She could not know what he was thinking, could she? Was that an invitation? He'd—

He could *not* accept. He must remember the footman. A moment's pleasure now would lead to a lifetime of doubt. No matter how much she pleaded, he would remain resolute.

She was braiding her hair and staring at him. She did not look as though she was waiting to be ravished.

"Why aren't you getting ready for bed? Do you need help getting your coat off?"

Of course. Bed. No, *sleep*. Only sleep. "No, thank you. When I travel, I make sure to wear only coats I can remove without assistance." He shrugged out of the article of clothing in question and threw it over a chair. Then he shed his waistcoat and cravat.

Should he stop there? He had only a limited number of shirts and pantaloons, and they were still a few days from London. He would much rather not sleep in his clothes, and he hadn't brought a nightshirt. Hell, since he usually slept naked, he wasn't entirely certain he still owned one.

He looked at Jess. She'd turned away to stare into the fire as her fingers worked to finish plaiting her hair. There really was no need for false modesty. They were married, and Jess had seen innumerable men naked; she'd had her hands on that bloody footman. He would make the sensible choice to be comfortable.

He removed his shirt and pantaloons; he had his hands on his drawers when she turned back to face him.

"Are you finally—oh!" Her eyes widened and then traveled all over him from his shoulders to his chest to his stomach and hips. She examined his drawers rather too intently; he was not about to look to see what she might be viewing, but he'd wager that there was an impressive tent in the fabric.

"Roger was right," she breathed. "You *do* strip to advantage."

Damnation, she'd been discussing him with the footman?

He should be angry or at least insulted, but the look of appreciation in Jess's eyes drowned everything but an odd feeling of male pride and a roaring lust. His fingers itched to jerk down his drawers and show her his body in all its exuberant glory.

He could not do that. Remember the footman. Remember the need to be certain any child she bore was his. Remember—

She was walking toward him, looking very much as if she was going to touch him. All of him.

God, the bloody succubus. If she did that, he'd not be able to help himself. He'd have her on her back and his cock deep in her body in a trice, pumping his seed into her sweet, warm depths.

That would be a fatal mistake.

He left his drawers firmly on his nether regions and turned abruptly toward the bed. "I'll take the side nearest the door."

"Oh." She stopped, looking momentarily disconcerted. "All right."

It was a reasonably sized bed. If they each stayed to their respective side, there would be plenty of space between them—and at the next inn he would see that they had separate bedchambers.

"Shall I snuff the candle?"

"Yes." Jess pulled back the covers on her side of the bed and smiled. "Good night, Kit. Thank you again for not embarrassing me in front of Winthrop."

He frowned. "I would never do that." They might have their problems—obviously they did have their problems—but he would never air his dirty linen in public. "Good night, Jess." He leaned over and doused the light.

He'd no sooner plunged the room into darkness—except for the dim light of the hearth fire—than he heard Jess gasp and make an odd squeaking sound.

He turned quickly. "Are you all ri—*ack!*"

It was anyone's guess when Winthrop had last tightened the ropes that supported the mattress. It hadn't been anytime soon. The thing sagged horribly. Ash slid down the steep slope to the center, coming up against Jess's soft body.

He put out a hand to push himself away and instead wrapped his fingers around one of her warm, firm breasts.

He was in serious trouble.

Chapter Six

In love, expect the unexpected.

—Venus's Love Notes

Oh! Kit's body was heavy on hers, pressing her more deeply into the sagging mattress. She'd put up her hands when she'd sensed him sliding toward her, and now they were splayed across his chest. His hard, naked chest with its dusting of soft hair.

All she could see was him above her, his broad shoulders and strong jaw and thin, sculpted lips, all shadowy in the darkened bed. She was surrounded by him, by his heat and his smell, and it was wonderful.

And then his large hand brushed against her breast, and heat flooded her, extinguishing all rational thought. Her nipples tightened into hard nubs. She held her breath, hoping he would touch her there, but his fingers glided past, moving down her side instead.

He was torturing her. She wanted to run her hands over his shoulders and back, to slide her fingers under his drawers, to find his lovely, long, heavy cock—it must be as beautiful as the rest of him—but she couldn't move. His weight held her captive.

Her mind—a tiny thread of sanity—struggled to be heard over the need humming through her body. Whether Kit meant it or not, this was a test. He thought she'd entertained countless men in her bed. If she gave in to the wanton abandon her treacherous body was urging, it would just confirm his belief that she was no better than a whore.

His fingers were now trailing across her hip. She pressed her lips together, but a small moan still slipped out.

Closer. Closer.

She should push him away. If he lost control and gave her a child, he would wonder forever if the babe was Roger's . . . unless she bled. Then he would know she was still a virgin.

But what if she didn't bleed? She'd heard sometimes women who rode horses broke their maidenhead before marriage.

She'd ridden hard, and sometimes astride.

His fingers dipped between her legs, and she couldn't stop herself. She moaned again and pressed against his hand. Her damn shift was very much in the way.

"You're damp."

His voice had an odd note of wonder in it—or perhaps she wasn't hearing him clearly. The desire raging through her drowned out everything, even common sense. It had definitely killed her ability to have any sort of coherent conversation. "Uh."

He moved his fingers, exploring her through the fabric, rubbing, pressing, all with a gentle, maddening touch.

She should stop him. Nothing good could come of going down this road.

Her body insisted something very good indeed was just around the corner, coming closer with each brush of his fingers.

Kit put his mouth over her nipple.

"Oh! Oh, Kit!" She threaded her fingers through his hair to hold him close as he sucked on the hard point. Exquisite sensation shot down from her breast to the place between her legs where his finger was still playing.

She gave up trying for any semblance of control. She panted and moaned, her hips twisting and arching, no longer caring what he thought of her. Everything in her strained toward the place he was taking her—

Kit's finger moved once more, and waves of pleasure rushed from the little point between her legs through her womb to her breasts. She tightened her grip on him; he was her anchor in a world suddenly convulsing.

And then the storm passed. Every muscle in her body relaxed, and she pressed a kiss on Kit's shoulder. "Mmm. That was wonderful." She dropped her head back and smiled at him. She loved him so much.

He did not smile back. She couldn't see his expression clearly in the bed's shadows, but she could feel his tension.

Of course. He'd brought her this wonderful release, but he hadn't found any himself. His cock was still hard and stiff against her leg. If only she was truly as experienced as he thought her.

But they loved each other. The years of separation were over. He could tell her what he wanted, how she could help him. He could teach her; she was eager to learn.

She reached up to trace his brows with her finger but he reared away, lurching out of the bed.

She struggled to sit. "What is it, Kit? What's the matter?"

Stupid question. One look at his drawers made it abundantly clear what the matter was. He must be very uncomfortable.

"I see why you are so popular, madam."

"Popular?" What was he talking about? She most certainly wasn't popular. Hadn't she told him already that the local people shunned her?

"Yes." His expression was as hard and stiff as his cock, his voice harsh and condescending. "You are clearly highly accomplished in the bedroom arts. If it happens that you do not retain your position as marchioness, you should be able to command an excellent living as a courtesan."

He hadn't touched her, but she felt as if he'd slammed his fist into her stomach. She gasped for breath. "Damn you, Kit." She grabbed for something to throw at him; all she had at hand was a pillow. She flung it at him, wishing it were something far harder. "Go to hell."

Jess had finally stopped crying.

Ash shifted on the floor where he'd stretched out by the fire. Jess's dog blocked most of the heat, but he'd wrapped himself in his greatcoat. He was warm enough. That wasn't what was keeping him awake.

Jess had sobbed for at least half an hour and then whimpered for another thirty minutes. Or maybe it had been an hour. It had seemed like forever. He had never seen her cry before. Never. Cicely and Ellie cried—well, Cicely had cried at anything—but not Jess.

He'd tried to apologize twice, but she'd snarled at him and refused to listen to a single word. He couldn't really blame her.

He shifted again, trying to find a comfortable position. The floor was bloody hard.

He should never have said what he had. It had been insulting and cruel and beneath him. And it had cheapened the experience. Just thinking about how she'd shuddered and whimpered and moaned as he'd touched her made his cock harden again. He'd always assumed the act was enjoyable because of the physical release it would give him, but he'd been wrong. Or partly wrong. He shifted yet again. He definitely would have liked to have found his own release.

Oh, Zeus. Now her dog was whining and twitching as if

he were chasing rabbits in his sleep. Ash moved farther away from him and from the fire.

He'd always known Jess was passionate. She'd been so intense about her art, and she'd ridden like the wind, taking jumps fearlessly, racing anyone foolish enough to challenge her. But he'd never guessed she'd be so explosive in bed. Seeing her overcome by his inexperienced touches—it had made him feel powerful, almost like a god.

He frowned up at the ceiling. He'd heard whores were accomplished actresses, especially if they thought it would get them a bigger purse or a secure position as a mistress, but he'd swear on his life that Jess hadn't been acting.

Perhaps she merely had a hot nature, requiring regular carnal intercourse to remain content, and hadn't been able to help herself with Percy and the footman and all the others. If that were the case, once she had him near at hand to attend to her needs, she should be faithful.

Zeus, he might need to attend to his own needs with his hand. But if his cock survived the next month or two, he would be delighted to give Jess all the carnal exercise she required.

He could not think of that now, though, or he would never get to sleep. He turned over again and began to count sheep. They all bore a striking resemblance to a large, bearlike dog.

When Ash woke the next morning, he saw Jess had managed to scramble into her clothing by herself. In fact, she had her cloak on and was tying her bonnet.

Her dog barked and got up, almost stepping on Ash's hand. He snatched it out of the way just in time and pushed himself to a sitting position. Damnation, his body ached in every place but his groin this morning. "I'll take your dog out for you, Jess."

Her face was pale, with dark shadows under her eyes. She addressed a point somewhere over his head.

"Thank you, Lord Ashton, but that will not be necessary."

So they were back to Lord Ashton. No surprise there. It would likely take a good long while before he could work his way back into her good graces. "Jess, about last night—"

"Please!" She put up a hand as if to ward him off, her cheeks as red as they'd been white a moment before. "Let us not speak of last night. I apologize for my unseemly behavior. I—"

It was his turn to interrupt. "No, Jess, I am the one who must apologize." He got to his feet, though he had to use a chair to help himself up. He was too old to be sleeping on floors. "I should never have said those things to you."

"But you thought them."

Even Jess's dog gave Ash an accusatory look.

Damn dog. Didn't he have any loyalty to his sex?

Jess still would not look at him. "There's no point in delaying the inevitable, Lord Ashton. You were correct—our marriage is beyond mending. I'll go back to the manor, and you can go on to London to start divorce proceedings."

No! Panic gripped his throat. He could not let Jess go now. She might be right about their marriage, but he wasn't ready to concede that. He certainly felt far more, ah, emotion for her than he had for that barmaid last night or any other woman he'd ever encountered.

He crossed the room in two strides and gripped her shoulders. "Jess."

Her dog growled low in his throat.

"Quiet, sir. I put up with you snorting and snuffling and blocking the fire all night; you can allow me a moment with your mistress, who, I might add, is my wife."

The dog thought about that for a moment and then sneezed and went back to lie down by the fire.

"Traitor." Jess only muttered the word, though, and without heat. She seemed to be darting glances at his shoulders and chest....

Ah, that's right. He'd left his greatcoat on the floor, so all he had on was his drawers. At least he was still too worried about her leaving for his cock to misbehave. But if she truly had a hot nature, perhaps his near nakedness would help convince her to stay.

That, and a sincere apology. He did owe her that. "Jess, I truly am sorry for what I said to you last night. I was..." She had experience; she must know how it was with men. "... frustrated, and I took it out on you."

Her face flushed, but she managed to tear her eyes away from his chest to meet his gaze. "I would have..." She cleared her throat. "If you'd told me what you wanted...." She looked down again and whispered to his chest, "I would have done whatever it was. You just had to tell me."

Oh, damn. His cock jumped up, ready to tell her exactly what it wanted. He moved his hips back slightly. Much as he'd like to hope otherwise, this was not the time for such activities.

Perhaps tonight he could ask her to—

No. No matter what Jess had been to other men, she was his wife. He could not use her as a light-skirt.

"Come with me to London, Jess. Please? You were right. We should give ourselves some time together. We were friends once. Perhaps we can be friends again." And lovers. His cock was rather insistent about that. "Surely it would be better for both of us if we can find a way to make our marriage work."

She scowled at him. "I will not be insulted again. If I agree to come with you, you must swear you won't call me a wh—whore."

Hearing her say that ugly word tore at his gut. He gripped

her shoulders a little more tightly. He didn't know what she was, but he was willing to grant that she wasn't that.

"I promise." He owed it to her to be honest. "But I can't promise I won't lose my temper again."

She frowned. "You didn't used to have a temper." She smiled a little. "Except for the time you and Percy got into that fight over the snow fort."

"Oh, I got angry all right. I just tried not to show it." A duke should always be in command of himself, and one day he would be duke. But no one had ever made him as angry as Jess had when he'd seen her with Percy and then with the naked footman. Usually when he was angry, he felt cold, but with Jess—Zeus! With her he'd felt a hot, stomach-churning fury.

That damn footman was lucky he was still breathing.

"So will you come, Jess? I'm sure I won't be so, er, difficult once we have better accommodations." And surely once he wasn't so tired, he wouldn't have to keep fighting the urge to pull her into his arms and kiss her—and then take her back to that dreadful, sagging mattress and do what he hadn't done with her last night.

She hesitated, and then nodded. "Very well."

His arms wanted to pull her close, but he forced himself to release her and step back. He shouldn't push his luck. And he wasn't completely certain this was luck; he just wasn't ready any longer to cut off all hope of salvaging their marriage. "I'd better get dressed."

"Yes." She'd tilted her head and was studying him, especially his arms and chest. Was there lust in her eyes, perhaps?

No, they were narrowed in her painterly expression.

"Is there a studio in your London house?"

He pulled on his breeches. "Yes, or at least there was. I haven't used it for years—I haven't been to London for years—but I can't imagine my parents would have done away with it. It's up near the old schoolroom." Of course, once Mama finally had a grandchild, the studio might get sacrificed.

"Will you pose for me?" She flushed.

Now he felt as if he were flushing, and of course it made him think of that damn footman. The words were out before he could stop himself. "Naked?"

She nodded. "And clothed. We could do clothed first, if you prefer, but I should like to . . . that is, you really do have classical proportions. Er, or at least I think you do. I don't know for certain, of course, since I haven't actually seen"—she gestured toward his groin—"everything."

He wanted to show her everything, but it was too soon for that.

He smiled as he sat down to pull on his stockings and boots. She was nervous. "Very well, if you'll pose for me." He looked up. "Naked."

Her eyebrows shot up. "You draw buildings."

He certainly preferred drawing buildings. Their straight lines and angles were very satisfying. But he drew other things, too, though perhaps not so much recently. "I used to draw figures. I believe I was drawing a heron when I first met you, wasn't I?"

Her eyes widened as if she was surprised he remembered. Of course he did. How could he not? He'd been sitting by the river, sketching, when a girl he'd never seen before had come running over the grass.

Everyone else, even his family, treated him with a certain amount of deference due his rank, but not this girl. He was mildly insulted and intrigued.

And annoyed. She'd scared away his heron.

She'd stopped by his side and stared at his drawing. And then she'd looked directly into his eyes.

He'd felt as if he'd taken a punch to the gut. Her eyes—a violet shade he'd never seen before—were full of intelligence and wonder. It felt silly to think it, but she'd seemed to vibrate with life, and all her attention and energy had been focused completely on him.

He was used to people pretending an interest in his drawings. Well, not pretending exactly. His parents, his brothers, the vicar, Cicely and Ellie and even Percy acknowledged he could draw, and his parents were clearly proud of his talent. But none of them really understood. They didn't feel the passion—the magic—of capturing angle and light and shade, of making a scene with volume and depth appear on a flat, blank paper.

Jess understood, and she'd wanted him to teach her how to do it right then.

He pulled his shirt on over his head. The times they'd spent drawing and painting together in the cottage were some of his fondest memories. Or had been. Seeing her there with Percy had rather soured things.

Jess shrugged. "I suppose I do have the straight lines you favor in your architectural designs, don't I?"

He picked up his cravat and tied it. Was she serious? She wasn't buxom, true. In fact, many would call her thin—and her outdated frock certainly didn't help matters—but he'd had his fingers on her soft breast and slender waist and swelling hip.

"I believe I discovered last night that you have delightful curves, my dear marchioness."

"Oh."

Now he'd managed to get her to blush. He walked closer. He felt different, more . . . alive. The stuffy old Marquis of Ashton had given way to Kit, a man unencumbered by title and expectations. "So will you pose for me?"

She backed up a step and bumped into the bed. "If you wish."

He grasped the bedpost and leaned in so he had her trapped.

"Dressed only in your lovely long, dark hair." He wished she wasn't wearing her damn bonnet.

"I have never posed before," she said. Her voice sounded a bit breathless.

"Nor have I."

"You will be drawing, remember. You won't be able to"—she frowned at him—"you won't *want* to do anything else."

"No?" Oh, he would definitely want to do something else. It was true an artist saw his subject differently, with his eyes more than with his heart, but he didn't plan to draw Jess until he could see her as his wife. As his lover. "Perhaps you are right. So do we have an agreement?"

"Yes." She extended her hand.

He took it, but he used it to pull her toward him. He intended to seal this bargain with a kiss. He had to dip his head to avoid her blasted bonnet, but he managed to find her mouth and brush her lips with his.

He felt the contact like lightning flashing through him to lodge in his heart . . . and another prominent organ. He heard her quick intake of breath—or maybe it was his breath he heard—and leaned forward to take a deeper taste. . . .

And then her damn dog barked.

"Oh!" She jerked back out of reach. "What is it, Kit?"

He would tell her. He—

Blast it, she was talking to the dog. It had got up and was now whining, its nose against the door.

"Oh, you poor thing." She slipped around him to go to her pet. "You need to go outside, don't you?"

Jess slid to the far side of the wagon's seat, putting as much space as possible between her and Kit, as her dog stretched out among their valises in the back. Kit didn't appear to notice; he was too annoyed at having to travel in the wagon.

"We'll be lucky if we make it a mile in this thing," he said as he gave poor Chester the signal to start. "How did you manage with it all these years?"

"It was fine for my purposes."

The old horse looked back, clearly irritated at being asked to pull a heavier load than usual, but at Kit's insistence, he blew out a long-suffering breath and grudgingly ambled into motion.

"I'll engage a coach and coachman when we get to the next town. I'm sure the inn there will have them for hire."

"Quite likely." And then she would have to share a confined, private space with him. She'd prefer keeping to the wagon. Now she only worried about having her teeth jolted from her head. In the coach, she'd have to worry about her heart.

Thank God for the canine Kit. She could use him as a furry shield against the human Kit's blandishments. If he kissed her again like he had in the inn bedroom, she was afraid she'd do anything he wanted.

And what would be the matter with that? He was her husband.

But he didn't trust her, and he certainly didn't love her.

"I should have seen you had a decent carriage. I don't know why Walker didn't mention it in his letters to me."

"He didn't mention it because we didn't need it. I told you I never went visiting."

She'd kissed men before without love. Years ago, when she was a girl, out of curiosity she'd let men steal a few kisses, but those had been no more than a furtive mashing together of lips, disappointing and slightly disgusting. Kit's kiss had been completely different. His mouth had barely touched hers yet, like a spark falling into a pile of dry leaves, it had lit a smoldering fire that was threatening to consume her and all her common sense.

And last night . . . oh, God.

She'd never felt anything like what she'd felt last night. Yes, she'd had that encounter with Percy, but that had been rough and cold and unpleasant.

She shifted on the hard wagon seat, but she couldn't escape that memory.

She'd been so stupid. When Percy had appeared at the cottage, he'd seemed like the answer to a prayer she hadn't yet thought to address to the Almighty.

With her father gone, she could no longer stay at the castle, even if the duchess would let her. But what could she do? Where would she go? No one would hire a female groom, and no one wanted a female painter, especially one who didn't paint flattering portraits. She could read and write, add and subtract, but she hadn't the patience to be a governess, and most employers wouldn't want a governess who wasn't from the gentry.

Even the lowest scullery maid had more useful skills than she did.

She'd known Kit was coming for his mother's house party. The hope of seeing him had been the only thing keeping the panic that fluttered in her breast from spreading its wings and stealing her fragile composure.

And then Kit had not come. She'd heard he'd arrived at the castle, but an entire day passed—it had felt like years— and he hadn't come to see her.

Of course he hadn't. She heard the whispering. Everyone said he was going to marry the beautiful Lady Charlotte. He had more important things to concern himself with than the feelings of a groom's daughter.

So when Percy had appeared, she'd seen opportunity. He'd been sniffing around her skirts for years. She'd thought he'd be willing to marry her.

Ha! How naive.

Percy had offered to pose for her. She hadn't realized he'd meant to shed his clothing until he was halfway out of his pantaloons. She should have stopped him—she'd smelled alcohol on his breath and of course any idiot knew what he was doing was so far beyond accepted behavior the sun should turn red and swoon from the sky—but her damn curiosity had got the better of her. She was an artist and yet she'd never seen a naked man. And she'd thought Percy wouldn't expose himself like that if he didn't mean marriage. He was wild, but she hadn't thought him that far beyond the pale.

He'd looked better with clothes on. His chest was flat and pasty; his legs, spindly and covered in curly, black hair. And his male bit—it was small and droopy and snakelike until she'd stared at it. Then it had grown, swelling and stiffening until it stood straight out from his body.

Oh, God. She'd actually asked him if he was in pain. He'd laughed and said yes, and she was the one who could ease his suffering.

She'd still thought he'd meant marriage when he'd pulled her into his arms. She'd wanted to push him away, but she'd reminded herself she needed a roof over her head.

He'd held her so tightly she'd been barely able to breathe. He'd covered her mouth with his and thrust his tongue between her teeth, making her gag. And then he'd jerked her bodice down, pinched her breasts, and pushed her onto the couch, pulling her skirts up and shoving himself between her legs.

She'd just thought that was the way of it. Men satisfied themselves and women endured.

But last night . . .

She clenched her teeth harder as a very sensitive part of her shivered at the memory. It had been wonderful—until Kit had called her a whore.

Her stomach knotted. She'd never thought . . . but perhaps she hadn't been so different from a whore that day with Percy. She'd been desperate enough to let him take what he wanted in exchange for marriage. And if Kit hadn't offered for her, she might very well have had to work on her back to keep a roof over her head and food in her belly.

"You didn't even visit the vicar and his wife?"

Kit's voice interrupted her ugly memories.

"No."

"Why not?" He looked genuinely puzzled. "I thought it was a vicar's duty to minister to his flock."

Oh, yes, the vicar had wished to minister to her in exactly the same way Kit had "ministered" to so many ladies of the ton.

She frowned. But if Kit was a rake, shouldn't he have been able to tell last night that she had no bedroom experience? And when he'd been helping her out of her gown, he'd been so clumsy and slow. One would think a man as rakish as the Marquis of Ashton was reputed to be would have expert fingers.

He *did* have expert fingers, but with more intimate skills than unbuttoning frocks. His touch—

She could not think about what he'd done to her in bed last night. It would be far safer to think about the disagreeable vicar. "Have you ever met the man?"

"Of course I have. Reverend Clintfield has been the vicar for ages."

"*Had* been the vicar. He retired shortly after I arrived. Reverend Pierson has the living now."

Kit's cheeks turned red from more than the cold air. "Oh, yes, that's right. Now I remember. Is the new fellow not satisfactory?"

"Oh, I'm sure everyone else finds him admirable. He's a very saintly man, far too principled to have anything to do with as great a sinner as I."

Unless she was willing to sin with the vicar, which she

wasn't, as she'd told him in so many words the one time he'd called at the manor.

They hit a particularly nasty rut, and she was thrown up against Kit. He put his arm round her to steady her.

"Are you all right?"

"Yes. Of course."

As soon as he removed his arm, she scooted back to her side of the seat and found a secure handhold. She was not going to go flying into him again if she could prevent it.

Oh, God. She'd *felt* like a loose woman after Kit had gone to lie down on the floor with her dog last night. Perhaps it was her lowborn nature coming out. Perhaps that was why Kit thought her accomplished. Likely proper society ladies didn't feel such wild, physical needs.

She had no idea how proper lowborn ladies behaved either. Her mother had died when she was very young; she'd only hazy memories of a black-haired, green-eyed woman with an Irish brogue and a warm hug. Had her mother felt the hot, embarrassing things Jess felt?

Perhaps.

When her father had heard the rumors that she'd let a few men kiss her, he'd sat her down and, with much hemming and hawing, had told her that women had needs—that she was likely a lusty girl like her mama—but that she should never let a man, especially one with a title, take her virtue unless he first gave her a wedding ring. She'd remembered his words that dreadful day in the cottage and had stopped Percy just in time.

Well, it would have been much better if she'd stopped him before he'd got between her legs. As much as she hated to admit it, she understood why Kit had such a hard time believing her protestations of innocence.

"Hallooo!"

She snapped her head up to see who was calling to

them. This could not be good—she couldn't think of a single person she'd wish Kit to meet.

Oh, blast. It was George Huntington, the worst of the local men. He was one of Percy's friends and had made her life hell her first few years at the manor. Fortunately, he was usually in London now, but she'd had to apply her knee forcibly to his groin just a few days ago when she'd encountered him in the village.

"Well, look who's here," Huntington said, drawing level with them and reining in his horse. He was wearing his usual unattractive sneer. "So this is why you turned me down last week, Jess. You'd rather entertain a farmer than the future Squire Huntington." Clearly, he was looking at the wagon and not at Kit.

She looked at Kit. His jaw had tensed as he struggled to control his temper. He wasn't going to try to fight, was he? She didn't want him getting hurt.

She could handle Huntington.

"I'm surprised you are out riding at all, Mr. Huntington. I must remember, if I'm ever so unlucky as to be subjected to your attentions again, to use more force in discouraging you."

She was happy to see the worm turn a little green and shift in his saddle. She'd thought she'd used plenty of force. He'd grabbed his privates and fallen to the ground cursing in a most satisfactory fashion.

"Did this fellow insult you, Jess?" Kit's voice was icy, a distinct thread of danger in it.

Mr. Huntington's color went from green to white.

It was surprisingly pleasant to have a man defend her, not that it was necessary. "Yes, but I dealt with the situation. Let's drive on. Good day, Mr. Huntington."

Huntington did not care to be dismissed so cavalierly. His anger trumped his good sense, as usual, and he grabbed Chester's bridle before Kit could put him back in motion.

"On second thought, I'm not surprised you'd prefer this pretty farmer to me. After all, he's of your class, isn't he? You must feel right at home in the hay." He turned to Kit. "I hope the jade hasn't misled you, my friend. She may call herself Lady Ashton, but she's really just an Irish strumpet."

She was going to jump out of the wagon and strangle the bloody miscreant. "And you are a despicable, lying toad."

He sniffed. "I was prepared to offer you some excellent carnal exercise, Jess, but you have lost your chance at that." He looked back at Kit. "I hope you didn't pay too much for her. You've likely discovered what my friend, Sir Percy, says—she isn't worth more than a farthing or two."

Chapter Seven

Gossip often lies.

—Venus's Love Notes

A red haze shimmered in front of Ash's eyes. He was going to murder the blackguard. "You—"

Jess touched his arm. "Don't," she whispered. Her brow was tented in what looked like worry.

"Don't what?" He struggled to keep his voice down. At least the fool was beginning to look somewhat concerned. "He just called you a strumpet." He wouldn't point out all the other ugly things Huntington had said. They didn't bear thinking of, let alone repeating. And then to have mentioned Percy as well—

He was going to haul the vile wretch off his horse and grind his fist, if not his heel, into his ugly face.

"I know. He's not the first to do so."

Damn! Guilt punched him in the gut. "I apologized for—"

"I didn't mean you." She leaned closer. "He's reputed to be excellent with his fists."

"Good." He turned his attention back to Huntington and raised his voice. "Then I won't feel bad when I darken his daylights and smash his damn nose." There was no fun in pummeling a man who couldn't defend himself; in fact, honor would demand he show some mercy. But if the fellow fought back, he needn't strive for restraint.

The blackguard's expression was suddenly markedly less cocky. "Good God, man. There's no reason to shed blood over a common whore."

Jess moaned, though she muffled the sound almost immediately.

Bloody hell, his head was going to explode with anger. He struggled to maintain some control. "You are speaking of my wife, sirrah."

"Wife?" Huntington's voice actually squeaked.

Jess put her hand on his arm. "Please, let's just leave."

"What do you mean 'wife'?" Huntington said. "She's not your wife; she's Ashton's." His eyes widened. "Did she actually get you to marry her? That makes her a bigamist."

Perhaps the man was too stupid to fight. It wouldn't be sporting to drub a half-wit. "I *am* Ashton, you fool."

"But Ashton never comes to Blackweith. He's abandoned his wife. Everyone knows that."

Hell, he *had* abandoned Jess. He'd never considered how that would affect her status in the community—well, he'd thought she was too busy working her way through the neighborhood men to care about anything else—but he should have considered it. He should never have left her exposed to such insults.

"Well, he is here now, Mr. Huntington," Jess said. "If you will be so kind as to let go of our horse, we can be on our way."

The blockhead narrowed his eyes. "I don't know that I believe you, Jess. Why would the Marquis of Ashton be driving your old wagon?"

The frayed thread of Ash's patience snapped. "Good God, man. No one cares what you believe, though I'll be happy to leave the imprint of my signet ring on your forehead, if that will help convince you."

Huntington must have believed he'd do exactly that, because he finally let go of their horse's bridle and backed his own horse away. "I was just trying to look out for Jess's welfare."

"*Lady Ashton* to you, sirrah." By God, he wanted to bash the fellow's brains out.

"But, er, Lady Ashton and I are friends. We just had a slight misunderstanding."

Jess snorted. "Friends? A *slight* misunderstanding? I sincerely detest you, sir. You've been spreading nasty rumors about me since I arrived at the manor, besides subjecting me to your very unwelcome advances."

Huntington laughed. "Oh, come, Jess—"

"*Lady Ashton*. Do I have to pound that into your thick skull, Huntington? Are you that slow a learner?" Zeus, how he wanted to feel the satisfying crunch of the miscreant's nose under his fist.

Huntington smiled weakly and ran a finger around his cravat. "Come, Lady Ashton, I will admit to a little flirtation, but it was all in fun."

"Oh, yes," Jess said. "I had great fun thrusting my knee into a rather sensitive part of your anatomy the other day to deter your 'little flirtation,' and I thoroughly enjoyed hearing you scream as you fell to the ground. Watching you writhe in the dirt was highly entertaining as well."

"Heh." Huntington was looking a bit nauseous. "You have such a delightful sense of humor, Je—" He paused and looked at Ash. "Lady Ashton."

"I am not joking."

Damnation! "I regret dueling is illegal, Huntington," Ash said, "but I shall take great enjoyment in thrashing you soundly should you ever annoy my wife again. Do I make myself clear?"

"Oh, well, I'm sure there's no need—"

"*Do I make myself clear?*"

The man straightened, backing his horse farther from the wagon. "Yes, quite clear. There is no need to make such a point of it. I can see Lady Ashton prefers we not continue our friendship now that you have returned, my lord."

"There was never any friendship to continue, you dastard!" Jess looked as if she wished she had something to throw at the man. Her sharp tone caused her dog to start barking.

Huntington's horse took exception to the sudden, deep noise and reared, almost depositing Huntington on his arse. It was a near thing, but the man managed to keep his seat, though he did lose his hat.

Meanwhile the dog, likely encouraged by the commotion he'd caused, leapt to his feet and redoubled his efforts. Huntington's horse was having none of it. It took off at a flat-out gallop.

"Shush, Kit. Sit down and compose yourself."

Since he was already sitting, Ash concluded Jess was addressing her dog. The animal, after one last parting bark, flopped back down in the back of the wagon. Jess turned around to pat him.

"Good boy. That's the way to send George running."

The dog licked Jess's face.

"Has Huntington truly been a thorn in your side all these years, Jess?" Now that he wasn't so blindingly angry, Ash realized the name was familiar. Had Walker, his estate manager, mentioned him?

No, it had been Percy. He'd overheard Percy talking to some fellow at Mama's house party the year after he'd left Jess at the manor. He'd been out on the terrace alone, trying to compose himself—it had been especially hard to endure Mama's matchmaking parties those first few years—and Percy had been inside, likely unaware that Ash could hear him. He was certain Percy had said Huntington was one of the many men who'd enjoyed Jess's favors. He remembered the incident because his pain was still so raw; it had just underlined how little he meant to his absent wife.

"Yes, though fortunately he does spend most of his time in London now." She frowned at him. "I try to avoid him whenever he's here, but I didn't know he was back in the area until I ran into him in Mr. Sheldwick's shop a few days ago. He insisted on walking me home."

"And you went with him? That doesn't seem wise."

Her frown turned to a scowl. "You don't know Mr. Sheldwick." She sighed and looked out over the fields. They'd resumed their plodding pace toward the next town.

"Mr. Sheldwick is a sweet old man and completely oblivious to gossip. He heard Huntington's offer to escort me and insisted I accept. He doesn't think I should be walking by myself."

"He's right about that. You should have taken one of the footmen or at least your dog."

Jess snorted. "This is the country. I'm perfectly safe by myself."

"Oh? And were you perfectly safe walking with Huntington?"

She looked somewhat chagrined. "I don't like him, but I didn't think I was in danger." She raised her chin. "I'm quite capable of taking care of myself."

Blast it, Jess had always been far too independent and headstrong for her own good.

Perhaps she'd encouraged the fellow.

No, she'd have to be an amazing actress to feign such anger. "I cannot believe the fellow would so abuse the Marchioness of Ashton."

"Well, people don't consider me a marchioness; they think I'm just a mistake you'll eventually get around to correcting."

Damnation. He gripped the reins too tightly, and the

horse tossed its head. He forced his fingers to relax. "Our marriage is no one's business but our own."

She laughed at that. "Come, Kit. Whatever I am, you are definitely a marquis, one day to be a duke, one of the most powerful men in England. Of course your marriage is everyone's business." She looked him in the eye with the same defiant expression she'd so often used as a girl when she was trying to pretend her feelings hadn't been hurt.

Something near his heart twisted.

He remembered the exact moment when she'd gone from childhood playmate to . . . to something else. He'd been sixteen, and she, fourteen. They'd been out riding early in the morning as they often did, when the grass was still wet with dew and they had the world to themselves. They'd reached the north field, and Jess, as usual, had challenged him to race to the old oak tree. And then she'd taken off, and he'd taken off after her.

She'd inherited her father's magic with horses; she could ride like no one else he knew. But he could ride, too. Her horse flew over the grass; he leaned low and urged his horse faster.

He always beat her, but this morning they reached the tree at exactly the same time.

Jess had let out a very unladylike whoop, and when she'd ridden back to him, she and her horse had been almost dancing.

He'd expected to feel annoyed, but when he saw her so happy and excited, the sun, filtering through the oak leaves, lighting her face, he'd had an almost overwhelming urge to kiss her.

And then she'd laughed, and the spell had been broken.

Nothing had been the same since. He'd watched her flirt with Percy and the other men, yet he could never bring himself to try to attract her interest. She was so different from him—a bonfire to his flickering candle.

And he hadn't had time for a flirtation or a courtship. He was going to be the duke one day. He'd been away at school or busy with his father, learning what he needed to know to manage the duchy.

And, yes, perhaps he'd been . . . not afraid, but overwhelmed by the emotions Jess made him feel, and had taken refuge in his studies and his architectural drawings. Those were orderly, factual, predictable. They didn't involve messy things like love and desire and jealousy.

If he were completely honest, coming upon Jess with Percy had given him the golden opportunity to get the woman he wanted. Except he hadn't managed even that. He'd married Jess, but then he'd sent her away.

Stupid, and yet what else could he have done? She might have been carrying Percy's child. He'd thought, once he was certain she wasn't increasing, that he could put the ugly scene behind him, but he'd underestimated its power over him.

And he hadn't realized how much she desired sexual congress. He'd heard all the rumors. Percy hadn't been the only one whispering about the disgraced Lady Ashton. He'd had firsthand experience of her wildness last night, hadn't he?

He shifted on the wagon's hard, wooden bench to take some of the pressure off his growing desire and encouraged the horse to pick up its pace. The sooner they got to the next town the better.

He glanced at Jess. She was looking away from him at the passing scenery, which was mostly just muddy fields and hedges.

He'd forgotten the full effect her presence had on him. He felt a bit giddy, a little irresponsible, always on the verge of doing something he'd regret when he was with her. Like what he'd done last night in that dreadful bed. Though he didn't quite regret that. . . .

Damn it all, she made him painfully, desperately, mad with desire. His blasted cock was going to explode. He shifted his weight again, but it didn't help. There was no comfortable position to be found on this unforgiving bench.

Why the hell wasn't he like other men? Most male members of the ton didn't let marriage vows prevent them from enjoying a mistress or two. And now that he'd signed that damned paper, he had one more vow keeping him celibate. He couldn't honorably find a willing barmaid to ease his pain and give him some sorely—ha! *very* sorely—needed experience.

If he was ever free to take Jess to bed and try for an heir, she would laugh at his fumbling.

Though she hadn't been laughing last night, had she?

The surge of pride that came with that thought only made his cock grow stiffer.

He shifted position once more. They had better reach the damn inn soon.

Why did Huntington have to come along? Not that her conversation with Kit had been going well, but Huntington had just made things worse.

Jess glanced at Kit. He was fidgeting on his seat as if he couldn't wait to reach the inn and put more space between them.

Had he believed her when she'd said she'd never had anything to do with Huntington? She knew people said that she had. The local gossips claimed she'd been in almost every man's bed in the county, though how anyone could believe that was beyond her. But believe it they did.

Dennis and Roger went to the tavern on occasion and heard the local men talking. They wouldn't tell her precisely what the fools said, but they'd admitted some of it, especially after the third or fourth or fifth round of ale, was highly uncomplimentary. Charlie, the footman who'd been at the door—or who should have been at the door—when Kit arrived, had let slip, before Dennis shushed him, that it was the common belief the manor staff was her male harem, a fact he found extremely funny. Of course if the villagers knew the staff's true interests, she and the men at the manor would have an entirely different set of problems. There were definitely benefits to her social ostracism.

But none of the local men had better be boasting he'd been in her bed. If that was going on, she'd like a list of the liars so she could give them a piece of her mind, and have Kit—her dog, Kit—take a large piece out of their arses.

She glanced at her husband Kit again. He was scowling at Chester's tail. She'd swear he'd actually been on the verge of hitting Huntington. Huntington had seemed to think so, too, and had been frightened by the prospect.

Perhaps Huntington wasn't such a skilled pugilist after all. And Kit *was* quite imposing—tall and broad shouldered. She could definitely attest to that fact.

Mmm, yes, indeed. For the first time her excitement at the thought of painting the male figure wasn't solely artistic.

Would Kit really pose for her when they got to London?

She shivered with what must be anticipation.

"Are you cold?" Kit asked.

"Ah . . ." No, she was actually rather hot, but she couldn't very well say that.

"Would you like my coat?"

His coat, warm with the heat of his body.

"No, of course not. I'm fine—and see, there's the church steeple up ahead. We're almost there."

He frowned down at her, concern in his eyes. "You're certain you're not cold?"

"Yes."

She forced herself to look away and take a deep breath

as Kit navigated a curve and the town came into view. She could not let herself fall back into love with Kit so easily.

All right, she'd never fallen out of love with him, but she mustn't let herself act on the feeling yet. Kit might be solicitous at the moment, but that was only because he needed an heir. Did she really want to be nothing more than his brood mare?

They clattered over the narrow, cobbled street, past shops and the church.

"The inn must be on the other side of town," Kit said.

The image of his body—broad chest, sculpted muscles, flat belly—flashed into her memory. And that very large tent in his drawers.

Yes, perhaps she did.

No! Where was her pride? He'd dropped her at the manor eight years ago like a rotten fish, and he'd not seen nor written to her—likely he'd not even thought of her—in all those years. Oh, no. He'd been too damn busy raking his way through the female members of the ton.

She might be spurned by the local gentry, but somehow they had managed to see that she heard *that* gossip.

And why was their gossip about Kit any more believable than their gossip about her?

She froze. Where the hell had *that* thought come from? Kit was a marquis. Everyone knew that was the way the male members of the ton lived. Look at Huntington. Look at Percy.

Look at Kit's father, the Duke of Greycliffe.

Ah.

She glanced at Kit, his face intent as he guided old Chester. He was nothing like Percy or Huntington.

Perhaps the gossips had exaggerated. Perhaps there was hope she could persuade Kit, even if he *had* had many lovers, to limit himself to her bed. But it was too soon to know. She could not give in to her attraction now. Yes, she had his name, but she wanted his heart.

And even if she threw herself naked into his arms, he'd only push her away. He still thought Roger had been much closer a friend than he had been.

"Ah, here we are." Kit sounded exceedingly relieved as they clattered into the Singing Maid inn yard. A young boy ran over to take Chester's bridle. "Let's go in and see about rooms."

With luck they'd be able to get separate bedchambers, and she wouldn't have to test her resolve. Her head was determined to wait, but her body, the treacherous thing, desperately wanted more of what Kit had done last night.

She started to get down.

"Wait for me to help you." Kit swung out of his seat and hurried over to her side. Damnation. She could have scrambled off the wagon's bench by herself. She'd certainly done it countless times these last eight years.

But Kit would not have liked her rejecting his assistance, and she'd admit it would have given a very odd appearance. The inn's servants who had occasion to be in the yard were staring. *They* didn't mistake Kit for a farmer.

She let his strong fingers grasp hers and ease her down from the wagon. Her silly heart fluttered, and—

Kit, her dog, whimpered.

Excellent timing. "You go on. I need to walk my dog."

Kit, her husband, raised his brows. "Then I shall accompany you."

"Why?" She'd like some time away from him. His large presence was unsettling. It was difficult to think clearly. "I walk him by myself all the time."

"And that is another thing I shall add to my list of issues to discuss with Walker when he and I next meet."

"I do not understand why you would raise the subject with Mr. Walker. He is not my keeper. And, in any event, in case it has escaped your notice, Kit is large and protective." Apparently like his namesake. "No one bothers me when I have him with me."

She heard the stable boy gasp as her dog jumped down to stand next to her. "See?"

"Yes, indeed. I see you are being difficult and overly independent to the point of ignoring your good sense."

"I am not." Kit had not been so overbearing when they'd been children. "I assure you I've walked my dog many, many times by myself." She should have seen this coming. She'd wanted to take her dog out alone before they'd left the White Stag, but her husband had insisted on accompanying her then, too.

She'd never been a dependent female, and eight years virtually running Blackweith Manor by herself had only strengthened her independent inclinations. If Kit thought she'd be some pliable, submissive wife, he was going to be very much disappointed.

Kit leaned against the wagon, looming over her in a very annoying way. "That may be true, but you are not walking him alone here. You do not know the area nor does your dog. He may be very intelligent and protective, but he is only an animal. He could take off, chasing a rabbit or a squirrel, and leave you at the mercy of any passerby." He straightened. "Where is his lead?"

"In the back of the wagon." Kit had insisted she use the lead at the White Stag, so it was, unfortunately, in plain sight. Otherwise she might have insisted her pet could not wait while he looked for it.

"Ah yes, I see it."

He proceeded to attach it to Kit's collar—and the damn dog allowed him to do so.

"There we go." He turned to the stable boy. "What's your name, lad?"

"Jake, sir." The boy couldn't be more than ten. He kept staring at her dog, his eyes huge. "Is that a bear, sir?"

Kit laughed. "No. He's just a very large dog. Would you like to pet him?"

And now Kit was introducing Kit—her dog, Kit—as if he were his. She watched Jake cautiously put a hand on Kit's head.

"Can you see that someone takes care of our horse, Jake?"

"Y-yes, milord. Of course, milord."

"And tell the innkeeper that the Marquis of Ashton would like two rooms for the night."

Jake's eyes grew even wider. "Straightaway, milord."

"Splendid." Kit gave the boy a coin and extended his arm to Jess. "Shall we go?"

Did she have a choice? "Very well." She put her hand on his sleeve just as a woman and two men rode into the inn yard.

"What is this wagon doing here?" the thinner of the men asked. His face was pinched with distaste.

"Blast it all," Kit muttered. She felt his arm tense under her fingers.

"It is rather in the way, ain't it, Hal?" The other man was much broader, tending toward fat, with a reddish, bulbous nose.

"Yes, indeed," Hal said. "Take it away, boy. Or better yet, find the farmer it belongs to and have him remove it."

Jake's mouth dropped open, and he looked at Kit.

The woman sniffed. She was strikingly beautiful with heavy-lidded eyes, very full lips, and clothes that must have come directly from London. "I hope we won't find manure tracked inside. I thought you said the Singing Maid was a better sort of inn."

"I assure you it is, my sweet," Hal said. "I have never

had a problem before. I will definitely have a word with Belmont, the innkeeper. He—"

The woman's eyes had been wandering while the man talked. Now they touched on Kit and widened briefly. Her lips slid into a very unpleasant smile. "Stop chattering, Hal. We must greet Lord Ashton and his . . . friend."

Jess did not like the way the woman paused before saying "friend." Kit's other hand came up to cover hers in a gesture that could only be intended as reassuring. She glanced up at him. His jaw was clenched.

"Ashton?" the other man said, looking Kit over as if he were a rare animal in a menagerie. "Good God, are you certain? I thought he never left Greycliffe Castle."

"Of course I'm certain. I was just at his mother's infernal house party, remember?" The woman nudged her horse closer. "So lovely to see you again, Lord Ashton."

"Lady Heldon," Ash said, bowing very, very slightly.

"You know Lord Hallington,"—she gestured toward the thin man—"and Lord Pelthurst, don't you?"

"I don't believe I've had the, ah, pleasure." Kit looked as if he'd be very happy to forgo that experience now as well.

Lady Heldon examined Jess rather as she imagined a hungry cat might examine a mouse. "And who is your lovely companion?" She tittered. "Or can you not present her to me?"

"Yes, indeed," Pelthurst said. "You may not be able to introduce the gal to Imogen, Ashton, but Hal and I would very much like to make her acquaintance. We're always looking for another comely armful—when you are done with her of course."

Lord Hallington nodded. "We've just finished up a rousing good party—Imogen here came over from your mother's do and assures me my gathering was far more enjoyable." He winked at Kit. "Why don't you and your companion sample Belmont's ale with us and then come back to my estate? Five is a good start on a second gathering, I'd say. Your friend would be a lovely addition to our games."

Good God, was this the sort of behavior she had to look forward to in London? She should set Kit—her dog, Kit—on them, but she didn't want to distress their horses. At least Kit, her husband, was also furious. His arm felt like steel; his nostrils flared.

"This *lady*," he said, his voice tight with anger, "is my wife, the Marchioness of Ashton."

All three dropped their jaws as one. Jess had to bite the inside of her cheek to keep from laughing.

"I'm sure you will understand when I tell you I do not wish to introduce her to you. Now if you will excuse us? Her dog has been patiently awaiting his walk."

With that he turned and led her away.

Chapter Eight

Good advice can be found in surprising places.
—Venus's Love Notes

"I'm sorry you were subjected to those three, Jess." Sorry hardly began to describe his emotions. He was disgusted and angry—and insulted anyone would think he, a married man, would parade a paramour around a country village.

Well, yes, many married men probably did just that and Jess had said she'd heard rumors that he was among their number, but he'd truly thought everyone expected him to hold to a higher standard. He was the son of the Duke of Greycliffe, after all, who was famous for being madly in love with and completely faithful to his wife.

Though perhaps people could be forgiven for not thinking him madly in love. Because he wasn't. Not precisely. But he was a man of his word. He took his marriage vows seriously—and perhaps he *would* be free to love his wife madly if this experiment or trial or whatever it was with Jess worked out.

He looked over at her. She was studying the ground. It was true the walkway was littered with the normal filth of village life—dust and mud and dog droppings—but navigating the mess didn't require quite so much concentration.

Blast it, he remembered that expression. He'd seen it

often enough when she was a girl. Her jaw was set and her lips were forced up into a tight smile. She'd always been determined not to show pain when someone hurt her. She was far more likely to laugh than cry.

Guilt and remorse cramped his belly.

Now Jess's dog was sniffing rather too intently near a shop's doorway. That would be a disaster. In his experience, the bigger the animal, the bigger the, er, deposit. He pulled on the lead and persuaded the beast to move along. He did hope Jess's pet could control himself until they reached the fields he saw up ahead.

"I'm used to people thinking the worst of me," Jess said, "though it's true I rarely have to hear it to my face."

Zeus, no matter how many times he insisted she'd brought on her own exile, he couldn't forgive himself for leaving her at the manor and making her the target of such gossip.

"You should not have been subjected to them. They all three skate on the very edge of respectability; Lady Heldon is hardly better than a light-skirt. I cannot imagine what provoked my mother to invite her to the house party."

Jess glanced at him. "Perhaps your mother thought you'd enjoy the woman's company." Her tone left little doubt as to what sort of enjoyment she meant.

Bloody hell! Did Jess truly think him—and his mother—so base?

"She did *not* invite her for me. Mama's goal is matchmaking, and she is very much aware that I am already matched."

"To her—and your—dismay."

What was Jess's point? "Yes. Of course she's unhappy about our situation. She's the Duchess of Love, not misery. She doesn't like to see husbands and wives at odds with each other."

"Especially when the husband in question is her son."

"Yes, especially then. I think worry must come with being a mother."

"I wouldn't know." Jess's tone sounded a bit wistful, but then she frowned, her cheeks suddenly red. "That is, my mother died when I was too young to remember her."

A man driving a wagon down the street turned his head to gawp at Jess's dog and almost ran into a gig coming from the other direction. The altercation caught the dog's attention; Ash had to pull on the lead to get him to move along.

Did Jess wish to have a child? Was that what was behind her offer to give him an heir? Motherhood had been Ellie's goal this year, so much so that she'd been considering marrying someone other than Ned, whom she'd loved for as long as Ash could recall. But then Ned had finally come to his senses and proposed.

Jess was two years older than Ellie; perhaps she, too, was feeling a growing desire for children. If so, she might be more willing to make their truce work.

No, Jess was nothing like Ellie. Ellie, until this party, had been quiet and meek, while Jess had always been fiercely independent, never hesitating to speak her mind. If she wanted a child, she would say so.

He wished she would say so. He would like to raise the issue himself, but her attention was focused straight ahead, as if she was determined not to look at him. He might—

What the hell was he thinking? Walking on an unfamiliar street with a large dog very much in need of finding a suitable out-of-the-way spot for his needs was not the time to discuss the matter of procreation. Not to mention the fact that she was barely speaking to him.

Unfortunately his wayward cock was *very* interested in pursuing that topic. Enthusiastically interested, probably obviously so. Thank God he was wearing his greatcoat.

Suddenly Jess's dog lifted his head from the pavement, sniffed, woofed, and lunged, jerking Ash forward.

"Hey there, sir." He pulled back on the lead. "Remember your manners."

The dog looked at him as if to beg pardon and then moved ahead again, at a pace only slightly more decorous than a run.

Ash lengthened his stride. "How do you manage this animal, Jess? He must weigh as much as you do."

Jess was almost trotting to keep up. "I usually let him run off lead, if you must know."

"Hmm. Does he come when called?"

"Y-yes."

She didn't sound completely confident in her answer.

"Always?" They passed the last house and started down a well-worn path. Ah, there was a stream up ahead. That must be what the dog was after.

"Almost always."

Sadly, almost was not good enough. He would have to keep hold of the lead. At least the animal had found a relatively discreet place to relieve himself, off the path near a bush, safely out of the way of any unsuspecting walker's foot.

Ash turned away to give the beast some privacy. Jess was breathing a little heavily, causing her bodice to rise and fall—

He must not look at her bodice.

She'd always been able to keep up with him when they were children. She had such long legs—

He must not think about her legs.

So what could he think about? "Why did you name your dog Kit?"

Jess's eyes widened in surprise, and then she flushed slightly and laughed. "Something about him reminded me of you."

"Good God, what? I hope I am not large and hairy and slobbery."

She grinned up at him like she used to do. "You *are* large. And Kit doesn't slobber so very badly."

Zeus. She looked so pretty and so achingly familiar. He wanted to—

The lead jerked in his hand. The dog had finished his business and apparently wished to continue on to the water. Ash held firm, though his shoulder was in danger of being dislocated.

"He's not going to try to swim, is he?"

"He might."

Damn. He would have to risk losing Jess's pet; he did not wish to go for a swim himself. He bent and unfastened the lead.

The dog gave a joyful bark and tore off down the hill to splash in the stream. He and Jess followed, stopping a safe distance away to watch.

"I cannot call your dog Kit, you know." He couldn't even think of the dog by that name.

"Why can't you call him Kit, Kit?" Jess laughed.

"You see the problem? It's a very unpleasant echo."

The dog had found a stick and was bringing it their way—fortunately after shaking the water from his fur. Ash did not care to get showered.

"Does he answer to another name?"

Jess's pet dropped the stick at Ash's feet and looked up at him expectantly.

It was more than how silly the name sounded. Jess had been the only one ever to call him Kit. It had felt special. He didn't want to share that with an animal.

He stooped, picked up the stick, and threw it—and watched the dog tear off in pursuit. It was probably a good idea to have him burn off some energy before spending another night in an inn bedchamber.

"Sometimes I call him Fluff."

"Fluff?" The poor animal. He couldn't call a dog that was the size of a small bear "Fluff."

The dog trotted back and dropped the stick at his feet again; he tossed it in a different direction.

"He *is* very fluffy, especially after he's had a bath." Jess watched the stick sail through the air. "It goes much farther when you throw it than when I do."

So perhaps she hadn't been walking the dog hand in hand with the footman. That was good. "How often do you bathe him?"

She laughed. "When he's rolled in something truly revolting. He likes to sleep in my bed, you know."

That would have to change if he and Jess settled their differences. He wanted a marriage like his parents'; he wanted Jess in his bed every single night—without her very large dog.

Fluff dropped the stick at his feet once more. He would have to get used to that name; he'd make it up to the poor animal when they got to Greycliffe House. A nice bit of meat or a large bone should do it.

"How long does, er, Fluff play this game?"

"Until your arm falls off."

He raised his brows and looked down at her.

"Though perhaps you will wear him out sooner, since your throws are so much farther."

He considered the eager dog. It really was too bad to stop, but the sun was starting to go down, and there was an increasing chill in the air. Jess was trying unsuccessfully to mask her shivering.

If they resolved their issues, he would move to the manor and they could walk Fluff—the name became somewhat easier to stomach with repetition—regularly. Though first he would have to do something about the household staff.

No, first he would have to reconcile with Jess.

"Last time, Fluff." He flung the stick as far as he could.

Jess watched Kit bound off, barking excitedly.

No, *Fluff*. Now that the real Kit was back in her life, she agreed it was confusing, and a bit disorienting, to call her dog by his name.

Poor Fluff had always been a bit of a placeholder. Oh, she loved him for himself now, but in the beginning her feelings for him had been all mixed up with her feelings for her husband—the anger, the shame, the sadness, the longing, and the love. Now that the man was here, she could focus all those emotions where they belonged.

Of course her feelings weren't as raw as they'd been at first. She was older—twenty-eight instead of twenty. Far more mature.

Except she didn't feel more mature as she watched Kit play with her dog. She felt like a silly girl again—possibly sillier than she had been as a girl. She didn't remember having this deep yearning before.

Kit had lost the gangly look of boyhood. He was broader, stronger. She could rely on him—

No. She could rely on no one but herself. To think otherwise was to invite disaster.

Fluff came back with the stick, and Kit bent to put the lead on. "Time to go, I'm afraid, old boy." He scratched her dog's ears, and Fluff's tail and entire back end wagged with happiness.

Jess laughed. "I think Fluff is going to want to share your bed tonight instead of mine."

Which was exactly the wrong thing to say. She should not mention beds to Kit. He looked at her, and she knew he was remembering the bed last night, just as she was, and what he'd done to her there. And, worse, she wanted him to do it again. She wanted to share a proper bed with him and—

She looked down at Fluff. *Please, God, don't let Kit be able to read my mind.*

"I think it's safer if the dog stays with you," he said.

Ah, yes, of course he would think that. Likely there would be no room in his bed—he'd be sharing it with a barmaid. He was probably concerned Fluff would bark and cause a disturbance when he brought the girl up. She might even scream; people who didn't know Fluff were often afraid of him.

But if the rumors were wrong . . .

It didn't matter. She had to believe them, at least until she knew otherwise, or her foolish heart would have her throwing herself into Kit's arms.

"Why? Are you worried he'll spoil your plans?"

Kit gave her a puzzled look as he offered her his arm. "The only plans I have are to eat supper and go to sleep. I was thinking the dog would be protection for you in the unlikely event some fellow forced himself into your room."

"Oh." So perhaps he didn't intend to invite an accommodating light-skirt to entertain him. Good. She should let the subject drop.

Something perverse in her, like the urge to pick at a scab, refused to do so.

She put her fingers on his sleeve. "But dare you let Fluff be my only watchdog? Aren't you worried I'll lure some man into my bed?"

His eyes widened. "That was not my thought, no."

Fluff was looking at them, probably wondering why they weren't moving. He barked and pulled on his lead.

"Perhaps you'd better stay with me again," she said, a

little breathlessly. "You don't want to have to worry that I went astray while you were sleeping."

His brows snapped down into a scowl. Would he tell her he trusted her or would he decide to spend the night in her room?

She wasn't certain which she wanted.

Fluff barked again, but Kit ignored him. "Have you forgotten the paper we both signed, Jess? You gave me your word you'd sleep alone, just as I promised to do the same. I trust you to honor your promise as I hope you trust me to honor mine."

Blast, she was losing her mind. "Yes. I'm sorry. Of course I won't break my word."

Kit's expression shifted from serious to slightly embarrassed. He clasped her shoulder in a bracing sort of way. "I know it will be hard for you, Jess, but it should only be for a month or two at the most, I should think."

"What will only be for a month or two?"

"That you'll need to give up male, er, companionship." Kit was definitely blushing now. "Once we know you aren't increasing, I promise to see to your needs."

She opened her mouth, but no sound emerged. Kit thought . . . Kit was willing to . . .

Her *needs?*

She felt her face turn a burning red. She wasn't just embarrassed, she was mortified . . . and she was suddenly one throbbing, quivering mass of need from the top of her head to the tips of her toes, with a few places in between threatening to explode on the spot.

He ran a finger down her cheek. He'd taken his gloves off to deal with Fluff's slobbery stick; his skin was cold and slightly callused.

"If it gets too bad, let me know, and I will try to help you like I did last night." He smiled a bit tightly. "But I can't do that too often. I'm afraid I don't have unlimited self-control."

She nodded. She didn't trust herself to speak; at the moment she was afraid she had *no* self-control. She wanted to throw her arms around him, pull him down on the grass next to where Fluff now sprawled panting, and—

She didn't quite know what she would do, but she was certain it would involve divesting him of his clothing, which definitely would not be a good idea in such a cold and public place.

"Perhaps your urges will subside once you are carrying my child."

"Ah." Carrying his child . . .

She was going to melt into a puddle of need right where she stood.

"Now shall we go? Poor Fluff has been most patient."

She swallowed, nodded again, and placed her hand on his arm, letting him lead her back to the village. At least no one could see her lustful thoughts—

Oh, blast! A man and his companion were staring at her.

No, they were staring at Fluff.

She needed to get a grip on herself.

"I do hope the Singing Maid's cook is better than the White Stag's," Kit said.

Trust a man to think of his stomach.

"Yes." But it was better to think—or at least speak—about that sort of hunger than the one that was currently consuming her. Not that she remembered last night's dinner. She'd been far too nervous to care if it had been duck or shoe leather on her plate.

"I think it might be wisest if we eat in my room again," Kit said. "I don't wish to encounter Lady Heldon and her companions, do you?"

"No, indeed." Thinking about those three unpleasant

individuals quickly cooled her blood. "I suppose it's too much to hope they will remain in the country?"

"I'm afraid it is. Whatever their original intentions may have been, I'd wager a significant sum they now plan to head for London as soon as possible. They must be more than eager to tell the ton they saw the Marquis of Ashton with his heretofore absent wife." His lips twisted in disgust. "They will be the center of attention. The blasted gabble-grinders will hang on their every word."

Her stomach clenched. "Perhaps we should go to the castle instead of Town, then. Your parents cannot be as bad as the London gossips." And there were only two of them.

"I'm not so certain. Father shouldn't be a problem, but Mama . . ." He shook his head. "It might be better to face a city full of gossips than Mama's focused interest. You know how she can be."

She didn't know, at least not firsthand. As the head groom's daughter, she hadn't had much direct contact with the duchess. But she'd heard what everyone said. Kit's mother was kind but devious when it came to matters of the heart.

It seemed like a very bad idea to let the Duchess of Love anywhere near Jess's confused heart.

"Don't worry," Kit said, gripping her hand in a comforting way. "We won't be at any social events." He grinned. "The ton is mostly a nocturnal animal. Society will be fast asleep while we go about during the day."

"Oh." All right, perhaps it wouldn't be too terrible. And she'd dealt with gossips before. She could probably handle them better than she could handle the Duchess of Love.

Just then a well-worn ball bounced off the side of a building and rolled down a narrow lane into their path. Fluff gave a joyous woof and picked it up in his mouth.

Kit chuckled. "I suspect we'll see a young lad show up in just a moment."

He was right, except it was two young lads. Kit and Jess heard them before they saw them.

"Why didn't you catch it?"

"You threw it too high."

"I did not. You just can't catch."

"Can too!"

"Where'd it go?"

"Down the hill. I'll get it."

"No, I will."

The boys, who looked to be seven or eight years old, appeared from behind a large white building and started running down the lane. They came to a skidding stop when they saw Fluff. Their eyes widened.

Now that they were closer, Jess could see one was an inch or two taller than the other, but beyond that they looked very much alike. They must be brothers.

"Zeus, Clive, the pony's got our ball."

"It ain't a pony, Oliver. It's a bear."

Fluff, sensing new people to play with, dropped the ball and barked—loudly as always—tail wagging furiously. The boys gasped and jumped back, so Fluff picked up the ball and tried to follow them. Kit brought him up short, holding the lead in an iron grip.

"It must be a dog," Oliver said, continuing to back away.

Clive, the taller and likely older one, was made of sterner stuff. He held his ground and looked up at Kit. "Sir, your dog has our ball."

"Yes, I know. I'll get it for you." Kit turned away to murmur to Jess, "Is your pet good with children?"

"I'm not sure," she whispered back. "He's never been around any." Children did not come to Blackweith Manor. Likely they'd been warned to stay as far away from the disreputable Lady Ashton as possible. "But he's never been vicious with anyone before."

Kit nodded and turned back to the boys. "He only wants to play. Would you like to meet him?" He stooped, moving his grip to hold the dog's collar. "His name is Fluff."

"Fluff?" Clive laughed and stepped closer; Oliver edged closer, too, but kept Clive between him and Fluff. "What sort of a name is that for a dog, especially such a big one like yours, sir?"

Kit grinned. He suddenly looked young and carefree, like a boy himself. "Actually, the dog belongs to the lady."

"Ah." The children nodded. Apparently that explained matters.

Fluff dropped the ball again, wriggling with delight, but Kit still kept a strong hold on him so he couldn't jump or get closer to the boys than they wanted.

Clive reached out to pat Fluff's head, and Fluff managed to twist around to lick Clive's wrist—the boy must have grown recently because his sleeves were too short.

Clive laughed. "That tickles."

"Lick *my* hand, Fluff," Oliver said, pushing his brother aside.

And then they were both patting and hugging the dog, their ball momentarily forgotten, and Kit was petting Fluff, too, and talking to them.

Jess had never seen Kit with children—they'd been hardly more than children when he'd left her at the manor—but he seemed very relaxed with these two. Not high in the instep at all, even though he was a marquis. Not stiff or standoffish or awkward.

He'd make a good father.

Her heart twisted. If things had been different—if they'd been truly married eight years ago—they might have a son close to these boys' ages. A son and a daughter and maybe more. They'd lost so much time. And she was getting older. Her chances for motherhood were slipping away. Would she have a child before she turned thirty?

Certainly not if they didn't manage to mend their marriage.

"Does he give rides?" Oliver asked. "I bet he could."

Clive nodded. "Likely we're too big, but I bet Fluff could carry babies."

"Like Annie and Meggie and Madge."

"Our little sisters," Clive explained. "You could charge a few pence or maybe even a shilling a ride and make some money."

"Or Fluff could pull a cart," Oliver offered.

Clive punched him in the arm. "Where would you get a cart, silly? A pony cart would be too big. And what would you use as a harness?"

Oliver frowned and rubbed his arm where Clive had hit him. "I bet Mr. Ludding, the blacksmith, could make something."

Heavens! She'd forgotten how Kit and his brothers had often greeted each other with a shove or a punch. It had seemed a natural form of affection and communication for them.

Perhaps she should hope she had only daughters—but Kit would need a son—

What was she thinking? First things first. She and Kit had to come to an understanding and then . . . Well, then they would see. She'd never given much thought to being a mother. She wasn't at all certain she'd be a very good one.

Not that her mothering aptitude was of any relevance. Kit needed an heir regardless. If she lacked the skill to raise his children, he would provide them with an army of nurses and governesses and tutors.

Likely he'd provide the army anyway and send her back

to the manor once she'd presented him with his heir and spare.

She clenched her jaw. Let him try.

Kit was laughing. "I don't know Fluff's opinion on the matter, but I must tell you we are only here briefly. We leave for London in the morning."

The boys looked horrified.

"I doubt Fluff would like Lunnon, sir," Clive said earnestly. "I've heard it's very noisy and dirty and crowded."

Oliver nodded, wrapping his arms more tightly around Fluff's neck. "He'd be much happier here."

"You are probably correct," Kit said, scooping up the ball and handing it to Clive, "but I'm afraid we really must go on to Town. And now we need to be off to have our supper."

The boys sighed, recognizing defeat.

"Yes, sir," Clive said. "Good-bye, Fluff."

"Bye, Fluff." Oliver gave the dog one last hug, and then he and Clive walked away, steps dragging for all of about a minute. Then Oliver snatched the ball from Clive and Clive yelled and the two of them went running up the hill, chasing each other and shouting.

Jess suddenly wanted to cry. Tears welled up.

Kit touched her arm. "What's the matter?"

Damnation, his eyes were far too sharp. "Nothing." She searched for her handkerchief. "I must have got a bit of dust in my eye, that's all."

"That must be it. I cannot imagine why you'd be sad to see those two rapscallions take off." He laughed. "Can you imagine? They wanted to hook your dog up to a cart. That sounds like something Jack would have come up with as a boy."

"Yes." Jack had always been the adventuresome brother, full of ideas and schemes. "And he would have egged Ellie on to be the first one to ride in it."

"He would have." They started walking back to the inn. "He was egging her on again at Mama's party. I think it was his urging that finally got her to do something about Ned." He grinned. "Ned can be a little thickheaded on occasion."

Kit seemed genuinely happy about Ned and Ellie. Perhaps those rumors had indeed been wrong. Or perhaps Kit and Ellie had simply parted ways. They might just have both been lonely and had found comfort in each other. She understood loneliness.

She glanced up at Kit. Or perhaps she should simply believe Kit. But—

She bit her lip. *Had she really been using the rumors to feed her anger so she wouldn't feel so terribly sad and lonely?*

"Jake!" They'd reached the Singing Maid, and Kit spotted the stable boy.

"Yes, milord?" Jake came running over. "Yer horse is in the stables, and yer rooms are all ready. I took yer bags up myself."

"Excellent. Do you suppose you might be able to find something for our dog here to eat?"

Jake grinned and patted Fluff's head. "Aye, milord. I'll see he's fed and walked again, if ye like, and then bring him up to yer room later."

"That would be splendid." Kit looked at Jess. "That is, if it's all right with you, Lady Ashton?"

"Yes, of course." She should not let Kit take care of such details, but she'd admit it was nice not having to tend to everything herself.

Kit handed the lead to Jake along with a coin. "Oh, and could you tell me if Lord Hallington and his companions are still here?"

"No, milord. They left right after ye went off with yer dog. They were in a hurry—didn't even go inside."

"Thank you." He slipped the boy another coin and looked at Jess. "It seems we'll be able to eat downstairs after all. I assume the inn has a private room available, Jake?"

"Yes, milord. I'll tell Mr. Belmont ye'll be needing it on my way to the kitchen with yer dog." Jake scratched Fluff's ears. "What's his name, milord?"

"Fluff."

Jake gawped. "F-Fluff?"

"He's really Lady Ashton's dog."

"Oh." Jake gave Fluff a commiserating look. "That explains it then. Mr. Belmont's daughter named her cat Snuggles." The look of disgust on the boy's face left no doubt as to his feelings on that matter. "I'll show ye to yer rooms. Come on, Fluff."

"Perhaps we should come up with a different name for my dog," she murmured to Kit as they followed Jake and Fluff upstairs.

"Oh, no. I think one name change is enough for the poor animal. At least he's familiar with Fluff and seems willing to answer to it."

"Here ye be," Jake said, opening a door. "As ye asked—two rooms." He pointed to the wall. "There's even a connecting door."

With a sturdy lock, Jess hoped—and swallowed a somewhat hysterical giggle. Kit might need it to keep her from attacking him in his sleep. Though now, seeing her valise on the bed, she felt more tired and sore than amorous.

"Do you want a moment before we go down to eat?" Kit asked as Jake and Fluff left. "I think an early night would be a good idea."

"Yes." Suddenly all she wanted to do was crawl into bed, but she knew she should have dinner first.

He opened the connecting door. "I'm right here if you need me."

"Thank you."

Kit went into his room, and she turned to her bed, opening her valise. There was no point in unpacking as they would be leaving in the morning, but at least tonight she could sleep in her nightgown. And perhaps she'd do a little sketching when she got back from dinner. She'd like to capture the images of those two boys and Jake and Kit with Fluff. She reached into her valise....

What was this? Oh, right. That packet of papers. It must be the advice sheets Roger had said he'd put in her bag. How ridiculous.

She picked it up and read the first page—

"Eek!" She dropped the packet as if burned. Perhaps it *had* burned her. Her eyes certainly felt as if they were burning. She—

"What is it, Jess?"

She whirled around. Oh, God. Kit was standing in the doorway.

"Is something wrong?" He started walking toward her.

"No!" She whirled back to her valise, stuffed the copies of *Venus's Love Notes* inside, and slammed it shut. Then she turned to face Kit again.

"Let's go down to eat," she said. "I'm famished."

Chapter Nine

*Embrace your beloved's family,
especially his mother.*

—Venus's Love Notes

Ash sat up on the coach box with the grizzled coachman and Fluff. It was a tight squeeze.

"Ye can go inside with yer lady, milord," Darby, the coachman, said for the fourth time. "I don't mind the dog, and now that he's out in the open, he seems fine."

"Thank you, but I feel better keeping an eye on him myself." And keeping an eye on Darby. He'd swear the fellow would not see his seventieth year, but Belmont, the innkeeper, had assured him the old man would get them to Town safely. And Ash hadn't had a choice. Darby was the only coachman for hire. Darby's son, the Singing Maid's main coachman, was laid up with the ague.

"Lady Ashton would be very unhappy if something happened to her pet." Ash smiled. "And you need to keep your full attention on your horses." Though there was little danger those poor creatures would bolt. They were rather elderly themselves, older even than the horse he'd driven from the manor.

No, the real reason Ash was sitting out in the chilly March air was to keep his attention off Jess, though that was proving to be well-nigh impossible. No matter how hard he tried to concentrate on other matters—like Darby's plodding driving—his thoughts kept circling back to her.

What were those papers she'd thrust back into her valise last night—love letters from the naked footman? He'd wanted to grab them out of her hands, but he'd restrained himself.

Just barely.

What the hell was wrong with him? He was always in strict control of himself—except around Jess. All during supper and as he was escorting her back to her room, he'd had to bite his tongue to keep from mentioning those damn papers. If he'd had to ride the whole way to London in the carriage, he'd have severed that organ from his mouth. As it was, the first few miles had been passed in uncomfortable silence.

Frankly, he'd been delighted when Fluff had shown signs of carriage sickness.

He frowned at the passing scenery. What the hell did it matter if Jess was in love with the footman? The man was back at Blackweith Manor, too far away to get into her bed. And while the fellow might be in Jess's heart, it wasn't her heart Ash needed: it was the temporary use of another of her organs. Once she gave him two sons, she could take her heart and her . . .

She could take herself back to her footman with Ash's blessing.

Well, with his grudging acquiescence.

Whom was he kidding? He'd want to fight tooth and nail to keep her, but he wouldn't hold her against her will.

He shifted on the hard coach box. He simply didn't like uncertainty and emotionally messy situations. Not that *his* emotions were involved. Oh no. His heart was completely whole. All would be well once this untidy detail from his past was resolved.

A young London buck in a curricle, pulling alongside

them to pass, made the mistake of glancing over. His hands dropped with his jaw—he was clearly not expecting to see an enormous dog sitting on the box—and his equipage shot forward.

"Damn idiot," Darby muttered as he and Ash watched the fellow fly down the road in front of them, struggling to get his horses back under control. "Good thing nobody was coming the other way."

"Yes, indeed." Ash watched the curricle disappear into the distance, conscious of a faint touch of envy. Their progress could most charitably be described as lumbering.

"At least the dog didn't bark at 'im." Darby wheezed in apparent laughter. "That would have sent the fool's horses running all the way to the sea."

"Quite likely." Fluff had greeted Darby with some enthusiastic barking, and the poor old man had turned white as a ghost. Ash had expected him to flee back into the Singing Maid, but now he was smiling at Fluff as if Fluff were his own dog.

"Look at 'im, milord. Can ye see how much 'e likes the view from up 'ere? 'e's a regular coachman's dog, 'e is."

Fluff was indeed surveying the countryside with what looked like great satisfaction.

"Well, he'd best not get too attached to the position. He'll be walking once we're settled in Town."

Fluff gave him a reproachful look.

Darby laughed. "Has yer lady brought the dog to Lunnon afore, milord?"

"No. This will be his first visit to Town."

The coachman frowned. "Ye know a dog that size is going to need a lot of walking."

"Yes, I suspect you are right." With luck there'd be a sturdy footman at Greycliffe House who liked dogs. . . .

Damn it, the footman had better not like women as well—or at least not Jess. Surely any man his father had in his employ would value his position too much to dally with the heir's wife.

But would Jess refrain from dallying with the footman? His hand balled into a fist.

He forced his fingers to uncurl. Zeus, he had to rein in this blasted jealousy if he hoped to have an ... arrangement with Jess. She had, rightly, objected to his calling her a whore, and she had signed the paper he now carried in his pocket. She'd agreed again yesterday to honor it. If he watched her constantly, questioned her interactions with every male who crossed her path ... She wasn't stupid. She'd know he thought her a light-skirt without his saying the words, and that would put paid to their truce.

He shifted on the box again and looked out over the passing scenery. The snow had all melted here, and the trees were beginning to bud. Spring was coming. He'd always liked spring, even with the mud and the rain. He liked the warmer weather and the longer days. It made him feel hopeful. He'd like to feel hopeful about his marriage—or at least his chances of getting an heir.

"I hope ye don't mind me offering ye a wee word of advice, milord," Darby said suddenly.

"Advice?" What possible advice could this ancient coachman have for him?

"Aye." Darby sent him a sidelong glance before turning his rheumy eyes back to his plodding cattle. "I know ye aren't sitting out here just to watch the dog. Yer in trouble with yer lady, ain't ye?"

Ash forced his brows up into his haughtiest expression, the one that usually shriveled encroaching mushrooms. He was not about to discuss his marriage with this old man. "I beg your pardon?"

"Oh, don't get all stiff with me, young lord. I may be only a coachman, but I've learned a thing or two about the fairer sex. I should 'ave. I've been married over fifty years."

"My felicitations." Ash gritted his teeth. It looked like, short of leaping from the coach box or opting to join Jess inside, he was doomed to hear the fellow's advice.

"'ere's the thing, milord. Women ain't the same as men."

"Ah."

Darby wheezed with laughter. "Well, of course ye know that. Ye've eyes in yer head." He went so far as to waggle his brows in a knowing way. "They've got curves where we don't, eh?"

"Mr. Darby, I fail to see the point of this conversation. Perhaps you should attend to your horses. We are approaching London, and traffic is increasing."

Not that he was really concerned. The horses showed every sign of plodding along at their steady, excruciatingly slow pace until Judgment Day.

"The point, milord, is that it's not just their lovely curves that are different. They're different up here, too." Darby pointed to his head in case Ash missed his meaning. "They think different." He leaned closer, his horses all but forgotten. "They want soft words and kisses and cuddling afore they'll let us men get down to the interesting part." He shrugged. "Whores are different—it's all business to them, o' course. But wives—they want love."

Husbands want love, too.

No. Ridiculous. He wanted an heir and a spare, that was all.

Darby jerked his head back toward the coach's body. "Ye should be in there with yer wife, milord. Yer both still young. Ye should be billing and cooing and making the coach rock." He winked. "It's still a ways to Lunnon. Ye could have yer heir growing in yer lady wife afore we get to Piccadilly."

Oh, damn. His cock was enthusiastically urging him to follow Darby's advice, but what his cock—and perhaps even his heart—wanted, his brain knew was a very bad idea. He reminded his unruly organ that it was too soon. He had to wait to be certain the naked footman's seed wasn't already planted in Jess's womb. "You presume too much."

Darby turned his attention back to his arthritic cattle. "Aye, I do. And I'll presume a bit more and tell ye that it's a very bad idea to leave a woman alone with only 'er thoughts for company. Women stew and fret and make mountains out o' molehills until what we think was a little mistake turns into a killing offense." He snorted. "Don't be surprised if ye get yer 'ead bitten off when she comes out of that carriage. It'll be like letting a tiger out of its cage. I'd stand back, if I were ye."

Jess did have a prodigious temper, but Ash had done nothing to anger her—well, not recently. It was partly to avoid doing so that he was sharing this chilly coach box with Darby and subjecting himself to the man's unwelcome advice. "Er, thank you. I'll consider what you say."

Darby laughed. "Oh, no ye won't. Ye young fellows are all the same. Ye think ye know the way of it, and no old graybeard can tell ye differently." He shot Ash a glance before turning back to his driving. "Now that my son's older, 'e'll sometimes admit that I'm right—after 'e's ignored my advice and suffered the consequences, o' course."

There didn't seem to be a reply to that, so Ash merely grunted in a noncommittal fashion and looked out over the passing fields again. Except there weren't empty fields any more, but houses. They were clearly getting closer to Town.

Perhaps he *should* join Jess. It seemed highly unlikely that anyone would recognize him, but if the newspapers were to be believed, London was chockful of gossips. A dog Fluff's size riding on the coach box was certain to draw attention, and of course when they pulled up in front of Greycliffe House, anyone might guess who he was—

and wonder why he wasn't sitting inside. When they saw Jess emerge . . .

There was already far too much speculation about his marriage.

"Perhaps I will join Lady Ashton, if you truly think you can manage the dog."

Darby waggled his brows and grinned broadly at him, revealing several missing teeth. "Shall I drive around until ye tell me to stop, milord?"

"That will not be necessary."

"Yer sure?"

"Quite." He would not wish to lose his virginity rolling down London's streets in a hired coach even if he were free to do so, which he wasn't. He must not forget the naked footman.

The old man's face fell. "There's plenty o' time for a quick bit o' sport, even with the kissing and the cuddling"—he shrugged—"but suit yerself. I swear I'll never understand ye nobs."

Darby brought the coach to a stop, and Ash climbed down. "Stay with Darby, Fluff."

Fluff barked and beat his tail on the seat, clearly happy to remain where he was. He seemed like an intelligent dog. Hopefully he could control himself if he caught sight of a cat or some other animal and not leap off the coach box in pursuit.

Ash pulled open the door. Jess was so lost in her sketchbook, she didn't hear him. She looked perfectly content to be drawing in solitude. Well, it was too late to change his mind—and he must remember the gossips.

"I've decided to—"

"Ack!" Her head snapped up, her eyes widened, and then she slammed her sketchbook shut. "Oh. I wasn't expecting you."

"Clearly." He climbed in. As soon as he pulled the door

closed, the coach rolled back into motion and, off balance, he fell somewhat heavily onto the seat next to her.

"Are you all right?" she said as she scooted as far away from him as she could. She was almost plastered against the coach's opposite wall.

"Yes." He looked at the sketchbook on her lap. He could reach over and take it. . . .

She shoved it into the space between her body and the wall.

He felt his face and the back of his neck tighten. What had she been sketching? Or rather, whom? Guilt was writ large on her face. "May I see?" He held out his hand.

She laughed weakly. "See what?"

"What you were drawing."

"Drawing? Oh, I wasn't drawing anything, really."

"You seemed very intent on what you weren't drawing when I came in." He should let it go. She must have been sketching the naked footman. It would only hurt him to see what she'd drawn. Jess put her feelings into her art for the world to see. Her skill and, more, her courage in doing that had always shocked and awed him.

Seeing her feelings now would only depress him.

I don't need her heart. Just her body. Just long enough to get my heir and spare.

He could not make himself believe that.

Oh, blast. If Kit really wanted to see her sketchbook, he would. She had no illusions that she could fight him off; he was far stronger than she. But he wouldn't insist . . . would he?

Perhaps she could distract him. "How is Fluff managing?"

He was still staring at the spot where she'd shoved her drawings. She shifted closer to the wall.

She'd been sketching him, of course. She'd meant to

draw him as he'd looked when he'd left with Fluff—tight lipped, jaw clenched. But somehow the picture had turned into how she'd imagined him above her on that damn bed the first night. She'd thought his face had been tense then, too, but not with anger. She wanted to believe there'd been desire in his eyes, and maybe even love.

She was an idiot. She would tear the sheet out as soon as she was alone again, crumple it into a ball, and throw it into the nearest fire.

"Is he getting along with Darby?" she asked.

He frowned at her. "Is who getting along with Darby?"

"Fluff. Weren't you listening?"

She had the worst luck. Last night it had been the damned *Venus's Love Notes*. She'd seen Kit's face when she'd stuffed them back into her valise. She'd been embarrassed, but to him she must have looked guilty. He'd scowled, glared at her bag, opened his mouth—and then shut it. His brow had bunched into a deep frown as they'd gone down to dinner in silence.

The question of what she was hiding had certainly sat at the table with them. She'd hardly been able to eat, waiting for him to ask it. But he hadn't asked, not then, not when he'd walked her to her room, not when he'd come down for breakfast, not in the coach even though the bloody question had taken up so much room she could feel it pressing against her chest.

And then Fluff had started whining. She'd never wish her pet ill, but she'd been immensely relieved when Kit had taken the dog out to sit with the coachman, leaving her in blessed solitude.

"He's fine. Darby thinks he has aspirations of being a coaching dog."

She snorted. "I don't think that will work. Even if I would give him up, which I won't, he's too large to sit on a coach box all day."

She should have told Kit last night—there was too much pain between them to add to it with something as silly as a collection of *Venus's Love Notes*—but she hadn't been able to make herself do it. It was too embarrassing. And he'd be horrified if he knew she had his mother's pamphlets in her possession. None of the brothers liked to admit the duchess was the ton's matchmaker, and they certainly didn't wish to acknowledge she was also the ton's counselor on marital matters.

Back when Percy and Kit were fifteen or sixteen, Percy had found an edition of *Venus's Love Notes* in his mother's sitting room. Of course he'd had to torture Kit and his brothers with it, but before he could read the first word, Jack had tackled him. That had been a bit of luck, since Jack was four years younger. But then Ned had sat on him while Kit tore the paper up and stuffed the pieces into Percy's mouth.

No, she could not tell Kit. She'd be happy to throw the papers, along with her sketch, into the first fire she came upon, but Roger wanted them back.

What the hell was Roger doing with copies of *Venus's Love Notes*? Worse, why had he told her she should read them? She most certainly did not want to know her mother-in-law's thoughts on marital love.

"I don't think there's much danger Fluff will run away to ride the highways and byways on the coachman's box," Kit said, "but he did seem content to remain where he was, so I felt it safe to leave him with Darby."

Kit had been gone at least two hours. Surely it hadn't taken him that long to reach this decision. "But why did you come inside now?"

Likely to quiz her.

His jaw hardened. Oh, damnation. He was going to ask about the damn sketchbook. Or the *Love Notes*. Could she pretend to swoon or have a fit of hysterics?

She had no idea how to do either of those things.

"We are approaching London. I felt I was a bit conspicuous sitting where I was. Gossips are everywhere, you know."

Her stomach tightened. "I thought you said we could avoid the gabble-grinders."

"I hope we can—which is why I removed myself from the coach box. Your dog is enough of an oddity." He switched seats so he was facing her and stretched his legs out, brushing against her skirts.

Her heart, the stupid thing, fluttered in her chest. If she moved her right leg just slightly, it would be pressing up against his.

And Kit would just move away. The coach was confining, and he was a tall man. He meant nothing by their proximity and would be horrified if he could hear her treacherous heart beating faster.

He couldn't hear it, could he?

"If I were driving the vehicle, that would be one thing. That might be considered somewhat dashing or dangerous. But sitting like a lump next to a dog and the coachman? No. Well, you can imagine what people would say, especially once it came out that you were with me."

"Oh yes." She could imagine all too well. *Why* hadn't they gone to the castle instead? Well, it was too late now. But to think she'd have all the London women—and men, too—looking at her and talking about her . . .

Her stomach clenched into a hard knot. "Everyone would say you found me so abhorrent, you braved the weather and contact with servants and animals to avoid me."

Kit frowned. "I believe you overstate the case, but yes, that would likely be the gist of it." He cleared his throat. "But I wasn't avoiding you, of course. I was just tending to your dog."

No, he'd been doing both.

"I'm sorry about Fluff," she said. "I had no idea he was prone to carriage sickness. I've never taken him anywhere in a closed coach like this—he's only ever ridden in the back of the wagon. And I suspect the cook at the Singing Maid spoiled him dreadfully, so he ate far more than he should have. How did you recognize the problem?"

Kit smiled. "Ned was afflicted with carriage sickness when he was a boy. Whenever we traveled together Father would have him sit with the coachman, until he was old enough to ride a horse. I just assumed your dog might be the same."

"I didn't know that about Ned." As a child she'd played with Ned, but of course she'd never been in a carriage with him. She was just a servant's daughter.

But she was in a carriage now with his brother, so close she could touch him without reaching. Alone, without even Fluff to chaperone them. Private. No one could see them.

Kit was so much larger than she. His hair was windblown; there was a slight shadow of stubble along his jaw. His right hand—he had shed his gloves—rested on the coach seat. It was broad and capable, with lovely long fingers that were so clever with a pencil . . . or, as she'd discovered the other night, with a woman's body.

She took a deep breath. His scent—a mix of cologne and soap and him—warmed her. She wanted to feel his touch again. . . .

"Why should you have? I think the only ones who knew Ned got queasy were my parents, Jack, and me. Ned wasn't proud of it. I'm afraid it was just one more thing for him to worry about."

Ned had always been the worrier of the brothers, the one who spoke the word of caution when they were climbing trees or sledding or doing anything that carried the slightest risk.

She could use a word of caution right now. Her fingers itched to touch Kit's knee, to slide up his leg—

He would only swat her hand away. He would have nothing to do with her until he knew she wasn't carrying Roger's child.

Which was a good thing. She didn't want to be just the mother of Kit's sons. She wanted a true marriage; she wanted Kit to love her and, perhaps even more, trust her. Respect her. Attacking him in the carriage would only confirm his opinion that she was no better than she should be.

But she still wanted to touch his knee.

Zeus, Kit's nearness and his scent were muddling her thoughts and eroding her self-control. She clasped her hands tightly in her lap and searched for a conversational topic that had nothing to do with Kit's knee.

"It must have been horrible for Ned when Cicely died."

Ned and Cicely had married about three years after Kit left her at the manor. Kit hadn't written to tell her about the wedding or about Cicely's subsequent pregnancy and death. She'd learned everything she knew from the newspapers and from Dennis Walker, who got some information from Kit's letters on estate business.

And this was the man she was struggling not to throw herself at?

She welcomed the spurt of anger.

It would be one thing if she were some London lady, but she'd grown up with Ned and Cicely. True, she'd thought Cicely an annoying, spineless, mewling ninnyhammer, but that hadn't meant she didn't mourn her passing. And she'd been very sad for Ned. She'd only hoped he'd soon realize he'd been . . . well, not lucky precisely, but that he still had hope for a happy future. She could not imagine being compelled to live one's life with a person as meek and helpless as Cicely.

But then, there was no accounting for taste when one's heart was involved, was there? She could hardly fault Ned for loving Cicely when she was stupid enough to love his brother.

Kit grunted. "Yes. It did rather reinforce his tendency to fret about everything."

She tightened her laced fingers to keep them from touching him and drew in a sustaining breath—and with it another lungful of Kit's scent.

Oh, God. It would be a very good thing if they arrived at Greycliffe House soon. Perhaps she should open a window. The cold air might clear her head. She fumbled with the latch.

"Here, let me help you with that."

"No, I can do it. I—oh!"

Kit reached over so his arm pressed up against hers as his fingers brushed hers aside. His scent enveloped her completely, making her feel a little giddy, as if she'd had one glass of wine too many.

His face was so achingly familiar with its high cheekbones, strong chin, and gray eyes fringed with long, dark lashes. She wanted to trace the tiny scar on his temple that he'd got when he was twelve and jumped out of a tree. Well, he'd said he jumped; she'd thought Percy had pushed him, so she'd pushed Percy into a large, fresh pile of horse droppings.

But there were lines there, too, that hadn't been there eight years ago—lines across his forehead, at the corners of his eyes and mouth. He was older, the boy in him harder to see.

Or perhaps she was fooling herself, and the person she'd dreamt of no longer existed. Eight years *was* a long time.

She watched his capable fingers force the latch open. She must look older as well. She bit her lip. Of course she did. Years were never kind to a woman's face; he must think her a complete quiz, especially compared to the beautiful women of the ton.

"There you go." He grinned as he shoved the window open. "What do you think of the place?"

She'd been aware of a rumbling in the background, but now she heard the cacophony all too clearly—carriage wheels clattering over cobblestones, people hawking their wares, dogs barking.

"It's very"—she had to raise her voice—"noisy."

And dirty with coal dust and smelly with stinks she'd rather not identify. She wrinkled her nose and reached for her handkerchief.

Kit laughed and closed the window again. "You'll get used to it—or at least you'll come to tolerate it. I confess on this I agree with my father: I much prefer the country."

"You really don't come to London often?" He'd said so, but she'd found it hard to believe. London must be like a sweets shop for a rake.

"I haven't been here in years." He looked at her, his face expressionless. "Not since we married."

"Oh." She looked out the window to avoid his gaze.

Hadn't the rumors specified London?

Perhaps not. Perhaps she'd just assumed he'd been in Town to have been able to "entertain" so many women. He could have taken full advantage of the society house parties he'd surely attended. They would be more convenient for his purposes anyway. Each night would offer a new bed with a new lady.

"Look up ahead, Jess. We're approaching the Thames and London Bridge."

She leaned forward. Yes, she could see the river; it was larger than she could ever have imagined, with ships of all sorts plying the water. And up above, a dome. "Is that St. Paul's?"

"Yes." His voice filled with enthusiasm. "I'll take you there. It's a magnificent building, and you can see all of London from the gallery at the top." He raised an eyebrow. "You don't have a fear of heights, do you?"

"Of course not."

The coach crossed the bridge and started up the hill.

"And what's that?" A large, stone column stood by itself, towering over the surrounding buildings.

"That's the Monument. It was erected to commemorate the Great Fire. We can climb all three hundred and eleven steps, if you like. It has a splendid view, as well."

"That might be nice." Anything to get above the crowds. She'd never seen so many people, moving in streams on either side of the road—and sometimes in the middle of it. And there were carts and wagons and carriages and dogs and—

"I hope Fluff stays with Darby."

Kit smiled reassuringly. "I'm sure Darby will stop if there's a problem. I suspect poor Fluff is glued to his seat, overwhelmed by all the noises and smells and sights."

As was she.

They turned west and followed the main road past St. Paul's. The streets gradually got broader, but they were still crammed with people.

"Good heavens, look at that!" A tall, very thin man with an impressively hooked nose and shirt points so high they brushed the corners of his eyes was walking a small pug on a pink lead. "It's a wonder he doesn't poke his eyes out with those shirt points."

Kit leaned forward to peer out, too. "I think he must already be blind to wear such an outlandish outfit."

He was right. The man's collar was the least of his peculiar appearance. He was also wearing red and white striped baggy trousers that looked like they'd be at home in a harem, a green coat with very long tails, a pink floral waistcoat, and a large ostrich feather pinned to his high-crowned beaver hat.

"I wonder who he is."

Kit snorted. "Just another of the eccentric members of the ton. His tailor should be shot."

"I can't imagine he'd want people knowing he made those clothes. Perhaps he swore the man to silence." She looked at Kit. "Are we going to see many such popinjays?"

Kit sat back, obviously tired of craning to see out the window. "I sincerely hope not, or if we do, only at a distance. I believe they tend to flock to the ton events, which we shall be giving a wide berth."

Their carriage had finally turned off the main road and was now approaching a broad square with a large fenced garden in its center. Another traveling coach—a much better looking conveyance—was drawn up in front of the largest house. The house they seemed to be headed for. The house that was supposed to contain only Kit's youngest brother.

She did not have a good feeling about this.

"Did Jack travel to London in a large carriage?"

Kit looked at her as though she'd just stepped out of Bedlam. "No, of course not. Why would he do something daft like that? He took his curricle." He paused, a furrow forming between his brows. "Why do you ask?"

They rocked to a stop.

"Because there's a large traveling coach parked right in front of us."

Kit's head snapped around, and he leaned forward to stare out the window. "Zeus," he muttered. "It couldn't be. They're at the castle."

"What couldn't be?" There were only two people who

were supposed to be at the castle—the duke and the duchess. Unless . . .

"Might it be Ned?"

"Perhaps." Kit's tone, however, said "not bloody likely."

Mr. Darby opened the door, Fluff at his side. "Sorry, milord, but there's a coach in my way. Ye want me to see if I can get them to move?"

"No, no, that's fine, Darby. Lady Ashton and I will get out here."

Kit bounded out of the carriage and, not bothering with the steps, grasped Jess by the waist and lifted her down just as the house's front door opened. He kept one arm around her, clasping her close to his side in a shockingly intimate manner, but she decided not to protest. She suspected she'd need the support. Fluff crowded against her other side; she rested her hand on his head.

A footman came out first, dressed in the duke's livery, and then a man and a woman—she recognized Ned and Ellie. And behind them came Jack with a girl she was fairly certain she'd never met. And then, of course, the duke and duchess themselves.

She must have moaned, because Kit hugged her closer and murmured, "Don't worry. Perhaps they are all leaving."

Only if she and Kit suddenly turned invisible.

"Look who's arrived, Mama," Jack said. Of course it had to be Jack, though the duke was looking at them, too, his expression inscrutable.

Jess pressed against Kit. She wanted to hide behind him. Yes, it was a cowardly thought, but she wasn't feeling especially brave at the moment.

"Who's arrived? What do you mean?" The duchess looked up at Jack, who nodded in their direction.

"Behold," Jack said. "The Duchess of Love's family is all in the same place for once."

The duchess frowned, clearly puzzled, and then her eyes widened. She made an odd sound—a yelp or a squeak—and came hurrying toward them.

"Oh, God," Jess muttered, and forced her feet to stay where they were, no matter how strong her urge to jump behind Kit. She was *not* a coward.

And if she told herself that enough times, perhaps she would actually believe it.

Chapter Ten

*But sometimes you will want to keep
his family at arm's length.*

—Venus's Love Notes

Mama had her arms out as if she would hug Jess, but she caught herself at the last moment and merely took her hands.

"Oh, it is *so* good to see you again, my dear. You haven't changed a bit." She looked up at Ash. Good God, were there tears in her eyes? "I'm so happy you two have resolved your differences."

Jess looked up at him, too, clearly wanting him to clarify matters.

"Er, well, as to that—"

But Mama rushed on like a flooding river. "And how kind of you to join us here. I assume Mr. Dalton told you we were in London when you got back to the castle? He is the best of butlers; he must have hinted we would love to have you come up to Town. Though of course he didn't know everything that's been happening—I haven't had time to send him word." Mama was still holding Jess's hands; thankfully, Jess wasn't struggling.

"Ah. Well, we didn't actually . . . that is, we never went to the castle."

Mama laughed and winked. "So you've spent all this time at the manor, getting reacquainted, have you? Well, of course you have. You've so much time to make up for." She must have squeezed Jess's hands, because Jess winced slightly. "Perhaps we will have another grandchild to welcome in the not-so-distant future, hmm?"

Oh, God, could Mama be more mortifying? Poor Jess. He should—

Wait a minute.

"Another?" He glanced at Ned and Ellie. Ellie was blushing, and Ned was trying not to look too proud of himself.

His brother had obviously been extremely efficient.

He looked back at Mama and Jess to find Jess frowning at him, inclining her head toward Mama and wiggling her brows significantly and with perhaps a touch of panic.

What was he to do? Tell his mother he had not, in fact, been sleeping with his wife? Oh, no, he was not going to broach that subject. Just the thought of discussing such a topic with his mother made his blood run cold—and his stomach churn.

"I will tell you, Ash, I was more than a little worried as the days went by and we didn't hear from you," Mama said. She looked back at Jess. "But isn't that just like a man? They are such dreadful correspondents when they have something—or *someone*"—Mama winked again—"more immediate to occupy their thoughts."

Jess smiled weakly. She looked a bit ill.

Mama finally released her to put a hand on his arm. "But we've been very busy with your brothers, Ash. We have so much news!"

"Which we'd best communicate inside, don't you think, my dear duchess?" Father had paid off Darby, directed footmen to take Ash's and Jess's bags inside, and then come up, hopefully to restrain Mama. Everyone else was wisely staying a safe distance away.

"Oh, yes, what am I thinking? We don't want to entertain the neighbors with our business, do we? But I am just so happy, I can hardly contain myself! Come, you must tell me how you've been getting on, Jess." She took Jess's arm and started toward the house.

Jess sent him a look of definite panic. He tried to smile reassuringly. He couldn't very well wrest her away from Mama. That would look very odd.

Mama paused and glanced down at Fluff, who was following Jess. "Oh, heavens! The coachman forgot his dog."

"The man claimed the dog was Jess's," Father said.

"Oh?" Mama looked slightly disconcerted. "He's very large, isn't he? What's his name, dear?"

"Ki—"

"Fluff!" Ash said quickly. His parents might not use his Christian name, but they certainly knew it.

"Fluff," Jess agreed while sending him a look that clearly said her pet would become "Kit" again if he failed to protect her from his mother.

Mama was still considering Fluff, who wagged his tail in a friendly fashion. Fortunately, he refrained from barking. "Do you think he'd be more comfortable in the stables? He's almost the size of a pony."

"But he's very well behaved," Jess said. "He's lived in the manor with me for years. He won't cause any trouble."

"But how is he with other dogs?" Father asked.

"Oh, yes." Mama nodded. "A very good point, my dear duke. We can't have him fighting with Shakespeare."

"Shakespeare?" Ash frowned. Mama had a thieving cat named Sir Reginald who stayed at the castle, but he'd never heard of any creature named Shakespeare.

"A dog I've recently acquired," Jack said, stepping forward to take Jess's free hand. "Hallo, Jess. It's been too long."

"Yes." Jess smiled. "It's good to see you again, Jack."

"May I make you known to my wife, Frances?"

"Wife?" Ash stared at the woman next to Jack. Good God, did nothing make sense today?

Jack laughed. "And this lobcock, Frances, is my older brother, the Marquis of Ashton."

Jack's wife smiled. "It's a pleasure to meet you, Lady Ashton, Lord Ashton."

"You must call me Ash," he said, trying to marshal his thoughts. "Everyone does." Except, of course his wife. "Ah, no, the pleasure is all ours, Miss—I mean, er, that is, Frances."

The girl was pretty enough, though her hair was startlingly short and very red. But she was clearly in love with Jack—and Jack seemed to be in love with her, judging by his besotted expression.

"And please call me Jess." Jess smiled and then turned to greet Ned.

"Ned," Mama said once Jess moved on to speak to Ellie, "you can't leave now. Send poor John Coachman back to the mews and come inside with us for a nice cup of tea."

"But, Mama . . ."

"And don't dillydally." Mama reclaimed Jess's arm and almost towed her along toward the house. "We can all catch up inside." She looked over her shoulder at them. "As your father so wisely pointed out, we don't want to give the gossips more to chew on. They will be excited enough that Jess and Ash are in Town."

Damnation. Mama was likely all too correct about the gossips. Ash glanced around furtively—and thought he saw the curtains on one of the neighboring houses twitch back into place.

Ned sighed and looked at Ash. "This is the second time

we've had the coach all packed to go back to the country, and the second time we've had to stay."

"And for excellent reasons," Ellie said. "First Jack's wedding, and now Ash's and Jess's arrival." She came up to touch Ash's arm. "I'm so happy you and Jess have mended things between you. I told you she loved you."

"Ah." Ellie had indeed said that at Mama's house party. She was wrong, of course, but he couldn't tell her that, just as he couldn't tell her he and Jess hadn't mended anything. "Er. Yes. Exactly."

Why the hell did his entire family have to be in London?

Ellie frowned. "You and Jess *have* settled your differences, haven't you?"

He hated lying to Ellie, but telling her the truth felt like betraying Jess. "We have . . . that is, we are . . ." He forced a smile. "We're in agreement." *About trying to come to an agreement.* "Frankly, we were hoping to spend some time alone together, which is why we came here instead of going to the castle."

"Trying to avoid Mama and Father, hmm?" Ned said, having bowed to the inevitable and sent the coach away.

Poor Jess had been swept along with Mama into the house, but at least Jack and his wife—*Good God, Jack had a wife!*—had gone with her.

"Yes."

Ellie giggled. "Your expression! Oh, poor Ash. You look so beleaguered, but you know you will just have to accept that you are trapped. You might as well enjoy it."

"Enjoy it? You know my mother is going to drag me and Jess around to every social event she can find." He'd never liked the idle, inane chatter that passed for conversation at ton parties. "I'd rather be boiled in oil."

"I'm sure you would," Ned said, "but that's beside the point. Mama believes she knows what's best, and much as I hate to admit it, she is often right."

"Not in this case." Ah, perhaps he saw a way to wriggle free. "Jess doesn't have the proper wardrobe."

Ellie laughed. "Frances tried that excuse, and your mother was having none of it. Well, I needed all new clothes also, and, as you can see"—she extended her arms to show off her new dress—"the duchess solved that problem, too. Truthfully, I think she was delighted to look at pattern books. She didn't get to do that before, having only sons." Ellie led the way through the front door. "And Madame Celeste will be overjoyed."

"Who's Madame Celeste?" Ash asked, following behind Ned.

Ellie looked back over her shoulder. "The London dressmaker. She—oh!"

Ellie stumbled, and Ned lunged to grab her, but she caught her own balance.

"Are you all right?" Ned's voice was far too sharp for such a minor event.

"Yes, of course," Ellie said, smiling. "I just didn't pick up my feet. I'm fine."

Poor Ned. His tendency to worry had only got stronger with his first wife's and his son's death in childbirth. And now with Ellie. . . .

"Did I understand Mama correctly and congratulations are in order?"

Ellie's smile was blinding. "Yes. We are delighted, aren't we, Ned?"

Ned looked more anxious than delighted. "I'll be happier once the baby's born."

Ellie shook his arm slightly. "Remember, you promised not to worry."

With Ned, that was like promising not to breathe.

Ellie must have realized this, too, because she laughed. "Well, not worry too much."

"I'm trying," Ned said, putting his hand over hers, the love he felt so clear in his eyes even Ash could see it.

If only *his* love was as uncomplicated as Ned's, Ash thought as he watched his brother escort Ellie into the blue drawing room. But then Ned had never had to face betrayal. He'd married Cicely, whom he'd loved and who had loved him as best she could, and when she'd died...

Ah, yes, there *were* some things worse than being cuckolded. As much as Jess had hurt him and as much as her demise would simplify his life, he couldn't wish for her death. Just the thought was unbearably painful, especially now that he'd seen her again.

"Lord Ashton!" Braxton, the butler, approached from the back of the house, a small—well, small in comparison to Fluff—brown dog with floppy ears and a plumed tail at his heels.

"Hallo, Braxton. Do you have a pet now?"

"A pet? Oh, no." He chuckled. "This is Shakespeare, my lord. Lord Jack's dog. Richard—one of the footman, you know—came down to the kitchen to say some cakes and biscuits and tea were needed at once in the drawing room, so Shakespeare, being very interested in cakes and biscuits, came up to investigate, isn't that right, sir?"

Shakespeare barked once and wagged his tail emphatically.

"He's a very talented animal, my lord. Say good day to Lord Ashton, Shakespeare."

Shakespeare sat and offered his paw.

Ash took it. "My wife has brought her dog with her, Braxton. I hope Shakespeare will welcome him also."

Braxton sucked in his breath sharply. "Lady Ashton is here as well?" He grinned broadly. "Oh, my lord, that is wonderful news. We have all hoped this day would come. I know I speak for the entire staff when I say we are so happy you and Lady Ashton have reconciled."

Ash forced himself to smile. "Yes, well. Thank you." Good God, he knew the servants wanted him to resolve his marital issues, but he'd thought their concern was largely for their own well-being—not that their employment was at all at risk with Ned and Jack able to continue the line. But Braxton seemed happy for Ash himself—Ash as a man, not as the heir. He suddenly hoped he wouldn't disappoint him.

"Ah, and here is Richard now," Braxton said, "and William as well. I see Cook took the precaution of sending up plenty of provisions. Your brothers do like their cakes, my lord, and they are always hungry. I imagine you might be a bit sharp-set yourself."

"Yes, I suppose I am."

He followed the servants into the drawing room. Jess was on the settee next to Mama, but the place next to her was empty, partly due to the fact Fluff was sprawled over the floor by her feet. She shot him a look of both anger and desperation as he came in. He felt a twinge of guilt; he had rather deserted her, though he hadn't intended to do so.

"Ah, here's Shakespeare," Jack said. "Now we'll see how he and Fluff get along."

"Fluff is very calm and well behaved," Jess said. Her voice was firm, but her eyes flicked nervously to Shakespeare as he gave an excited yip and trotted over to make Fluff's acquaintance.

Ash strode over to separate the animals if necessary, but Fluff merely yawned as Shakespeare sniffed around him, and then shifted position so Ash could sit next to Jess.

"Shakespeare, come here." Jack snapped his fingers, and Shakespeare reluctantly left Fluff to sit by Jack.

"At least we aren't going to have a dog fight in Mama's drawing room," Ned said as he reached for the tray of cakes William had just put down. "You were taking a bit of a chance, Jack, introducing them like that."

"I didn't introduce them, if you'll notice," Jack said. "Ash is the one who let Shakespeare in."

"Your dog let himself in." Ash helped himself to a slice of seedcake. "Would you care for something, Jess?"

She shook her head a bit too sharply. Her eyes still had a glimmer of panic, and her lips were pressed tightly together.

"Do have some tea, dear," Mama said, handing her a cup.

Jess had no choice but to take it; it rattled in its saucer, and she put it down at once.

Seeing her with Mama this way—now that Ash thought about it, Jess had never attended any of his mother's parties. She'd never taken tea or had supper with them. Once he'd stopped climbing trees and catching fish with her, he'd seen her only riding or painting in the studio.

Of course she hadn't been at his mother's house parties. She was only the head groom's daughter.

No. He'd told her the disparity in their social standing had never mattered to him, and it was true. He felt far more at ease with her than he did with the women of the ton. They saw him as the future Duke of Greycliffe. Jess saw him as Kit. She understood him—

Bloody hell! If she understood him, she'd never have let Percy get between her thighs, not to mention the naked footman and who knew how many others—

No. He was not going to indulge in that line of thought again. He would simply hope her behavior all stemmed from her hot nature, which would no longer cause her to seek male companionship once she had him standing—or lying—by, ready to satisfy her needs.

He shifted in his seat. Blast it, that thought had had its predictable effect.

"Quite a lot has happened since last we saw you, Ash," Father said, clearly trying to draw Mama's attention away from Jess. He was successful.

"Oh, yes." Mama bounced slightly in her seat and leaned forward. "I'm sure you will not be completely surprised that Ned and Ellie have wed. You were there at the ball when they announced their betrothal, and you likely knew they were already—"

Father cleared his throat. "Yes, my love, but perhaps you don't wish to say precisely what they were already doing?"

Ellie's face was bright red. She was studying her fingernails while Ned examined the cakes even more closely.

Mama grinned. "Suffice it to say that Ellie is expecting an interesting event."

"And you, my dear, are expecting a grandchild to spoil."

"As are you. Admit it!" Mama laughed, clearly delighted.

If he and Jess had had a true marriage, Mama might have any number of grandchildren to spoil now.

Damnation.

Father grinned. "I will not deny it."

They shared one of their looks that always made Ash feel as if he and everyone else in the room had ceased to exist for them.

And then Mama bounced again and turned back to him. "And the day you left for the manor, Ash, we received a note from Jack asking us to come up to London to help him resolve a small problem—"

Father choked on a piece of seedcake and reached for his tea. Mama gave him a quelling look before she continued.

"And we found Frances"—she beamed at the girl—"who happens to be the long-lost granddaughter of the Marquis of Rothmarsh. And Frances and Jack fell madly in love and married this morning."

With such rushed nuptials, he'd wager Jack had anticipated his vows as well.

Blast it, far from anticipating *his* vows, Ash still hadn't managed to consummate his damn marriage—and he'd been wed for eight bloody years.

Mama frowned. "If only we'd known you were coming, Ash, we could have waited until tomorrow to hold the ceremony."

Thank God they hadn't known. He did not care to witness his brother's wedding when his marriage was still in such a shambles. "Ah, well, that's quite all right. No need to wait for us. I can see Jack and Frances are very happy." He smiled at Frances, who looked almost as anxious as Jess to be free of this family gathering. Mama could be a bit overwhelming. "Does this mean, now that all your sons are wed, you'll hang up your matchmaking mantle, Mama?"

Father's eyes brightened. "By Jove, yes. You don't need to hold those beastly monthly Love Balls anymore, do you, my dear duchess? And you certainly don't need to invite the silly spawn of the ton to that yearly torture—er, party—in February." He grinned. "I'd say this calls for something more than tea." He got up to fetch the brandy bottle. "Anyone else care for a glass?"

"Yes!"

"Please."

Jack and Ned didn't hesitate. Ash nodded, too, and glanced at Jess. She looked as if she'd dearly like some brandy as well.

He should find a way to free her from Mama's clutches. He looked down at Fluff, but the dog was contentedly resting his head on his paws. No excuse there.

"I still have to find a match for Miss Wharton," Mama said.

"I thought you'd decided Percy would do for her, much as that seems like throwing a kitten into the jaws of a lion." Father's face was carefully expressionless as he handed Ash his brandy.

Ash hoped his face was equally unreadable, since his brothers, mother, and Ellie were all regarding him with varying degrees of sympathy. At least they were looking at him and not at Jess, though he'd swear he heard a very faint moan come from her direction.

"So Percy's in Town, is he?" Perhaps that was for the best. If he was going to resolve his marital difficulties, he might as well face them head on. If Jess couldn't control her passion for Percy, then there was no hope for the continuation of their union.

"Yes." Jack glanced at Jess and then back at Ash. "Causing trouble as usual."

"Oh, but I do think he may have formed a tendre for Miss Wharton," Mama said. "And we need to find her a husband before the Season is over or her dreadful parents will force her to marry their ancient neighbor."

"But will Percy be worse than the neighbor?" Ned asked. "Aren't you afraid he'll ruin her life?"

"No, not at all. I think she may save his." Mama's eyes drifted toward Jess. "Or at least I hope so."

Jess turned white. Fortunately, Braxton appeared at the door just then.

"Lord and Lady Ashton's room is ready, Your Grace. Mrs. Watson will show them up, if they are ready to retire."

Thank God. Ash surged to his feet. "If you'll excuse us, Mama?"

Jess hadn't been certain that her legs would support her weight, so she was extremely thankful when Kit offered her his arm. She gripped it as they crossed the room. She'd never been so happy to leave a group of people in her life. Not that anyone had been the least bit rude. Oh, no. They'd all been unfailingly polite, even when Percy's name had been mentioned.

Oh, God, Percy! She'd seen him once since that dreadful afternoon in the studio at Greycliffe Castle. He'd had the unbelievable effrontery to present himself at Blackweith Manor a few months after she'd arrived. She'd been there long enough to have got over her initial fury at Kit for abandoning her and to have settled into an extended fit of the blue devils.

The butler at the time had heard the rumors about her disgrace and had apparently thought he was assisting an illicit assignation when he brought Percy directly up to her bedroom. The chamber pot whizzing past his ear had disabused him of that notion. She'd gone after Percy with the fireplace poker. Fortunately Dennis had been upstairs also. He'd heard the commotion and had come running, disarming her before she broke Percy's head.

She did not want to see Percy again, especially in London with Kit and his parents and brothers and all the nasty ton watching.

Mrs. Watson was waiting just outside the door. She beamed at Kit. "Oh, Lord Ashton, it is so good to see you!" And then she looked at Jess and said, ice in her voice, "Lady Ashton."

Jess expected to be disliked; she'd been more shocked at Mr. Braxton's pleasant welcome than Mrs. Watson's cold one. The Greycliffe servants had always been intensely loyal to the duke and his family; they must see her as having ruined Kit's life and thus the lives of his mother and father. At the very least, she'd cut up the duke's and duchess's peace for eight long years.

If this were the Dark Ages, she'd worry that someone might slip poison into her tea.

Mrs. Watson led the way up the stairs, chattering to Kit while Jess and Fluff followed behind. The woman was amazingly well preserved. Her hair under her cap was gray and she was rather stout, but she could still climb the steps and keep up a steady stream of talk without becoming the slightest bit breathless.

"It's been so long since we've seen you here in Town,

my lord, but don't worry. I've kept your room well aired in the hopes you might see fit to pay us a visit someday. Once the duke and duchess arrived with Lord Ned and Miss Ellie, we were so hoping you'd come, too. It is too bad you missed the weddings, first Lord Ned's and then Lord Jack's. I tell you, we haven't had so much excitement at Greycliffe House for as long as I can remember."

They reached the top of the stairs, walked down the corridor, and stopped at a door at the end. Mrs. Watson opened it.

"Here you go then, my lord. It should be all as you remember it." Mrs. Watson bustled over to tug one of the curtains straight.

The room was large and quiet and tasteful. The heavy mahogany furniture was covered in blue and green upholstery, and the carpet, bed hangings, and coverlet were blue and green as well. Jess felt as if she'd wandered into a secluded forest glade—with a jay screaming disapprovingly from the bushes.

To be fair, Mrs. Watson was a cooing dove where Kit was concerned, but when her eyes encountered Jess, her brows and mouth snapped down and her nose wrinkled as if she smelled something rotten.

It *had* been several days since Jess had had the luxury of a bath, but then it had been equally long—perhaps longer—for Kit.

"*Your* things are here by the wardrobe," the housekeeper said, not quite looking at Jess. "Shall I send up a maid to put them away?"

Oh, damnation. Some supercilious young girl would have her fingers all over Jess's outdated and threadbare clothing, and then go gossip about Lady Ashton's shabby wardrobe with the other servants.

She shouldn't care. She wouldn't care if she were back

at the manor. Well, at the manor no female besides Dennis's rose-mad sister Helena ever saw her, and Helena certainly didn't care what Jess's clothes looked like, even though taking care of them was ostensibly her job. If they didn't have leaves and thorns and petals, they weren't of any interest to Helena.

Kit glanced at her, and Jess was desperate enough to shake her head slightly, hoping he'd take her hint even if he didn't know her reasons.

He gave her a puzzled look, but said, "No, thank you, Mrs. Watson. I believe we can manage well enough on our own."

"Very good, my lord." Mrs. Watson looked at Jess, sniffed, and headed toward the door, but paused on the threshold. "Shall I have water sent up for a bath?"

Kit grinned. "Yes, thank you. That would be splendid."

Mrs. Watson nodded. "I shall ask William and Richard to bring it up directly, my lord." She cleared her throat, pressed her lips together, and finally managed a stiff, "my lady." She left, closing the door behind her.

Kit turned to Jess. "I hope you don't mind?"

"Not at all. I would like to use the water when you are done." Rinsing the grime of the trip off her skin and out of her hair sounded wonderful. Being clean might help her face Kit's family with more fortitude.

"Of course. I will even let you use it before I do." He grinned. "If it is not too indelicate for me to say so, I suspect I am far dirtier than you. I must smell like horse."

"Oh, no, you smell—" Like home. Like Kit. "You smell fine. I'm the one who smells of wet dog." She ran her hand over Fluff's ears. "Fluff insisted on sleeping with me last night."

And now she was blushing, blast it. She couldn't think about beds without thinking about what Kit had done with her in one particular bed. She hurried to pick up her valise.

"I'll just take my things to my room. Come, Fluff." She looked around. Where was the door to her bedchamber?

"Er, Jess . . ."

Kit looked uncomfortable, as if there was something unpleasant he needed to tell her. Well, she would listen to him in a moment. "I know this is silly, but I don't see the connecting door."

"That's because there isn't one."

Even better. No connecting door meant no late night temptations. She headed for the corridor—

"Not that way, Jess."

She frowned, even as her heart started pounding. She must have misunderstood. He couldn't mean . . . "Pardon me?"

He smiled cautiously. "*This* is your room."

"Oh." She bit her lip and put down her bag. Now she was having trouble breathing. "But then where is yours?"

He must be teasing her. She was certain this was his room. Mrs. Watson would not have brought them to her room, and the woman had definitely said "your" room when she'd been talking to Kit. . . .

Oh, God. "Where are you sleeping?"

"Here." He shrugged and gestured with his head to the bed. "There."

Her mouth opened, but she couldn't make any words come out. Specks of lights danced in front of her eyes.

She felt Kit's strong fingers grip her arms. He shook her slightly, and her vision cleared.

"It will be all right, Jess. This bed is bigger and firmer than the one at the White Stag." He flushed. "We can put something down the center to divide it, if you want. It will be almost as good as separate beds."

She wet her lips. "There must be another bedchamber I can use. This is a big house."

"But we're married, Jess. Mama and Father believe

married couples should share a room and a bed. If I insist you have your own room, everyone will know we haven't reconciled."

"But we haven't." Fluff, the traitor, had left her to make himself at home in front of the fire.

"We are trying to reconcile though, aren't we?" He dropped his hold on her and stepped back. "I know it's awkward, but especially with both my brothers married, it would be more awkward if we didn't share a room. The servants would talk, and I'm sure that would get the damn ton talking as well. And with Mama and everyone here, I can't see any way we can avoid attending at least some social events."

He shoved his hands into his pockets and turned to look at Fluff and the fire. "Blast it, I can't believe Jack is wed. I swear he didn't know this woman when he left the castle just weeks ago."

She'd inhaled, ready to argue about sharing a room and going off to balls and parties, but she let her breath out when Kit changed the subject.

Ned wasn't the only one who worried. Kit did, too. It wasn't easy being the heir, feeling responsible for everyone from his brothers to the boot boy, knowing one day they would all depend on him in one way or another.

"Perhaps he's known her for years, Kit. You say you're never in London, so it wouldn't be surprising if you weren't aware of their friendship. If she's the granddaughter of a marquis, they must move in the same circles." She'd never been to London before and had been ostracized by everyone near the manor, but she knew that the ton was a very small, very select world where everyone knew everyone.

"No. Remember Mama said Jack's wife was Rothmarsh's 'long lost' granddaughter. It sounds as if she was a complete surprise."

She might have been a surprise, but a marquis's

granddaughter—unlike a groom's daughter—belonged in the ton's drawing rooms. London society would be more than surprised—it would be horrified—when the notorious Lady Ashton made her appearance.

"Well, she seems very nice, and your parents appear content with the match. There's really nothing you can do but accept her."

Kit blew out a long breath. "I know, but what chance of success does Jack's marriage have when they know so little about each other?"

She tasted bitterness—or maybe it was despair.

"Perhaps they know enough. As we have illustrated all too well, long familiarity doesn't guarantee marital happiness."

He looked at her, his eyes as bleak as she felt. "Jess—"

But then the door swung open.

"Your bath's here, my lord," Mrs. Watson said.

Chapter Eleven

What the eye sees, it doesn't forget.

—Venus's Love Notes

Two footmen maneuvered a large copper slipper tub into the room and over to the hearth. Fluff, perhaps thinking the bath was for him, scrambled to his feet and fled, tail between his legs, to hide behind Jess's skirts.

Kit laughed. "I thought he liked the water."

"He does. He just doesn't like baths."

Fluff whined and peered around her as a procession of housemaids filled the tub.

"He'll have to have one, you know. I thought he might go in after we're done."

Mrs. Watson's eyes snapped from supervising the tub filling to stare horrified at Kit. "My lord, you can't give that animal a bath up here! Think of the carpet."

"Oh, yes, quite right. The carpet. But what about the dog, Mrs. Watson? You may not have noticed, but he smells."

Mrs. Watson wrinkled her nose. "Yes, I'm afraid he does." She gestured to the taller of the two footmen who were still in the room, waiting for the housemaids to stop filing through the door with their water pitchers. "Perhaps Richard could bathe him. He was able to get Shakespeare clean."

Richard did not look thrilled. "Shakespeare liked bathing, my lord, and he is considerably smaller."

"You might need some help, then." Kit looked at the other footman. "William, isn't it?"

"Yes, my lord." William sounded as unenthusiastic as Richard.

"I'm sure the two of you can manage to get Fluff presentable. Have you any advice, Lady Ashton, to make the experience easier for all involved?"

"I do." Roger had managed, through trial and error, to perfect a dog-bathing routine. "It's best not to actually say b-a-t-h. Fluff is very bright." Fluff had moved to her other side to get farther from the tub. "I'd use the largest t-u-b you have; I think that makes him feel less cramped—or he just thinks he's in a deep puddle. And hide the s-o-a-p until you have him in the water."

"Yes, my lady," Richard said, "but how do we keep him in the ba—"

Fluff moaned and backed up to hide behind the bed.

"That is," Richard corrected himself, "how do we keep him in the water?"

She laughed. "He likes to be sung to."

Richard and William exchanged an alarmed look.

"But it doesn't have to be good singing. In fact, it can be terrible singing." She grinned at them. "Sometimes Fluff will sing along."

"Oh, my word, that is all we need," Mrs. Watson said. Clearly she disapproved of Fluff as much as she did of Jess. "A dog howling in the kitchen."

"And perhaps Shakespeare will join in," Kit said. "Can you persuade Fluff to leave with Richard and William, my dear?"

"As long as I'm not going toward the t-u-b, I can." She looked at the footmen. "You might wish to wait in the corridor."

The men left the room, and she grabbed Fluff's collar,

pulling him toward the door. Once it was clear they weren't headed toward the tub, he stopped resisting.

"Go with Richard and William now," she said when she'd got him out of the room.

Fluff looked at the men and then at her. Jess stroked his ears. "Don't worry, I'll be fine. And I bet Richard and William can find something nice for you to eat."

Fluff's tail started wagging, and he looked at the men hopefully.

"Yes, indeed," Richard said. "Cook's taken to saving tidbits for Shakespeare; I'm sure there's some to spare. Come along, Fluff, and we'll see what we can find, shall we?"

Fluff woofed happily, all reservations gone, and followed Richard and William downstairs.

Mrs. Watson was shaking her head as Jess came back in. "At least you're all here now. I don't think we'll be getting any more beasties underfoot."

"But think of poor Ned, Mrs. Watson," Kit said. "He has no pet of his own."

The housekeeper almost smiled. "He has taken to sharing Shakespeare with Lord Jack, so don't you worry about him, my lord." She put the towels she'd been holding on the bed and started for the door. "Oh, and the duchess said supper will be put back so you can have your baths. You're to join everyone in the blue drawing room in two hours." She closed the door behind her.

Jess tried not to let out a sigh of relief. "I don't think she likes me."

"She'll come around." Kit walked over and took one of the towels and a cake of soap off the bed. "Some of the servants chose sides when we separated."

"No, they didn't. They couldn't have. There was only one side for them to choose. I know that." Oh, dear. Until now, she'd only considered the question of being Kit's wife and having his children; she hadn't thought how difficult it would be to assume the role of Lady Ashton and take charge of Kit's household. The servants would never accept her. *They* knew she was more properly one of them.

Of course, if she didn't come to an agreement with Kit, the servants' opinions of her wouldn't matter.

He brought her the towel and the soap. "I don't think it's as bad as all that. In fact, I suspect some of them blame me for letting matters remain in limbo so long."

"They think you should have divorced me." She took the things from him. The towel was softer than any she'd felt before, and the cake of soap smelled of lavender.

"No, they think I should have brought you back to the castle and made you my wife in truth years ago, once it was clear you weren't carrying Percy's child."

There had never been any danger of her becoming *enceinte*, as she'd told him before, but she wasn't going to start that argument again. "But I was only a servant like themselves—worse even, I was the Irish groom's daughter. They could not have wanted you to stay married to me."

"No one saw you as a servant, Jess. As I told you before, I certainly never thought of you that way."

Perhaps he hadn't, but his parents certainly must have. Their nuptials had been more like a funeral than a wedding. The duke had been stony faced; the duchess had cried. Even Ellie's father, who'd officiated, had had a furrow of worry between his brows from the moment he'd opened his prayer book. And Kit—Kit had stood stoically at her side, reciting his vows woodenly.

She should have stopped it, but she'd been too young and stupid and desperate—and oddly numb—to do so. Too much had happened to her in too short a time. She'd felt as if she were caught in a bizarre dream from which she'd soon awaken.

"I'd better get my bath before the water is cold," she said.

He smiled. "Yes, indeed. Especially since I have to use that water after you."

"Ha. A cold bath will be good for you."

She said it without thinking, but Kit's expression suddenly sharpened, reminding her how Roger and Dennis and the other men at the manor would talk about taking a cold bath or a dip in the frigid pond to cool their ardor over some unrequited love.

Damnation. She hadn't meant it that way.

"I'll hurry." At least she could get herself out of this dress and her stays without his help. She turned, looked at the tub, and stopped. Oh, blast. "Kit."

"What is it?" His voice sounded tight. She glanced at him. He still had an oddly pained look on his face. Likely her comment wasn't going to help the situation.

"There's no screen." She waved her hand at the tub. "I'll be . . . that is, you could . . ." She wasn't usually one to mince words, but this didn't seem like the time to point out in such detail that she'd be wet and naked and exposed to his view. "I won't have any privacy."

The pained expression intensified. "Oh. Yes. I see." His voice was rather hoarse; she watched his Adam's apple bob as he swallowed. "I shall just turn my back."

She looked at him and then at the tub. She wanted a bath so badly, and she trusted Kit to keep his word, but it would be so easy for him to look. . . .

What was the matter with her? She was used to nudity. She'd painted any number of naked men. She'd even agreed to let Kit paint her unclothed.

She shivered. That might not have been such a good idea.

But painting wasn't lascivious. When she had a brush in her hand, she was looking with an artist's eye at line and light and volume and proportion. She might feel happy or satisfied or frustrated, depending on how well she felt the painting was coming along, but she never felt—heat swept up her neck to her face—*lustful*.

"I will turn the wing chair over there around and read a book." Kit grabbed a volume from the bookcase and strode across the room to the big leather chair, wrestling it so it was facing away from the fire. "Just let me know when it's my turn." He sat down—and disappeared from view.

If she couldn't see him, he certainly couldn't see her, and even if he peeked—which she really did trust him not to do—he wouldn't be able to see anything. The bed and bed hangings were between them, and the tub had high sides.

But he might get impatient.

She scrambled out of her dress and underthings, dropped them into a pile on the floor, stepped into the tub, and sank into the water. Ohhh. It felt wonderful. If only she could soak here until the water chilled, but Kit deserved some warm water, too.

She washed her body and then wet her hair. Water cascaded down her face and into her eyes as she felt around for the cake of soap. Where was it? Ah, here it was. She grabbed it—and it squirted out of her fingers.

Blast. From the sound of it, the soap had landed on the carpet.

She wiped the water from her eyes and peered over the edge of the tub. No soap. Where the hell—

Oh, Lord. Her heart sank. The damn thing had flown quite a distance.

She stared at the glistening soap. She could skip washing her hair, but it was already wet and it had been days since her hair was clean.

Perhaps if she stretched, she could reach it. She tried, but as she leaned farther, she felt the tub begin to tip. Oh, that would be perfect, to go sprawling like a caught fish, flopping around naked in a pool of water—not to mention the fact she'd soak Mrs. Watson's precious carpet. She would just climb out and snatch it; the carpet would only get slightly damp then.

She tried to stand up, but her feet slipped on the tub's slick bottom, and she plopped back down, sending a little wave of water over the side. Damnation. And even though she was next to the fire, the air was cold on her wet skin, especially as the soap had taken off on the side away from the fire.

She looked at the soap and then she looked across the room at the wing chair. Unfortunately, if she was going to wash her hair, there was only one solution to her problem.

Oh, blast. He'd picked up Ovid's *Ars Amatoria—The Art of Love*. What the hell was that doing in his room?

He heard the sound of cloth rustling, of stays dropping to the floor. *Zeus.* He'd imagined Jess naked in as much detail as he could—he'd seen her body outlined by the fire through her shift at the White Stag—but he didn't really know what she looked like without her dress and chemise and stays. He could find out now. . . .

No. He'd given her his word that he wouldn't peek, and she would expect him to honor it.

Of *course* he would honor it. He was an honorable man . . . who at the moment was suffering from a terrible case of lust.

He laid *Ars Amatoria* on his lap. It was a heavy book—it should keep his unruly cock where it belonged. And then he squeezed his eyes shut, gripped the chair arms, and pressed his head against the chair back. He would stay where he was if it killed him, and it probably would.

He could shut his eyes, but not his ears, not and keep hold of the chair. He heard splashing and a small feminine moan of pleasure as Jess sank into the water.

Mmm. He could imagine how her wet skin would glisten in the firelight. She'd lie back, and droplets of water would slowly trace their way from the base of her throat down her body. Her hands, slippery with soap, would slide over and under, around and between her beautiful firm breasts with their perfect rose-colored nipples, and then they'd move down over her flat belly to the place between her thighs—

He squinted down at *Ars Amatoria,* expecting to see it had risen several inches, but apparently it was still winning the battle with his cock. But only just. All his blood must be concentrated in that poor organ. He certainly felt light-headed—

"Kit."

He'd swear *Ars Amatoria* jumped. He tightened his grip on the chair arms. He was so lost in lust he was hallucinating. He'd thought he'd heard Jess—

"Kit!"

Good God, he *had* heard her. Was she done with her bath already?

"Kit, I need your help."

To wash her back? He swallowed, pressing *Ars Amatoria* firmly down on his frantic cock. He was not going to attack her. He was not. He would go slowly—or he would try to—tracing the water drops with his lips, with his tongue—

No! He must not forget the naked footman. It was too soon.

"Kit?"

He cleared his throat. "What is it, Jess?"

"I've . . . I've lost the soap. Could you get it for me?"

"Lost the soap?" He had a very, er, elevating vision of fishing around in the bathwater, under her legs and around her arse—

He pushed down harder on the book.

"Yes. It slipped out of my hands and onto the floor. It's too far away for me to reach, and I still have to wash my hair."

He cleared his throat again. "I"—more throat clearing—"see."

"So would you get it for me without . . . without, ah . . . you know."

"I know?" Without attacking her like an animal? She couldn't mean that.

"Without peeking. You can . . ." She paused, and then her voice sounded stronger, as if she'd thought of the perfect solution. "You can tie your cravat around your eyes."

That was ridiculous, but he probably shouldn't say that. "How shall I find the soap when I'm blindfolded?"

"I'll direct you."

"Oh, very well." It would be better for his sanity if he didn't see Jess naked. He had to wait at least a month—more likely two—before he could be sure her encounter with the footman hadn't had any permanent consequences.

He put Ovid safely on the floor, tied his cravat over his eyes, and stood. It was odd and a bit disorienting not being able to see. "I haven't been in this room in years, you know, so I can't be certain I remember the positions of all the furniture. You will have to guide my every step."

"You can feel your way around the bed, can't you?"

"Yes." He remembered where the bed was; it was hard to forget that. He took a few steps. "Ouch! Bloody hel—" He pressed his lips together and bent down to rub his shin.

"What is it? What happened? Are you all right?"

At least she sounded truly concerned.

"I just forgot the bed steps were here. You don't see any other hazards, do you?"

"No. You should be fine as long as you keep a hand on the mattress."

He inched along, sweeping a foot cautiously before him, to the first bedpost and then along the bottom of the bed to the second. From here he'd have to cross the room without support.

"Anything in my way?"

"No."

He put his hands out in front of him and continued his shuffling gait. He heard poorly muffled sniggers.

"If you're going to laugh at me, I'll just take this damn blindfold off."

"Oh, no. I'm sorry. You just look . . . I mean, I do appreciate your understanding. Ah, there. The soap is just by your right foot—oh!"

He kicked something with his left foot. "Did you mean my other right foot?"

"Yes. I'm sorry. I'm not always good with directions."

He was usually very good with directions, but the insistent thrum of lust vibrating through his body was extremely distracting. He stepped cautiously to the left.

"There it is. Just by your right foot."

"You mean this foot?" He lifted his left.

She laughed. "Yes."

He stooped cautiously and felt around. His fingers closed on the soap.

"Splendid!" Jess clapped. "Now if you will just hand it to me."

"My pleasure."

He didn't need any further guidance; he could tell from her voice where she was. He took a quick step—and stumbled over something lying on the floor. He tried to regain his balance, but the thing—or things as it must be her discarded clothing—wrapped around his feet, defeating his efforts to save himself. He went pitching forward.

He heard Jess squeak in alarm as he threw his arms out to break his fall. It didn't help. He splashed face first into the tub.

The next few minutes were a mad scramble. His first priority was breathing; his second, keeping the tub from capsizing and spilling water and Jess and him all over the floor. And his third—

"Oh, Kit! Are you all right?" He felt Jess's hands on his shoulder and then his face. She pulled off his blindfold.

Yes, he was all right, but apparently he couldn't talk. The edge of the metal tub was sticking into his chest, but, more importantly, his hands had just slid off a naked thigh. And now he could see the thigh and the sweet place where her legs met. . . .

Look at her face, for God's sake, you idiot!

He sucked air into his lungs. "Are *you* all right? I didn't hurt you when I landed, did I?"

"No." She shrugged, and he forced his eyes to stay on her face, though fortunately he had excellent peripheral vision. "Well, perhaps a little. I might have a bruise there tomorrow."

He fought the urge to see if she had a bruise there now. "I'm sorry. I tripped over your clothes."

"I shouldn't have left them there." She flushed. "Your coat is all wet."

And he was hovering over her naked body. He needed to give her back the soap.

What had he done with the soap?

It was probably floating in the water somewhere, and much as he'd like to hunt for it, he seriously doubted his self-control was up to that task.

If he were a true rake, he'd know how to kiss her and suggest they finish the bath together. And she would enthusiastically agree. He looked at her lips and swore her chin tilted up ever so slightly. . . .

Of course it did. She was the one with all the experience, wasn't she? A succubus. And much as he might like to be seduced, he couldn't allow himself that pleasure. Not yet.

He hauled himself up to stand and tore his gaze away

from her lovely naked body. Not that he needed to look at it. He was quite certain it was burned into his memory.

He stared at a fat cherub perched on the mantel instead. Yes, think of the spiritual, the noncorporeal, the chaste. His body was having none of it. He stepped around the foot of the tub to get closer to the fire, turning his back to Jess to restore her privacy—and his own. His cock was far too prominent.

He shivered. But the cold air and uncomfortably wet clothing would help cast a literal damper on his physical enthusiasm. "If you don't mind, I think I'll stand here until you are finished. I'm afraid I'll take a chill—and ruin the leather on the chair—if I return to my previous place."

"Oh, yes, of course."

Did she sound a little disappointed that he'd pulled away from her? No, that was likely only wishful thinking.

"I'll hurry."

"No, no. Take your time. Did you find the soap? I'm not quite certain what happened to it when I fell."

There was some splashing, and then she said, "Yes, here it is. It somehow got under my . . . er, that is, I was sitting on it."

"Ah." Her lovely, rounded arse, which was below her narrow waist, which was below her two beautiful—

Even the damp and the chill couldn't keep his cock down. "I'm glad you found it."

"And I promise to use it quickly." There was a great quantity of splashing. "Shouldn't you remove your wet clothing?"

God give him strength. "*All* my clothing is wet, Jess. I cannot think you wish me to stand here naked."

"Oh. N-no, of course not. You would be shivering terribly. I'm almost done. I just need to rinse the soap out of my hair and—" She paused.

He watched a piece of ash float up the chimney. "And what?"

There was more splashing, and then she finally answered him.

"Do you have a spare banyan I could borrow? I'll need to sit in front of the fire to dry my hair, and I obviously can't do that now. But if I put my clothing back on, my dress and other things will get soaked."

He had only one banyan, but he was happy to lend it to her. He certainly wasn't going to use it. He was going to bathe and dress as quickly as he could, and then flee the room before his cock persuaded him to do something very stupid. "Of course."

He rescued his banyan from his valise and walked back toward the tub, keeping his eyes on the ground so he didn't trip again—or stare at Jess. "Are you ready for it?"

"Just a moment. Let me just get my towel. I—oh!"

God or the devil or some other divine being clearly was determined to tempt him past sanity. He snapped his head up in time to see Jess catch her foot on the side of the tub and start to fall. He dropped the banyan and extended his arms to catch her as her naked, wet body came crashing into his.

He took a couple steps back to regain his balance, clutching her tightly, one hand on her back, the other on the rise of her soft buttocks. He should be chilled—she was soaking the last dry spots of his waistcoat and shirt and breeches—but the heat surging from his groin threatened instead to turn the wet patches to steam.

"Oh. I'm so sorry." She looked up at him. "What a clumsy pair we are today."

If he bent his head just a little, his lips would meet hers. His hands itched to move, to trace the swell of her buttocks or slip around to explore her breasts. With her vast experience, she must know the bulge pushing against her belly was his painfully swollen cock.

She wasn't struggling in his arms. She would welcome his advances. It had been days since she'd had the attentions of the naked footman. She must be feeling the need—

What the hell was he thinking? Yes, it had been days since that damn footman had been between her thighs. Days. Not weeks, not months. *Days.* He couldn't let his damn cock lead him down the path it wanted. That would be disastrous. He needed some control. He needed to think of something besides the feel of Jess's skin under his fingers.

Fortunately Jess kept her wits about her. Of course she did. Being naked in a man's arms was nothing new for her.

"I'll just get the towel, shall I?"

"Yes, of course." He released her and went to pick the banyan off the floor. When he turned back, she'd wrapped her hair in one towel and was holding the other in front of her like a shield.

"Mrs. Watson only left us two towels, so I'm very glad you're loaning me your extra banyan."

"It's my only banyan." He averted his eyes and held it up for her. "But don't worry. I plan to bathe quickly, and then dress and go down to the study, so you can dry your hair in peace."

"Thank you." She closed the banyan and handed him his towel. "I'll go sit in the chair now. Would I like what you were reading?"

"No!" God, no. If she were already familiar with *Ars Amatoria* he didn't want to know it, and he particularly didn't want her to know he'd been reading the book—which he hadn't been, actually. He would take it downstairs.

He strode over and scooped it up, carefully keeping the title covered, and then scanned the bookshelf. There was nothing else as scandalous, thank God, but nothing very interesting either. "I haven't been here in years; I think they must have taken to storing the books no one wants to read in my bookcase."

Jess looked at the offerings, too. "Oh, I don't know. I assume *someone* might be interested in reading *A Treatise on Sheep Breeding* or *Some Thoughts on Eradicating Vermin in the House,* even though I'm not."

She craned her neck, trying to read the spine of Ovid's book, but he wasn't about to allow her to do that. He put it behind his back.

"Why won't you let me see what you were reading?"

"Because it is completely inappropriate. Here." He pulled *Favorite Household Remedies for All Manner of Ills* off the shelf and offered it to her. "This looks interesting."

She made a face. "It does not."

He pushed it into her hands. "Well, I shall be very quick, so if you'll go over and sit down, I can get on with it."

"Oh, very well."

He watched her disappear behind the chair back and then he hurried over to the tub. Would she try to peek at him? He glanced back. No. Why did he think she would even consider such a thing? She'd seen plenty of naked men.

He stripped off his clothes and stepped into the tub. The water was ice cold.

Chapter Twelve

Your family will always discover your secrets.

—Venus's Love Notes

". . . but do you think—" Ned broke off as soon as the study door opened.

Hmm. Ash noted his brothers looked quite guilty. What were Ned and Jack doing here? They were newly married men; he'd expect them to be spending time with their wives instead of each other and Shakespeare and Fluff. The dogs got up to greet him; his brothers did not.

"Should my ears be burning?" he asked as he patted the animals. They were both slightly damp; Shakespeare must have joined Fluff in his bath.

Shakespeare went back to stretch out by Jack's chair, but Fluff stayed with him.

"Yes." Jack held up the brandy bottle. "Want a drink?"

Ash was tempted to claim some just-remembered engagement that required his immediate presence elsewhere, but his brothers would see through that ruse in an instant. He'd just got to London; he could have no appointments. And with Jess upstairs drying her long, lovely black hair in front of the fire, he couldn't retreat to his room. It was too late to bolt for White's, not that he wished to spend time at that gentlemen's club with strangers who would only gossip about him. And if he wandered the house, he might encounter Mama, which would be much, much worse than facing his brothers. Mama was extremely skilled at prying uncomfortable information out of her sons.

A dose of brandy might be just the thing to steady his nerves. "Yes, thanks." He took the glass from Jack and sat on the sofa. Fluff put his head on his lap.

"Well, at least you're getting along with Jess's dog," Jack said.

Ash took a healthy swallow of brandy. He did not wish to discuss Jess. As the proverb said, attack was the best form of defense. "Yes, but you are the one with real news, Jack. Tell me how you find yourself with a dog and, more importantly, a wife. I don't believe either one had yet entered your life when last I saw you."

"That's right," Ned said, frowning. "Can you believe Jack first met Frances at the Crowing Cock the night he left the castle? She was traveling to London disguised as a boy." He scowled at Jack. "It was an incredibly dangerous plan."

Jack scowled back at Ned. "Yes, but she had what she thought was a good reason for her masquerade, Lord Worry, and nothing dreadful happened to her."

"Except she was compelled to wed you."

"She did *not* have to marry me."

Ned sniffed. "It was the only way to repair her reputation."

"It was not." Jack had lost his customary good humor. "Mama and Lady Rothmarsh had addressed the issue, as well you know."

Ned shrugged. "They'd done their best, but I still think if you hadn't married her, Frances would have had an uncomfortable time of it."

Shakespeare and Fluff started to whine, clearly unsettled by the harsh voices. Jack looked like he was on the verge of throwing his brandy into Ned's face. From there the "discussion" would undoubtedly degenerate into fisticuffs.

Ash did not relish separating the two with a fireplace poker as he'd done on one occasion back at the castle. "But are you happy, Jack? That's what's important."

Both Ned's and Jack's attention snapped back to him. Damn. He'd made a serious tactical error.

"Yes, actually, I'm very happy," Jack said. "Are you?"

"Er . . ." He loosened his cravat. The room was suddenly infernally warm.

"That's what we were discussing when you came in, Ash, as you probably surmised." Ned leaned toward him. "Have you finally resolved your difficulties with Jess, then?"

"Ah . . ." There was no point in lying; his brothers would root out the full story eventually. Well, likely in a matter of minutes. They'd had years of experience at uncovering each other's falsehoods and partial truths. "Not exactly, but we have agreed to work on our problems."

Jack smacked his forehead and looked at the ceiling, clearly not believing he was related to such a blockhead. "So why the hell did you bring her to Town, if you haven't put your marriage back on rock solid ground? At the first whiff of trouble, society will be on you like the ravening pack of wolves it is, tearing your union with Jess to shreds."

That was encouraging. Fluff whined, and he stroked the dog's head.

"Yes, Ash," Ned said, "why didn't you take Jess to the castle and the relative privacy of the country?"

At least Ned and Jack were now in agreement about something.

"I thought Mama and Father were still at the castle. The only person I expected to find here was you, Jack, and I was hoping you could tell us how to avoid the ton."

Jack snorted. "There's no way in hell you're going to dodge the gabble-grinders now, my dear brother. I suspect Mama is making plans as we speak to trot you and Jess around to all the Season's events."

That's what he'd been afraid of. "Perhaps if I reason with her, Mama will let us go back to the castle by ourselves."

Ned and Jack stared at him.

"Reason with the Duchess of Love when she thinks she can finally show all the old cats that her oldest son and the heir to the duchy is truly, happily married?" Jack raised an eyebrow. "How much detail are you willing to share with Mama?"

Ash shifted on the couch, causing Fluff to look up at him. He didn't wish to tell Mama anything. "I'll merely say Jess and I still have a few things to work out, and we need privacy to do so."

Jack's other eyebrow went up. "And you think that will work?"

No, he didn't. It *should* work. Mama was a reasonable woman—except when it came to matters of the heart; then there was no fathoming her thought processes.

"Mama probably feels she's the best person to help you solve your marital difficulties," Ned said. "She *is* the one who pens *Venus's Love Notes*."

Ash's stomach twisted as it always did when he heard those words. "That thing? No one actually reads it, do they?"

"Oh, yes, they do," Jack said. "Avidly, though fortunately not publicly. And since its readership is largely female, we can usually avoid hearing about it. Jess, however, may have a harder time of it."

"Ellie confessed that some girl hinted to her . . . well, said outright, really . . ." Ned's face turned red and he took a quick swallow of brandy.

"It was Miss Patton, one of the boldest of the society misses," Jack said. "She told Ellie and Frances how lucky they were to have married us, since, being the Duchess of

Love's sons, we must have made losing their virginity quite painless. Frances reported the incident to me in horror."

"Bloody hell. *This* is how society women behave these days?" Ash's stomach tightened into a hard knot. How would Jess react if some spoiled daughter of the nobility said such a thing to her? She had quite a temper, but she wouldn't admit she hadn't had the dubious pleasure of being deflowered by a Valentine, would she?

At least she didn't know his darkest secret. For some reason, she seemed to think he was a rake.

"It's the way Miss Patton behaves," Jack said. "I'd advise avoiding her if at all possible—and definitely keep Jess away from her."

"I shall do my best."

"Unfortunately that will be a bit difficult. Her mother is one of Mama's circle. Miss Patton is the youngest of Lady Widley's brood and quite spoilt."

"And she apparently reads all of Mama's scribbling." Ned sighed heavily. "Ellie says the girl can recite some of the choicest bits by heart."

This was terrible news, indeed. They all stared at their brandy glasses in silence for a moment.

"But the main problem," Jack said finally, "is now everyone knows you're in Town. If you leave precipitously, it will set the gabble-grinders to speculating, which is never a good thing. You'll be all the old cats talk about for weeks."

"Wait a moment." Jack was making no sense now. "We just arrived a few hours ago. No one knows we are here."

"Ah, Ash." Jack shook his head. "You don't know the ways of London. Eyes and ears are everywhere. What happens outside the Duke of Greycliffe's house is of intense interest to all London society. I'll wager that if we went to White's right now, we'd hear every last man discussing the

Marquis of Ashton's arrival and speculating whether the woman with him was his wife."

"No! You're exaggerating." God, he hoped Jack was exaggerating, but even his admittedly limited experience of society made him fear his younger brother was correct. Zeus, he hated London.

Ned sent him a sympathetic look. "I wanted to go back to the country almost immediately, too, but Jack and Father convinced me to stay. They said it was important to attend some social events so the gossips could see me with Ellie and stop making up outlandish stories." He smiled ruefully. "I hate to say it, but I do think they were correct."

"Of course we were correct. And it is especially important for you and Jess to show yourselves, Ash," Jack said. "The gossips have been speculating about your marital status for eight years. I told you back at the castle that things had reached a fevered pitch with the approach of your thirtieth birthday. The betting book at White's is full of wagers, and more are being added every day." Jack shrugged. "Hell, there are probably at least twenty new ones since you stepped out of that hired coach." He reached for the brandy bottle. "Care for some more?"

Ash extended his glass and watched the amber liquid splash into it. If only he could turn back the clock and decide to go to the castle instead of London.

He took a large swallow. No, if only he could go back further in time and decide not to marry Jess. His life would be so much simpler. He would have wed one of the girls his mother had found for him and might now be the proud papa of three or four sons.

And be completely miserable. He stroked Fluff's ears. The truth was, all the society girls had seemed brainless and annoying.

He wouldn't have wasted eight years of his life as a bloody virgin if Jess could be so easily replaced.

"And there's another problem," Jack said, exchanging a significant glance with Ned.

"Another problem?" Zeus, didn't he have enough problems?

"Yes. Percy."

"Ah, yes. Percy."

After he'd dropped Jess at Blackweith Manor eight years ago, Ash had gone back to the castle to beat Percy to a pulp, duels being, unfortunately, illegal. But he hadn't had the opportunity—Percy had left. He wasn't even in London. Months went by before Ash saw the man again, and by then he'd heard enough rumors about what Jess was doing at the manor to conclude she'd likely seduced Percy rather than the other way round.

And then, of course, Ned had married Percy's sister, and Ash had been forced to learn to tolerate him as part of the family.

"Percy hates you, Ash." Ned had his familiar, worried expression. "Even Cicely noticed that, though she never understood why."

Jack snorted again. "Well, I hope you'll forgive me for saying so, but Cicely wasn't the most perceptive of individuals. The problem was painfully obvious."

Ned scowled at Jack. "Then perhaps you could explain it to me." He looked at Ash. "Or you can."

"Actually, I'm as much in the dark as you are. Pray, enlighten us, Jack."

"You mean you really don't know?" Jack was looking at him as if he were a complete blockhead, damn it.

"No, I don't. I assumed he didn't care for the fact that I would be duke one day, while he would only be a baronet."

"Oh, no. That wasn't it at all, or at least it wasn't the heart of the problem."

"So what *was* the heart of the problem, Jack?" Ash

didn't have the patience for guessing games. "Stop being such a pain in the arse and spit it out."

Fluff whined and gave Ash a concerned look. He smiled as reassuringly as he could and patted him. The heavy weight of the dog's head in his lap was rather comforting. No wonder Jess was so attached to her pet.

Was she still drying her hair in front of the fire, dressed only in his banyan? Mmm . . . He took a swallow of brandy.

"I really thought you knew," Jack was saying. "Percy was indeed jealous, but not of your title. He loved Jess, but she was hopelessly in love with you."

Blast it, taking a drink right then had been an unlucky decision. The brandy that didn't threaten to choke him shot up his nose. He coughed violently, causing Fluff to yelp and scramble away.

"Are you all right?" Ned leapt up to pound him on the back.

"Y-yes." He flung up his hand to hold Ned off. "I'm f-fine."

"You didn't know, did you?" Jack was shaking his head.

He didn't know because it wasn't true. No one but he and Percy—and Jess and Morton and Alfred, the footman—knew what had happened in the studio that day. If Percy had loved Jess, he could have—should have, even if he hadn't loved her—offered for her. And he'd point-blank refused.

"I very much doubt Percy is jealous of me because of Jess."

"I don't know, Ash," Ned said. "Ellie told me Percy wanted Lady Heldon to seduce you at the house party. She thought he was motivated by something more than idle mischief, and apparently Ophelia thought so, too. Ellie overheard Ophelia tell Percy she couldn't forgive him his obsession with you, and she ended her long affair with him shortly thereafter."

"I imagine Ophelia broke off with Percy because she finally realized he wasn't going to marry her."

"Look," Ned said, "Percy hates me, too. He blames me for Cicely's death—"

"What?" Ash sat up, spilling a drop of brandy. "That's ridiculous." Poor Ned had been devastated by losing his wife and child; he certainly didn't need Percy piling on guilt. "Cicely died in childbirth."

"Yes, but Percy isn't completely rational about it. And he isn't at all happy I cut off his funds—I suspect he'd been sponging off Cicely from the moment we wed. But no matter how much he dislikes me, he's never tried to cause me trouble the way he does you, Ash." Ned took a sip of his brandy. "And if you don't believe me, Ellie, too, thinks Percy loves Jess."

"He doesn't."

Jack almost rolled his eyes. "Whether Percy loves Jess or not," he said, "he hates you, Ash, and he can cause you far more problems in London than he ever could at the castle."

Ash drained the last drops of his brandy. "I'm not afraid of Percy."

"I'm not saying you are; I'm just telling you that you need to watch out for him." There wasn't the faintest shadow of a smile on Jack's lips or in his eyes. "Percy will make your stay in Town—and, perhaps more importantly, Jess's stay—pure hell. You can't ignore him here as you do at the castle."

"I don't see why I can't. London is far larger than Greycliffe Castle. There must be more than one event in an evening."

"Yes, but Percy is certain to find out which one you are attending and be there, too. And even if you could avoid him, what about Jess? Will she ignore Percy?"

Ah, no. He was very much afraid Jess would *not* ignore Percy. That was the problem, wasn't it?

Ned leaned forward, worry creasing his brow. "Jess always had a prodigious temper, Ash, which she never bothered to control."

It wasn't Jess's temper that concerned him. He was afraid she'd feel a completely different emotion when she saw Percy again.

He would not stand for any trysts.

Jack was nodding. "Precisely. And if she tears into Percy, the London gossips will tear into her. They will have no mercy."

"What?!" Anger erupted in Ash's gut. "They damn well better not bother Jess." Jess might not love him, she might be little better than a light-skirt, but she *was* his wife. "Jess is the Marchioness of Ashton, and I shall not tolerate anyone being disrespectful to her."

Jack suddenly grinned and raised his brandy glass. "Thank God for that. Perhaps there's still hope for you."

Now why did he feel as if he'd passed some bizarre test? Damn it, he wished he still had brandy in his glass so he could toss it in Jack's face.

Jess looked glumly down at her turtle soup. It was one of her favorite dishes, and this particular bowl looked and smelled wonderful. But then the Greycliffe cook could probably turn an old shoe into a feast; a mediocre chef would not be tolerated in a duke's kitchen.

She brought a spoonful to her mouth—and then put it back down. She was far too nervous to eat; sitting next to Kit's mother had her completely on edge. She'd been trying to answer the duchess's many questions while not revealing too much about her travels to London or the uncertain state of her marriage.

She wished, not for the first time, that Kit was sitting next to her, rather than at the other end of the table.

"Don't you care for turtle soup, dear?"

She startled, bumping the table. Her soup and everyone else's, along with the wine and any other liquid in the vicinity, threatened to splash onto the tablecloth. Thank heavens she'd returned her spoon to her bowl or she'd very likely have soup adorning her bodice.

"Oh, no, Your Grace. I'm quite partial to turtle soup."

Now why the hell did the duchess's eyes suddenly gleam with what appeared to be delight? Kit's mother could not possibly care if Jess liked turtle soup or not.

"I see. So you have no appetite?"

She tried to smile. "No, Your Grace, I'm afraid I don't."

She'd hoped Jack, her dinner partner on her right, would help her manage his mother, but he was too busy talking to his wife. Ned was across the table, laughing with Ellie, and Kit was far away, next to his father, sending her worried looks and making her even more nervous.

If only she could have taken a tray in her room, but how could she have explained that? And, really, there was no point in putting this off. The duke and duchess weren't leaving Town anytime soon, and if she and Kit ironed out their differences, she would have to learn to deal with them eventually. It might as well be now.

"You must be tired"—the duchess winked—"from your trip."

Oh, God, she was in over her head and sinking fast. She knew nothing of the ways of dukes and duchesses. Why had Kit's mother winked?

She took a deep breath and dipped her spoon back in her soup. She was letting her nerves rob her of her common sense. The duchess hadn't winked. Of course not. What would the duchess have to wink about? She'd likely got an eyelash in her eye.

"I suppose I am a little tired."

Now the duchess was beaming at her. "I'm sure that will pass with time."

"Y-yes. A good night's sleep will have me fit as a fiddle again."

Though how she was ever going to get a good night's sleep sharing a bed with Kit was anybody's guess.

He'd seen her naked. He'd had his *hands* on her.

Oh, God.

What a disaster. Why the hell did the soap have to go squirting through her fingers? It never did that when she took a bath at the manor. If only she'd been more careful—more sensible—the entire embarrassing, mortifying scene could have been averted. She should not have dropped the soap. She should have tried harder to reach it herself. And she should never have had Kit walk across the room blindfolded. She was very lucky he hadn't hurt himself.

"Sleep is very important for a woman in your condition."

When Kit had looked at her breasts, she'd felt her nipples tighten. Dear heavens. He hadn't noticed, had he?

He was a rake. Of course he'd noticed.

And then when she'd tripped getting out of the tub . . . His chest had been like a wall, his arms strong around her. His hands hot on her back and buttocks . . .

Need shivered low in her belly.

And then there'd been that breathless moment when she'd been certain he was going to kiss her—

What had the duchess said? Something about sleep.

"Yes, sleep is—" She snapped her eyes from her soup to Kit's mother. "My condition? What condition would that be, Your Grace?"

She could not let her attention wander when she was talking to the Duchess of Love.

Kit's mother was watching her intently. "A condition that makes women unusually tired."

The duchess was speaking in riddles. "I'm afraid I don't follow you."

"Are you nauseous first thing in the morning?"

"No, of course not. I'm quite fit, Your Grace. I'm just not hungry this evening. As you say, I'm probably overtired. I'm not used to traveling, having spent eight—" No, no, *no!* Don't say that. Don't refer to the many years she'd spent alone, rejected at the manor. "I'm just not used to traveling. I'm sure I'll be fine in the morning."

Her Grace looked disappointed.

Jack leaned over and smiled at Jess. "Mama thinks you might be increasing."

"What?"

Oh, no, that was a mistake. She should not have sounded so shocked. It would not be surprising that a married woman might be increasing. The duchess thought Kit had gone directly from the castle to the manor, but even so . . . wasn't it too soon to know if one were in the family way?

It didn't matter. She wasn't *enceinte,* but she wasn't about to tell Kit's mother why she was so certain of the matter.

"I'm only tired from traveling, Your Grace, and I'm not so very tired at that. My appetite will pick up, I'm sure." She would force the rest of the courses down her throat if it would stop the duchess from speculating about her womb. Though with her luck, that would only cause the duchess to conclude she was eating for two.

Jack sniggered, and then looked at his mother. "Leave poor Jess alone, Mama. She's just getting used to us."

"But she and Ash were in the bath so long." The duchess turned back to waggle her eyebrows at Jess. "Not that I was noticing, of course."

Was this how it was going to be, the duchess drawing salacious conclusions every time she was alone with Kit? Oh, blast. Jess felt as if the walls were beginning to close in on her.

"Keep that up, Mama," Jack said, "and you'll have Jess running back to Blackweith Manor."

That sounded like a splendid idea.

The duchess frowned. "Oh, no, dear. You can't do that. That would be fatal."

To whom? Staying in London—in this house—felt like a death sentence. But she wasn't about to argue with the Duchess of Love. She smiled weakly and let William take away her soup bowl.

"Mama's right, you know," Jack said. "I was telling Ash the same thing a little earlier. You must stay in Town and face down the gossips."

Did Jack think *that* would help her appetite? "Ah. Yes. Of course."

He grinned at her.

"I confess I was surprised Ash brought you to Town," the duchess said. "I would have thought he'd have wanted to stay in the country. You didn't have a real honeymoon before, did you?"

Jess thought it best simply to shake her head.

William put the fish platter in front of her. The plaice's dead eye stared up at her accusingly.

Blast it, she was really losing her grip on reality if she was letting the food judge her.

"But as it turns out," the duchess continued, "it was a brilliant decision. The gossip has got completely out of hand because of Ash turning thirty, Jess. But once society sees the two of you dancing and strolling happily together, everyone will stop talking." She beamed at her.

Jess nodded, tried her best to smile, and declined a serving of eels from Jack.

"Don't you think Percy will try to stir up trouble, Mama?" Jack asked.

"Oh, Percy." The duchess made a dismissive sound and flicked her fingers. "We can deal with Percy." She smiled in a rather satisfied way. "And I think Miss Wharton will take care of him."

"Miss Wharton?" Jack shook his head. "I think Father has the right of it, Mama. Matching Miss Wharton with Percy is indeed like throwing a kitten to a lion."

"Nonsense. Women are far stronger than men give them credit for. Isn't that right, Jess?"

At last, something she could agree about wholeheartedly. "Yes, Your Grace, it is."

Chapter Thirteen

If you pry, you'll see things you'll wish you hadn't.
—Venus's Love Notes

Jess closed the bedroom door and leaned against it, sighing with relief. Thank God she was finally, blessedly alone. She'd escaped when the women left the men at their port after supper.

She should have gone on to the drawing room with the duchess and Ellie and Frances. She knew that. She'd even decided during dinner to do so. She was a grown woman and Kit's wife, the Marchioness of Ashton. As Roger had said, she must pluck up her courage.

She pressed her head back against the door. Hell, it was all well and good to remind herself of her title when steeling herself to face an innkeeper, but when facing the Duchess of Greycliffe, the Duchess of Love . . .

Kit's *mother*.

She took a deep breath. She *knew* there was no point in hiding from the duchess. It was impossible, especially as they were living in the same house. But when the moment had come to sail, head high, into the drawing room, she'd turned craven. She just couldn't face another hour or two of dodging questions. She'd stopped as they'd passed the stairs and said she was going up to bed.

A poor choice of words.

The duchess had raised her eyebrows—likely remembering Jess was at heart nothing but a servant and unschooled in the social niceties—but she hadn't tried to insist or argue. She'd merely wished her good night, and then, with an alarmingly knowing expression, said she'd send Kit up promptly.

Oh, God! Jess covered her face with her hands. Had she ever felt more embarrassed?

She'd insisted that it wasn't necessary, that she knew Kit would want to spend time with his family, that she was very tired and was going straight to sleep—

She'd been babbling and must certainly have confirmed to the duchess—and to Ellie and Frances, too—that what they must all think was going to happen in that damn bed was indeed going to happen.

Why did Kit's family have to be in London?

She pushed away from the door. Surely Kit wouldn't take his mother's hint—or outright suggestion, since she doubted the duchess would waste any time beating around this particular bush—and come right up. But just in case, she'd get changed immediately. She certainly didn't want him watching her disrobe—

She paused, hand on the wardrobe door, and closed her eyes, but that only made the memory come into sharper focus.

Kit already knew what was hidden under her dress. He'd seen her completely naked. He'd had his hands all over her.

She moaned, but perhaps not entirely from mortification.

Damn it! She snapped her eyes open to scowl at the innocent wardrobe. Enough foolishness. She would change and then perhaps sketch a bit.

She scrambled out of her clothes and into her nightgown. The poor garment had been mended so many times it was more darns than fabric. Well, the duchess had said at dinner that the dressmaker would be coming tomorrow—

Oh, God. She closed her eyes again. And then Kit's mother had leaned close to whisper, in a very significant way, *"and she'll make you some under-things and nightgowns, too."* Thank heavens Jack had been talking to Frances and hadn't heard or he'd have been sure to tease her about that.

She shook her old dress out and hung it on a peg in the wardrobe. Even with the impending embarrassment of buying stockings and chemises and stays and nightgowns, she had to admit to feeling excited about the dressmaker. She loved color and texture. She was a painter, after all.

She'd never had nice clothes. Her father certainly hadn't been able to afford silks and laces on his groom's earnings, but there'd also been no need for her to have such finery. The horses she rode didn't care, and it was far better to spatter paint on homespun than satin.

Girls of her station often did get some special clothing for their wedding, but her marriage had been such a scrambling affair, she'd not got a trousseau. Nor had she needed one during her long exile at the manor. She shrugged. And even if she'd got clothes then, they'd be sadly out of date now.

She reached for her sketchbook, but what her fingers closed on was Roger's pink-ribboned collection of *Venus's Love Notes*.

She snatched her hand back. She didn't want to know what her mother-in-law thought of love.

And yet . . .

The duchess had been happily married to her duke for over thirty years, and she'd made countless successful society matches. Roger, though he definitely had some unusual proclivities, was no idiot. If he'd carefully saved the duchess's leaflets and loaned them to her, he must think Kit's mother had something useful to say on the matter of love. She certainly knew more about it than Jess did.

She shifted from foot to foot and glanced at the clock on the mantel. It was early. Kit was likely still at table drinking port with his father and brothers. She would just have a quick peek.

She picked up the packet, untied the ribbon, and started reading the first page.

Men are not women dressed in breeches.

Well, of course they weren't. Even she knew that.

They are far more aroused by their senses than we are.

Hmm. That might be correct. Men certainly did a lot more obvious ogling than women did.

Thus if you wish to seduce—

"What are you reading, Jess?"

"Ack!" Her hands flew up, and the papers sailed off in all directions.

Kit was standing in the doorway with Fluff.

"I'm sorry. Did I startle you?"

She scrambled over the floor, scooping up the errant leaflets. "No, I always scream and throw things when people enter the room."

He put the brandy decanter he was carrying on the bureau. "Here, let me help—"

"No!" She dove to grab a sheet at Kit's feet before he could pick it up.

Fluff, having sniffed the paper and found it completely uninteresting, went off to lie in front of the fire.

Kit scowled at her. "Why don't you want me to see what you were reading?"

Had she got them all? She looked around wildly. Yes, she thought she had. "Believe me, you don't want to see these papers any more than I want to show them to you."

He closed the door. "What, are they love notes from the footman?"

"Er..." If he only knew how funny his question was. "Not exactly. That is, yes, Roger gave—or, rather, lent—them to me, but he didn't write them." She stuffed them back in her valise and shoved the bag into the wardrobe. "I believe I will go to bed now."

Kit was still scowling at her, but there was really nothing more she could say. Roger had been quite right. She definitely could not show those papers to Kit.

He scowled at the wardrobe for good measure, and then turned back to her. Thank heavens he was too honorable to rummage through her things.

"I was concerned when I didn't see you in the drawing room. Mama said you'd gone to bed. Are you not feeling well?"

"I'm fine. I'm just tired and a bit overwhelmed by your family." Might as well say precisely what she meant. "By your mother."

Kit grimaced. "She, ah, means well."

Oddly enough, she was willing to grant him that. The duchess hadn't been unkind or even high in the instep.

"Did you know at supper she was hinting that I might be increasing?" She hadn't meant to tell him that. It had just popped out, probably because she was still in a fluster over his finding her reading *Venus's Love Notes*. "I can't promise I'll behave if she keeps looking at my stomach."

Which of course made *him* look at her stomach, which wasn't well shielded since she was wearing only her nightgown.

Her threadbare nightgown.

... if you wish to seduce ...

She did not. Well, at least not tonight. She scampered over to the far side of the bed, climbed in, and pulled the covers up to her chin.

Kit moved farther into the room and removed his cravat. Her stupid heart beat faster at the sight of his naked neck.

"I imagine she is just engaging in wishful thinking," he said. "She assumes we've been together all this time."

"Yes, but wouldn't it still be too soon to know such a thing, even if we had . . . that is, even if we'd been . . ." Her face must be red enough to glow. "You know."

Kit was staring at her. Surely he was thinking, as she was, about what the exercise of getting a child entailed, though of course his thoughts must be far more detailed, since he'd actually performed the deed.

"I don't know." His cheeks looked rather red as well. "I have no idea how long it takes for, er, signs that one is increasing to appear."

She watched him pull his shirt over his head. Oh! Her heart had gone from a quickened beat to pounding, her blood pulsing in her chest and head and locations rather lower down. He hadn't got his flat belly and muscled arms from sketching building plans.

She really would love to paint him naked, though she would have to overcome this overwhelming . . . hunger if she wished to get any good work done. At the moment, she wanted to run her hands over his broad chest far more than she wanted to brush paint over a canvas.

She gripped the coverlet to keep her hands from misbehaving.

He sat down to remove his shoes and socks. Once that was done, all he'd have left to take off would be his pantaloons and drawers. And then she would see—

A drenching heat flooded her, pooling in her lower regions.

No! It was too soon. He still didn't trust her.

"What do you want to put on the bed?" she asked, rather too breathlessly.

He frowned at her, a sock dangling from one hand. "Pardon me?"

"You know—as a wall? You stay on your side, and I stay on mine?" She had to get this settled so she could blow out her candle and close her eyes or she would see more than her willpower could withstand. She did not want to suffer the humiliation of attacking Kit and having him push her away.

He looked extremely annoyed. "You can trust me not to take advantage of you."

Blast it, he didn't comprehend the situation at all. But why should he? He didn't feel this overwhelming attraction. "Perhaps you can't trust me."

His eyes widened in shock.

Why the hell had she said that? "Don't worry. Your virtue is safe. Fluff can serve the purpose admirably. Fluff!"

Fluff's head came up, and he gave a happy woof before launching himself onto the middle of the bed.

Venus Valentine, the Duchess of Love, put down her hairbrush and sighed.

Her duke, propped up in bed, reading glasses perched on the end of his nose, turned a page in his book.

She sighed again, louder.

"If you wish to say something, Venus, just say it." Drew glanced up at her over his glasses. "You are not usually one to beat around the bush."

"Yes, I know, but in this case I don't know what I wish to say."

It was Drew's turn to sigh. He closed his book and put it on his nightstand with only a very brief look of longing as he laid his glasses on top of it.

"I can see I am never going to finish the *History of the*

Peloponnesian War." He patted the bed beside him. "Come over and tell me what is troubling you."

Venus needed no second invitation. "I don't know why you persist in reading that dusty old tome." She slid under the covers and under his arm, putting her head on his shoulder and snuggling up against him. Mmm. He and his side of the bed were wonderfully warm. She could feel the tightness in her neck and shoulders begin to loosen.

"Perhaps because I'm interested in Greek history?" He pulled her closer.

She put her free hand on his chest. She could feel his heart beating slowly, steadily, calmly. "Pshaw. All that fighting happened years ago."

His fingers smoothed her nightgown over her hip. "Yes. That is why it is called history."

"Very funny. Aren't you concerned about Ash and Jess?"

"No. Should I be?"

She raised her head to look at him. He was not joking. The man was impossible. "Of course you should be. You were extremely concerned just a few months ago."

He shrugged. "Yes, but that was before Ash went to Blackweith Manor. Now they are together again."

"No, they are not." Drew was usually far more perceptive than this.

He raised his eyebrows, clearly surprised. "Excuse me? They are both here, are they not?"

"Yes, of course, but they are not *together*."

His brows furrowed. "I fail to see your point. They are in the same bedroom. I assume they are even in the same bed. That is rather together, wouldn't you say?"

"No." Surely Drew realized it was possible for a couple to be physically touching yet have an unbridgeable chasm separating them.

"Then perhaps you had better explain the matter to my poor male intellect."

Venus leaned up on her elbow so she could see him better. "You must have noticed how shocked and dismayed they looked when they saw us come out of the house."

"Of course they were shocked and dismayed. They thought they were going to have the place to themselves." He reached out and pulled her back down next to him. "You are letting too much cold air in under the coverlet."

It *was* warmer down here next to Drew. His body was like a furnace.

His fingers were beginning to stray where they shouldn't, at least not yet. She captured them and put them on his chest.

"No, it wasn't that. I thought so at first, but after watching them . . ." How to describe that intangible connection, the unspoken communication, that existed between two people in love, and that was so notably missing between Ash and his wife? "They aren't comfortable together. I don't think they even like each other."

"Oh, I think they do. There was far too much desperation in the air for them to be indifferent."

"Hmm." She laid her head on Drew's chest to think about that. "Yes, you may be right. But Jess is so tense. I don't think she cares for me."

"She hardly knows you, Venus." He freed his hand to rub her shoulder in a comforting way. "Ellie is from the gentry; her father was one of my school chums. It was easy for her to become part of our family even before she married Ned. But Jess's father was our head groom. Far more skilled and appreciated than most servants, but not quite gentry, either." He smiled. "And Irish. I'm not sure he wanted to be too accepted by us English."

"He was rather proud and independent, wasn't he?"

"As is Jess."

"Yes." Now that she thought of it, she'd seen both those traits in Jess, even when she was a little girl. "But she played with the boys when she was young. We never made her feel like a servant."

"Didn't we? You never invited her to your parties."

"N-no, but that was for her benefit. You know our guests would not have been kind to her. They would have given her the cut direct."

"Very likely, but does Jess know that?"

She lifted her head to frown at him. "She must. She's not naive."

"No, she's not. But did we ever explain to her that *we* didn't feel she was unworthy? She may well have taken the lack of invitations—especially when Ellie *was* included—as a judgment rather than an attempt to shield her from pain."

She'd never considered things in that light, but Drew might well be right. A sick, heavy feeling weighted her chest. She would never have wanted to insult or wound the girl. "But you know it would never have worked."

"I know, and I'll wager Jess knows." His mouth tightened. "Even better now."

That sounded ominous. "What do you mean?"

"Just that I believe Jess has had a rough time of it these past eight years. From what I can gather, she's been ostracized by everyone, even the damn curate."

"That's terrible. Why didn't you do something?"

Drew's frown deepened into a scowl. "I gave Blackweith to Ash—it's his estate and his wife. And . . ." He rubbed her shoulder again. "You know as well as I do that there was something seriously amiss between them even on their wedding day."

"Yes." That had been a horrible time. "Remember how Ash looked when he told us he was marrying Jess? It was during that dreadful house party right after her father died."

Drew nodded. "He looked grim. Thank God he found

us alone. I wouldn't have put it past him to have blurted out his plans in the middle of a drawing room full of your damn guests."

Yes, Ash had seemed distressed enough—almost wild, really—to have done that. "And then he left to get the special license. He seemed so angry."

"I tried to find out what the problem was," Drew said, clearly reliving the events as she was, "but he wouldn't say anything." He stroked her hair. "I even asked the servants, and you know how I hate to do that. I never want the boys thinking we are spying on them."

"No, indeed."

"No one seemed to know anything . . . except Alfred. But I couldn't force myself to make him tell me."

"What?" She sat up. "You think one of the footmen knew what had caused Ash to go rushing off for a special license, and you didn't demand he tell you everything?"

Drew pulled her back down. "No, I didn't. It felt dishonorable, and, well . . ." Drew's jaw clenched.

"Well what?"

His eyes held worry and pain. "Alfred was angry about the situation. I think Jess had been hurt in some way. . . ."

Shock hit her like a blow to the stomach. "You think Ash raped her?"

"N-no." Drew was scowling again. "I would swear there was no way in hell Ash could do something that heinous, especially as he'd been so close to Jess since childhood, but something was clearly very, very wrong. I thought perhaps in the heat of passion, he'd taken an amorous encounter farther than he'd intended. You know he always held himself to such a high standard. Feeling guilty and trapped at the same time might have explained his anger and sense of desperation."

"Yes, I suppose it might have." She liked that possibility far more than the thought her son could have forced himself on Jess. "Oh, why didn't she talk to me?"

"Why would she? You are the duchess and Ash's mother."

"But I'm also a woman. I would have helped her." Guilt joined her churning feelings. "I should have helped her. I saw she wasn't happy, that Ash wasn't happy. I should have insisted on finding out exactly what was going on."

Drew shook her gently. "Don't castigate yourself, Venus. I could have done more, too. But I thought, as you did, that Ash truly cared for Jess and that all would be well."

"Oh, I *wish* I had done something." Guilt overwhelmed her. Her heart twisted. "If only I'd tried to help, I might have saved them eight years of loneliness and a lifetime without love."

Drew cupped her cheek and tilted her face toward his. "That doesn't sound like the Duchess of Love speaking."

"It's not. It's just a worried mother."

He clucked his tongue. "Don't despair. I think Ash and Jess do love each other."

"And that sounds like what I should be saying." Venus laughed, though the sound was a bit watery. She sniffed and blotted a few tears with her fingers. "I thought you swore you would never turn into the Duke of Love."

Drew grimaced. "Good God! Forget I said anything. They hate and detest each other." He grinned and kissed the top of her head. "But I think it will be very interesting to see how they survive sharing a room and a bed."

"Yes, but . . ." Worry rushed back. "Do you think I should move Jess?"

"Oh, no. Definitely not."

"But if Ash is . . . if he might . . . Do you think he would . . . ?" She couldn't say the ugly word.

"No. If he'd been going to do something like that, he would already have done so. They've been together quite a number of days now. Jess may be angry and uncomfortable, but I'd swear she's not afraid of Ash. And did you see the protective way he held her—and how she leaned into him—when they got out of that hired coach and saw us?"

"Yes. Yes, I did." She grinned. Perhaps things were not so bleak after all. "You're quite right about that."

"However, I would advise against hinting any more about grandchildren."

She flushed. "Yes, of course. I got a bit carried away at dinner."

"And speaking of getting carried away . . ." He traced the rim of her ear. "I would like to get carried away with my wife."

"Oh." Ten minutes ago—even just five minutes ago—she would have sworn she had no interest at all in marital relations, but after thirty-one years, Drew knew exactly where and how to touch her to make her forget everything but him. She sighed with pleasure and let her worries go as she sank into the heat of her duke's embrace.

Ash woke up slowly. His head was pounding, and his mouth felt like it was full of sawdust. Blech. He should not have drunk all that brandy last night. He'd brought the decanter up thinking another glass or two might help him sleep, and he'd planned to offer Jess a glass as well, but then she'd run for the bed as if she was afraid he'd ravish her.

Mmm. She *had* looked rather ravishing in that nightgown. It was as translucent as the shift she'd worn at the White Stag. In the fire's glow, he could see all too clearly her delightful curves—her breasts, her waist, her hips, her long, lovely legs, and the darker shadows that were her nipples and the curls at the juncture of her—

Zeus! His damn cock jumped at the memory, tenting the coverlet.

He turned quickly on his side, but he needn't have worried. The bed was empty. Jess must have woken and taken Fluff downstairs for a footman to walk. Ash had been so dead to the world, he hadn't heard her leave.

Well, of course he'd been dead to the world. Once Jess—and Fluff—had gone to sleep, he'd donned his banyan and sat up drinking. When he'd finally lain down, he'd tossed and turned, listening to Jess's soft breathing and Fluff's snuffling and intermittent moaning—and shoving back against the damn dog when he tried to crowd him out of the bed. The animal was *not* sleeping with them again.

He pushed himself to sit. The room spun briefly, but then settled down . . . as did his stomach. No more brandy for him for a while. He'd drunk the whole bloody decanter.

He staggered over to the washbasin. The water was cold, but that was just as well. He splashed it on his face and began to feel marginally better.

Should he say something to Mama so she'd stop hinting about the state of Jess's womb?

His stomach heaved, but he swallowed determinedly and regained control.

No, he couldn't speak about it to Mama, at least not yet. It was all too complicated, and he owed it to Jess to keep things in confidence. Mama had always been far too skilled at getting him and his brothers to spill all their secrets, even when they'd firmly decided to remain mum.

But what if Mama's questions goaded Jess into losing her temper? Jess was in an uncomfortable situation. Like a cornered animal, she might snap.

He let out a long breath. He would just have to stay close when she was around Mama.

One would hope the Duchess of Love would be sensitive to the nuances of such matters. Perhaps last night had been an aberration. Mama had probably been so happy to see him with Jess that she'd jumped to a very wrong conclusion. At least, that's what he'd hope.

God, sometimes he hated being the heir. His brothers could give Mama and Father grandchildren, but only he could present them with the next little duke.

He dried his face on a towel. How long would it be until he could be certain Jess wasn't carrying the footman's child? He knew next to nothing about the matter. He remembered Cicely's pregnancy, but he hadn't paid attention to when her condition had become obvious.

Ellie knew she was in the family way, and she wasn't yet showing. There must be signs that a woman noticed before anyone else guessed her condition. So perhaps Jess would know in another week or two. . . .

Oh, God. He gripped his head to keep it from pounding. If she *was* increasing, Mama would notice and think the child was his. That would be beyond dreadful. Mama would be so happy—Father, too—and then he'd have to dash their hopes and go into all the awful, mortifying details.

His stomach rebelled again, but he mastered it, though only just.

The bloody footman. If the blackguard were here right now, he'd beat him senseless. No man of honor would consort with another man's wife when she'd yet to give him his heir and spare.

And, worse, Jess was still pining for the fellow. She'd admitted the papers she'd been reading last night had come from the man. If they'd been completely unexceptional, she would have shown them to him.

His stomach finally won the battle, and he emptied its contents into the basin. Ugh. At least there wasn't much. He would deposit the mess in the chamber pot and rinse out the basin once his head stopped spinning.

He looked over at the wardrobe. He should read the damn letters and see exactly how bad things were.

No, that would be dishonorable. Jess's behavior was not an excuse for him to betray his principles. He would bring her up to the room instead and demand to read them in her presence. And once he'd read them . . .

He would decide then how best to proceed.

Yes. Now he had a course of action. Splendid. He would empty the disgusting contents of the basin and go in search of Jess.

He looked for the chamber pot in the bedside cabinet, but it wasn't there. It must be under the bed. He peered into the shadowy space. Ah, yes, there it—

Wait a moment, there was a sheet of paper on the floor as well.

He stared at the white rectangle. It must be one of Jess's letters. They'd fallen all higgledy-piggledy last night.

He should pick it up and, since he didn't know for a fact what it was, he would have to glance at it. That would be enough to determine if it was personal correspondence, and of course if it was, he would read no further.

He pinched the offending paper gingerly between his index finger and thumb. Suddenly his heart was pounding, and his stomach threatened to misbehave again. He took a deep breath and steeled himself to face whatever he would find.

He turned the paper over.

Oh, God!

He was staring down—in horror—at a copy of *Venus's Love Notes*.

Chapter Fourteen

Try not to kill the messenger.
—Venus's Love Notes

"Lady Ashton, I would be happy to walk the dog for you," William said for the fourth time. He was following a few steps behind her and Fluff as they made their way to Hyde Park. "Or, if the animal can wait, I'm certain Shakespeare will be up and ready for his walk shortly, and then Lord Jack and his lady can accompany you. They generally take him to the park at nine o'clock."

Ah, yes. Jack and Frances, the newlyweds. They would love to have Kit's estranged wife tag along with them, keeping them from their private conversations.

"As you can see, Fluff wishes to go out now, William, and I would like some fresh air"—hopefully the air would be fresher in the park—"and some exercise myself." She came to a corner. "Which way should I go now?"

"Hyde Park is to your right, my lady."

"Thank you." She had to tug a bit on the lead to persuade Fluff to change direction, but he eventually acquiesced. "You know it might be easier if you just walked up with me. It's a bit distracting to have to speak over my shoulder."

"Oh, I couldn't do that, my lady. That wouldn't be at all proper." He paused, and she could almost hear him wringing his hands. "Are you quite, quite certain Lord Ashton knows you're taking the dog out? I would think he would wish to come with you, especially as it's your first outing in Town."

"I told you he's still asleep, William. Of course he doesn't know."

She'd swear William moaned.

"But I brought you along, didn't I? That should satisfy even the highest sticklers." She would have preferred to take Fluff out alone; she'd walked miles with just her dog for company at Blackweith Manor. But even she would admit country manners were different than London ones. It was also true that she didn't know her way around, and with all the new sights and smells, she didn't trust Fluff to find their way back to Greycliffe House. She'd likely get completely lost without William.

Fluff lifted his head and gave a joyful woof. He must smell the park. He was certainly moving more quickly. She had to almost run to keep up.

And then she saw it, a great green swath of grass and trees and country.

"Mind the carriage!"

"What? Oh!" She pulled back on Fluff's lead just in time. They had almost stepped in front of a curricle. The driver gave them a very nasty look as he bowled past.

"Idiot," she muttered, looking cautiously both ways before allowing Fluff to cross. "He was driving far too fast."

"Yes, my lady. That happens early in the morning when there isn't much traffic."

Fluff towed her through the park gate and then turned left. He seemed quite certain where he wanted to go. She glanced over her shoulder. William was mopping his brow with a handkerchief. Poor man. "What's in this direction?"

"The Serpentine, my lady. And Rotten Row, where all the haute ton go to be seen, though not this early, of course." He smiled weakly. "They are all still abed."

"Splendid. I'm not especially anxious to encounter any of polite society." Now that she considered the matter, anyone who saw them would probably assume she was some sort of servant, given her country clothes, and leave her alone. Excellent. It was better for everyone that she remain anonymous.

A light breeze stirred the ribbons on her old bonnet, and she tilted her face up to the warmth of the sun. She felt free for the first time since Kit had appeared at her studio door. It was only an illusion of freedom, of course, just like this large, lovely park set in the midst of England's largest city was only an illusion of the country. But she would believe it for a little while and enjoy it. Too soon she'd have to go back to Greycliffe House and Kit's parents and brothers. And Kit.

Oh, God, what was she going to do about Kit? She definitely wanted him, but did she love him?

Did it really matter?

She was so confused. Yes, she'd loved him as a girl, but in an ethereal sort of way. He was her friend; he was handsome and honorable. She'd thought him male perfection. And she'd dreamed of him for years while exiled at the manor. But she'd never experienced this breathless, churning desire before.

She'd watched the men at the manor pant after each other, and she'd thought them very silly.

Ha! Now she began to understand. Kit didn't know how thankful he should have been for Fluff's large, furry presence in the middle of the bed last night.

If she'd loved Kit as a girl, she wanted him now as a woman. His brief kiss had shaken her to her soul—and had shaken other, much less spiritual places. She'd *never* wanted to see a man naked except as a model, her paintbrush in her hand, and now she wanted to strip Kit bare, inch by inch, and run her fingers . . . and her tongue—

She waved her hand in front of her face. It was rather warm in the sun.

She must remember lust was not love, and her image of Kit might be as much an illusion as this park.

All right, she'd *seen* his chest and shoulders.

She dodged a low hanging tree limb.

Oh, who the hell cared? She was Kit's wife. He could give her pleasure and children. Wasn't that enough?

They had come to a group of trees; beyond them, down a broad expanse of lawn, was the Serpentine. Fluff barked and tugged on his lead. She was tempted to let him go, but she saw there were swans by the water. She didn't want him worrying the birds.

"We're going down to the lake, William," she said, turning to look for the footman. He'd fallen behind and was clutching his side as if he had a stitch. He must not be used to walking so quickly. "Come along at your own pace. Don't worry, you'll be able to see us."

"Yes. My. Lady," he panted.

She let Fluff pull her down the slope. They were almost at the water when she heard a man call her name. Her heart leapt in response, but she quickly realized it wasn't Kit's voice. Who could it be?

"Jess!" he called again.

She looked around and saw a stylish fellow in a beaver hat, blue coat, tan riding breeches, and glossy boots coming toward her on a beautiful brown horse. She would swear she'd never seen him before, but Fluff gave his friendly woof and changed direction.

The man swung down and scratched the dog's ears. "How do you like Hyde Park, Kit?"

The voice was definitely familiar. She studied his face. Good God! "Roger?"

He gave her an exaggerated bow. "The same, though

you should more properly address me as Lord Trendal now, you know."

She threw her arms around him. She was so happy to see a familiar face—a *friendly* familiar face.

He laughed, hugged her briefly, and then set her away. "I think you're scandalizing that fellow up on the top of the rise, Jess."

She turned and looked. "Oh. That's William, one of the Greycliffe servants. He insisted on accompanying me and Fluff."

He frowned. "Fluff?"

"Kit—my husband—thought it was too confusing having a dog with the same name. And I did sometimes call him Fluff, you'll remember." She grinned. "The dog, that is, not the husband." She took his arm, and they started walking toward the water, he leading his horse, she being led by Fluff. "When did you get to London?"

"The day before yesterday. I left the morning after I dropped you at the White Stag."

"You made much better time than we did, then." Fortunately. She would not have wanted to run into Roger on the road. Kit would not have taken it well.

"I was on horseback, and you were in that dreadful wagon."

She laughed. "It is dreadful, isn't it? We rented a coach at the Singing Maid." If Roger was here in Town and going about as Baron Trendal, he must have reconnected with his family. That was good. She'd been after him to go home. "Was your mother happy to see you?"

He smiled and nodded. "Very. I was the prodigal son returned. Apparently she's been rather worried."

"Of course she's been worried." He'd written his mother only sporadically in the years he'd been at the manor, usually at Jess's urging. "You are her child, her firstborn. She loves you."

He shrugged. "I suppose she does."

"Of course she does."

Would *she* ever have a child to love?

Only if she came to some agreement with Kit.

She'd never thought much about children. What was the point when her husband was miles away and detested her? She'd never had much experience with children or family, either. As long as she could remember, it had been just her father and her.

She'd envied Kit his family. He had his parents and his brothers, and they seemed to genuinely like each other, no matter how much they might tease and argue. And now his family was expanding with sisters-in-law and a niece or nephew on the way. Perhaps, if she gave Kit a son, they would accept her, too.

The swans saw them approaching and hurried off to the other side of the Serpentine, so she let Fluff off his lead. He bounded into the water.

"Looking at him splashing about like that," Roger said, "you'd never guess he hates baths."

She laughed. "Perhaps his distaste actually stemmed from your poor singing. Apparently he was transfixed by the Greycliffe footmen's duet yesterday and was as meek as a lamb in the tub." She looked back at William, who'd run down the hill once Roger had arrived and was now hovering only steps away. "Fluff's going to need another bath I'm afraid, William."

"Yes, my lady."

Now what was the matter? He was scowling at her quite ferociously. Perhaps he didn't want to have to bathe Fluff again. And he really was standing far too close. Roger was always extremely careful about what he said, but it would be disastrous if she should slip up and give some hint of his secret proclivities. "Wait here and hold Lord

Trendal's horse, will you, William? We wish to go closer to the water."

Good heavens, William's expression grew even darker. He looked like a thundercloud—an extremely disapproving thundercloud.

"Yes, my lady."

"You know you'll have some explaining to do when you see your husband," Roger said once they were well out of William's earshot.

"What do you mean?"

"I'm quite certain William suspects we've arranged a lovers' tryst."

"Oh, surely not." She looked back again. If it were physically possible, darts would be flying from William's eyes to lodge in her chest. "Oh, dear, I believe you are correct. That's likely what he'll tell Kit. Do you suppose I can persuade him to hold his tongue?"

"Not a chance. If you suggest it, you will look very guilty indeed."

"Damnation."

He patted her hand. "I take it things do not go well with Lord Ashton?"

She did not wish to discuss Kit with Roger. "Things are still uncertain. Was your brother as angry at your welcome as the prodigal son's brother?"

He raised his brows, but let her change the subject. "Not at all. Archie was delighted to see me. He's taken good care of things in my absence, as I was certain he would, and he's on the verge of getting betrothed to a lovely young woman." He smiled. "I think he suspects what I am, yet seems not to think me a demon. I will probably take him into my confidence shortly. It's only fair he know the title will come to him or to his son eventually."

"Yes, I suppose you are right." Fluff had finally tired

of running in and out of the water. He shook himself off and came over to flop down in the grass by her feet.

"I believe I am." He looked at her.

Blast, he was going to start in on Kit again. She bent over to pat Fluff.

"Frankly I'm shocked to see you here," he said to the back of her head. "I would have thought you'd go to Greycliffe Castle. Ashton doesn't frequent London, but he must know Town is the very worst place to be if you have any secrets."

She straightened, but kept her gaze on Fluff. "We thought the duke and duchess were still in the country. Even I know His Grace hates London."

"That's very true. I discovered the story at White's last night. Apparently there was some scandal with Jack—not that there isn't always some scandal with Jack—but this time it was more serious, so Greycliffe and Her Grace came up to help resolve the issue." He laughed. "And the resolution included a wedding."

She looked at him then. "A happy wedding. Jack and his wife are staying at Greycliffe House, too. They seem very much in love." If only her own scandal could have ended in such harmony, but she'd wager her scandal had been far, far worse than anything Jack and Frances had been involved in.

"Which reminds me." He grinned. "Did you read the *Love Notes*?"

She flushed. "Damnation, Roger, what did you mean by putting those sheets in my bag?"

His grin widened. "The Duchess of Love is very wise, Jess. Read them and see for yourself."

She bent down to put Fluff's lead back on. "I wish I'd known I was going to run into you today. I could have brought them and given them back to you." She was not about to admit any interest in Kit's mother's marital writings, especially to Roger.

"Humor me and read them. You'll thank me eventually."

"Oh! You are absurd. I—"

"Look who's here!"

Bloody hell, she recognized *that* voice. It had echoed in too many of her nightmares.

She looked up to see Percy coming toward them on a big black horse, Mr. Huntington riding a chestnut at his side.

She'd not seen Percy since he'd made his ill-advised visit to the manor shortly after she'd arrived, and she'd gone after him with a fireplace poker. The years hadn't been kind to him. Dissipation clung to him like the musty smell of an old, long-closed trunk.

"Huntington here told me you'd left the manor, Jess," Percy said, "but I didn't expect to see you in Town." He looked at Roger. "Are you going to introduce us to your companion?"

Oh, dear. Percy might not have seen Roger before, but Huntington must have. He went to the local taverns and the cockfights where the gentry rubbed elbows with the local servants.

Roger stepped into the silence her panic had created and bowed slightly. "Lord Trendal at your service, gentlemen."

His voice broke her paralysis. If Roger could be calm, so could she. And, thank God, Huntington seemed not to have recognized him. "Oh, please excuse me, Lord Trendal. May I present Sir Percy Headley and Mr. George Huntington?"

Percy nodded at Roger, but then his attention returned to her. "I didn't realize you had friends in London, Jess. How very . . . interesting. Does your husband know you are sauntering through the park with this fellow?"

She opened her mouth to blister Percy's damn ears, but Roger spoke before she could.

"And do you know that your tone is insulting, sirrah?" His voice could cut glass. "You seem to be insinuating that Lady Ashton is doing something improper."

She was happy to see Percy turn a shade or two whiter.

"No offense meant, of course. Jess is a childhood friend. I would hate to see her take a wrong step so soon after her arrival in Town."

Ha! Now there was a whisker if ever she'd heard one. "Don't worry, Percy. I was out walking my dog with one of the Greycliffe footmen"—she nodded toward William—"when we encountered Lord Trendal quite by chance."

"I . . . see."

Ooh, she'd love to punch the slimy blackguard. His words were unexceptional, but his tone was not. She felt Roger bristle.

"Lord Trendal." Huntington looked as if he'd suddenly recognized the name—but still not the face, thank heavens. "I remember now. You're the 'Missing Baron' everyone was talking about at the clubs last night."

Roger bowed again. "The ton does like to make a fuss about so many silly things, does it not? I've merely been traveling while my brother saw to the estate."

Percy waggled his brows. "One wonders where you encountered Jess."

Damnation. "I'll thank you not to wonder—not to *think*—about me at all, Percy. What I do is none of your concern."

"And there is nothing to wonder about." Roger sounded delightfully haughty. "I stopped by Blackweith Manor very briefly in my travels, of course." He offered Jess his arm. "Now I believe Lady Ashton is ready to return to Greycliffe House."

"Yes, indeed. I'm suddenly not enjoying the park as much as I had been."

Roger gave her a warning look before nodding at the men. "If you'll excuse us?"

"Yes, of course." Percy laughed. "Jess always was quite tetchy."

Oh, she'd show him tetchy. She'd get Fluff to charge the horses and—

Roger put his hand over hers and squeezed warningly. "Shall we go?"

"Yes." She tugged on Fluff's lead. "Good day, gentlemen."

She and Roger—and Fluff and William—turned and headed back toward Greycliffe House.

"Zeus," she muttered so only Roger could hear. "Weren't you afraid Huntington would recognize you?"

"Not at all." He smiled at William, who was still glowering at him, though not with quite the same ferocity. He must have approved of how Roger had handled Percy and Huntington. "I'm going to walk with Lady Ashton, William, to be certain she isn't disturbed again."

"Very good, my lord."

"I'm sure that's not necessary."

"Don't argue, Jess. You're merely wasting your breath."

"Oh, very well." They started up the hill, leaving William huffing behind them. She wasn't finished with Roger anyway. "Why weren't you afraid you'd be discovered?"

"Because the nobility and gentry never actually look at servants; they look through them," he said. "And they judge people by their clothing. I'm dressed as a lord, so of course that's what I am. I'll wager not a single member of the ton would believe you if you told them I'd been your footman."

"But aren't you—" Jess stopped. She heard a dog barking up ahead. She couldn't see it yet, but it was coming closer. Fluff woofed in response and pulled on his lead. Oh, dear. She did hope they weren't in for a dog fight. . . .

No, thank goodness. It was Shakespeare. He appeared at the top of the rise with Kit.

Kit did not look happy. He scowled at them as he strode down the hill, keeping pace with Shakespeare. His eyes slid past her to focus on Roger.

Kit looked as though he was contemplating murder—if he didn't suffer an apoplexy first.

"Well," Roger murmured, "perhaps there is *one* member of the ton who will recognize me."

Bloody hell! The naked footman was in London. He was tricked out in gentlemanly attire, but Ash would recognize those dark, cocky eyes anywhere.

Cocky . . .

His eyes dropped without his conscious bidding to the bounder's fall. At least the damn reprobate's male organ wasn't advertising its enthusiasm for Jess—

Unless it wasn't announcing its presence because it had already enjoyed its sport?

Zeus! He drew in a lungful of the chill spring air as he tried to beat back the red madness that threatened to overcome him. Think! They were in one of the most exposed sections of Hyde Park, and William was with them. They had a dog and a horse. They could not possibly have engaged in sexual congress.

Could they?

"Lord Ashton." The blackguard bowed. "I don't believe we were properly introduced when we met before. I am Lord Trendal."

Ash managed to nod in acknowledgment. Speech was still beyond his capabilities. He glanced at Jess. She looked worried, damn it. What had they been doing?

He could ask William. William would tell him if they'd been . . .

He took another deep breath. The scoundrel was still talking, looking damnably at ease, even smiling in a friendly sort of way.

He'd show the bloody vermin friendly.

"I just arrived in London the day before yesterday and was delighted—and surprised—to stumble upon your charming wife when I was out for my ride this morning."

Ash grunted, but it sounded even to his own ears more like a growl. Jess made a small sound of distress, and William straightened, ready to defend the Greycliffe honor, no doubt, even as he still held the miscreant's horse. Even Shakespeare and Fluff stopped sniffing each other to look at him.

The only one who seemed completely unaffected was Trendal.

"I must tell you, however," Trendal said, "that we just encountered two men who I feel very strongly do not have your wife's best interests at heart."

"And you do?" The words were almost ripped from his throat.

Trendal looked him straight in the eye and said calmly, "Yes, I do. Jess—Lady Ashton—and I have been friends for years. I care about her as a friend—as a *sister,* if you will."

Ash almost said something extremely crude, but managed to hold his tongue. There was something strangely convincing about Trendal's words.

"As your wife will explain to you later."

Jess frowned. "But, Roger—"

"No, Jess. Lord Ashton needs to know about me and about Blackweith Manor."

What was this? Had the manor turned into a brothel, then? "What about the manor?"

Jess and Trendal ignored him.

"Are you certain?"

"Yes. It's time. Things can't remain as they are; everyone knows that." Trendal laughed. "Or at least all the men who have any sense know it."

Good God, had Jess indeed slept with all the servants? Or was she running some odd sort of reverse whorehouse, where women paid men to perform? "What the *hell* are you two talking about?"

He was shouting now, damn it. He'd made the dogs start whining. Their tails dropped between their legs.

He took another deep breath, drawing the air in through his nose and letting it out through his mouth. "Pardon me. I should not have raised my voice."

"No, you should not have—"

Trendal put his hand on Jess's arm, stopping her. "Lady Ashton, your husband's concern is completely understandable. Don't let your temper get in the way of your good sense—or of what you truly want."

All right, so perhaps Trendal didn't deserve to be beaten to a bloody pulp . . . yet.

And what the hell did he mean, what Jess truly wanted?

Jess glared at Trendal—she'd never taken well to being reined in—but then she swallowed her spleen and nodded.

Trendal turned back to him. "Lord Ashton, now that you are here I can put Lady Ashton in your capable hands and be off about my business. But before I go, I must warn you about the men we encountered—Sir Percy and George Huntington."

"Percy." He must have put a wealth of disgust into his voice, because Trendal nodded.

Well, it was past time to settle the issue of Percy. Ash was very tired of that bounder trying to make mischief for him.

"I know the man only by reputation," Trendal said,

"which is sadly quite black, but Huntington I've had the misfortune to see in action. He's one of those unsavory fellows who likes nothing better than to whisper unfounded, reputation-ruining rumors to as many people as he can. He's the perfect tool for an unscrupulous individual—in this case, Sir Percy—because he never considers whether something he's been told is true. He just passes it along, taking great pleasure in seeming to be in the know."

Ash nodded. Perhaps Trendal had *some* redeeming qualities. "I've made Huntington's acquaintance, and I must agree with your assessment. In fact, I promised him a thorough drubbing if he insulted my wife again. I shall be delighted to make good on that promise."

Jess reached out to grip his arm. "No, Kit." Her brow was creased with worry. "I told you he's reputed to be quite dangerous. I don't want you getting hurt."

"I'm not going to challenge him to a duel, Jess. I'm just going to bloody his face and blacken his eyes." He grinned. "And break his blasted nose."

She dug her fingers into his arm. "But didn't you hear me? Huntington is supposed to be very handy with his fives."

"As am I." He couldn't decide if he was flattered or insulted that she was so concerned for his safety. He looked at Trendal—the man was laughing.

"I told Jess you'd strip to advantage," he said, "but she wouldn't believe me. Apparently you weren't much of a fighter when you were a boy."

Jess whipped her hand off Ash's arm, her face suddenly flushed. "You know I used to have to defend you from Percy."

"You *thought* you had to defend me."

"What do you mean? I kept him from hitting you."

"Only when you pushed yourself between us. I will say

that for Percy; he wouldn't hit a girl. We settled things later, after you'd gone home."

Jess's jaw dropped. She was staring at him as if she'd never seen him before.

Trendal made a sound suspiciously like a snigger and took his reins back from William. "I'm off then." He swung up onto his horse. "I'm sure our paths will cross at some blasted society affair."

"Yes," Ash said. "I'm sure they will." He looked from Jess to Trendal. He didn't know what had been between them, but he was willing to accept that it hadn't been physical, at least not recently. Which meant he had to accept that the naked footman had been only Jess's model when he'd walked in on them at the manor.

All right. He was an artist, too. He understood how drawing—or painting—turned the simple act of looking into an intellectual exercise. And that naked hug—

That was rather harder to swallow, but it was true they hadn't been kissing or . . . or engaged in any other amorous activity when he'd opened the door. And while Jess's hair had been down, her clothes had all been in their proper places.

Thank God.

He bowed slightly to Trendal. "I appreciate you protecting my wife from insult this morning."

Jess bristled. "Don't be ridiculous. Roger didn't protect me from anything. I didn't need protection."

Trendal inclined his head. "It was my pleasure."

"Are you both deaf?" Jess's voice was thick with annoyance. "I said I didn't need protection. I can protect myself. I'm not afraid of Percy or Huntington."

Trendal continued to ignore her. "And it was a pleasure to finally meet you, Lord Ashton. May I suggest, since I fear Sir Percy and Huntington will spread tales that

I was misbehaving with your wife, we appear to be on good terms when next we meet?"

"Of course you should be on good terms. Nothing happened." Jess frowned at Ash. "I've told my husband that you are only a friend, Roger."

Perhaps he was being a fool, but for some reason at the moment he believed her. "I can be cordial if you can, Trendal."

Trendal nodded. "And Jess?"

"How nice you noticed I was still here."

The man grinned. "Be sure you do tell Lord Ashton about how things are at the manor."

Trendal rode off, but Ash didn't bother watching him.

"How things are at the manor?"

"Er, yes." Her eyes slid over to William, and she leaned closer, dropping her voice to a whisper. "It's a bit, ah, irregular. I'd rather only you heard the tale."

This was somewhat alarming, but at least she was willing to confide in him. And if she was going to admit to shocking behavior, it was indeed best William not hear it. He turned to the footman.

"I'm going to walk with Lady Ashton, William. Could you take both Fluff and Shakespeare back to Greycliffe House?"

William looked a little doubtful, but clearly he felt Ash should have things out with his wife. "I'll do my best, my lord. Perhaps Shakespeare can show Fluff how to go on."

Chapter Fifteen

Listen.

—Venus's Love Notes

Ash offered Jess his arm and led her off toward a less frequented section of the park. A breeze blew past, sending a loose strand of her hair across her face. She batted it away—and said nothing.

What could be so shocking she couldn't tell him within William's hearing?

He was back to thinking her a whore or a madam.

No, he wasn't. He'd been insanely angry about the naked footman, and yet that had turned out to be wasted emotion. He would wait to see what she had to say before he lost his temper.

If she ever said anything. She did not look like she was going to speak anytime soon.

They strolled along the path, completely alone except for the birds calling in the trees and a pair of squirrels chasing each other over the grass. Ash watched as one caught the other and mounted—

Oh, damnation. He looked away. Well, it *was* spring. It was the time for mating. . . .

Hmm. If Jess had not had relations with Trendal, then she wasn't increasing, which meant he could—

No. Not yet. He had to hear her story first. Perhaps there was someone besides Trendal who'd visited her bed.

"When you abandoned me at the manor, Dennis—Mr. Walker—took pity on me."

And he still had some rough patches to smooth over before he could hope for sexual congress with his wife.

"I'm sorry, Jess. That was not well done of me. I should never have left you like that."

She waved away his apology. "It was a difficult time. I was at fault, too."

She certainly was. Zeus, he'd forgotten about Percy. There was no way he could have misconstrued *that* encounter, but at least it sounded as if Jess and Percy were no longer on familiar or even civil terms. Still, he'd keep an eye on Jess as they went about to see how she acted around the blackguard.

And around other men. She was so beautiful with her black hair and violet eyes and alabaster skin, she'd likely have all the damn dandies buzzing around her, even though she was past the first blush of youth. Or perhaps *because* she was—and was married and experienced.

They'd best not think she was available for dalliance.

"I was concerned that the household was completely male," she was saying, "especially after what you thought happened with Percy—"

"What I *saw* happen with Percy."

She shrugged, clearly unwilling to pursue that topic at the moment. "As I say, I was concerned, but Den—Mr. Walker assured me I was quite safe because . . ." She flushed.

"Because . . . ?" Where the hell was she going with this?

She stopped and turned to face him. "Kit, you must give me your word that you'll keep what I'm going to tell you secret."

He didn't have to do anything. "Why? Has Walker been doing something illegal?"

"No—" She flushed and looked away. When she looked back, her expression had hardened. "No one is being hurt by what happens at the manor."

Good God, Walker *was* breaking the law. "I will not harbor criminals. I expect my employees to carry out their duties with honor."

"And Mr. Walker does. He's very honorable. And kind."

What the hell could the man be doing? "Is Walker the only one involved?"

"No."

She was not going to make this easy for him. "I suppose Trendal must be part of it, too, but is there anyone else?"

"Yes."

Who else could . . . damn. Jess knew about it, and she was clearly uncomfortable with this conversation. "So you participated as well?"

She turned bright red. "No! I couldn't . . . I mean, that is the whole point . . . well, not precisely, but—" She broke off, crossed her arms, and glared at him. "This is ridiculous. Either you swear you will keep my confidence and do nothing to cause harm to Dennis, Roger, and the rest of the staff, or I shall not say another word."

"Zeus! The entire staff is involved?" This was what happened when you ignored a property as thoroughly as he'd ignored Blackweith Manor. As the damn proverb had it, *When the cat's away, the mice will play.* He'd not only been away for eight bloody years, he'd made it exceedingly clear he was never again setting foot in the place. He shouldn't be surprised the mice had set up their own kingdom. He was lucky the manor hadn't become notorious.

At least he hoped it wasn't notorious. Surely even if he hadn't heard anything, Mama or Father would have, if there was anything to hear.

"Except Helena, my sometimes maid." Jess's jaw hardened. "So will you swear to keep mum or not?"

Clearly, if he wished to get the story from her, he would have to promise not to report his staff to the proper authorities. "Very well. I will keep your confidence and not have anyone arrested, but I reserve the right to fire the lot of them without references."

Jess sighed and nodded. "Well, I do hope you won't act so rashly, but all right, I accept that condition. I think most of the men will be leaving the manor now anyway." She took a deep breath and looked him in the eye. "The reason I was so safe at Blackweith Manor was. . . ." She flushed again.

The secret must be extremely embarrassing.

"Was because none of the men had amorous feelings for me." The words tumbled out in a rush.

Ash stared at her. "I'm sure you mistake the matter. They may not have acted on their feelings, but they had them. Any man would. You are very beautiful."

Her flush deepened, and he thought he saw happiness spark in her eyes, but the expression was gone before he could be certain. "No, I am not mistaken. I know beyond the shadow of a doubt that the men at the manor don't have those feelings for me. They don't have those feelings for any women."

What? "You aren't making any sense. Do you mean they're all monks?" Celibacy wasn't illegal, though it was damn uncomfortable—he could vouch for the truth of that.

"Damnation, Kit!" She looked rather harried. "You aren't usually so slow witted. No, they aren't monks. They just don't do . . . that with women. They, ah, prefer"—she swallowed—"each other."

They preferred each other? That would mean . . .

"Good God—you were living in a house of sodomites!"

"Shh. Don't shout." She looked around, but they were still alone—except for the birds and the squirrels.

"That's disgusting." To think she'd been surrounded

by . . . That she'd been exposed to . . . That *he'd* just been talking to . . .

So *that's* what the fellows who'd answered the door when he'd arrived at the manor had been doing.

"It was not disgusting at all. Dennis made certain everyone was discreet, so I was never put to the blush." She sniffed. "I don't know what you are so scandalized about. I think your orgies must be far more disgusting."

"My orgies?" Now what nonsense was she spouting?

"Oh, yes." She poked him in the chest. "I may have been living in the country all these years, but I read the newspapers—at least until I couldn't bear to read about your raking any longer. But I needn't have worried I'd miss any details. The local gabble-grinders, including that fool Huntington, were always kind enough to see I was kept abreast of your shameful activities."

She'd mentioned rumors before, but he'd been too angry about the naked footman to give her words much thought. "You can't believe everything you read in the gossip columns, Jess, or hear from prattle boxes, especially that bounder Huntington."

"Oh? So you haven't littered the countryside with broken hearts"—she curled her lip—"or by-blows?"

"I have not." This was the perfect time to confess that not only had he never attended an orgy or fathered a child, he'd never even—

"There you are!"

What the hell—? He looked in the direction of the sound. Blast! Jack was striding down the path toward them.

"Sorry to intrude," Jack said, "but Mama sent me to fetch Jess. The dressmaker has arrived."

"And why are you Mama's errand boy? Couldn't she have sent William or Richard or another of the footmen?" He tried to swallow his annoyance, but Jack's elevated eyebrows and quickly suppressed grin indicated he hadn't been entirely successful. "I'm surprised she could pry you away from Frances."

That had probably been uncalled for, but he was feeling distinctly out of sorts. He'd been on the verge of confessing his darkest secret, for God's sake.

"She did ask William first, but he had to help Richard haul the dressmaker's bolts of fabric upstairs, and"—Jack cleared his throat and glanced from Ash to Jess—"for some reason Mama felt a family member might have more success dragging you back to the house. I had the misfortune of being the one closest at hand." He raised one eyebrow and said blandly, "Frances is still asleep."

Bloody hell. Which likely meant Jack had kept her busy all night. Why did his brothers have to be happily, *actively* married? "Can't the damn dressmaker wait?"

"Apparently there is much to be accomplished and little time. Mama seems to feel your wardrobe is in dire need of refurbishing, Jess."

Jess laughed. "She is right about that. I suppose I had better come along then."

There was no point in arguing. The moment was lost anyway. He certainly wasn't about to confess in Jack's hearing.

He offered Jess his arm and listened to her chat with his brother about Frances and London and the infernal Season and Ellie's interesting condition as they walked back to Greycliffe House.

The dressmaker, a plump woman of indeterminate age, clapped when Jess entered the sitting room. "Ooo, Your Grace, she is *très, très jolie!* The black hair, the violet eyes, the white skin—" She clasped her hands to her bosom, apparently overcome with delight.

Ellie giggled. "Oh, Jess, if you could see your face!"

Jess hoped she didn't look quite as incredulous as she felt. "I'm not usually greeted with such enthusiasm." She glanced at the sitting room sofa; bolts of fabric were spread out like a rainbow. She felt a thread of excitement.

The duchess was chuckling, too. "Do come in, my dear. This is Madame Celeste. She can be a bit French at times, but she is quite right—you *are* lovely."

"Thank you, Your Grace." Kit's mother was smiling at her, looking sincerely delighted—and not looking at her stomach. Jess smiled back.

"But the dress—" Madame Celeste twisted her face as if in pain. "The dress, she is *une* disgrace." She turned to the duchess. "How is eet, Your Grace, that *tous* your *belles-filles*, they wear such horrible rags? Your sons, do they like to *regardez* such . . ." Words failed; madame simply pointed at Jess's frock.

Jess would agree it wasn't stylish or even especially presentable. It was . . . she thought back. Yes, it was one of the dresses she'd had made years ago, shortly after Helena arrived at the manor. Helena was a passable needlewoman when her roses weren't demanding her attention.

"I believe my sons fall in love with the person, not the presentation, Madame Celeste. But I agree my daughters-in-law have had unfortunate wardrobes. Unless . . ." The duchess looked again at Jess. "I do not mean to be insulting. Do you like that dress, dear?"

"Oh, no, Your Grace. It's ugly and old and worn. I would be delighted to have a new one."

"A new one?" Madame Celeste looked at the duchess. "Many, many new ones, yes?"

"Of course," the duchess said. "Morning dresses and walking dresses and ball gowns and riding habits—everything."

"*Magnifique!* We begin then. Raise your arms, madame, *s'il vous plaît,* so I can take the measurements."

Ellie laughed again as Jess dutifully raised her arms. "You look as if your eyes are going to pop out of your head, Jess."

"I feel as if they are going to. I don't suppose there's any point in suggesting a bit of restraint?"

"None at all." The duchess patted her shoulder. "You'll see. You will need everything Madame Celeste makes—isn't that right, Ellie?"

Madame tightened her measuring tape around Jess's bust, calling off the number for her assistants to record.

"Yes. I couldn't believe it either, Jess, but I've worn almost all my new things, and I've only been here a few weeks. People in London change their clothes three or four times a day."

Was Ellie teasing her? "That seems like a colossal waste of time."

Madame Celeste paused before she snaked the tape around Jess's waist. "*Non, non,* madame. You *must* be *à la mode*. Eet is *très* important. Everyone, they will look at you. They will wish to see the mysterious Lady Ashton, no? It is all they talk about."

Good God! That was alarming, but perhaps the dressmaker was simply exaggerating. "What do you mean?" Jess looked from Madame Celeste to Ellie to the duchess.

The seamstress abruptly filled her mouth with pins; Ellie studied her fingernails.

"People do like to speculate about Ash," the duchess said. "I suppose it's because he'll be the next Duke of Greycliffe."

Madame Celeste choked, and Jess was afraid she'd swallowed one of the pins.

"What do they speculate about exactly?" For once she hoped it was Kit's many indiscretions.

The duchess smiled kindly. "Well, Madame is correct—they do wonder about you, especially in the last few days. Lady Heldon has been telling anyone who would listen that she saw you and Ash together at that inn in the country." She frowned. "I do wish I hadn't invited her to the last house party. I had no idea she was quite so objectionable."

Jess took a deep breath, causing Madame Celeste some consternation.

"*Non, non.* Breathe, madame. The measurements, they must be correct."

She forced herself to exhale.

Oh, God. And now she'd be dropped in the middle of the ton to be mocked and gossiped about. She had no experience whatsoever with society ballrooms, and what little contact she'd had with the male members of the aristocracy had not been good.

She suddenly knew how the Christians must have felt when facing the lions in the Roman Colosseum.

She felt a soft touch on her arm and blinked. The duchess was looking at her, her eyes full of concern.

"Don't worry, Jess," she said. "Ash will be by your side. We all will."

She swallowed. Perhaps Kit's mother didn't think she was a dirty little servant girl after all.

But she *was* a dirty little servant girl. She was an Irish groom's daughter. That fact would just make the ton's gossip all the more delectable.

"Of course we will." Ellie smiled and put her hand over her belly, an action she was prone to these days. "Well, I'll be at your side in my thoughts. I wish I could go to the parties with you, but I tire so easily now and Ned wants to be certain I take care of myself." Her lips twisted. "He's naturally a little overprotective after what happened with Cicely."

"I do think Ned is handling his concern better now," the

duchess said. "He's been limiting his warnings to a half dozen or so a day."

Ellie laughed. "Well, he shares rather more of them with me, but yes, he's trying very hard to remain calm. Still, it will be a tremendous relief once the baby's born, and Ned sees all is well."

"We'll all be relieved." The duchess grinned. "And delighted. Have I said how much the duke and I are looking forward to greeting our first grandchild?"

Ellie rolled her eyes playfully. "I believe you might have mentioned it once or twice."

If only things had been different between Kit and me...

No, there was no point in regretting the past. And the future was far from determined. If Kit couldn't bring himself to forgive her and trust her, there would be no babies in her future.

A large pit opened where her stomach should be.

No! Not having babies was fine. She had her art; she had that plan with Roger. And really, she did trust Kit to keep his word and provide for her if he divorced her. She was no longer worried about having a roof over her head.

She might not have love, but she'd have friendship, at least Roger's and Dennis's. Everyone else, including the duchess and Kit's brothers and Frances and likely even Ellie, would give her the cut direct, but that was better than living with a husband who despised and distrusted her, wasn't it?

Yes. It must be.

If she didn't love Kit, she might be able to manage being his wife. It would be a business arrangement, a marriage of convenience. But she did love him. She couldn't treat him like a polite stranger whose only interest was the use of her body for procreative purposes. And that wouldn't even be the worst of it. Any children they had would be swept up into Kit's loving family while she stood on the sidelines, tolerated, perhaps, but, especially if Kit did not respect her, not embraced. And then her children would come to see her as a necessary embarrassment—or perhaps not even necessary.

Madame Celeste was now holding lengths of fabric under Jess's chin. "What do you think, Your Grace? The deep colors, no?"

"Definitely."

She should look—she was the artist. She could tell if a color was right for her.

At the moment she didn't care. They could drape her in black bombazine, and she wouldn't bat an eye. In fact, she wished they would. Funeral garments matched her mood.

"That shade of blue is perfect on you, Jess," Ellie said. "When you walk into a room, everyone's eyes will follow you."

The duchess nodded. "Yes, indeed."

All three women beamed at her.

Oh, God.

"I believe Jess and I need a moment alone," she heard the duchess say from what seemed like a long distance. "If you'll excuse us?"

Kit's mother led her out the door and across the corridor to a smaller room, where she gently pushed her to sit before sitting beside her.

"I seem to be making a habit of this," the duchess said, smiling. "Frances was also quite distressed when Madame Celeste was measuring her for new dresses. Perhaps I should change mantua makers."

"Oh, no, it's not Madame Celeste." But Kit's mother knew that. She was the Duchess of Love, the ton's matchmaker. She knew London society as well as anyone. "Your Grace, I can't . . . you know I can't . . . it would be a disaster for me to . . ."

The duchess's fingers covered Jess's where they were clawing at her dress. "Breathe, Jess. Relax."

That was a good idea. She tried it. It worked—until she let the notion of ballrooms creep back into her thoughts. "Ohhh."

Her Grace clasped both Jess's hands in a strong grip, shaking them a little. "It will be all right."

She didn't understand. She couldn't. She was a duchess, for God's sake. "I'm a groom's daughter."

"Yes, you are, but you are not just any groom's daughter. Your father was very well respected, you know, and much in demand. He had a special talent with horses—everyone said so. The duke had to go to some trouble to hire him, as I remember. You must try to take pride in that."

"Ah." Yes, Papa had been good with horses, and perhaps a few of the older men might remember him. But society in general? The gossipy women and disdainful fops? No.

The duchess squeezed her hands. "I must beg your forgiveness, Jess. Eight years ago I was distracted by the house party and didn't properly convey how saddened the duke and I were by your father's death. I had meant to discuss things with you once our guests left, but then suddenly you were married and gone." She dropped Jess's hands and looked away. "It was a very . . . confusing time."

"Yes, it was." Confusing was one way to describe it. Disastrous was another.

"Did . . ." The duchess looked down. Her fingers pleated her skirt as if *she* was the one discomposed. "Ash didn't do anything he shouldn't have, did he?"

Besides marry her? "No."

Kit's mother met her gaze, a shadow of desperation in her eyes. "Then he didn't, ah, force himself on you?"

"No!"

The duchess's shoulders slumped with relief. "I thought not, but the circumstances were so odd, the duke and I did wonder." Her voice strengthened. "Then was Percy to blame?"

Jess stared at Kit's mother. She must look terribly guilty, but if the woman didn't know the details of that dreadful scene in the studio, Jess certainly was not going to tell her.

"It wouldn't be surprising. I saw how Percy and Ash were both in love with you growing up, and Percy has taken every opportunity since your marriage to cause trouble for Ash. I think he must still be jealous."

"Ah." Percy in love with her? Why did anyone think that? Percy could have married her if he'd wanted. Kit had just about demanded the worm offer for her in the studio that day. But instead Percy had stomped all over her . . . reputation. Not her heart. He'd never had her heart.

And Kit? If he'd loved her once—and she doubted the duchess was correct about that, too—his love had died in that damn studio.

"Oh, I don't think Percy could be jealous."

"Hmm."

Oh, hell. Now the duchess was looking thoughtful, as if she was devising some unpleasant—unpleasant for Jess, at least—scheme.

"You know you are certain to encounter Percy at the various society events. He is invited everywhere."

Another reason this was all a terrible mistake. "I've already encountered Percy, Your Grace. I spoke to him in Hyde Park this morning when I took Fluff for his walk."

"Did you?" The duchess smiled and sat back. "That's good, then. The first meeting is often the most difficult."

If only that were the case. "I think Percy intends to make all our meetings difficult, Your Grace, and busy himself spreading unpleasant lies about me." Dear God, she hadn't considered that the duke and duchess would hear Percy's calumnies, but of course they would. "And I do assure you they are lies."

The duchess nodded. "It is good to be prepared. I had thought his affection for Miss Wharton would have softened him, but perhaps I was mistaken. Well, we shall hope for the best and prepare for the worst. And you, my dear, must hold your head high and ignore him."

That sounded like an excellent idea, and she might have been able to do it if she were still at the manor. But in a London ballroom? "I shall try."

She must have sounded as doubtful as she felt, because Kit's mother touched her hand again.

"Remember, your father may have been a groom—a very skilled groom—but your husband is the heir to a duchy. You have no reason to hang your head." The duchess smiled. "You will be the Duchess of Greycliffe one day—though I hope you won't fault me for praying that day doesn't come soon."

Did the duchess not know her son was considering divorce? "But that is another part of the problem, isn't it? Our marriage is rather irregular."

The duchess nodded, her expression suddenly concerned. "Well, yes, that's true, but the point is you *are* married. As long as that's the case, most people will give you the benefit of the doubt." She paused and then shrugged slightly.

"Well, most people will at least pretend to give you the benefit of the doubt. No one wants to offend the Duke and Duchess of Greycliffe—current or future. It would be social suicide." She frowned, suddenly looking rather fierce. "And believe me, the duke may appear pleasant and somewhat mild mannered, but everyone knows he will brook no insult to his family."

That was lovely, except many people would say *she* was the insult. Certainly anyone who believed Percy's stories would say so. Kit would . . .

The duchess patted her arm. "Don't look so bleak. You

and Ash are together now. That is something to be very happy about."

"But we're not, Your Grace. Not really." She bit her lip. She must not confess everything to the duchess, no matter how sympathetic a listener she seemed.

"I mean you are finally in the same location. That is much better than the foolish way Ash has had you live miles away all these years. I don't know what he was thinking, and of course he wouldn't discuss it with me or his father."

Kit's mother sighed. "Young people! If they would only listen to wiser heads . . . But I suppose when I was young I felt the same way." She laughed. "Only my parents had their heads stuck in ancient Greek texts all the time. If I'd asked them for advice, they would have directed me to Plato." Her lips slid into a sly smile. "However, if you would care for some suggestions, I'd be happy to give you copies of my *Love Notes*."

"Ah." Jess was not about to admit she already had a collection of the papers. "Well . . ."

"Splendid! I'll get them for you once we are done with Madame Celeste, whom we should probably be getting back to."

She stood, so Jess stood, too, but the duchess made no move to leave. Instead she took Jess's hands again. "As I'm sure you know, Jess, Ash can be very stubborn. But then, men are often blind when it comes to matters of the heart, aren't they? We women must show them the way."

Jess looked longingly at the door. She would dearly love to make her way out of this conversation, but Kit's mother wasn't finished.

"The duke and I are both hoping you two can manage to overcome your differences." She leaned forward slightly, her expression intent, and her grip on Jess's hands tightened. "We will do anything we can to help. And do not think it is because we wish to see the succession assured. Ash has not been happy for a long time, Jess. Not since he came home from leaving you at the manor."

"Oh, surely you are wrong, Your Grace."

"No, I'm not." The duchess suddenly grinned and let go of Jess's hands. "But at least now I'm hopeful." She finally started for the door. "Now let us go see if Madame Celeste can make you a wardrobe that will charm the ton and seduce that blockheaded husband of yours."

Chapter Sixteen

*Men would rather die than admit
they need marital advice.*

—Venus's Love Notes

"Drew!" Venus had spent the last fifteen minutes searching for her husband. She'd only climbed the stairs to the old nursery in desperation, never guessing that's where he'd hidden himself.

Drew sighed and stood to greet her. "Yes, Venus?"

"I've been looking all over for you." She frowned at the book in his hands. "Are you reading that Peloponnesian War tome again?"

He smiled a touch wistfully. "I am trying to."

Typical. Trust Drew to hide when there was work of the matchmaking variety to be done.

"Well, this is no time for idle reading." She closed the door behind her. She couldn't remember the last time she'd been up here. She looked around. The room was a bit dusty and faded, but it brought back wonderful memories of when her sons had been young. "Oh, Drew, isn't it splendid that we'll have a baby in the family again?"

"Yes. And even more splendid that it will not be ours. Babies are a lot of work."

"But worth every minute." Drew might pretend to be unmoved, but she knew he was just as delighted as she was. "We'll be using this nursery again." She looked around once more. "I think the curtains need to be replaced."

"Quite likely."

"And there is only one comfortable chair." They would need at least two—one for her and one for Drew. Well, and others for the nursery maid and Ellie and Ned. The room was large; it wouldn't be too crowded.

"You are welcome to it." He eyed the sheaf of papers in her hand. "I see you have brought your own reading material."

She laughed. This was going to be the tricky part. "Oh, no. This is for you."

Drew knew her too well. His brows shot up, and then he got what she'd come to call his wary expression. "Thank you, but as you can see"—he lifted Thucydides—"I have plenty to keep me busy."

She walked closer, smiling. Drew backed up, frowning, until he bumped up against the mantel.

"Well, it's not for you precisely. It's for Ash."

"Then why don't you give it to him yourself?"

"He'd much rather get it from you."

"If that is true, then I venture to say he'd much rather not get it at all."

Likely Drew was right about that. "Well, perhaps he'll be unenthusiastic at first, but I'm sure he'll thank you later."

Drew was not convinced. "That sounds like something you say before administering a purge."

"Don't be ridiculous." Though now that he mentioned it . . . "However, I do think a dose of this information might cure whatever ails Ash's marriage."

Drew's jaw hardened. "Venus, I am not going to discuss Ash's marriage with him."

How could he say that? Didn't he want Ash to be happy?

"But he's your son. I'm sure if I had a daughter, I would have a frank discussion about marital matters with her."

"You do not have a daughter, so we cannot put that theory to the test. Besides, men are not like women. We do not discuss such things."

She'd overheard enough male conversations to know differently. "Of course you do. You just use cruder words and snigger a lot. And the discussions are usually not about wives."

Drew's eyes widened. "Good God, Venus, how did you form that opinion?"

"I eavesdrop at society events, of course. It's one of my main ways of identifying suitable matches." She smiled. "People seem to think if they can't be seen, they can't be heard. They say some of the most amazing things. For example, just the other night, old Lady Pentworth was standing behind some potted palms in Lord Eddington's ballroom, telling—"

"Stop!" Drew threw up his hands, clutching Thucydides like a shield to block her words. "I do not wish to hear what Lady Pentworth said."

"But you would be most diverted. She's such a hunched-over, ancient thing, and yet she and Lord Eddington—"

He now had his forehead pressed against his book. He looked as if he might be in pain. "No. Please. Spare me. I shall have nightmares for weeks if you continue."

She giggled. "Very well. I promise not to tell you, if you promise to give this to Ash." She extended her papers again.

He lowered his book to glare at them as if they were a nest of vipers. "Blackmail, my dear duchess, does not become you." But he put Thucydides down and took them. His mouth tightened as he read the title. "*How to Woo Your Wife?* Good God!"

"It's something new I've been working on. The *Love*

Notes are very popular, but they are really more for women. Men can use marital advice as well."

Drew raised an eyebrow.

"Except you, of course." And that was almost true. "Actually, I was hoping you might read it through and give me your suggestions for making it more useful." She smiled. "You being a man, you know."

He bowed slightly. "I'm so glad you noticed, but no, I shall not be reading this. I cannot think Ash will read it either."

"But it has lots of good advice!" How could she help men find love if they wouldn't open their minds to new ideas? It was all very well to make a match, but marriage required more than a wedding. It was a journey two people took together, and if it was going to be a pleasant journey, both the man and the woman had to work to keep the spark burning.

There was still a spark between Ash and Jess. She could feel it. But it was in grave danger of going out if they didn't resolve whatever it was that was keeping them apart. And she would swear one of the things keeping them apart involved the bedchamber. She couldn't put her finger on why she thought so, but she trusted her instincts on this.

"You *must* give it to Ash," she said. "The fate of the succession depends upon it."

"Venus, I am not going to insult Ash by suggesting he doesn't know what to do in bed with his wife."

"It's not about that, precisely." Drew could be so infuriating sometimes. "If you will just read the pages—"

"No."

"—you will see the advice is mostly about how to strengthen the bond between husband and wife in such a way that women want to engage in bedroom activities." She grinned. "Enthusiastically."

Drew still did not look persuaded. "It doesn't matter what your pages say. Ash will not want to read them. Haven't you seen how our sons turn green when anyone mentions *Venus's Love Notes*? They do not want to know what their mother—or their father, I suspect—thinks about marital love."

Drew might have a point. "Then don't say I wrote the pages. You can see I've put 'by Anonymous' as the author. Tell him a friend penned it."

"I can't lie."

"You won't be lying. I am your friend, aren't I?"

"Venus, Ash will be mortified if I give him this, no matter whom I say it's by. He's a very proud, private person. You know that. Look at how he never breathed a word about his marriage difficulties in eight years, even when we began to push him to resolve matters."

She did not want to agree with Drew, but, yes, she could see how Ash would not wish to accept advice, even though he clearly needed it. Anything he did would have to be his own idea. . . .

"I have it! We will arrange it so he stumbles upon the pages himself."

Drew looked skeptical as he handed the bundle back to her. "I don't know how you're going to manage that with the house so full. Jack or Ned is equally likely to find it, and we know *they* don't need any advice of this sort."

"Oh, dear. You are right, as always."

Drew snorted. "Right as always? May I have that in writing?"

"You are very silly."

"Why don't you just hand the papers to Ash and ask *him* to give you his opinion? You can tell him I flat out refused to read any of it, which is true." He smiled suggestively. "I know very well how to woo my wife."

"Yes, you most certainly do." Venus moved to kiss him on the cheek, but he caught her around the waist and captured her lips with his instead.

Mmm.

"I confess I feel the need to dispel any lingering doubts you might have on the subject of my wooing," he murmured in her ear. He picked her up and carried her to the chair; she was delighted to discover that two people could indeed be quite comfortable in it.

She put her fingers on Drew's lips as he tried to kiss her again. She wished to finish this topic before they moved on to what promised to be a very long, very engrossing "discussion."

"Do you think Ash will read the pages if I give them to him, Drew?"

He brushed her fingers with his lips. "If he can get past the shock and mortification of the title, he might, especially if he's feeling desperate enough." He frowned. "And I am definitely sensing desperation there."

"Yes, I agree. And Jess is not feeling very content either."

"Just don't give him the impression that you think he needs your advice."

"Of course not. I shall be very tactful."

Now why did Drew look so doubtful? She was the personification of tact.

"Are we finished talking about Ash's problems now?" Drew's clever fingers were teasing her earlobe.

"Yes, I suppose we are."

"Splendid." He took her papers and put them on the floor.

And that was the last she thought of them again for quite some while.

* * *

Ash stared glumly at his coffee. He felt as if his head was stuffed with old rags, and the sight—and the smell—of breakfast repulsed him.

He could not go on this way. He'd stayed up late drinking to be certain Jess was asleep before he went to bed—Ned and Jack had both given him pitying looks when they'd left him in the study, but had wisely held their tongues—and then he'd hauled himself downstairs before she'd awakened. Even Fluff was still asleep. He snorted. The dog had sprawled over his side of the bed the moment he'd vacated it.

"Sleep well, dear?"

Oh, God. Mama was revoltingly cheerful in the morning. Why couldn't she take toast and tea in her room like a proper duchess? "Well enough."

She clicked her tongue. "You don't look like it." Then—good God!—she waggled her eyebrows. "I see Jess is still abed."

He was going to vomit right here on the table. Perhaps a piece of toast would settle his stomach and have the added benefit of preventing him from talking. "Have you the morning papers?" he asked before grabbing the toast. It was cold and somewhat soggy. Disgusting.

He took a bite.

"No, but I have something else for you to read."

All his body's inner alarms went off, and he choked.

"As I assume you must know, I write a little leaflet with advice of a romantic nature."

"Uh." He could bolt from the room, but that would only put off the inevitable. Mama was just like a terrier after a rat when she had something she wanted to convey.

"Well, it isn't a secret, is it? I don't suppose you've read any of my *Love Notes*?"

"*No!*"

Don't shout. Remain calm. Try to smile as if this was a normal sort of conversation.

Unfortunately, it *was* all too normal where Mama was concerned. "I thought those were directed at women."

Oh, damnation. He'd said the wrong thing. Mama's eyes lit up with the gleeful expression a fencer must have when he sees the opening he's been looking for, right before he runs a man through with his sword.

"Precisely! Which is why I, er, that is, why a friend wrote this." She pulled out a stack of papers she'd hidden behind her skirts. "It's marital advice specifically for men. But I—that is my friend—would really like to have a male's opinion before publishing it." She tried to give him the papers.

He wrapped his hands around his coffee cup. "You should ask Father."

She laid them on the table by his elbow. "I have, of course, but he refused to read the first word."

"Ah." He glanced over at the papers and saw the title.

Hell! He jerked and spilled his coffee all over his fingers. At least it was already lukewarm.

"Oh, I don't mean to suggest that *you* need any advice on how to woo your wife."

Mama laughed, but her eyes were watching him like a hawk, so he concentrated on wiping his fingers and mopping up the puddle in his saucer. He'd got much better at hiding his feelings now that he was an adult, but having Jess around had unsettled him. His control was shaky.

"Why don't you ask Ned or Jack to read it?"

"Perhaps I will once you are finished, but I particularly want your opinion."

He risked looking at her. She was smiling, but now there was a crease between her brows and her eyes had their worried look.

Of course she knew there were still problems between him and Jess.

"Please, Ash? I truly think it would help."

Damn. He knew whom she thought it would help, and it wasn't the author. And perhaps she was right. It couldn't hurt.... Well, it would indeed be painful to read, but if he learned something that would show him how to resolve his issues with Jess, then it would be worth the suffering.

At least he hoped so.

"Very well. Though I can't say when I shall be able to get to it."

He'd swear she was going to clap her hands, but she managed to catch herself at the last minute and adjust her fichu instead. "Of course. I understand. Whenever you have a moment would be fine." She smiled again. "But it would be splendid if you could read at least a few pages before we go to the Palmerson ball tonight."

"Yes, well, I can't promise. And now I hate to leave you alone...." He'd hate more to stay and risk being quizzed about his relationship with Jess or, even worse, for Jess or one of his brothers to discover him with such embarrassing reading material. "But I'm afraid I really must depart." He picked up the papers and stood.

Thankfully Mama didn't ask him where he needed to be so early in the day, but she did frown at his plate. "You hardly ate any breakfast."

"I'm not hungry." He bowed and fled, though he did try to make his retreat look like a leisurely stroll rather than a panicked rout.

He paused in the entry hall. He couldn't retreat to the study to read Mama's booklet. Ned, or especially Jack, might come in and find him; they'd plague him unmercifully if they caught sight of what he was reading. Normally he'd go to his room, but Jess was there—

Damnation, he heard dog nails on the stairs and voices. Someone was coming with Fluff and Shakespeare.

"Madame Celeste is very quick." That was Frances's voice.

"Really? I can't see how she can have a dress ready by tonight. She only took my measurements yesterday."

And that was Jess. He saw their slippers. In a moment they would reach the landing and turn to see him—and ask him what he had in his hands.

He took his only path of escape—the front door.

Fortunately it was a warm morning, but he couldn't very well sit on the stoop to read. He'd go to the park in the middle of the square. As he remembered, it had a few benches in among the trees. He'd be comfortable and, more importantly, he'd be hidden from view.

"Don't worry," Frances said as they reached the bottom of the stairs. "I didn't have any suitable clothes either when I arrived in London." She laughed. "Suitable? I was dressed as a boy, so obviously my situation was dire indeed. But Madame Celeste had two dresses ready in less than twenty-four hours. I'm certain you'll have your gown in plenty of time for the ball tonight."

"Oh. Th-that's good then." Jess's stomach sank. It would be better if Madame Celeste was not quite so efficient. Attending her first ton event was going to be stressful enough, but attending it without Kit's support—

Stupid! Why the hell had she thought she'd have his support? He hadn't cared enough about her to spend last night in their bed.

No, that wasn't quite true. The bedclothes on his side *were* mussed this morning. He must have arrived after she'd fallen asleep and left before she'd woken.

How . . . annoying.

She flushed. She should never have looked at the duchess's shocking leaflets, but she'd skimmed through them after supper and had planned to try some of their suggestions. She'd been very, er, *anxious* to try them. Very, *very* anxious.

She'd waited expectantly for Kit to appear, but as the clock ticked the time away, she'd gone from excited—that was one way to describe the churning, needy feeling—to impatient to angry. She'd finally given up and blown out the candle. And then she'd tossed and turned for what had felt like hours. Fluff had almost abandoned her for the hearth.

Kit must have been in someone else's bed. Where else could he have been? Talking to his brothers until all hours of the night? Not bloody likely.

No, he'd been out "visiting." He had many beautiful women anxious to entertain him and a lot of time to make up for, since he hadn't been able to indulge his lecherous urges on their trip from the manor.

Her flush deepened. Well, he *had* exercised those urges briefly when he'd touched her at the White Stag—and then he'd blamed *her* for being a light-skirt!

Damn it. The ton was certain to be gossiping about his nocturnal activities at the ball tonight, making her even more of a laughingstock.

Ohhh! If Kit were within reach right now, she'd kick him in the place that would do the most damage to his profligate ways. And to think she'd begun to doubt the rumors. She was such a fool.

She'd had enough. She would have it out with him tonight, after this dreadful ball they were committed to. She'd beg off going at all if she didn't think the duchess would ask embarrassing questions—or, worse, waggle her eyebrows in that hideously knowing way.

William appeared from the back of the house and noticed the dogs—or the dogs noticed him. He was becoming quite their favorite. They rushed over to greet him.

"Hallo, boys," he said, patting them. He smiled at Frances and her. "Shall I take them down to the kitchen, then, and find them some breakfast?"

Shakespeare sat up and begged, and Fluff so forgot himself as to woof with enthusiasm.

"I think so," Frances said, laughing.

The dogs knew the way to the kitchen quite well and took off, leaving William to catch up.

"And now let's have our breakfasts," Frances said, leading the way into the breakfast room.

Jess followed her—

Blast, there was the duchess, sitting alone at the table. She'd been eyeing Kit and Jess all during supper the night before, clearly trying to divine what it was that was keeping them apart. Ha! She should tell the duchess where her son had been last night—or, rather, where he hadn't been. *That* would stop the woman's speculations.

Or, perhaps it wouldn't. It was hard to tell with Kit's mother. Best to hold her tongue and eat quickly so she could leave quickly. Her control was very fragile after such a trying—and lonely—night.

"Good morning." The duchess beamed at them. "Did you run into Ash in the hall? He was just here."

Oh, God. Jess reached for some toast and took a large bite. If she was chewing, she couldn't say things she shouldn't.

"No, Your Grace," Frances said, "we didn't."

"Really?" Kit's mother frowned. "I don't see how you could have missed him. He left no more than a minute ago." She shrugged, smiling again. She was sunnier than the damn celestial orb itself. "Well, it doesn't matter. We don't need him until it's time to leave for Lord Palmerson's." She took a sip of tea. "Where's Jack, Frances?"

"He got up early to visit his children."

Jess inhaled a crumb and started coughing. Jack had children? She reached for her teacup.

"I was surprised, too," the duchess said. "But it turns out Jack has set up a foundling home in Bromley. Can you believe it? And here I'd thought he was rather irresponsible."

"He doesn't want the ton to know what he's doing," Frances said, a slight frown appearing between her brows, "so please don't say anything, Jess."

"Of course I won't." Even if she were one to blab, which she wasn't, she wouldn't have the opportunity. Much as the duchess might think otherwise, the ton would give Jess the cut direct or, if not that, then avoid her as though she was carrying the plague. Which she was in their minds—she had the blood of an Irish groom in her veins, no matter how talented and respected he was.

Even Papa would say it was best to breed quality to quality if you wanted a good racehorse . . . or a future duke.

Kit should have thought of that eight years ago.

She glared at her toast. The playwright William Congreve had got it exactly right: "Married in haste, we repent at leisure."

Why *had* Kit married her?

The duchess spread jam on her toast. "I'm glad you're here—I wished to speak to you both about tonight's engagement. I'm afraid it will be a terrible squeeze"—she smiled at Jess—"since word is sure to have got out that you and Ash will be attending. It might be hard to edge through the crowd, so I plan to arrive early and get settled in a comfortable spot." She smiled again. "That might also curtail the number of people goggling at you and Ash, Jess."

They wouldn't be staring at Kit, they'd be gawping at her. Navigating a crowded room would not be a problem. The duchess need only let her lead the way. The crowd would part as though she were ringing a leper's bell.

The duchess frowned slightly. "I hate to say this, but..." She leaned toward Jess. "Most people will be polite, but there is always one or two who won't be."

"Like Percy." *Of course. It always came back to Percy.*

"Yes, I'm afraid so, though I truly am hoping Percy behaves." The duchess sighed and shook her head. "I really thought Miss Wharton would be the making of him, but if he doesn't offer for her soon, I shall have to find her another gentleman. Her parents have threatened to marry her to an elderly neighbor if she doesn't catch a husband by the end of the Season."

"I thought Percy was on the verge of asking for her hand a few days ago when I saw him with Miss Wharton at Lady Wainwright's Venetian breakfast," Frances said.

"Yes, I thought so, too." The duchess looked at Jess. "But now..."

Oh, God. Now her presence in Town would dash some poor spinster's hopes in addition to everything else.

Why the hell did Percy still care what she did? He'd ruined her life and Kit's—his job was done.

"Jack told me no one liked Percy growing up." Frances helped herself to a slice of ham.

"I do feel sorry for the boy." The duchess looked at Jess. "You must have known his parents were very unpleasant."

"Yes, Your Grace. I had heard they were." Of course she'd never met Percy's parents. A baronet and his wife weren't going to have anything to do with a groom's daughter. Everyone—except her—knew what use the heir to a baronetcy would have for such a woman, and it didn't involve introducing her to his parents.

But servants did gossip. Lady Headley was said to have been an overbearing woman who would pinch a penny until it howled for mercy. She reputedly bullied her husband and son shamelessly. Once she died, Percy's father ran through all the family's funds and expired nine months after his wife while in bed with two of the maids.

"I invited Percy to the Valentine house party year after year," the duchess said, "hoping he'd find a nice girl who would settle him down. And I kept hoping he and Ash would resolve whatever it was that stood between them"—she smiled at Jess—"and become friends again."

"They were never really friends," Jess said.

"Well, yes, that's true. But I'd hoped they'd at least come to terms with . . . things"—the duchess smiled again—"so Percy would stop spreading nasty rumors about you."

"Which Ash believed." That had always hurt, that Kit could think so little of her. But then why wouldn't he? He'd caught her with Percy in such damning circumstances.

"Yes," the duchess said, "just as you believed the rumors about Ash."

Jess smiled weakly and concentrated on her toast. Of course Kit's mother would say that.

She wished the duchess was right. Just yesterday in the park, Kit had told her she couldn't believe everything she heard. He hadn't denied the rumors completely—she'd noted that—but she'd thought he'd been on the verge of telling her the truth.

But then Jack had arrived, and the moment was lost.

Damn it, they could have discussed all that last night if Kit had come to bed at the proper time.

She forced herself to take a bite of toast and chew it thoroughly. The duchess and Frances had moved on to discussing some eccentric old woman who dressed her cats in silver and gold livery.

She'd grant that people enjoyed exaggerating and distorting things, but there was almost always some kernel of truth to the tales. Take the ugly rumors about her. She'd never done the things people said she had, but she had indeed behaved scandalously with Percy. Once, but once was enough.

And really, why wouldn't Kit enjoy himself, especially since he believed his wife was little better than a doxy? He was only doing what the rest of his class did.

Well, enough was enough. She was determined. After the silly ball was over, she'd settle things with the Marquis of Ashton.

Chapter Seventeen

A woman's feelings require careful handling.
—Venus's Love Notes

"You look beautiful, Jess," Ash said, hoping to ease the tension in the room.

Fluff had retreated to the hearth to sprawl in front of the fire, his head on his paws, his brows tented, watching them from a safe distance. Ash would like to remove himself as well, but his gut told him that would be a colossal mistake.

Jess had been snapping at him ever since they'd come up to get ready for the Palmerson ball. Mary, Mama's maid, had just left after arranging Jess's hair, and now Jess was standing stiffly in front of the cheval glass, scowling at her reflection.

Why the hell was she scowling? She took his breath away. Her dark blue gown hugged her small breasts, barely covering them, and her lovely black hair was swept up to expose her shoulders.

God, he wanted to run his hands over her, pull her back against him, and kiss his way along the exquisite curve of her neck to her delicate jaw and then turn her and—

And that sure as hell wasn't going to happen. She'd likely jab her sharp elbow into his stomach. For some damn reason she was angry with him.

He took a deep calming breath. He'd read the handbook

Mama had given him. It wasn't a long or difficult text. Some of it was more than a little scandalous, so he sincerely hoped Mama hadn't written it—though he was very much afraid that she had—but other parts had suggestions that could be implemented without blushing, such as: *Compliments, as long as they are sincere, will go a long way to warming your wife's heart.*

Well, *that* hadn't worked, and he was sincere, very, very sincere. He had never seen Jess look more beautiful. She would have every man at the ball lusting after her—including Percy.

Bloody hell! If Percy stepped even a quarter of an inch over the line of proper behavior, Ash would rip his head off.

Unless Jess wanted Percy's attentions. But she didn't . . . did she?

The fear of that was why he'd forced himself to read every damn word of *How to Woo Your Wife*.

"You're certain the neck isn't too low?" Jess turned one way and then the other, studying herself in the mirror. "I really do think a fichu might be a good idea, no matter what Mary says."

Sometimes a woman needs reassurance, not reasoned argument.

Right.

"I'm sure Mary must know what's proper for a London ballroom. Mama certainly relies on her."

Jess bit her lip, her eyes still studying her reflection. "Yes, I suppose you are right."

She did not look convinced.

"And Madame Celeste definitely must know. She wants everyone to admire your dress so they'll come to her for their clothing, doesn't she?"

Jess frowned. "Remember that popinjay we saw on the

street when we first arrived in London? His tailor must have thought people would admire that outlandish outfit, too."

Oh, for God's sake! Now she was being ridiculous. But he swallowed his impatience.

"Jess, you look nothing like that man." He stepped closer, but still not close enough to present a target for her elbow. "You really are beautiful."

"Really?" She glanced up at him. He saw doubt and perhaps a flicker of hope in her eyes—and then a flash of anger again. "I suppose you should know, being such an accomplished rake."

It was almost as if she was trying to pick a fight.

He would let it go. This was no time to get into that. It was just her nerves speaking.

"All I know is what I see. I'm telling you the truth, Jess." Should he mention how she would draw all the male eyes? No. He would have sworn just a few weeks ago that she'd want to hear exactly that, but now he thought not.

What had the damn pamphlet said? *Ask her how she feels. Listen to her.*

Why anyone would want to talk about feelings was beyond him. Frankly, the notion gave him shivers, like hearing fingernails scraping on slate. It must be a female quirk.

"Are you nervous?"

Her jaw hardened. "No." And then she sighed and looked back at the mirror. "Well, maybe a little."

Perhaps Mama's handbook had some value. He thought he could sense her softening toward him. He might—

No, he might not. He clasped his hands behind his back. *Listen means listening,* not *touching. Keep your hands to yourself.*

That was his advice, not the pamphlet's.

"I'll stay by your side if you wish."

"Would you?" Her lips wavered in and out of a smile.

"Of course." He wanted to say more, but he held his tongue. Their connection was so fragile, anger might come rushing back at the first wrong word to sever it.

Her eyes flared with warmth, and then she flushed and dropped her gaze.

He felt quite hot himself. And he'd almost forgotten. "I have something for you."

Mama's handbook had said women liked gifts as long as they were really gifts and not bribes.

He'd never given Jess a gift. He should have given her something when they'd wed, but he'd been too . . . upset at the time. Perhaps this could be a new beginning—a courtship. The handbook said women liked to be courted.

"You do?" She smiled. "Some paints? I haven't painted since I left Blackweith Manor."

Should he remind her who she'd said would be her next subject? No. From the color flooding her cheeks, she'd just remembered. If they weren't going to the ball . . .

But they were going. Mama and Father were correct. Now that society knew they were in Town, the gossip would only become more outrageous if they didn't attend at least some events and give everyone a chance to stare at them.

And he must remember, the way Jess was acting, she might skewer rather than paint him if he armed her with a sharp-handled paintbrush.

"I'm afraid not paints. We can get those later." He reached into his pocket and pulled out a jeweler's bag. He'd dashed over to Rundell and Bridge this afternoon and found something he liked. He hoped Jess liked it, too. He spilled the pearl necklace onto his palm.

"Oh!" Jess sucked in her breath. "Is that for me?"

He laughed. "Well, it's certainly not for me."

She laughed, too. "No, I suppose it would look odd with your cravat."

"Most definitely. Here, let me put it on you." He dropped the bag on her dressing table and stepped close behind her. Mmm. She smelled of lavender.

He draped the pearls over the creamy expanse of her chest. The blue dress was barely modest; if his hands slipped, they could easily reach below the scrap of fabric and lift her lovely, soft breasts free—

His body had the predictable response. He pushed his hips back so the bulge that had suddenly appeared in his pantaloons would not startle her.

Blast it, all the bloody men at the ball would have the same reaction. Jess would have her pick of the damn scoundrels.

"Is something the matter?"

He met her gaze in the mirror. Worry and uncertainty clouded her eyes.

Kill suspicion before it kills your marriage.

Those had been the hardest words to read in Mama's handbook. He knew what Jess had done with Percy; he'd seen that with his own eyes. But it had happened eight years ago. All the other tales of Jess's infidelities were hearsay, and some of the rumors had her consorting with the Blackweith staff. After meeting the footman—no, *Lord Trendal*—in the park, and hearing what Jess said was the truth of Blackweith Manor, he was willing to concede that those stories were false.

He would try to trust her. He wouldn't trust blindly— he'd keep a close eye on her—but he would try to give her the benefit of the doubt.

"No, nothing's the matter." He fastened the clasp and rested his hands on her bare shoulders. Her skin was so soft. He swept his thumbs back and forth over it.

He'd swear the wide expanse of her chest turned pink, making the white of the pearls more pronounced.

"The n-necklace is beautiful," she said, raising a hand to touch it. "I-I don't know what to say."

He rather enjoyed seeing his independent, strong-willed wife at a loss for words.

"Just say thank you." He desperately wanted to kiss the curve of her neck, but that would be rushing his fences. She might interpret the pearls as a bribe to get into her good graces. He stepped back.

"Thank you." She looked at her reflection again. "It fills in the bare space quite nicely." She smiled at him. "I feel less naked." And then she blushed.

He would like to see her naked, to sketch her wearing only the pearls. . . .

There was no point in following that line of thought.

He pulled another, smaller jeweler's bag out of his pocket. "And here are the matching earrings."

"Oh!" She took the bag and opened it. "They are beautiful, too." She looked up at him. "But what is the occasion?"

"Your entry into society." *Sometimes honesty really is the best policy.* "And to mark our first public appearance as husband and wife."

She stared at him. "It is, isn't it? Our first appearance as a married couple"—she pulled a face—"even though we've been married eight years."

"Yes. We didn't start off well, did we?"

She shook her head. "No, we didn't. And it was my fault."

"It was my fault, too."

She was frowning again. "Percy—"

He put his finger on her lips. "Let's not talk about Percy now." There was a limit to the subjects he could listen to. "Not before your first ball."

She nodded. "I do hope Percy's not there tonight."

He hoped so, too, but he wouldn't wager any money on Percy's absence. "You can't avoid meeting him at these things. He must go to them all, if just for the free food. He's always short of blunt."

"But I wish I could avoid him." She turned to put on the earrings. "I hate him."

Mama's handbook said there was often a very fine line between love and hate, that passion of any sort begat passion. That had been true for him, though the love and hate he'd felt for Jess had existed together in a tight, messy knot.

Would Jess's hatred of Percy turn to love? Zeus, he hoped not, but it would be best to find out now before he let her back into his life.

Hell, it was far too late for that. She'd been part of his life since she'd first arrived at the castle as a girl.

He'd thought he could keep his feelings for her locked away, that he could keep their interactions superficial and physical. He'd thought the use of her body would be enough.

He'd been a fool.

And he was a fool now. He couldn't allow himself to wallow in these maudlin thoughts. He needed an heir. He was married to Jess. If she would swear to be faithful to him until his second son was born, then that would *have* to be enough. It was the practical, sensible thing to do.

Even if it felt like it would kill him.

Jess waited to climb the stairs to Lord Palmerson's town house while a battalion of servants carried an elderly couple in bath chairs up the steps. She had her hand on Kit's arm, but it felt as if Kit himself was miles away. He'd been like this since just after he'd given her the pearl earrings. What had happened?

Yes, she'd still been angry with him when they were in their bedroom getting ready for the ball. She'd spent the day reminding herself of what the duchess had said at breakfast—that she was as guilty of listening to rumors as Kit was. But the bed was right there, a silent reminder of his absence the night before.

And then he'd been so kind. He'd complimented her and given her the beautiful pearls—she'd never had a gift so fine. He'd been friendly—more than friendly. He'd looked at her with what she would have sworn was desire—

Of course! How stupid could she be? He'd given her jewelry, hadn't he? That was the bribe men used to lure silly women into their beds.

But Kit's gift hadn't felt like a bribe, and he hadn't tried to seduce her, even though he'd made her want to be seduced. He hadn't even kissed her.

She was so confused. She hated feeling off balance and out of control.

She looked up at him. His eyes were on the commotion with the bath chairs—the elderly man must be rather deaf, because he was shouting directions so loudly Dennis could probably hear him back at Blackweith Manor—but she doubted Kit actually heard or saw anything. His profile was set, his jaw hard. He looked angry and sullen, a man forced to offer her his escort.

Damn it. Couldn't he pull himself out of his funk? He knew she was nervous. She'd told him so.

She welcomed the spurt of anger. She'd much rather feel angry than awkward.

The duchess glanced at them and frowned. "Smile, Ash. You look like you're going to a funeral."

"Your own," Jack said. Frances, standing by his side, quickly muffled a surprised giggle. He tilted his head and looked Kit up and down, while Kit glared at him. "No, on second thought, not a funeral. A murder."

"You're a blo—" Kit pressed his lips together.

Jack laughed. "You're here to calm the old cats, Ash,

not stir them into a gossiping frenzy. If you walk into the ballroom looking like that, they'll think you're planning to poison Jess and drop her body in the Thames."

Jack's eyes moved to regard her. "And frankly, Jess looks like she might do the same to you."

"Don't be absurd." Kit's expression darkened even more.

"Oh? I wouldn't say I'm being absurd. What do you think, Jess? Doesn't my brother's scowling face make you shudder?"

"Of course not." But Jack was probably right about the gossips. She forced herself to smile at Kit. "You do look as though you'd like to be somewhere else, though." She paused, and then said quietly, only for his ears, "And with someone else."

That got his attention. His gaze sharpened as if he were suddenly focusing on her instead of his black thoughts. "It's true I'd rather be somewhere else—this infernal ball will be crowded and hot and full of the worst idiots—but if I have to suffer through it, and I realize I do, I wouldn't want to be with anyone but you."

"There you are, Jess," Jack said. "You are Ash's chosen partner in hell."

"Damnation, Jack. That's not what I meant."

"Well, that's what you said."

"I did not, and you know it."

The duke turned around then. "Perhaps you two might stop squabbling before we enter the ballroom? There will be enough rude speculation without you adding to the spectacle."

Kit's jaw hardened again, but Jack laughed.

"Of course, Father," Jack said. "We will be models of deportment."

The duke snorted. "I do not ask for miracles."

"Perhaps you should," the duchess said. "The Almighty might be feeling generous." She took his arm. "Come along. They have finally managed to wrestle Lord and Lady Smittle into the house." She paused on the first step and looked back. "Do try to smile, Ash. Jack is quite right. Everyone will think you are contemplating murder."

"I am." He glared at his brother. "Jack's."

"I should like to see you try," Jack said, grinning.

They made their way up the stairs and into the ballroom without further conversation. Jess's knees were trembling so much she had to focus all her attention on walking. She certainly did not wish to trip and go sprawling on the floor. Just the thought made her tighten her hold on Kit's arm.

His hand came up to cover her fingers. "Courage," he whispered.

Yes, courage. Surely she could discover some modicum of that virtue in her breast. After all, she'd endured years and years of gossip when she'd lived at the manor. How bad could a few hours be?

Very bad.

True to her word, the duchess had got them to the ball early, but there were still quite a number of people present, all of whom stopped their conversations to stare the moment Jess was announced. It was quite remarkable, really. The steady drone cut off abruptly for a beat or two of complete silence and then started up again, louder and at an almost fevered pitch.

She would not have credited it, but in some regards it was easier to be gossiped about behind her back than to her face—well, in front of her face. She was quite certain none of those present would actually tell her what they were saying, though she could guess. She could guess very well.

"Ignore them," Kit said. He looked rather fierce again, but this time his anger was clearly directed at the ton. "They are all chattering dunderheads."

"Who can make my stay in London very unpleasant."

His jaw hardened to granite. "It doesn't matter what

they say. You are my wife, the Marchioness of Ashton, and the daughter-in-law of the Duke of Greycliffe."

If only she were his wife in more than name. If only she were his love.

"And Mama is not only the Duchess of Greycliffe, remember. She's the Duchess of Love. None of the mothers with daughters on the marriage mart dare offend her."

"Of course." But it was often difficult to trace down the authors of rumors, especially if everyone was whispering the same thing. There was safety—and anonymity—in numbers.

The duchess smiled and nodded to everyone who greeted her, but she didn't stop until she'd reached a corner with some exuberant potted palms and windows that opened onto the terrace.

"Trust Mama to find the coolest place in the ballroom," Jack said.

"I have not spent years attending these events without making note of the best spots to, ahem, enjoy the festivities." The duchess looked at Jess and Frances. "I should warn you both that Lord Palmerson's garden is exceedingly large and dark, so don't go into it without Ash or Jack at your side. Some men cannot remember their manners."

Jess flushed. The duchess made a show of addressing Frances, too, but she knew to whom Her Grace's words were really directed. She—

"Don't worry, Your Grace," Frances said. "I have no intention of going out into a garden by myself or with anyone but Jack ever again." Even though she smiled, her voice trembled.

"I should hope not!" Jack, his face devoid of humor for once, grasped Frances's hand. "Let's go see where Lady Palmerson has hidden the refreshment room. You look like you could use a glass of lemonade."

Kit watched them leave. "What was that about? Is Frances afraid of gardens?"

"No." The duchess shook her head. "Well, not precisely."

"There was a madman loose in London when we arrived," the duke said, "luring women into dark corners and slashing their throats."

"Yes, and he almost got Frances," Her Grace added, "but thanks largely to her quick thinking, he was captured."

"Thank God for that." Kit looked at Jess. "You'll be careful, won't you?"

"Of course." She had no desire to tour the garden. Since it was too dark to view the foliage, the only purpose would be to misbehave, and no matter how much Kit might think otherwise, she did not wish to do that. Unless, perhaps, she was misbehaving with him, but that wasn't going to happen tonight. "But if the man has been apprehended, he's no longer a threat."

"True, but you never know what other threats will pop up, Jess," the duchess said. "London is nothing like the country."

"And speaking of London threats . . ." the duke said.

"What? Oh, blast." The duchess swiveled her head to look in the direction the duke indicated. A determined-looking woman with graying hair was bearing down upon them. "It's Lady Dunlee. You may want to take Jess to the refreshment room, too, Ash. No need starting the evening off with London's biggest gossip."

Jess stood next to Frances, happy to have a moment's respite. She'd danced every dance, though that was likely because the duchess—or the mothers of hopeful daughters and long-suffering sons—had shooed men her way. And the men . . .

She scowled, causing a nervous-looking little fellow to

make a hundred-and-eighty-degree turn and vanish into a sea of plumed chaperones.

Many of the men who'd danced with her had acted as if she were a light-skirt, damn it, though they had enough fear of Kit's family not to be blatantly rude—which almost made things worse. They didn't say anything she could call them on; they just hinted, smirked, waggled their brows.

At least Percy had kept his distance.

"It's too bad Ellie and Ned aren't here," Frances said, "though of course it is wonderful that Ellie is increasing."

"Yes, indeed." Jess missed Ellie's quiet support, and Ned would have stood up with her without making her feel like a doxy.

Kit hadn't made her feel that way either—

No, that wasn't quite true. He hadn't treated her with disrespect, but moving in time to the music with him, touching hands, looking into his eyes—all had provoked hot, needy feelings in her breast and, er, other places.

"It's nice to sit out a set," Frances said. "I confess I find dancing tiring."

After their dance, with the ton avidly watching, Jess hadn't been able to think of a single thing to say. They'd stood there awkwardly until the duchess had come and dragged Kit away, saying people would think he didn't trust his wife to behave in society if he stayed glued to her side, looking like a thundercloud.

"The country dances can be a bit of an exertion," she said, smiling at Frances. Though she was happier when her partners were breathless; if they couldn't speak, they couldn't treat her to unpleasant innuendos and veiled insults.

Frances laughed. "Oh, I didn't mean physically tiring. It's the mental strain of concentrating that's so wearing." She smiled. "I've just learned to dance. I still have to count the steps under my breath most of the time."

Jess's eyebrows shot up. A marquis's granddaughter

who didn't know how to dance? Even Jess had mastered that skill. "Really?"

Frances nodded. "I used to think dancing was only for silly, husband-mad girls. I was wrong, of course." She laughed. "Jack teases me about it all the time."

"I hope you don't think he means anything by it, Frances." Sometimes Jack lost sight of the effect his comments had on people. "Jack likes to tease, but I can tell he's very much in love with you."

Frances's face lit up. "I know. And I am very much in love with him. Jack has changed my life, Jess. I was a lonely, angry person before I met him." She put her hand on Jess's arm. "I know he's been worried about Ash for years. I do hope you two can resolve your problems and be as happy as we are."

"Er, yes. Thank you." Jess did not wish to discuss her marriage, especially not here in Lord Palmerson's ballroom. When was Jack going to come take his wife away?

Soon. The set was ending; Jack was already looking their way, thank God.

And where was Kit?

He'd just come in from Lord Palmerson's large, dark garden.

Damn. Her stomach dropped.

Had he spent a few amorous minutes with one of the beautiful London ladies, perhaps the one whose bed he'd graced last night? Now he'd dodged behind some potted palms. What was he trying to hide?

Anger bloomed in her gut, and she looked away. She didn't want to see him flirting. She—

She saw Percy talking to a plump girl who had a mass of blonde ringlets on her head and a plethora of furbelows on her puce-colored dress. Well, it was more accurate to say the girl was talking to Percy. As Jess watched, Percy cut her off with a few words and a sharp chop of his hand and walked away.

The girl took a step after him, but stopped herself. She appeared to be on the verge of tears, poor thing. Jess glanced around. Thank God no one else seemed to be watching her. She must have realized she was in danger of making a spectacle of herself, because she looked around wildly and then darted out the closest door.

She should go after the girl and tell her how lucky she was to be free of Percy.

"Excuse me, Frances. I see someone I must speak to."

Frances nodded, but she probably hadn't heard. Her attention was all on Jack, who was making his way toward her.

Jess slipped around the perimeter of the ballroom, trying to stay out of Percy's sight. He appeared to be searching for someone, likely her. She dodged behind a potted palm, and then kept a large woman wearing an elaborate headdress between them. Finally, she got to the door the other girl had slipped through and made her own escape.

Chapter Eighteen

The truth is sometimes hard to believe.

—Venus's Love Notes

Ash stepped inside after a few moments on the terrace. Zeus, the ballroom was stuffy. He should see if Jess would like to stroll outside. Perhaps, if she was agreeable, they could wander into the vegetation.

He'd wanted to take her out into the garden earlier, after their dance, though that likely would have got all the gossips' tongues wagging. Hell, what he'd really wanted to do was find the nearest bed, rip off Jess's dress, and—

And he should have had that thought out on the dark terrace.

He ducked behind some potted palms.

Where was she now?

Ah, there with Frances, watching the dancers.

He'd never found dancing this, ah, stimulating before, but with Jess . . . She was so beautiful, so graceful, so alluring. He'd been so lust-crazed after the music had ended that he'd been as tongue-tied as a boy. He'd wanted to keep Jess from dancing with any other man.

It was a good thing Mama had come over then and dragged him away, though he did hope he'd made it look as though he'd gone willingly.

Oh, blast. Speaking of Mama, she was beckoning him now, some debutante at her side. He'd already danced with a legion of the young girls. Surely he'd earned one more dance with Jess? He would just—

He bumped into the back of another man. "Pardon me."

The man turned and smiled at him. Damnation, it was the naked footman.

No, he must call him Baron Trendal.

"Lord Ashton, I was hoping to see you again." Trendal nodded to the man he'd been talking to. "If you'll excuse me, Windon?"

"Of course." The man bowed and took himself off—after giving Ash a quick inspection and a slight, seductive smile.

No, he'd imagined that. . . .

Good God, he *hoped* he'd imagined it.

"No need to interrupt your conversation on my account, Trendal." The baron wasn't going to make an improper advance, was he?

Trendal shrugged. "Windon was becoming a bit of a bore. I was happy for the interruption." He raised a brow. "And no, you don't have to worry."

Damn it, he felt a hot flush rise up his neck. "Worry about what?" The fellow could not have read his mind.

Trendal just smiled. "I assume Jess told you about the staff at the manor?"

"Yes."

"Then I must thank you for keeping my secret."

Ash glanced around.

"Don't worry. There's no one within earshot." Trendal's mouth flattened. "I'm used to watching what I say."

"Yes, the walls have ears, do they not?" Ash, too, hated feeling as if he was always under observation. "And eyes."

He cleared his throat. "Well, I must be off. I believe my mother wishes me to dance with another wallflower."

"She has found someone else to do the honors." Trendal was now regarding him as if he were an odd species of insect. "And I have something I wish to say to you."

Hell, *he* wasn't the odd one in this equation. Ash glanced over at his mother. Yes, she'd indeed found another victim. And, as Trendal had said in Hyde Park, it would be best if they appeared to be on cordial terms.

"Very well. What is it?"

"You know," Trendal said, "I was certain I would thoroughly detest you if we ever met. I was very surprised—shocked, really—that I didn't."

There was a trap here somewhere. "I'm surprised, too. You must have comprehended that I would have gladly torn you limb from limb in that studio."

Trendal nodded. "Yes. I was actually happy to see your anger. It meant you still care for Jess."

The damn effrontery of the fellow. "Of course I care for her. Jess is my wife."

Trendal's brows snapped down. "Then why the hell did you abandon her for eight bloody years?"

"That is none of your bloody business." Ash struggled for control. Much as he'd like to rearrange the man's face, Trendal *had* stood by Jess. "I thank you for being her friend, but I do not discuss my marriage."

Trendal glared at him, and Ash glared back. Concern that the gossips might be watching them whispered through his mind, but he was too angry to heed it.

Trendal dropped his eyes first to examine his fingernails. "She loves you, you know."

Ash froze. Part of him wanted to scoff—how the hell did this Miss Molly know Jess loved him? And part of him wanted desperately to believe the man.

"I told her to go after you and settle things, but from

what I've observed tonight, nothing at all has been settled." Trendal looked back at Ash. "Have you seen her sketchbook?"

"Sketchbook? No." So Jess had shown the book to this fellow, but she wouldn't let him look at it?

Hurt mixed with his anger. He'd like very much to hit something. Perhaps Trendal. He clenched his fists. But not in Palmerson's ballroom in front of all the ton.

He'd give Trendal credit; the man never flinched, though he was clearly aware Ash wanted to pummel him.

"No, she didn't show it to me, but I suspect you should see it. Ask her to let you." Trendal inclined his head. "And now I hesitate to risk taking that flush hit you so wish to give me—which would delight the gossips and make Lady Palmerson's ball the talk of the Season—but I feel I should tell you Sir Percy has left the room—"

"I don't care where that blackguard goes."

"—through the same door Jess used just a few minutes ago."

"Bloody hell." So Jess was trysting with Percy again. He should let her go.

No, this was his chance to put an end to his foolish hopes once and for all. Jess didn't love him; she didn't even respect him enough to honor her written promise.

"If you'll excuse me, Trendal?"

Trendal stepped back. "Do try not to be a complete idiot, Ashton."

As soon as Jess opened the door to the room set aside for women to repair their flounces and attend to other matters of a personal nature, she heard sobbing. Damnation. She wanted to speak to the girl but she didn't relish dealing with a female watering pot.

Jess looked around. The sobber must be hidden behind

the privacy screen or one of the high-backed chairs. She flinched as the woman let out a particularly piercing wail. Anyone passing in the corridor might have heard that. She closed the door firmly behind her.

Was no one with the girl? She listened for the murmur of another voice offering words of comfort or at least a warning that she should try to muffle her misery.

Nothing. Only the deep wracking sobs.

The girl had to be the one she'd seen with Percy, but that blackguard certainly didn't deserve such tears; instead, whoever it was should be capering about with joy at being quit of him.

Jess cleared her throat, but got no response. She tried again. "Pardon me, but are you all right?"

She heard a gasp, and the crying stopped abruptly. The girl didn't show herself, but Jess thought she'd seen a flash of puce-colored fabric by the wing chair across the room. She headed in that direction.

"I'm f-fine. Go away."

The "away" stretched out into a wail followed by a hiccupped sob and then a low moan. Clearly she was *not* fine.

"Shall I get your mother?"

"No!" Panic vibrated in her suddenly shrill voice. "Good God, do not get Mama, I beg of you. That would be disastrous. She'd drag me home at once and make me marry old Mr. Wattles. He's already gone through three wives. I would be his fourth."

Another torrent of sobbing ensued.

Clearly this was not the time to point out Jess could add three plus one to get four.

"Then let me sit with you. I am Lady Ashton—"

"What?!" The girl jumped out of her chair and turned to glare at Jess. She looked like a deranged grape.

"You *jezebel!* Why did you have to come to London now?" Her bosom heaved; she dashed tears from her eyes.

"Why couldn't you have stayed hidden in the country for even one more week? Ohhh, I *hate* you."

Jess could only gawp. Deranged indeed. The poor girl. It was a wonder her relatives let her go about in society.

And then the girl slapped her hands over her face and started sobbing again. "I'm sorry. I shouldn't have said that. I'm just so . . . so . . ."

"Miss . . ." What was her name?

"Wharton."

"Miss Whar—" Oh, dear, did she hear voices in the corridor?

Miss Wharton must have heard them, too. Her entire body jerked. "Don't let them in. I can't . . . they'll see . . ."

Jess did the only thing she could think of. She ran to the door and leaned against it.

The doorknob rattled, and then the door started to open.

She dug in her heels and pushed back, gesturing to Miss Wharton to come help—they'd have better luck keeping the door shut if they used both their weights.

And they'd better keep it shut. It would look very odd indeed if they were discovered trying to prevent women from coming into the retiring room. She had a sudden memory of Charlie and Ralph darting, giggling, into the large linen closet at the manor.

Good God! People would begin to think she had unusual proclivities, especially given the peculiar state of her marriage.

Miss Wharton hurried over to add her considerable bulk to the effort.

"Something's wrong, Melinda," one of the women in the corridor said. "I thought the door started to open, but now I can't get it to budge."

"Let me try, Clarissa."

Miss Wharton turned white as a sheet. Jess elbowed her

and gave her a pointed look. This was no time to swoon, though at least if she went down, she'd block the door.

Miss Wharton nodded and pushed back harder.

"You're right," Melinda said. "I can't get it to give an inch."

"What could Lady Palmerson be thinking to lock the door to the ladies' retiring room during a ball?" That was Clarissa. "I need to piss in the worst way."

Miss Wharton made a strangled sound, which she quickly muffled.

"What was that?" Melinda asked.

"What do you mean, what was that?" Clarissa sounded very out of sorts and perhaps a touch desperate.

"I thought I heard a noise coming from that room."

Something thudded against the door, as if one of the women had thrown her weight against it. Jess was very glad she and Miss Wharton were working together. The door didn't move.

"I don't know how anyone could have got in there," Clarissa said. "Come on. Let's find Lady Palmerson before I need to go so badly I can't walk."

The women retreated.

"Oh, dear Lord." Miss Wharton was back to moaning. "I am ruined. I may as well let Mama take me home now and tell Mr. Wattles we will set the date."

"What do you mean? Who were those women?"

"You don't know?"

"I wouldn't have asked if I knew, would I?" Jess was beginning to lose patience with the girl.

"Clarissa," Miss Wharton said in the voice of doom, "is Lady Dunlee, the biggest gossip in London, and Melinda is Mrs. Fallwell, her bosom friend and London's second biggest gossip."

"Oh, I see." That *was* bad. "Then we had better settle your problem and leave as quickly as possible." Jess kept her voice down. They should stay pressed to the door in case someone else came along. "Why do you hate me? We've never met."

Wait, she had heard the girl's name before. "Oh, that's right. You're the woman the duchess is trying to match with Percy."

Miss Wharton turned her head to look at her gloomily. Apparently she'd spent her anger. "Yes. And you've gone and spoiled everything."

"How in the world have I done that?"

"Percy was just about to pop the question, and now all he can think and talk about is you. He's in love with you." And she started to cry again.

"Miss Wharton, please. Get a hold of yourself. We don't have much time. Lady Dunlee and Mrs. Fallwell might be back with Lady Palmerson at any moment."

Miss Wharton swallowed two or three times, but finally managed to stop the waterworks. "He said he's loved you since you were children, and you broke his heart."

"Gammon! If he truly believes that, he's a bedlamite. I no more broke his heart than Lady Dunlee broke this very solid door. He's using me as an excuse to avoid meeting you at the altar." Typical behavior for Percy, but she wouldn't say that. The girl looked to be sincerely attached to the worm. "I'm sorry."

Miss Wharton shook her head. "No, he really does love you."

How to explain her error without going into the gory details of that hideous afternoon in the Greycliffe studio? "Miss Wharton, I promise you, Percy could have married me if he'd wanted to. He was in a position to propose, and he declined to do so most emphatically."

Miss Wharton stared at her. "And I promise you he loves you." She shrugged and looked away. "It's almost an obsession. Lady Ophelia Upton, his longtime female companion, told me it's why she broke off her, er, connection with him."

Good God. If Percy loved her, he had a very odd way of showing it.

No, he *couldn't* love her. The notion was absurd. But Miss Wharton clearly believed that he did. "Even if he does love me, Miss Wharton, it makes no difference. I'm married."

Miss Wharton nodded. "And he hates Lord Ashton with a passion."

Ohhh, if Percy were in the room right now, she'd bash the chamber pot over his head.

"Do you love Percy?" Miss Wharton asked.

But first she'd use the chamber pot. Just thinking about Percy and his machinations made her stomach heave.

"Of course not. I love my husband." Fool that she was.

"But you've been estranged. Percy says Lord Ashton is going to divorce you."

"Percy knows nothing about my marriage, but even if Lord Ashton and I part ways, I would never *ever* have anything to do with Percy."

Miss Wharton looked extremely dubious.

"More to the point, do *you* love Percy?"

Miss Wharton nodded decisively. "Yes, I do. I'll admit at first I pursued him because I needed a husband, and I couldn't get Lord Ned or Lord Jack to propose."

Oh, dear. Hopefully Jess's shock and, well, amusement didn't show on her face. Miss Wharton didn't strike her as the type of girl who would appeal to Ned or Jack.

"But now I really do care for him."

"You shouldn't. You must see he's a nasty individual." The words were out before Jess could swallow them. It was none of her concern what Miss Wharton did, but still, she couldn't bear to think the woman would throw her life away on such a scoundrel.

Miss Wharton was shaking her head. "But don't you see? He's not nasty with me. He's kind and gentle."

"Percy?" If Miss Wharton could make Percy behave in a fashion even approaching kind or gentle, she was a magician.

"Yes. Oh, I know he's got a deep streak of anger, but he's never been angry with me . . . well, except just now in the ballroom. He was a bit short with me then. But that was only because you'd reentered his life. If it weren't for you . . ." Miss Wharton looked Jess in the eye. "If you will only stand aside, Lady Ashton, I think Percy will marry me. And I'm certain I can make him happy."

Jess felt a momentary urge to scream. "Miss Wharton, I cannot step aside because I've never been in the way. I'm already wed, and I want absolutely nothing to do with Percy. He's a complete and utter fool if he doesn't marry you, and I'd be delighted to tell him so." It was about time someone tried to force some sense into Percy's hard little brain.

"Would you?" Miss Wharton looked hopeful—but then she sighed and her shoulders drooped. "No, you can't. He won't listen."

Damn Percy. It was bad enough that he'd been making her and Kit's lives miserable all these years, but to play with Miss Wharton's affections, especially when he must know she needed a husband desperately, was unconscionable.

"He'd better listen, because I'm going to find him right now and tell him exactly that." She stepped away from the door and jerked it open.

Miss Wharton grabbed her arm. "Oh, no, please, Lady Ashton. Only consider! At Lady Palmerson's ball? Think of the scandal if you are discovered. I'm not worth that."

Jess shook off Miss Wharton's hold and stepped into the corridor. "You *are* worth it, Miss Wharton, but this is not only about you—or even largely about you. Percy has been a thorn in my side forever. He has much to answer for, and I believe the time has come for him to do so."

Miss Wharton followed, wringing her hands. "But perhaps you should wait until tomorrow? Give yourself a chance to sleep on it?"

"I have 'slept on it' for far too many nights. I don't intend to sleep again until I've confronted the blackguard." But where to find the worm? She'd haul him off the ballroom floor if she had to, but she would rather not, not so much because of the scandal but because someone might try to stop her.

"Oh, no, Lady Ashton. Percy isn't a blackguard, really he isn't. He just needs someone who understands him. His parents were horrible to him"—Miss Wharton flushed—"much as mine are to me."

Jess listened with only half an ear as she headed back toward the ballroom—

Wait a minute. Had she seen motion up ahead? Yes.

"Well, look who's here. Were you lurking in the shadows for me, Percy?"

Percy stepped out of an alcove he'd shared with the statue of some naked Greek god. "Of course, my dear. I began to think you were avoiding me."

"Well, I'm finished avoiding you now."

Miss Wharton inserted herself between them. "Percy, let's return to the ballroom."

Percy, the snake, brushed Miss Wharton aside. "No, Isabelle, you go back. I need to chat with Lady Ashton."

Miss Wharton turned to her. "Lady Ashton, will you return to the ballroom with me?" She looked at Percy and then back at Jess. "Please?"

"No, I'm sorry. As Percy says, he and I need to chat." Jess gestured to the open door behind her. "Shall we have our little discussion in a room or in the corridor?"

"Oh, a room, of course." Percy bowed and swept his hand forward, indicating Jess should precede him.

"But that's the ladies' retiring room." Miss Wharton's voice squeaked with shock.

Jess ignored her. The room could be Lady Palmerson's bedchamber for all she cared. She strode back into it as Miss Wharton hurried off with a moan of distress.

Percy closed the door behind him. "And now, Jess—"

"And now, Percy, we settle this once and for all." She wished she could challenge the snake to a duel, but instead of pistols or swords she'd have to make do with words.

"So dramatic." He sauntered farther into the room and picked a fat cherub off a table. He turned it over in his hands. "We'd best not dally, though." He looked over his shoulder at her. "I suspect Isabelle has gone to fetch Ash."

Wonderful. She certainly didn't need Kit finding her alone with Percy again.

"And Lady Dunlee needs to pee," she said. "This *is* the ladies' retiring room." How long had it been since Lady Dunlee and Mrs. Fallwell had pushed on the door? She and Percy likely had only a handful of minutes until they were interrupted. Well, it wouldn't take long to say what she needed to.

He snorted. "That's what I like about you, Jess. You've never strayed far from your roots."

"And what the hell is that supposed to mean?"

"Oh, come, you know exactly what it means. You're an Irish groom's daughter, crude and coarse and lower than even an English servant."

Yes, that was what she'd thought he'd meant. And Miss Wharton believed Percy loved her? If he did, it was a very odd sort of love.

"If I'm so below you, Percy, why did you play with me when we were children? Why did you steal kisses when I was a girl? And why did you try to . . . to do what you did in the Greycliffe studio?"

He laughed brittlely and put the angel figurine down.

"You are naive, aren't you, Jess? A child will play with anyone. And a man . . . I don't expect my whores to come from the ton. Any reasonably clean female will do. You offered. Why would I turn down a bit of sport?" His eyes looked rather bleak, very much at odds with his words. "You've got a lovely cun—"

"Stop!" She fisted her hands to keep her fingers from wrapping around his throat. How could he say such things? "I did *not* offer. You were the one who started what happened that day."

He flushed and shrugged. "Perhaps I did make the first move. I'd been drinking, after all, and you tempted me." His lip curled up. "You didn't try to stop me."

"Because I thought you meant marriage!"

An odd, almost confused expression flashed through Percy's eyes, but he shook it off and smirked. "Marriage? To you? The heir to a baronetcy doesn't marry an Irish servant."

"The heir to a duchy did." The words were out before she could stop them. But Kit *had* married her, even though she was exactly what Percy said she was.

Percy scowled. "He wasn't supposed to. I thought for certain he was such a bloody prig, he'd wash his hands of you." His voice grew harsher. "But no, the saintly Marquis of Ashton couldn't let a damsel in distress go unrescued."

He took a deep breath, clearly struggling to regain control. "Ah, well, it turned out far better than I'd planned. I'd no idea I'd devised the perfect way to torture Ash for years. It's been quite amusing watching him suffer."

Percy was making no sense. "Why did you want to hurt Ash?"

His lip curled. "You didn't have the *pleasure* of knowing my mother. She was forever holding Ash up to me as the prime example of manly perfection—and a measure of what a disappointment I was." His face twisted. "I don't think she ever managed to speak a sentence to me that didn't have 'Lord Ashton' in it."

Jess felt a flicker of sympathy, which she quashed. "That wasn't Ash's fault."

Percy went on as if she hadn't spoken. "Mother's greatest dream was for Ash to marry Cicely, but he married you instead. Poor Mother. She was inconsolable, until she realized she could get Ned to take Cicely. Then as long as you and Ash never reconciled, the title would come to Ned or to his son, and Mama would no longer be just the wife of a baronet. She'd be the mother-in-law and grandmother of a duke." His voice broke. "And then Cicely died with the damn baby."

Perhaps Percy *had* loved someone other than himself.

"My family's not had much luck with the Valentines." He smiled unpleasantly. "But I got back at them, didn't I? I kept the heir childless and separated from his one true love." He said the last three words in a sarcastic, saccharine tone, but Jess barely noticed it.

"*What?!* Are you daft?" She felt an odd spurt of panic. "Ash didn't—doesn't—love me."

Percy snorted. "Yes, he does. You were the only one who never saw it."

"But he never—"

"What? He never flirted with you or stole a kiss behind the stables? Of course he didn't. He was the bloody, saintly Marquis of Ashton, someday to be the Duke of Greycliffe. He couldn't go around stealing kisses." Percy almost snarled. "God, how Mother held that over my head." His voice grew high and priggish. "'Lord Ashton would never do that. Lord Ashton knows the proper way to go on.' Bah!"

"You're lying." This was just another of Percy's many attempts to hurt her.

But . . .

If she'd acted differently, could she really have had Kit's love all these years?

No. She could *not* believe Percy.

"I saw how he looked at you," Percy said. "Everyone did. The man was drowning in desire."

"Damn you, Percy." Before she knew it, she'd come up to him so they were only inches apart. She wanted to slap him or grab him around the neck and squeeze, but she gripped her skirts to keep her hands out of mischief.

He laughed and stepped back a pace. "Did you truly not realize you could thank me for all the outrageous rumors about your whoring—and Ash's raking?"

Oh, damn. Her stomach suddenly felt like it was full of lead. She pressed her fingers into her forehead. The rumors . . . Percy *must* be lying. "But the stories were in the newspapers."

"Jess, it doesn't take any effort at all to get gossip about the Marquis of Ashton into the papers. He's the ton's favorite topic—the Duchess of Love's loveless son and heir to the duchy." Percy shrugged. "As far as I know, your charming husband is as virginal as a blushing young maiden."

Oh, God! Had she unwittingly been Percy's marionette all these years? "I can't believe Miss Wharton thinks you love me."

She thought she saw pain in Percy's eyes before he looked away.

"I do love you, Jess." It sounded as if the words were being dragged out of him. "I always have, even though you were beneath me." He tried to laugh, but didn't quite succeed. "I was desperate for you, and did you even notice? No. Oh, no. You were too busy panting after the bloody marquis. God, I hate him."

Her hands tightened into fists. She wanted to kick him, to pummel him, to spit on him—

But this was her fault, too, wasn't it? She was the one who had believed the lies.

If they were lies. Kit hadn't been in her bed for most of last night, and she'd seen him come in from the dark, scandalous garden just this evening.

No, clearly Percy was doing what he did best: twisting things to confuse her. He simply wanted to extend his torturous hold over her.

Well, she hadn't got Percy here to discuss ancient history. She was here to help Miss Wharton.

"Percy." She took a deep breath and addressed his back. "Percy, you don't love me."

She held up her hand as he turned and opened his mouth to speak. "But even if you do, I do not love you. In fact, I detest you. I hate what you did to me and what you did to Ash." She took another deep breath. No, this was not about her, it was about Miss Wharton. "But that's the past. We can't change it. We *can* change the future. I don't love you, but Miss Wharton, poor girl, does."

He shrugged and turned away from her again. "Oh, well, poor Isabelle. She needs a husband, you know."

Jess grabbed Percy's arm and jerked him around. She poked him in the chest. "You're a bloody idiot, Percy, if you let Miss Wharton get away, not that you're good enough for her. But I suspect she's your only hope of pulling yourself out of your sick fascination with me and Ash."

He frowned. "I—" And then something changed in his eyes, and he suddenly pulled her into his arms.

What? Oh, God, now she heard it, too—the door opening.

Bloody hell! She was not going to let this happen again.

Chapter Nineteen

Men have very thick skulls.

—Venus's Love Notes

Blast it, one person after another waylaid him as he tried to leave the ballroom. Ash struggled to be polite. He shouldn't stir up the gossips more than they undoubtedly were: they must have noticed he was headed for the same door Percy had followed Jess through moments earlier.

He finally got free of Viscount Trent, Frances's cousin and one of Jack's friends, and took the last few steps to the door. Thank God! He slipped through—and almost collided with Miss Wharton.

"Oh, Lord Ashton!" She grabbed his sleeve. "Come quick. Lady Ashton is going to murder Percy."

He choked back a surprised laugh. "Pardon me?"

She tugged, clearly beside herself. "Your wife is going to kill Percy if you don't come now and stop her."

He sniffed. He didn't smell alcohol, but intoxication was the only explanation he could imagine for Miss Wharton's bizarre behavior.

"Oh, why won't you come?" She tugged again. "There is not a moment to lose."

Clearly it was best to humor her, so he allowed her to drag him down the corridor. "Where are they?"

"In the ladies' retiring room."

He choked back another laugh.

"And Lady Dunlee needs to use the chamber pot and has gone in search of Lady Palmerson, so Percy is sure to be discovered at any moment if your wife doesn't kill him first." She took a deep breath. "Or even if she does, I suppose, but then there will be nothing to be done about it." She looked back at him. "Though I imagine you would not care for Lady Dunlee to find Lady Ashton standing over Percy's lifeless body."

"Er, quite right." Had he somehow stepped into Bedlam? Miss Wharton had never appeared mad before, just annoying. "Miss Wharton, please compose yourself. I'm sure all will be well."

She gave him an exasperated look as if he were the bedlamite and stopped in front of a closed door. "They are in there."

Apparently it fell to him to open the door, though Miss Wharton looked quite capable of performing that task herself.

He took a deep breath. He was very much afraid of what he would find, and it would not be a dead body. But Miss Wharton was correct in that Lady Dunlee would be extremely scandalized should she enter the room now and see Jess in Percy's close embrace. He did not wish to give the ton even more delightfully shocking tidbits to feast on.

He would deal with the problem and then take Jess back to Blackweith Manor and quietly—or as quietly as possible—begin divorce proceedings.

He pushed open the door.

Oh, God. Even though he'd expected to see Percy's arms around Jess, the sight still hurt, like a lance shoved through his eyes. At least they weren't naked on the ground like last time. He would—

"Take *that,* you bloody blackguard."

Zeus! Jess had just driven her knee into Percy's groin.

Ash flinched in sympathy as Percy yelped and released her. And then as Percy doubled over, Jess's fist came up to hit him in the nose.

The man fell to the ground, blood everywhere. Jess pulled back her foot as if she was going to kick him for good measure.

Perhaps Miss Wharton's concern for Percy's life was not unwarranted. "Jess, that's enough. It's not sporting to hit a man when he's down."

She glared at Ash as Miss Wharton ran to Percy's side. "He's an Evil. Disgusting. Snake." She had to take a breath between each word, she was so angry.

"Oh, look what you've done." Miss Wharton started crying as she knelt next to Percy, wrapped her arms around him, and held him close, blood and all. "You've broken his nose."

"I hope I have."

Ash put a comforting—and restraining—arm around Jess. If Ned couldn't break Percy's nose—and he'd tried at the house party—it was very unlikely Jess could. No, he'd wager his nose wasn't the part of Percy's body that was paining him the most. "Noses tend to bleed a lot." Percy's blood was now all over Miss Wharton's bodice. "*Is* your nose broken, Percy?"

Ash tried to sound solicitous. He should be furious—Percy had clearly been taking unwelcome liberties with his wife—but he was actually having a hard time controlling his laughter. This was assuming all the aspects of a farce.

Percy glared at him over his handkerchief. "I don't think so."

"Oh, thank God for that," Miss Wharton said. "You poor, poor man." She glared at Jess. "Why did you hit him?"

Ash felt Jess, who'd relaxed slightly, stiffen again. He kept his arm around her waist. The last thing they needed was for Jess and Miss Wharton to pull caps.

"Because he was mauling me about, as I'm sure you saw." Jess transferred her attention to Percy. "That had better be the last time you try something like that, sirrah. You should be ashamed of yourself."

Percy flushed and, surprisingly, did appear mortified for once.

Miss Wharton, however, looked furious and started to get to her feet as if she intended to try out her pugilistic skills on Jess. "Don't you talk to Percy that way."

Percy put his hand on Miss Wharton's arm and stopped her. "She's right, Isabelle. What I did wasn't honorable." He sighed and looked from Jess to Ash. "What I've done for the last eight years hasn't been honorable. I've known that for a while, but I couldn't stop myself." He looked at Miss Wharton again. "Until you showed me the way, Isabelle." He grimaced. "And Jess knocked some sense into me."

"Oh, Percy." Miss Wharton sank back down by his side and put her head on his shoulder.

Egad, was that a look of tenderness that flitted across Percy's face?

"Well, I hope this means you will leave me and Ash alone from now on," Jess said, "and busy yourself about your own affairs."

Percy nodded as Miss Wharton took his bloody handkerchief and handed him her own.

"You know, I did love you, Jess. Desperately." Percy glanced at Ash. "And I hated you."

Jess drew in her breath as if she planned to give Percy another piece of her mind, but Ash tightened his grip on her, hoping she'd get the hint. She glared at him, but held her tongue. There really was no point in ravaging Percy further.

"Why the hell did you hate me?" He fished his handkerchief out of his pocket and gave it to Percy. Miss Wharton's frilly bit of cloth was already soaked through.

Percy dabbed at his nose and winced. "My mother constantly dangled you in front of me as an example of perfection."

"Good God. I'm sorry." That *was* revolting.

Percy flushed. "And I suppose I was envious, too. You had everything—money, prestige, a happy family, Jess. And neither you nor your brothers ever liked me."

Ash was tempted to point out that they hadn't liked Percy because he'd always been a royal pain in the arse, but if Jess could restrain herself, he could, too.

"You've had a very hard time of it, Percy," Miss Wharton said, patting him on the arm. "It's no wonder you lost your way and did things you wish you hadn't."

Surely the woman was joking?

Apparently not. She looked completely serious—and completely enamored.

"I know you don't want my advice, Percy," Ash said, "but you really are a fool if you don't ask Miss Wharton to marry you at once, before she regains her good sense."

"Oh, Lord Ashton, how can you say that? Any woman would be happy to marry Percy." Miss Wharton paused, likely realizing she'd overstated the case. "Well, any woman who understands him like I do."

A miracle occurred: a sliver of good sense wormed its way into Percy's brain box. His cravat covered in blood, Ash's handkerchief pressed to his nose, Percy turned to Miss Wharton.

"Isabelle, Ash is correct. I know I'm not much of a prize, and obviously I'm the greatest cods-head in London, if not in all of Britain, but I do sincerely care for you. You are a pearl of great price and would be very wise to decline my offer, but"—he shifted position so he was on one knee—"will you make me the happiest of men?"

Miss Wharton burst into tears again. "Oh, of course I will, Percy." She flung her arms around his neck.

"What in the world is going on here?"

Oh, blast. Ash turned to see Lady Palmerson standing in the doorway, Lady Dunlee and Mrs. Fallwell—and Mama—behind her.

"Good evening, ladies." Clearly, he was in the best position to attempt to gloss over the situation. "I'm sorry to say Sir Percy got confused and stumbled into this room by accident."

"Confused?" Lady Dunlee said, her sharp eyes examining every detail of the scene.

Ash cleared his throat. Percy deserved to suffer a bit; after all, the problem was mostly of his making. "I believe he might have had a few too many glasses of champagne."

Percy moaned convincingly.

"Good heavens, is that blood?" Lady Palmerson's eyes widened as she examined Percy more closely, and then she looked a little faint, but whether that was from the sight of Percy's blood or the worry that he might have dripped some of it on her carpet, Ash couldn't say.

"Yes, I'm afraid it is. As you might imagine, Percy was quite taken aback when he realized his error. He beat a hasty retreat, but unfortunately in doing so he stumbled and hit his nose." Ash smiled, hoping that would do.

Of course it wouldn't.

"And what are you doing here, Lord Ashton?" Lady Dunlee sniffed as if she could smell a lie—or perhaps just a whiff of alcohol. "Have you also imbibed too freely?"

"No indeed. When Sir Percy was injured, Lady Ashton naturally sent Miss Wharton to get me while she helped Percy."

Lady Dunlee raised a doubting eyebrow.

Mama smiled. "It looks more as if Miss Wharton is assisting Percy."

"Yes." Jess nodded. "And the good news is—" She put her hand over her mouth. Ash could see the wicked gleam in her eyes as she looked at Percy. "Oh, I suppose I shouldn't say."

"Say what?" Mrs. Fallwell pushed past Lady Dunlee, bumping into Lady Palmerson in her eagerness to hear a new bit of gossip.

Lady Palmerson gave her an annoyed look and then turned to Percy. "Yes, Sir Percy, what *is* this good news?"

Percy had by this time managed to get to his feet, though he still had Ash's handkerchief pressed to his nose. He took Miss Wharton's hand and pulled her up to stand beside him. "The news is that Miss Wharton has graciously accepted my offer of marriage, pending her father's consent, of course."

"Oh." Mrs. Fallwell looked at Lady Dunlee. Clearly the two ladies had been hoping for something more exciting.

"That's wonderful." Mama clapped her hands and brushed past the other ladies to hug Miss Wharton. "I knew you two would be perfect for each other."

Of course Mama was delighted. She'd just been responsible for another society match.

She put her hand on Percy's arm. "I think it would be best if you spoke to Miss Wharton's father tomorrow, don't you, Percy? Once you have, er, cleaned up a bit."

Percy bowed. "You are correct as always, Your Grace." He lifted Miss Wharton's hand and kissed it—and all the women in the room sighed, except Jess, of course. "I shall call upon your father in the morning, if that will suit?"

"Oh, yes," Miss Wharton said. "Papa will be delighted. He wants to get rid of me as soon as may be."

Mama cringed slightly and then smiled. "Percy, I imagine it would be best if you avoided the other guests. Lady Palmerson, could you show Sir Percy how he might depart unobtrusively?"

"Of course, Your Grace. Come right this way, Sir Percy."

Percy nodded farewell to Miss Wharton and then meekly followed Lady Palmerson out of the room.

"And now, Miss Wharton," Mama said, turning back to her, "perhaps you and I should go have a word with your mother."

"Oh, yes, Your Grace, that would be splendid." Miss Wharton was so happy her face almost glowed. "My mother will be so dazzled by your attention, you could tell her I was going to swim to the Colonies and she would agree it was an excellent notion."

Mama laughed. "Well, I do hope being married to Percy will be somewhat less arduous than paddling across the ocean." She took Miss Wharton's arm and raised her brows at Ash.

"I think Lady Ashton and I have had enough excitement for one evening, Your Grace. I believe we'll return to Greycliffe House." He turned to Jess. "Does that meet with your approval, my dear?"

Jess nodded, suddenly looking tired and a little nervous. "Yes, I would like to go home." She looked at Mama. "That is, if you don't object, Your Grace."

"Of course I don't object." Mama grinned, a bit too broadly in his opinion. "There will be many more balls for you to attend. I'll see you in the morning." She chuckled. "And we should definitely be off so poor Lady Dunlee and Mrs. Fallwell can put this room to the use Lady Palmerson intended."

Lady Dunlee blushed.

Lady Fallwell started inching toward the door. "I think perhaps I'll just return to the ballro—oh!"

Lady Dunlee's gloved fingers had wrapped themselves around Mrs. Fallwell's wrist in what looked to be an unbreakable grip.

"Oh, no, my dear Mrs. Fallwell. I must insist you keep me company."

"Ah, er . . ."

Mama smiled and ushered Miss Wharton out of the room. Ash followed closely behind with Jess; he had absolutely no desire to spend another minute with those two gossips.

Once they were out of the ladies' earshot, Mama chuckled. "Lady Dunlee is not about to let Melinda Fallwell get before her with a juicy bit of gossip."

She frowned slightly and touched Miss Wharton's arm. "A word of advice, my dear. I'm quite certain both ladies suspect that something more interesting than just your betrothal happened in that room. If anything did, it would be best not to mention it."

"Yes, Your Grace." Miss Wharton looked anxiously at Jess.

"I have nothing to say, except to give you my best wishes on your betrothal, Miss Wharton."

"Yes, indeed." Ash bowed. "Let me add my very sincere felicitations. I do hope Percy turns out to be an adequate husband."

Miss Wharton grinned. "Oh, I think he will, Lord Ashton. And he will certainly be leagues better than old Mr. Wattles."

Hell, she'd done it again—dropped an embarrassing mess in Kit's lap.

"It would help if you'd smile," Kit murmured as they reentered the ballroom, his hand warm on Jess's where it rested on his sleeve.

She forced her lips to curve up, but judging by the startled look the woman in the pink turban gave them, the expression didn't look particularly pleasant.

Jess didn't feel pleasant. It didn't matter that Lady

Dunlee and Mrs. Fallwell might not be able to guess exactly what had happened in the ladies' retiring room. If they just recounted what they'd seen, the ton would be in alt. Society loved to speculate about her and Kit and Percy. By the end of the ball, there might be a hundred stories circulating, one more salacious than the next.

At least she wouldn't be around to hear them. She and Kit were making their way to the front door and freedom.

Freedom . . . ha! Tomorrow Kit would take her back to exile at the manor—or, worse, send her with a servant—and begin divorce proceedings.

"Jess, you do an excellent impression of a thundercloud, but it really would help matters if you could stop. I believe you've just given poor Lady Cartley heart palpitations."

She looked in the direction he indicated. A plump woman in a blindingly yellow gown was pressing her hand to her breast—and whispering behind her fan to a sour-looking little man.

"You are also tilling society's soil so that any seeds of gossip Lady Dunlee and Mrs. Fallwell sow will flourish."

Jess wouldn't be in London to suffer the harvest, but that didn't mean she relished the idea of people spreading tales about her. However, it was deuced difficult to smile when one was contemplating a long life of loveless solitude, especially as she didn't have the acting skills honed by years of exposure to the ton. . . .

Wait a minute—what was she thinking? She'd just faced down Percy, something she'd wanted to do for eight years. She'd bloodied his damn nose. She wasn't about to creep and crawl across the ballroom like a frightened mouse.

"Let the blasted gossips say what they will. I don't care. If I wish to look like a thundercloud, I shall."

She wasn't about to creep and crawl around Kit, either.

She'd promised herself even before she'd done battle with Percy that she would settle a few issues with him tonight.

He laughed. "Yes, my lady. Whatever you say."

"Don't try to act meek, my lord."

His brows shot up, but his eyes were smiling. "I assure you, my dear wife, I am not acting. If poor Percy is any indication, you have a punishing right."

She grinned at him. "Oh, I suspect it was my first blow that really did the trick." Hopefully she hadn't done any permanent damage. Miss Wharton might like to have children.

"I suspect so, too." His eyes were still laughing, but there was an odd warmth in them as well. "I beg you not to resort to such tactics with me. A simple word will suffice to get my attention if you wish me to stop whatever I'm doing."

Ah . . . and what was he expecting to be doing that would require her to ask him to stop—or that would bring him in range of her knee, for that matter?

A little shiver of anticipation snaked up her spine—

No. They had much to discuss before she could allow anything of that nature to occur, if that was indeed the sort of activity he was hinting at.

"Lady Ashton, how pleasant to see you."

She turned to find Roger at her elbow. "Roge—"

Roger's eyebrows rose in warning at the same time Kit's fingers tightened on her hand. She wasn't a complete dunderhead—she got the message. "*Lord Trendal*. Lord Ashton and I are on the point of leaving. I'm sorry we didn't have the opportunity to speak earlier." Frankly, she'd thought Roger had been avoiding her.

"I won't keep you. I just wished to say I had the opportunity to chat with Lord Ashton earlier. He tells me you haven't shown him your sketchbook." Roger smiled. "You should share it with him, you know."

"Oh, I don't think so." She'd never shown that book to anyone. It included a few sketches of the Blackweith servants and the local shopkeepers and farm laborers and even the local gentry. She'd never been that interested in drawing landscapes. But most of the sketches were of Kit. "The drawings are very rough."

"I thought they conveyed uncommon emotion."

Kit stiffened. "And I thought you said just earlier this evening that Lady Ashton hadn't shown you those drawings, Trendal."

"I didn't show them to him." Her eyes narrowed. "You've never seen those sketches."

Roger grinned. "Actually I have. I went to fetch you one day from the studio a year or so ago. You weren't there, but the sketchbook was."

"And you opened it?" God! She felt betrayed.

"Oh, no. I never touched it. You'd left it open on your easel. I only looked at what was in plain sight."

All right, yes. It was possible she'd done that.

Roger turned his attention to Kit. "You *must* see these drawings, Lord Ashton. I believe they are some of your wife's best work."

"I'd like to see them." Kit looked down at her. "Perhaps you will show them to me tonight, Lady Ashton?"

"Perhaps." Or perhaps not. Perhaps she would throw the damn sketchbook in the fire as she should have done when she'd been packing to leave the manor. "I thought you wished to depart, my lord."

Roger, the blackguard, laughed. "Eager to be alone with your husband, are you, Lady Ashton?"

"No." Her knee twitched, begging to repeat its performance from the ladies' retiring room. "I seem to have suddenly taken ill." She smiled with gritted teeth. "Apparently something—or someone—in the vicinity puts me out of humor."

He laid a dramatic hand on his chest. "I'm cut to the quick, my dear Lady Ashton."

She snorted. "I don't believe that for one moment." She poked him in the waistcoat. "You are far too busy about other people's business, my lord."

Roger captured her hand and cradled it against his chest. "In this case, yes, I am, and I shan't even apologize. As long as my efforts bring about the desired results, I'm happy."

She jerked her hand free. "Ha! Results desired by whom?"

He smiled and turned to Kit. "Good luck, Ashton. I'm afraid she really will cut off her nose to spite her face if you let her."

"Why you—"

Kit covered her fist before she could swing it at Roger's face. "Perhaps it would have been wiser not to have said that, Trendal."

Roger grinned. "I am just getting her blood pumping. I've often found that one sort of passion leads to another." He waggled his blasted eyebrows.

Ohhh, she was going to stomp on his dancing slippers, not that that would do much damage, unfortunately.

"I do believe you are making things worse." Kit kept a very firm hold on her. "Come along, my dear. You can vent your spleen on me in the privacy of the carriage."

She treated Roger to her nastiest look as she spoke to Kit. "There is hardly time for that. As I remember it's a very short ride."

Kit inclined his head. "Then you can flay me with your tongue once we are safely inside Greycliffe House."

"Ah, now *that* sounds like fun." Roger winked. "A tongue can be a lethal weapon in so many ways."

Now what the hell was he getting at? And why was Kit suddenly blushing?

"Good evening, Trendal," Kit said. "Shall we continue, my dear?"

"Yes, indeed. We have lingered here"—she glared at Roger—"far too long."

They made their way around the perimeter of the ballroom. Jack and Frances were dancing; Kit's mother and father were on the other side of the room with Miss Wharton and a man and woman who must be her parents. Miss Wharton's mother looked remarkably like a peacock—or, rather, peahen. She had a very beaklike nose and a collection of plumes that trembled on her head. Her husband was more like a toad, squat and brown, but puffed up at the moment from the duke's and duchess's attention.

"Do you think Percy will actually present himself to Miss Wharton's father tomorrow?" She hoped so. Surely if Percy had a wife and family, he would leave her alone.

"Yes, I believe he will. I thought he appeared thoroughly smitten with Miss Wharton when he proposed, didn't you?"

She nodded. "It was as if all the anger and ill-humor had drained out of him like . . . like pus from a boil."

Kit chuckled. "There must be a more attractive way to say that."

"I think it's quite apt. Percy *has* been a painful, annoying boil on my side for as long as I can remember."

She could feel Kit looking at her. He must be thinking about that horrible afternoon in the Greycliffe studio. They would have to speak about that, likely tonight when they got back to Greycliffe House. That and the paper they'd signed at the White Stag and a few other things.

Her stomach tightened. She didn't look forward to that conversation, but it couldn't be avoided any longer.

And then she saw Mr. Huntington. Damnation. She didn't want to have another confrontation this evening.

Mr. Huntington caught sight of them—and jumped behind some potted palms.

"What's the matter with him?"

Kit grinned. "I believe he developed a hearty respect for me after our first meeting. He's been avoiding me whenever our paths threaten to cross."

"It is too bad you weren't at Blackweith Manor, then. I could have used someone to discourage the fellow."

Kit's hand squeezed hers. "I should have been there, Jess. I should never have left you so unprotected."

A lump blocked her throat; she swallowed it. "Oh, I wasn't unprotected. I had Roger and Dennis."

"You should have had your husband."

Yes, and she would have if she hadn't been so stupid that day in the studio. . . .

Or perhaps if Kit hadn't found her with Percy, he would never have married her. It was his sense of chivalry that had prompted him to offer for her, nothing else.

Or was Percy right? Did Kit love her?

She would find out tonight.

The lump in her throat grew and moved to her stomach.

Chapter Twenty

At some point, you just have to close your eyes and leap.

—Venus's Love Notes

"My lord!" Braxton's eyes widened as he opened the door. "We didn't expect you home so early." He peered over Ash's shoulder. "Is it just you and Lady Ashton, then?"

"Yes, Braxton." Ash forced himself to smile. "I believe London balls may require some getting used to after years in the country. They are very crowded, hot, and noisy. We decided we had had enough."

"Ah. I see."

Braxton's bewildered expression indicated he did not see at all. The man's gaze shifted to Jess, who was standing stiffly at Ash's side, and his face grew tight with worry. Damnation. Now the staff would be speculating about their marriage.

Whom was he fooling? The staff—both here and at the castle—had been speculating for eight years. He'd hoped to begin to resolve the issue in the carriage, but Jess had been correct: the ride had been far too short. He would have barely got her bodice loosened—

And he would have got his face soundly slapped. She'd moved to the far wall as soon as she'd got into the coach, much as she had on their trip from the country. They'd ridden the whole way in silence.

Clearly there was still rough ground to get over before he could hope for marital bliss. But now they would go to their room and talk and then—

Perhaps then. Talking had to come first. He could not allow himself to think about anything else or he'd be incapable of talking at all. He'd wish to rush directly to, er, doing, which would likely result in him encountering Jess's balled fist or worse.

His cock flinched at the memory of how she'd dealt with Percy.

"Are Ned and his wife still up?" He didn't particularly wish to speak to either of them, but Braxton would expect him to inquire.

"No, my lord. Lady Edward gets very tired, being in the family way. I believe they went up to their room several hours ago."

"I see." Good. No need to make small talk, or risk having Ned or Ellie guess they'd been involved in something other than dancing tonight. Some version of the story would be making the rounds tomorrow, but by then he hoped he wouldn't care what people said.

"Shall I have some tea and cakes sent up to the drawing room, my lord?"

"No, thank you, Braxton. Lady Ashton and I are going to retire for the night as well."

Braxton grinned. "Very good, my lord."

Oh, damn. Had Jess noticed Braxton's expression?

She had. Her jaw hardened. Ash hurried her toward the stairs.

"Good night, my lord, my lady," Braxton called after them, waggling his brows.

Well to be honest, Ash, too, hoped something more than sleep would occur this evening.

"I hope you're not thinking what Braxton is," Jess muttered.

Damn. "Er, what is Braxton thinking?" He remembered a caution from Mama's handbook: *Don't assume you know what is in a woman's mind.*

He was afraid he knew all too well what Jess was thinking, but it was far safer to pretend not to. He opened the door to their bedchamber and waited for her to precede him.

Fluff was lying in the middle of the bed. He lifted his head, gave a welcoming woof, beat the mattress a few times with his tail—and dropped his head back on Ash's pillow, damn it.

He was a smart animal. He knew when to lie low.

"That we will . . . that you will . . ." Jess stepped away and faced him. "Nothing will happen until we talk."

Did she think he was going to pounce on her like a wild animal?

His cock was quite taken with that notion.

He sent it a strong admonition to behave.

"Of course." He closed the door. "Let us sit and converse." He gestured to the settee.

Jess crossed her arms and glared at him.

Perhaps he really should have tried to coax her into conversation on their way home. Mama's handbook had said ladies sometimes worked themselves into a lather if left too long to muse on a problem. Hell, even Darby, the ancient coachman who'd driven them up to London, had said that.

"First, we need to discuss that paper you had us sign at the White Stag," Jess said. She lifted a brow. "Remember?"

"Yes." Where the hell was she going with this? She was definitely trying to pick a fight.

He tightened the reins on his temper. Giving in to his

urge to respond in kind would only earn him a large dog down the center of the bed again. And he should get the damn thing out anyway. He would not give up hope of burning it this evening. "I have it in my bureau. Shall I get it?"

"Please do."

He went over and pulled open his sock drawer, rummaging around until he found the sheet. "Here—"

Jess snatched it out of his hands. "Do you remember what you promised?"

"Yes."

She read it aloud anyway:

"I, Christopher, Marquis of Ashton, in consideration of my wife forsaking all others, swear that I will not engage in sexual congress with any other woman."

"And so I haven't." He grinned in what he hoped she'd take as a joking rather than lecherous way. "I haven't even engaged in sexual congress with my wife."

Oh, all right, that had been his cock talking, but damnation, he was frustrated.

Jess inhaled sharply, her brows snapping down as she slammed the paper on a side table. "So where were you last night?"

"What do you mean?"

"You weren't in bed."

"Yes, I was."

"Not when I went to sleep."

He was willing to grant that Jess was not quite as experienced as he'd first thought, but surely she must comprehend the effect she had on him. "No, I was downstairs in the study drinking—you can ask Ned or Jack if you doubt me. They were there"—he grimaced—"until they went upstairs to their wives."

Her frown lightened to a look of puzzlement. "So why didn't you come upstairs, too?"

Zeus! "Because I was afraid I would lose control and try to have sexual congress with my wife, of course. I am not a bloody statue, madam." His damn cock, apparently oblivious to the danger, was insisting that he'd like to have some sexual congress right now. It was getting hard—no, it was getting *difficult*—to think. "Can we sit down?"

She flushed and stepped away from him.

"Good God, Jess. I won't ra—" *No!* He had to get hold of his blasted tongue.

And now he couldn't think about tongues, not after Trendal's comment at the ball.

"You must know I won't touch you without your consent. You do not need to be afraid of me."

"I'm not afraid of you." She glared at him. "Perhaps *you* should be afraid of *me*."

What the hell did she mean by that? Was she struggling to restrain her own amorous urges?

More likely her urges involved a fist or knee applied vigorously to his person.

"We still have points to discuss before . . . before anything else may or may not happen." She crossed her arms—and his brainless cock hoped she did so to keep from reaching for him.

"Percy admitted that he'd been the author of many of the rumors concerning your raking, but I find it hard to believe he was behind all of them. A man of your age and rank surely must have a few indiscretions in his past. I need to know if I'm likely to run into any of your by-blows." Her flush deepened. "I merely wish to be forewarned, you understand. After years of living with people whispering about me, I've become a bit sensitive. I hate it when everyone else knows something I do not."

Ah, so Percy was the one behind her odd notions of his vast amatory experience. That wasn't a surprise. "You don't have to worry about by-blows."

Her eyes narrowed. "Why not?"

"Because I don't have any."

"How do you know?"

"I—" Cowardice raised its ugly head. He cleared his throat. "Men just know these things."

Zeus, lightning should strike him dead right where he stood.

Of course Jess didn't accept that. She frowned. "Are you impotent?"

"Good God, no."

"Do you have the pox?"

"No! Where are you getting these ideas?"

"The manor servants sometimes talked among themselves and forgot I was nearby." She chewed her lip. Suddenly her eyes widened. "Is that it? Do you prefer men? But I'm sure Roger would have told me if that were the case, and—"

"I'm a bloody virgin!"

All right, he shouldn't have shouted that. Fluff woofed again and glared at him. Thank God the door was closed. No one but Jess—and Fluff—had heard him.

He hoped.

Hell. He closed his eyes. What did it matter? The most important person had heard. Now Jess knew he was no better than a boy—*less* experienced, in fact, than most boys.

"But you're thirty years old."

"I *know* how old I am." He felt like a two-headed snake at a Bartholomew Fair.

Remember, the truth would have come out eventually, at an even more awkward moment. There was no hiding his ignorance.

He flushed. "You'll have to teach me all you know."

"Damn it, Kit. For the last time, I'm as virginal as you are."

"Ah." He wanted to believe her, but he'd *seen* her with Percy. "So then what happened that day in the studio?"

She exhaled a long breath. "Yes, we need to talk about that. We should have discussed it eight years ago. Let's sit down now and I'll tell you."

Kit led her over to the settee and sat next to her, his large body comfortingly close.

It was hard to believe he'd never been with a woman.

No, it wasn't. Her mind had been insisting she'd be a fool to think him anything other than what the rumors said he was—a typical male of the ton—but her heart had known the truth for a while.

But the truth was so preposterous. *Why* hadn't Kit done what all the other men did? Many married men had certainly propositioned her.

Could he . . . could he love her?

She would not hope.

"Why haven't you—" She blushed. "You know. No one would have faulted you."

He shifted on the settee. "I am married. I respect my vows."

So it was duty and honor that had kept him faithful.

Damn.

Kit squeezed her hand gently. "You were going to explain about Percy."

Yes. She needed to do that.

"That day at the studio . . . You know my father had just died."

Zeus, the memory of that horrible day when they'd brought Papa back on a hurdle, his neck broken, his face still and waxen was as clear as if the accident had just occurred. Papa had been laughing and arguing with her in the morning and by afternoon he was gone. It shouldn't have happened. He was an excellent rider, and he'd made that jump thousands of times.

"I know. I'm so sorry."

Kit's arm came around her shoulders. She thought his lips brushed her hair.

Oh, God. Something hard in her chest loosened.

"I had no skills. No family. No place to live. I didn't know what I was going to do. I'd thought you'd come to see me—"

She was going to cry. She could feel the tears pressing against the back of her eyes and the ugly, harsh sobs straining in her throat to get free. She pressed her lips tightly together. She never cried.

His arm tightened. "I should have come as soon as I reached the castle."

Oh, damn. She *was* crying. She'd never been a pretty crier like Cicely. Cicely's tears had trembled on her long eyelashes and then slid one by one down her cheeks—her nose hadn't even got red. And at least Ellie had been quiet when she cried. But when Jess cried, she gulped and wailed, her nose ran, and her face got all blotchy.

Kit pulled her against him, and she turned her face into his chest. His poor waistcoat was going to be soaked.

"I shouldn't have expected you to come straightaway." She saw that now. They'd been friends, not—then—husband and wife. He had other responsibilities. She swiped at her tears with her palms. "You came the next day."

"I should have come immediately, but I never thought you'd worry so." He wiped some of the wetness from her cheek with his thumb. "And I shouldn't have given Percy my handkerchief."

"He needed it, and I still have mine." Thank God Madame Celeste had included a small pocket in this gown. She blew her nose . . . loudly. There was no point in trying to be discreet.

She sniffed and blotted her eyes, and then crumbled her

handkerchief in her fingers, as if holding it tightly would make the next things she had to say easier.

It wouldn't. The rest of the story was very ugly, but it had to be told.

"I think I was slightly mad—I certainly wasn't thinking clearly. When Percy appeared at the studio that day—" She shook her head. "I felt as if I was drowning, and he was the only one who could save me." She looked up at Kit. "Can you understand that at all?"

He pulled her closer. "I suppose so. But I truly thought you knew my family would never cast you out."

"They had no reason to see to my welfare, Kit. I was only the groom's daughter."

He frowned. "Will you stop saying that? You were my"—he paused briefly. "You were my friend. And even if you had been 'only the groom's daughter,' you must know Mama and Father take their servants' welfare to heart."

"Yes, I can see that now, but then . . ."

Then she'd been blinded by panic and loss.

She took a deep breath and let it out slowly. "At first I thought Percy only wanted me to paint him." She flushed. "I certainly should have stopped him from taking off his clothes, but I . . . I was curious. I'd never painted the naked human form."

Kit smiled. "Ever the artist, hmm?"

"Yes." Perhaps Kit did understand, at least that part. He was an artist, too. "But then he kissed me." She shuddered. Hopefully that was enough detail. "It was horrible, but I thought he'd never behave that way if he didn't mean to marry me."

"And he shouldn't have," Kit said. "What he did was unconscionable, which I think from what he said tonight he now realizes." He rubbed her shoulder.

"Did you love him?" he asked, his voice gentle.

"No! Of course not. But I was willing to endure his

pawing for a roof over my head." Shame flooded her. "So I suppose in that way I was a wh-whore."

Kit turned her, shaking her a little. "No, you were not, Jess, and I am very, very sorry I ever used that word. Can you forgive me?"

His lovely gray eyes warmed her. She nodded, and blew her nose again. She still had to finish the story. It was almost over. Best just to say it quickly.

"Just before Percy—" She bit her lip. "Just before it was too late, I stopped him and asked if he had the special license already. He looked embarrassed, and that's when I realized he had no intention of marrying me." She swallowed. "And that's when you opened the door."

"Hmm." Kit frowned. "You know, I think Percy planned things so I would find him with you, though I don't suppose he could have guessed I'd walk in at such an especially scandalous moment."

"What do you mean? How could Percy have known you'd come to the studio?"

"Because he heard me say so." Kit's mouth flattened into a hard line. "We were up at the castle. I was trying to get free to come see you when Felix Morton cornered me. He fancied himself an artist and said Percy had told him I'd turned our cottage into a studio. Of course he wanted to see it. I tried to fob him off with a promise to show him the place the next day, but there was no dissuading him."

"Oh."

"Yes, 'oh.' Morton has a reputation for being infernally tenacious when he wants something. Percy left the room when it was clear I had no polite way to decline Morton's request. What Percy couldn't have known was that Mama delayed me a few more minutes." He smiled a little. "So perhaps he never meant for things to progress quite as far as they did. He was just carried away by his desires. You heard him say he loved you."

She snorted. "Spare me Percy's love, then."

"I think Miss Wharton has done that." He stroked her cheek with his thumb. "I'm so sorry Percy hurt you, Jess, but I'm even sorrier that I did."

Which brought her to the crucial question, the one she'd been too afraid to ask until now.

"Why *did* you marry me, Kit? You didn't have to. You weren't the one at fault."

He cupped her face in his hands and looked into her eyes. "I married you because I love you, Jess. I always have."

And then he kissed her.

Heat flooded her, and need. His tongue slipped between her teeth, deep into her mouth.

This was nothing like the ugly time with Percy. This time she wanted more, much more. As much as Kit would give her. Her hands slid over his body—

No, not his body. His coat and waistcoat. She growled in frustration, leaned into him—

And knocked him off onto the floor.

"Oof!" He flinched.

"Oh, dear. I'm so sorry. Are you all right?"

"Well, I'm afraid my rump is a bit sore, but there's no real damage done."

She scrambled down to kneel next to him. "You really do love me?"

He grinned at her. "Of course I do."

"But I'm only the Irish groom's daughter."

"*Will* you stop that?" He brushed a stray hair out of her face. "I used to think I was too boring for you. I was black and white and gray to your vibrant color. Measured lines to your bold strokes."

"But that is part of what I love about you, Kit. You're so intelligent and disciplined and controlled. You were my tether, my rock, my . . . except you weren't mine at all."

He grinned again. "I'm yours now, Jess. And as you know, I do want an heir." He leaned over and kissed her nose. "But more than that, I want my wife—my love."

She laughed, happiness bubbling up inside her. "Then what are you waiting for? I am at your complete disposal."

"I was so hoping you'd say that." He stood, pulling her up with him. "First, let's burn that silly agreement."

"Yes, indeed." She plucked the offending paper off the table, took it over to the hearth, and threw it into the fire. She stood with Kit, their fingers laced, and watched it curl and blacken and turn to dust.

"And now," Kit said. "I hope you don't mind, but I've waited eight years to consummate our marriage, and I'd rather not wait a moment longer."

"I've waited eight years as well. Quick is good." She was suddenly feeling quite desperate. The area he'd touched at the White Stag throbbed in anticipation. "Take off your coat."

He laughed. "I thought you'd disrobe first, but very well." He started to wrestle out of his clothing. "I think quick is not normally good, but I'm afraid it's all I can manage this time."

"Quick is what I need." She was almost panting. While he was busy with his coat, she unbuttoned his waistcoat and pulled his shirt out of his pantaloons.

Ah. Kit's body was beautiful, far more beautiful than any she'd painted. Of course now she was seeing with more than her eyes. She was seeing with her heart.

And she was doing more than looking. Her hands touched Kit's belly, warm and hard with muscle. They slid higher, taking his shirt with them. His chest was muscled, too, broad and—

Kit finally freed himself of his coat. "Good God, Jess, you're torturing me. Let me get my bloody waistcoat off, will you?"

"Go ahead. I'm not stopping you." She pressed her cheek against his chest and breathed in his scent. She heard his heart pounding. She brushed her lips over his skin.

He moaned.

"You're going to kill me, Jess." He tore off his waistcoat and started unwinding his cravat. "Or I may strangle myself with this blasted cloth. Why the devil are cravats so long?"

She slid her hands around to his muscled back. Mmm. Her fingers slipped lower. . . .

"Have mercy, Jess."

She smiled. The time for mercy was past. While he grabbed the hem of his shirt and pulled it up, she attended to his last set of buttons.

"Ah." Kit's male organ fell into her hands. It was beautiful, too, at least to her. It was hard, yet soft. Long and thick. She ran her hand over it all the way to the sacks at its base.

Love certainly changed how she saw things.

Kit jerked his shirt over his head, flung it on the floor, and grabbed her hands. "Jess, I can't take anymore. I am going to totally embarrass myself if you don't stop."

"I don't want to stop."

"Well, you're going to have to." He took her back to the settee and pushed her to sit. "Stay there. Please."

"Oh, very well." She grinned. "The view *is* quite appealing. Now if you'll just remove your pantaloons, I would be completely delighted."

Kit laughed. "Yes, I'm sure you'd be delighted by the spectacle of me falling on my arse. Let me get my shoes and socks off first." He went over to the wing chair to accomplish that task.

She watched him as she slipped off her earrings and necklace and put them carefully on a table. She didn't want to lose such precious gifts but neither did she want to miss—ah, he was standing again. He had long, muscled thighs, but it was the organ between them that most fascinated her.

She might not have experienced copulation, but she understood the theory. Frankly, she'd thought the whole business sounded extremely uncomfortable. She'd certainly expected it to be unpleasant when she'd faced Percy in the studio.

But now she was eager—*all* of her was eager—to embrace Kit. The most relevant part of her anatomy was almost crying with eagerness. It felt empty, needy—

"And now, Jess, it's my turn to undress you."

She'd thought Kit would pull her up to stand, but instead he knelt in front of her. He put his hands on her calves and slid her dress up, higher and higher, up to her thighs and then to her waist. She was completely exposed to his view.

She flushed—she was likely blushing down there, too. She tried to pull her knees together, but he stopped her.

"You're beautiful, Jess. Everywhere. Your knees." He kissed each one as he untied her garters. "Your soft white thighs." His fingers stroked the skin there.

She moaned and spread her legs wider.

He kissed one thigh and then the other as his hands slid down her legs to her ankles, taking her stockings with them. His mouth was getting closer to the tiny point that throbbed so insistently.

Embarrassment was only a vague memory. If she was flushed, it was with the heat of desire.

"You smell beautiful, too, Jess. You have your own perfume. Lavender and woman. Warm and welcoming."

"Ohhh."

"I wonder how you taste?"

She was panting, and the spot that had been throbbing now pulsed and ached. She jiggled her knees and arched a bit to encourage him to do the terribly shocking thing that his words had put into her head. She wanted him to—

His tongue touched her.

"Oh, oh, Kit." Her hips twisted, and she arched again. The sight of his head between her legs was beyond scandalous, so she closed her eyes—which made the sensations even more intense. "Yes. Please. Oh, God."

He made a tsking sound. "I'm not sure you should be using the Almighty's name in this situation, Jess."

"*Kit!* Stop. Teasing. Me."

"You were teasing me earlier if you will remember." He was laughing at her, clearly enjoying her desperation. "Shall I get back to removing your clothes?"

"No. Forget the clothes." She glared at him. "Just do it. Now." Zeus, she was going to go mad if he didn't do something immediately.

The blackguard grinned, though he did sound a bit breathless. "I'm afraid I cannot accommodate you, Lady Ashton. I may not be experienced in marital matters, but I do know a woman's first time can be painful—and messy. Think of dear Mrs. Watson's dismay if we stain the settee."

"I don't care about Mrs. Watson."

"You know, I suddenly realize I don't care about her either, but I'm still not going to take you on this very uncomfortable settee." He pulled her up to stand with him. "How much do you love this dress?"

"Very much." Why was he wasting time talking about her dress? It was very much in the way.

"Shall I remove it carefully? Or shall I tear it off?"

The servants would be scandalized and a beautiful gown would be ruined. "Tear it off."

Kit didn't actually tear the fabric, but a number of buttons were sacrificed without compunction. Her stays and shift followed in short order. Then he held her away from him and just looked.

She felt so hot, she suspected her clothes would have burned off her if Kit hadn't already removed them.

"God, Jess. You're beautiful."

"And you're handsome. Now hurry up and take me to bed."

He laughed and scooped her up, turning—

"Damn."

"What?" She looked at the bed and saw the problem. Damn indeed. "Fluff! Get down."

Fluff gave her a piteous look, but she was completely unmoved. "Go over to the hearth."

Fluff looked at Kit.

"Sorry, my friend, but I'm not sharing my marriage bed with another male—and such a hairy one at that. You need to go."

Fluff sighed and moaned a little, but he dragged himself off the bed and slowly walked over to the fire, the picture of a dog much put upon. He stretched out, propped his head on his front paws, and gazed mournfully at them.

"Poor Fluff." She did feel just a *little* bad. . . .

"Don't even think about inviting him back."

"Oh, I won't. I—*eek!*"

Kit dropped her on the bed and then joined her. She reached for him, but he propped himself up on one elbow, took her hands, and held them against his chest.

"I'm sorry I waited eight years to resolve the problem of our marriage, Jess."

Damnation, was Kit going to start castigating himself again? That was not going to soothe the insistent ache between her thighs. "Then please don't wait eight more years. In fact, don't wait eight more seconds. I am in dire need of some resolution."

He smiled. "You know I don't have any experience—"

"Then for God's sake, come get some." Ah, perhaps she

saw the way to urge him into action. She slid her hand down his body to his most prominent organ.

It jumped in welcome.

"Oh, no, you don't." Kit pulled her hand away from its prize.

"But you like it."

"Yes, but now it's my turn." His mouth came down on hers.

Oh! His touch made the fire in her roar even higher. She arched into him. She wanted to get closer.

His thumb flicked over her hard, tight nipple.

Sensation shot directly from her breast to the place between her thighs. Her hips twisted; her hands slid down his back.

His mouth moved to her jaw, her throat, and finally her breast.

She moaned and grabbed his head to keep him there. Her hips bucked with each rasp of his tongue, each pull on her nipple. She panted and whimpered.

What if someone hears me?

The thought whispered through her overheated mind. She didn't care. She couldn't. She was too focused on the tiny point Kit's tongue had touched on the settee, that his finger had first found on that sagging mattress at the White Stag. She desperately needed him to touch her there now.

His hand slid down her side, closer, closer.

"Please. Oh, Kit. Please."

He answered her prayer. His finger found her.

She thought she would die of pleasure.

Only not quite yet. Her body tightened with each light, teasing touch. Kit was drawing her closer to where he'd taken her at the inn. Closer. Closer. She was almost there. . . .

"You're so wet." His words whispered over her skin. "I want to taste you again."

His body left hers. It was cold without his weight. She

reached to pull him back—and then his tongue took the place of his finger, slipping over the hard point.

"Ohhh!"

Her hips tried to arch, but Kit held her still while his tongue touched her again, probing, sliding....

She panted faster, grabbing the bedclothes. She was almost there.

And then his tongue rasped over her once more, and she screamed, almost sitting up as wave after wave of intense pleasure broke through her.

She collapsed, completely sated.

Kit looked down at Jess, sprawled wantonly on his bed. He felt a flicker of pride at how he'd caused her to lose control.

But the pride was almost immediately drowned by desire. It was his turn. His time to finally shed his virginity. His cock was most insistent on the matter.

He fit himself between Jess's legs and touched her entrance. He had to go slowly, for her and for him. He didn't want to rush. He wanted to feel every inch as he slid deep inside her.

Mmm. She was so tight and warm and wet. The sensations threatened to overwhelm him, but even though he was a virgin—for a few more seconds—he was not a boy. He had some control.

Still, the experience was far more intense than he'd imagined, and he'd imagined it too many times to count, usually with his hand around his cock. Jess's body was so much better than that. That had been a solitary, physical thing. This was the exact opposite. It was deeply, soul-wrenchingly intimate.

"Oh!" Jess flinched.

He stopped. "Are you all right?"

She grinned up at him and ran her hands over his back. "Yes, but I'm not a virgin any longer."

He kissed her and pushed forward, sliding all the way into her so his entire length was embraced by her warmth. "And neither am I."

His body was screaming at him to move, but he held still a moment longer and kissed Jess slowly and thoroughly, savoring her taste. "I love you, Jess."

She smiled at him, holding his face in her hands. "And I love you, Kit."

He let his happiness at her words wash over him before he gave in to the insistent need and moved, in and out and in again, as close to her heart as he could go, his seed and his love flowing into her, into Jess, his friend and, at last, his wife.

Jess was glad her madness had passed so she could concentrate on the feel of Kit inside her: the slide of his cock, the slickness of his back, the tension of his muscles, of his face, and then, at last, the warm wash of his seed flooding her womb. Her heart.

She felt very married, and very, very happy.

He collapsed onto her, and she held him close.

"I'm too heavy for you."

He was, but she would never say it.

He lifted his body off hers, and then gathered her into his arms, close against his side. "I wish we hadn't waited eight years to do that."

"Mmm." She stretched against him. She was sore in new places. "We'll just have to make up for lost time."

"Yes, we will." He brushed his lips over her forehead. "Are you all right?"

"I'm splendid."

"But sore?"

She laughed. "Splendidly sore." She snuggled closer. "And I'm afraid there will be some blood on your sheets."

He didn't look happy to have her virginity confirmed. "I'm sorry. It does seem unfair men don't also have to suffer their first time."

Yes, it was unfair, but life wasn't fair, was it? She kissed his chest. "And was your first time all you'd hoped it would be?"

He grinned. He looked as happy as he had as a boy. "Yes." He kissed her forehead. "And I am so glad it was with you."

Fluff snorted in his sleep, and they both laughed.

"Say, are you going to show me the sketchbook Trendal kept talking about?"

She hesitated. She'd never shown those drawings to anyone—but she had nothing to hide from Kit now. "I'm too warm and cozy to get it."

"I'll get it."

"Very well. It's in the bottom of the wardrobe."

She watched him cross the room. It was cold without him next to her, but he did have a lovely arse—and he was back in just a moment.

He propped the pillows on the headboard, and she cuddled up against his warm side, her head on his shoulder. He opened the book and turned the pages. She waited somewhat anxiously for his reaction. He looked surprised. Would he be embarrassed? Horrified?

"Good God, Jess. They are almost all of me."

"Yes. You were always my favorite subject." There was a sketch of the day she first saw him drawing by the river and another of him building a snow castle and another of him riding through the fields and another—

She blushed.

"You seem to have left some crucial parts in shadow." He was laughing again.

"My imagination couldn't do you justice." She slid her hand down to cup one of those parts, which blossomed under her fingers.

Kit was still smiling, but his gaze had sharpened.

"I think I can do a better job now." She stroked him. "In fact, I'm looking forward to it."

He put her sketchbook on the bedside table, blew out the candle, and then wrapped his arms around her, holding her close. "And I'm looking forward to it as well."

Epilogue

Children grow so quickly.

—Venus's Love Notes

A year and a half later...

The Earl of Morane sucked on his father's cravat.

"Nate is hungry, Jess." Kit sniffed his son's posterior. "And he needs a change of clothes."

Jess laughed. "Nate is always hungry, and he always needs a change." She sat in her favorite chair and extended her arms. "Here, give him to me."

Nate heard her voice and started to fuss.

"Gladly, since I cannot satisfy his needs." Kit placed the infant safely in Jess's hands.

"And since he's quite smelly." She opened her gown, and Nate dove for her breast. "You'd think the poor baby was starving, and I fed him less than two hours ago."

"He's growing."

"Mmm." Jess looked down at Nate's beautiful fuzzy head as he began to suck. She felt the pull of his tiny mouth all the way to her heart. To think such a short time ago she'd been alone and desperately lonely, and now she had this precious child and her husband by her side and in her bed every night—and in her body many of those nights, now that she'd recovered from her lying-in. Not to mention she also had a mother-in-law and father-in-law and brothers-in-law and sisters-in-law and two nephews. She was suddenly surrounded by family.

She looked up at Kit: he was staring at Nate. His face held the same wonder hers must.

And his cravat was sadly bedraggled.

"You'd best change as well before we go downstairs."

He looked in the mirror and started to undo his cravat. "It's wasted effort, you know. I will look like I've been attacked by wild animals moments after we arrive in the parlor."

She laughed and put Nate to her shoulder. "They are only babies, Kit, and only Ned's son can move around. Wait until they are older. Your mother says that is when the damage will really begin." She patted Nate's back, and he let out a very loud, extremely inelegant belch.

Kit glanced over, looking absurdly proud. "That's my boy."

"Do not brag about this to your brothers!" She put Nate to her other breast. It was wonderful that they all had sons about the same age—and she loved having Ellie and Frances to talk to about child rearing—but the men sometimes became a bit competitive.

"He has strong lungs, as befits the future Duke of Greycliffe."

"I shall remind you of that the next time he's crying inconsolably."

"Thank God that doesn't happen often. Has he finished his meal?"

"He's digesting." A fact confirmed by another loud, rather ominous sound emanating from Nate's nether regions. "Now he is definitely in need of a change. Hold him for me while I get some clean clothes."

Kit held the poor baby at arm's length, but Nate just laughed and wiggled.

"Isn't this a job for his nurse?"

"Don't be silly. I like changing him." She laughed at Kit's expression. "Just wait until he's on solid foods. Ellie says then I'll want to hand him off to Anna."

Kit's nose wrinkled. "Spare me the details, please."

He laid Nate down so Jess could remove the baby's dirty clothes.

"Are you ready to see your cousins and grandmamma and grandfather, Natey boy?" Kit said in the high, sing-songy voice adults use to talk to babies.

Nate gurgled and laughed and waved his hands and legs.

"He does like his daddy, doesn't he?" Jess said, turning away to put the soiled laundry well out of reach. She'd once made the mistake of keeping it beside Nate when changing him, and he'd managed to get his hand in the dirt.

"Yes, he does." Kit sounded so happy, so different from the man who'd come upon her with Roger at Blackweith Manor.

She smiled. She had indeed painted Kit naked, many times, in that studio—and he had painted her, even when she was nine months pregnant. She hadn't realized how sterile her paintings had become until she was painting again with her heart. She—

"Ack!"

She spun around to see Kit using the end of his cravat to stanch the healthy stream little Nate was producing, a predictable reaction of a naked baby boy left uncovered.

"Oh, I'm sorry. I—" And then she was laughing too hard to say anything else.

Nate squealed and laughed, too.

"He's very proud of himself," she said, kissing Kit as she brought Nate his clean clothes.

Kit chuckled. "Yes, I can see that." He kissed her back. "I believe I should change my cravat again."

The Duchess of Love paused in the doorway to the blue parlor.

"Happy, my dear duchess?" the duke murmured, coming up behind her and wrapping his arm around her waist.

"Oh, yes." She leaned her head against his chest. "How can I not be? Look at them, Drew."

Their three daughters-in-law were sitting together on the far side of the room, chatting about baby matters no doubt. Their sons were on the near side with their children. Ned was bent over, shuffling along holding his son William's hands as little Will learned to walk. Ned laughed at something Jack said—Jack who was on the floor with *his* son, Adrian. Adrian had not quite mastered the skill of sitting upright, so Jack had to push him back up from time to time when he slowly toppled sideways. And Ash—

Ash was also laughing at whatever Jack had said. He was sitting on a chair, baby Nate straddling his knee, Nate's arms and legs moving with excitement as he watched his cousins.

"Did you ever think to see Ash so happy, Drew?"

Drew tightened his arm to hug her closer. "No, Venus. I confess I had given up hope."

"Now all we need is a granddaughter."

Drew laughed. "Do not tell our sons—or, more importantly, their wives—*that,* my dear duchess."

Will had heard his grandfather laugh. He looked up and his little face broke into a heart-melting smile. "Gamma! Gampa!"

The Duchess of Love could not resist such seductive words. She hurried into the room to gather her precious grandbabies close.

Author's Note

If you're a reader who studies book covers, you might be puzzled by the dog on the front of *Loving Lord Ash*. He's very cute, but you're right—he's not Fluff. Fluff is a LARGE dog, so large he apparently wouldn't fit in the picture!

I knew I wanted Fluff to be big—Jess didn't strike me as a small dog person—and he had to be a breed that was around in the Regency. Initially I was waffling between an Irish Wolfhound and a Newfoundland. I finally decided on a Newfie, though I suspect Fluff is a bit of a mutt.

All of the *Duchess of Love* books include pets. I find animals a great source of humor, and they help reveal who the hero and heroine are. But I also try to make my animals characters in their own right with their own distinctive personalities.

I didn't grow up with pets. Before I was born—or at least before I was old enough to remember—my family had a dog that chased cars and ate blankets. I did have a dime store turtle for a little while. It was quite the escape artist, climbing out of its plastic terrarium in the kitchen at night to be found in the morning two rooms over in the living room. And then when I had my own family . . . well, four sons seemed like enough living creatures to keep track of!

So I'll confess I take special delight when a story animal comes to life for me, and I can "see" him moving through the pages. I hope Fluff has come to life for you.

If you enjoyed LOVING LORD ASH,
don't miss Sally MacKenzie's delightful

SURPRISING LORD JACK.

Available as a Kensington eBook
and mass-market paperback, on sale now!

Appearances can be deceiving.

—Venus's Love Notes

Miss Frances Hadley staggered up to the Crowing Cock's weather-beaten door, her legs, backside, and feet throbbing with each step.

Blast it, men rode astride all the time. How could she have guessed the experience would be so painful? And having to walk the last half mile in Frederick's old boots hadn't helped. Damn icy roads.

She took a deep breath of the sharp, winter air. And if Daisy was lame—

She scowled at the door. If her horse was lame, she'd figure out another way to get to London. Hell, she'd walk if she had to. She was *not* going home to Landsford. To think Aunt Viola had been going to help Mr. Littleton with his nefarious scheme—

Oh! Every time she thought about it, she wanted to hit something—or someone.

She put her hand on the door. The drunken male laughter was so loud she could hear it out here. Pot-valiant oafs! At least drunkards were even less likely than sober men to see through her disguise. She almost hoped one of them would approach her. She'd take great delight in bloodying his nose.

She shoved open the door and was hit by a cacophony of voices and the stench of spilled ale, smoke, and too many sweaty male bodies. A barmaid, burdened with six or seven mugs of ale, rushed out of a room to her left.

"Where can I see about a bed for the night?" Frances had to shout to make herself heard. She had a deep voice for a woman, but was it deep enough? Apparently. The girl barely glanced at her.

"See Mr. Findley," she said without breaking stride, jerking her head back at the room she'd just left, "but we're full up."

Oh, damn. Frances's stomach plummeted.

She would *not* despair. If worse came to worst, she'd find a corner of the common room and sleep there. Or perhaps the innkeeper would let her stay in the stables. Even if Daisy were able to carry her, she could not go any farther. Night was coming on.

She went through the narrow doorway. A stout man with a bald head and an equally stout, gray-haired woman were sitting at a scarred wooden table, eating their dinner. Frances inhaled. Mutton and potatoes. Not her favorite dishes, but she was so hungry, the food smelled like ambrosia.

"Tonight's the duchess's ball, Archie," the woman was saying. She waved a bite of mutton at him. "Do you think Her Grace found a match for Lord Ned or Lord Jack this year?"

Archie snorted. "Don't know why this year should be any different than last year or the year before, Madge."

"I suppose you're right. I just—"

Frances cleared her throat. "Pardon me, but might you have a room for the night?"

The man looked over and frowned. "'Fraid every bed is full."

"I see." She bit her lip. Damn it.

"Oh, Archie," his wife said, getting up. "I'm sure we can find something for the poor lad. He looks exhausted."

"I *am* very tired, madam, and my horse is lame." Frances was suddenly a hairsbreadth from groveling. Lying in a real bed would be heaven, especially compared to sleeping on the hard floor with the tosspots in the common room or on straw in the stable.

Mrs. Findley clucked her tongue. "You're likely hungry as well."

Frances's stomach spoke for her, growling loudly. She flushed. She hadn't eaten since breakfast, eight hours earlier. She should have packed something, but she hadn't expected to be so delayed, and to be frank, she'd been too angry to think clearly.

And if she'd had a knife in her hand, Aunt Viola would not have been safe.

Mrs. Findley laughed. "Come, sit with us." She took Frances's arm and towed her over to the table.

"I-I don't wish to intrude. If you could just spare a slice of mutton and a potato, I'm sure I would do very well."

"Don't be ridiculous." The woman pushed her into a chair and started filling a plate with food. "You must be starving."

Frances's stomach growled again, and Mrs. Findley laughed. "Poor boy." She put the plate down in front of her. "Now eat before you fall over from hunger. I'm sure we can find you someplace to sleep."

Mr. Findley was less inclined to charity. "Madge, the only room we have free is the one I save for the Valentines."

"Well, none of them will be here tonight, will they? It's the birthday ball, remember? They won't miss it, no matter how much they hate attending. They're good boys."

Ha! Frances speared a bit of potato with her fork. Jack, the youngest of the Duke of Greycliffe's sons, was far from a "good boy." Aunt Viola was forever holding him up as an example of the evils of Town. A rake of the first order and likely a procurer as well, he was rumored to know—*intimately*—every brothel owner in London.

"I suppose you're right." Mr. Findley turned his attention to Frances. "What's your name, lad, and where are you headed?"

"Frances Had—" Frances coughed. She could use her Christian name—spelled with an *i* instead of an *e* it was a male name anyway—but perhaps she should be cautious about using her family name. "Francis Haddon. I'm on my way to London."

"London?" Mr. Findley's brows shot up and then down into a scowl. "How old are you? You haven't escaped from school, have you?"

"No, sir." She focused on cutting her meat so she wouldn't have to meet his eyes. "I'm, er, older than I look."

Mrs. Findley laughed. "What? Thirteen instead of twelve? Don't try to cozen us, young sir. We've raised three sons. Here it is the end of the day, and you don't have the faintest shadow of a beard."

This pretending to be a man was more complicated than she'd thought. Frances smiled and stuffed a large piece of mutton in her mouth.

"What can your mother be thinking to let you travel alone like this?" Mrs. Findley made a clucking sound with her tongue again.

Frances swallowed. "My mother died a number of years ago, madam. I live with my elderly aunt." Aunt Viola would not be happy with that description, but she *had* passed her sixtieth birthday.

"Well, I can't fathom even an aunt, elderly or not, letting a young'un such as yourself travel up to Town alone."

There was more than a hint of suspicion in Mr. Findley's voice.

"My aunt wasn't happy about it, sir,"—Viola had been shouting so loudly it was surprising they hadn't heard her at the Crowing Cock—"but I was desperate to go." She wasn't about to spend one more second under the same roof as that treacherous woman. "I'm to visit my brother. I would have got to London hours ago if the roads hadn't been so bad." She'd meant to stay the night with Frederick, see their man of business in the morning, and then go back to Landsford and wave the bank draft for the amount of her dowry in Viola's face before taking it, packing up, and moving out.

She frowned at her plate. She hadn't yet figured out where she'd go, but she bloody well wasn't going to stay one more night at Landsford. To think Viola had planned to drug her with laudanum, let Littleton into her bedroom, and then raise an alarm so he'd be discovered there by the gossiping servants.

She stabbed a bit of potato so hard, her fork screeched across the plate.

Mrs. Findley wagged her finger at her husband. "Don't glower at the boy, Archie. You're frightening him." Then she turned to wag it at Frances. "And a boy your age should not be traveling by himself. There are bad men—and women—at every turn, eager to take terrible advantage of a young cub like yourself, still wet behind the ears. I'll wager your brother hasn't the least idea how to take charge of you. How old is he?"

Frances blinked. She would like to see Frederick try to take charge of her. If there was any taking charge to be done, she'd be the one doing it. "Twenty-four." They were twins, but she was the elder by ten minutes.

"I don't know, Madge." Mr. Findley was still frowning. "It seems a bit fishy to me. I—"

"Mr. Findley," the barmaid said from the door, "there's a fight starting."

"Damnation." He glanced at his watch. "Right on time, the drunken louts." He looked at his wife as he got to his feet. "I suppose you're right, Madge. None of the Valentines will be needing the room, and I can see you don't want the lad sleeping with the men out there."

They heard a shout and what sounded like a table tipping over followed by glass shattering.

Mr. Findley sighed. "Get the boy settled while I go knock some heads together." He picked up a wooden cudgel leaning against the wall and left to do battle with the drunks.

"Are you ready to go, Francis?"

"Yes, madam." She didn't want to give the innkeeper's wife an opportunity to change her mind. She swallowed her last bite and stood. "Thank you."

"I still don't see how your aunt could have let you travel alone, especially after that dreadful blizzard. The roads were barely passable—well, not passable at all once it clouded up and everything refroze." Mrs. Findley led her out of the room and up the stairs. She looked back, frowning. "You didn't sneak away while she was busy elsewhere, did you?"

"Oh no, madam. My aunt saw me off." With a string of curses.

She looked down so Mrs. Findley wouldn't see the fury in her eyes. Thank God she'd overheard that louse Felix Littleton this morning. If she hadn't stopped in Mr. Turner's store to read Mr. Puddington's letter—if she hadn't dropped the damn man of business's note and had to crawl behind a case of candles to retrieve it—she'd never have learned how Viola had been colluding with the bloody little worm.

Mrs. Findley turned left at the top of the stairs, and Frances followed her down the corridor.

Littleton—she'd recognized his whiny little voice—and his friend, a Mr. Pettigrew, whom she hadn't been able to see but had heard all too clearly, had been laughing about the plot. Littleton had been home these last few weeks, apparently fleeing his creditors, and had been paying her court. He and Pettigrew had sniggered at how easy it was to get silly, old, *desperate* spinsters to lose their hearts.

She felt a hot flush climb from her breast to her cheeks. Mr. Lousy Littleton was flattering himself if he thought she'd fallen in love with him. *Love.* Ha! She was not susceptible to that malady. Yes, she might have begun to fancy herself attracted to the snake—he was very handsome and had been extremely attentive—but her heart had been quite safe.

But why Viola, who'd always told her that men were not to be trusted—and certainly the behavior of her absent brother and father supported that theory—would consent to help Littleton was beyond her. Frankly, she couldn't believe it at first, but when she'd come home and confronted her aunt, Viola's guilt had been written all over her face.

"Here you are, then." Mrs. Findley stopped at the last room and opened the door. "It's—"

They both jumped at the sound of another crash from downstairs.

"Oh dear, I'd better go help Archie. The men can get so obstreperous when they're in their cups, but they'll quiet down in just a bit." She smiled and patted Frances on the arm. "Do sleep well." She almost ran back down the passageway.

Frances stepped into the room, and her feet sank into thick carpet. Oh! She couldn't track mud and slush in here. She put her hat and candle on a nearby table, closed the door, and leaned against it to tug off Frederick's boots.

Ah. She wiggled her toes in the deep pile and looked around. Red-and-tan wallpaper covered the walls, heavy red curtains hung on the windows to keep out light and drafts, and a red upholstered chair sat by the fire. But the best thing of all was the big mahogany four-poster bed.

Which had likely been used by Lord Jack to entertain countless women. She wrinkled her nose as she jerked off her overcoat and hung it on a hook. As distasteful as the notion was, she was so tired, she couldn't muster much moral outrage. Perhaps in the morning she'd be suitably incensed, but now she just wanted to lie down.

She slipped out of her coat and started unbuttoning her waistcoat . . .

No, better leave that on, as well as her shirt and breeches and socks—all Frederick's castoffs. It seemed unlikely another traveler would arrive so late, but she couldn't take any chances.

She pulled back the coverlet and climbed onto the bed, stretching her aching body over the soft, yielding, wonderful feather mattress.

She was asleep even before her head hit the pillow.

GREAT BOOKS, GREAT SAVINGS!

When You Visit Our Website:
www.kensingtonbooks.com
You Can Save Money Off The Retail Price Of Any Book You Purchase!

- All Your Favorite Kensington Authors
- New Releases & Timeless Classics
- Overnight Shipping Available
- eBooks Available For Many Titles
- All Major Credit Cards Accepted

Visit Us Today To Start Saving!
www.kensingtonbooks.com

All Orders Are Subject To Availability.
Shipping and Handling Charges Apply.
Offers and Prices Subject To Change Without Notice.

Romantic Suspense from
Lisa Jackson

Absolute Fear	0-8217-7936-2	$7.99US/$9.99CAN
Afraid to Die	1-4201-1850-1	$7.99US/$9.99CAN
Almost Dead	0-8217-7579-0	$7.99US/$10.99CAN
Born to Die	1-4201-0278-8	$7.99US/$9.99CAN
Chosen to Die	1-4201-0277-X	$7.99US/$10.99CAN
Cold Blooded	1-4201-2581-8	$7.99US/$8.99CAN
Deep Freeze	0-8217-7296-1	$7.99US/$10.99CAN
Devious	1-4201-0275-3	$7.99US/$9.99CAN
Fatal Burn	0-8217-7577-4	$7.99US/$10.99CAN
Final Scream	0-8217-7712-2	$7.99US/$10.99CAN
Hot Blooded	1-4201-0678-3	$7.99US/$9.49CAN
If She Only Knew	1-4201-3241-5	$7.99US/$9.99CAN
Left to Die	1-4201-0276-1	$7.99US/$10.99CAN
Lost Souls	0-8217-7938-9	$7.99US/$10.99CAN
Malice	0-8217-7940-0	$7.99US/$10.99CAN
The Morning After	1-4201-3370-5	$7.99US/$9.99CAN
The Night Before	1-4201-3371-3	$7.99US/$9.99CAN
Ready to Die	1-4201-1851-X	$7.99US/$9.99CAN
Running Scared	1-4201-0182-X	$7.99US/$10.99CAN
See How She Dies	1-4201-2584-2	$7.99US/$8.99CAN
Shiver	0-8217-7578-2	$7.99US/$10.99CAN
Tell Me	1-4201-1854-4	$7.99US/$9.99CAN
Twice Kissed	0-8217-7944-3	$7.99US/$9.99CAN
Unspoken	1-4201-0093-9	$7.99US/$9.99CAN
Whispers	1-4201-5158-4	$7.99US/$9.99CAN
Wicked Game	1-4201-0338-5	$7.99US/$9.99CAN
Wicked Lies	1-4201-0339-3	$7.99US/$9.99CAN
Without Mercy	1-4201-0274-	$7.99US/$10.99CAN
You Don't Want to Know		$9.99CAN

Visit ou...nsingtonbooks.com